A TIME TO LOVE

Kathleen Bryant

HarperPaperbacks
A Division of HarperCollinsPublishers

This is a work of fiction. The characters, incidents, and dialogues are products of the author's imagination and are not to be construed as real. Any resemblance to actual events or persons, living or dead, is entirely coincidental.

HarperPaperbacks *A Division of* HarperCollins*Publishers*
10 East 53rd Street, New York, N.Y. 10022

Cover illustration by Carla Sormanti

First printing: January 1994

Printed in the United States of America

HarperPaperbacks, HarperMonogram, and colophon are trademarks of HarperCollins*Publishers*

❖ 10 9 8 7 6 5 4 3 2

PROLOGUE

Dear Willa,

Hi, Sis. I looked at the calendar today and thought of you picking blackberries on the island. You never could stand to wait until they were ripe. Remember the time you stepped on that hornet's nest and got stung all over? You didn't want Christian to see you cry, so you jumped into the lake and swam back to shore.

God, that seems like two lifetimes ago. It feels all right to be walking around again, but I just can't get used to it here. Most of these guys came from stateside. They've never even heard of Loc Ninh or Quang Ngai, and they all call me "the old man." Ha, ha.

Truth is, I feel like an old man sometimes. I

know this is going to sound crazy, Sis, but sometimes I wish I could go back to Nam. I guess what I really want is to do it all over again, like maybe this time it would be different, if I could save even one of my buddies. Toward the end, I'd lost so many friends that it was easier not to make new ones.

The docs here say I'm lucky to be alive. They don't understand why I wanted to reenlist. I'm not sure I understand, either. I get scared sometimes when I look at Caro and see our baby growing inside her. How can I take care of them? I don't know anymore if I can be the kind of father who laughs at knock-knock jokes or flies kites.

We used to do those things, didn't we? It all seems so far away. I think of it a lot, especially the summers at the lake. Fishing, going to Quinlan's store for an ice cream sandwich. I wish I could go back that far. But I'm not twelve years old anymore. I shouldn't be talking like this to you, but I don't want to worry Caro, and the folks wouldn't understand.

I don't think Christian would understand, either. He still thinks some things are worth fighting for. I don't, not anymore. Well, I guess I'd better get back to work. I'm supposed to be helping the quartermaster count inventory. It seems so stupid after spending the last lifetime trying to stay alive in the jungle.

Hey, pick some blackberries for me, okay?

Love,
Rick

1

The narrow causeway was an almost invisible thread between the white snowflakes that swirled against the windshield and the midnight black of the tall pine trees ahead. But it was more than the treacherous causeway Willa feared. There was also the uncertain reception that lay at the end.

After eighteen years, did her stern-faced Aunt Billie still have a soft spot for any stray that crossed the doorstep? She hoped so, because tonight Billie was going to get not just one, but two of life's losers—a washed-up singer and a troubled teenager. Willa looked over at the sleeping boy sprawled across the passenger seat next to her. There was no turning back now.

She put the car into low gear and gripped the steering wheel with palms gone slippery with sweat. The causeway was longer than she remembered—agonizingly so—and for a moment she was afraid she'd driven onto the frozen, snow-covered lake surface. As the wind buffeted the small car, Willa prayed they wouldn't skid off the causeway into the freezing waters.

Her prayers were answered when the beam of her headlights picked out a battered wooden gate and faded sign. They'd made it.

At one time the sign had welcomed visitors to Spirit Island on Pine Lake, "the home of Restless Spirit Resort, Pinecrest, Minnesota." Now, only the name of the resort was visible, and it seemed particularly apt. Willa had no idea where she would go from this point in her life. All she knew was that she needed to say goodbye to the past. Then perhaps her restless spirit would find some peace.

She noticed something else, something she'd missed at first. Tire tracks. Tall pines lined the long driveway ahead like sentinels, blocking the worst of the fierce wind. The dark tracks slicing through the snow were practically untouched. She hoped they didn't mean Billie wasn't home after all. Willa glanced quickly at the gas gauge. If she could turn the car around and recross the causeway without getting stuck—or worse—she could just make it to Quinlan's grocery. Quinlan's was still there after eighteen years.

Eighteen years. It was long enough so that she'd forgotten to take the customary winter precautions— blankets, extra fuel, candles, food, tire chains. The last time she had challenged country roads during a Minnesota blizzard was in her grandmother's Bel Aire, before she'd even gotten her driver's license. Rick and Christian had decided to teach her to drive into a skid, and she could still hear their howls of laughter at her white-knuckled panic.

This time she was thirty-three years old, all grown up, a widow even before her divorce had become final three years ago. She wasn't quite ready to panic—yet. She shifted into a lower gear, thanked God for front-wheel drive, and used the tracks ahead as a guide.

Her hope that Billie might be home fled when she saw the house. Black-leaded glass windows stared into the night like unseeing eyes. She shut off the engine and headlights, and the house's façade was thrown into darkness, masking the whimsical gingerbread and lacy fence work and making the sprawling edifice appear even more unwelcoming. The snow had momentarily ceased, and the uneven roof line of tower, gables, and chimneys formed a starkly jagged silhouette against the dull sky.

Willa felt a chill at the sight and wondered if she'd been wrong to leave Los Angeles after all. No matter how hard she tried she could never recapture the years of innocent bliss she'd spent here in her youth. She spared a quick glance at her still-sleeping companion before reaching behind the seat, her hand shaking. She didn't know if the tremors were a delayed reaction to the last difficult miles, or a sign of her nervousness for what lay ahead.

On top of the boxes and suitcases crowding the hatchback compartment was a shoe box. She pulled it toward her and untied the ribbon that held the lid.

The photograph was on top.

She held it in her hands like a talisman, and its presence soothed her even before she turned on the dome light to view it. It was a shot of the last time the three of them had been together, taken on the front porch of the house in front of her. The house had been freshly painted then, and leafy shadows gently dappled the sparkling white paint. She and Christian stood on either side of Rick, and the three of them were laughing.

The photo gave her strength and helped her remember the happy times, the youthful feeling of invincibility. During those summers, they'd been inseparable, and in their naïveté, they had assumed that was the way things would stay. How wrong they'd been.

She carefully placed the photo on top of the pile of yellowed letters and reclosed the box. It was time to start again. Her brother Rick was gone, but his son was here.

"Rod," she said, gently shaking the boy's shoulder. Coldness was beginning to seep into the car's cramped interior. "We're here."

The boy mumbled and tried to brush away her persistent hand before straightening up at last and rubbing his eyes with the back of one bony fist. Willa smiled. He looked younger than his seventeen years, with his sleep-swollen eyes and his hair sticking out in all directions. Like Willa's own, it was vivid red-orange, but it was straight as a stick, whereas hers fell in waves past her shoulders.

She felt another dart of apprehension but shoved it aside. "You'll wake up soon enough when you step outside," she told him.

Rod wiped the steam from the window next to him and looked out. The wind picked up and sprayed a cloud of snow in the clearing where the car was parked. "Holy sh—I mean, wow. It looks like the Munsters' house!"

Willa chose not to respond. She turned off the dome light and said, "We'll have to see if Billie is home before we carry our things inside."

"What happens if she isn't?"

Willa smiled to cover her concern. "She'll be here. I wrote and told her I'd be coming sometime this week."

But I didn't tell her about you, she added to herself. Rod was an unexpected addition to her plans. She'd stopped to visit her parents in Arizona, and Rod was there, sent by his mother in another attempt to "straighten him out," as Rod's adoptive father put it. Rod was clearly unhappy there, and when he asked

Willa to take him with her, she'd reluctantly agreed, thinking she would drop him off in Minneapolis, where his parents lived, before getting on with her own plans—whatever they turned out to be.

"Let's do it then," Rod said, his words putting an end to her hesitation. He was already halfway out the door.

They waded through snow to the veranda. Willa ignored the ornate brass knocker and rapped on the wood door with her bare knuckles. She shivered a little, thinking how foolishly she was dressed for a northern February. When the door opened at last, she smiled, ready to greet the aunt she hadn't seen in so long.

Then she saw the gun.

It was a full minute before she could even form a thought, let alone react to the twenty-gauge shotgun aimed at her chest. Even her vocal cords froze with fear.

Just when Willa thought she could manage to choke out a scream, the overhead light came on. She blinked and saw a vaguely familiar pair of blue eyes set into an unknown, well-lined face. Then the network of wrinkles turned up into a smile.

"Wilhelmina Mitterhauser, is that you?"

"Aunt Billie?" Willa couldn't erase the incredulity from her voice. Her aunt and namesake had been what people kindly termed "a handsome woman," square-jawed and lanky with unremarkable brown hair. Age had softened her. Her hair was a cloud of white around her lined face, and her eyes were still vibrant. Her expression spoke not of loneliness, as Willa might have expected, but of contentment.

"I thought you were the ghost," her aunt said. Before the strange comment had a chance to register in Willa's mind, her aunt leaned the gun against the wall and continued, "Well, get out of the way so I can close the door."

Willa stepped aside obediently, gesturing for Rod to

follow her into the hallway. When she looked back again at Billie, the old woman was staring at Rod, her eyes wide with shock. "Dear Lord. It *is* a ghost."

Willa knew exactly what Billie was thinking. Except for his bright hair, his resemblance to Rick was startling. If there had been a way to prepare Billie . . . But then Willa hadn't been prepared herself, she remembered with a pang. And neither was Rod, who stood there awkwardly, looking as though he wanted to shrink and disappear. She drew him further into the hallway. "Rod, this is your great aunt, Billie Mitterhauser."

"Oh, dear Lord," Billie said again, but this time she smiled, and her eyes were shiny with tears. "You're Rick's son." She patted him on the shoulder. "Come into the kitchen, both of you, and get warm," she said.

Willa started down the hallway, but Rod hung back. "If it's all right with you—" his eyes pleaded with Willa's "—I'd rather just go to bed. I'm pretty tired." He shoved his hands deeper in the pockets of his battered green parka. Willa could see weariness in every line of his lanky body.

"Sure," she said. "Why don't you help me bring in the overnight things from the car first." She looked at Billie apologetically, but her aunt was two steps ahead of her.

"You just go on upstairs when you're done," Billie told Rod. "You can sleep in my room tonight. It's at the end of the hall. I'll make up a room for you in the morning." She turned to Willa. "You can stay in the master bedroom."

Willa was mildly surprised that Billie hadn't moved into the large suite of rooms that once belonged to Willa's grandparents. After the rest of the family had left for Arizona, Billie was both mistress and master of the huge house. But for some reason, she'd chosen to stay in the room she'd used as a girl. Willa hoped Rod's long limbs would fit into the narrow sleigh bed.

After carrying the last bag upstairs and bidding Rod goodnight, Willa joined her aunt in the kitchen. Billie looked up from filling a teakettle with water.

"I'm sorry I surprised you with Rod," Willa said. "I just didn't know how to explain."

"It was a good surprise," Billie assured her. "And I have a surprise for you, too."

"Oh?"

Billie grinned at Willa's cautious look and shook a bony finger at her. "You'll have to wait until tomorrow to find out, but it's a dandy. Right now I thought we'd have a cup of coffee," she said. "Or is grape soda pop still your beverage of choice?"

Willa returned her aunt's teasing smile. "Coffee's fine. I'm all grown up now."

Billie's glance traveled over Willa's fashionable Aztec print jacket and narrow black wool pants. "That you are," she said with the briskness Willa remembered from her father's oldest sibling. "Not quite as coltish as you were at fifteen, and most of the freckles are gone. But your hair's still the same shade as a fox's coat and your eyes still look like the lake on a cloudy day."

Willa tolerated the exacting assessment much better than she would have as a schoolgirl. "It's good to see you, too, Aunt Billie," she said, then realized with surprise that she actually meant it. For the last few years she'd done her best to avoid family, and therefore this reunion should have been awkward. But Billie treated her as she always had, tempering her sternness with teasing, and Willa was immediately at ease, though she did wonder about the shotgun that was still leaning against the wall.

She watched Billie place the teakettle on the well-used commercial range that sat in one corner like a hulking behemoth. The pink enameled kitchen table, every bit as old as the range, was still in its place by the doorway. After Billie declined her offer of help, Willa hung her jacket over the back of a chair and sat down before asking, "So what exactly has Hulbert been up to this time?"

"Oh, you know. Typical ghostly deeds." Billie made a delicate, fluttering gesture with her hands that was totally out of keeping with her solid build. "Digging holes, howling and haunting—that sort of thing."

"You always used to say that Hulbert was only a public relations ploy created by Grandpa Johann." Willa remembered how her aunt had scorned the ghost stories Johann loved to tell as he was seated next to a crackling fireplace and surrounded by willing guests and wide-eyed children.

Billie shrugged and spooned instant coffee into two mugs.

Willa persisted. "Are you saying you believe in ghosts now? You think Hulbert's spirit is wandering the island looking for his lost fortune?"

Billie shrugged again. "There's something out there. Maybe just an old woman's imagination." She filled a mug with hot water and handed it to Willa, without quite meeting her questioning gaze.

"That shotgun certainly isn't imaginary." Willa took a swallow of coffee and grimaced. Instant coffee always tasted metallic to her, and Billie had made this batch strong enough to dissolve rust.

Billie stared at her for a long moment, then finally sighed. "All right, you don't believe me. I wouldn't either, as much as I'd like to forget the truth." Her voice lowered to a raspy whisper. "Someone comes here at night—unless ghosts leave footprints and break windows."

Willa thought of the tire tracks she'd seen, and a cold feeling of unease stole over her, prickling her skin and making her shiver. Billie lived alone on the island. It was only a few miles into town, but with the road almost impassable and the lake frozen, it could just as well be a few hundred.

"Who? And why?"

Billie shrugged. "Just kids, I think. That sorry old tale about Hulbert is still circulating around Pinecrest." She shook her head. "I suppose they think they'll find buried treasure, or maybe they get their kicks scaring an old woman. They've been showing up once or twice a week since fall. The storm kept them away tonight."

"Have you called the sheriff?"

Billie snorted. "Didn't do any good. Sam Pitzer's been sheriff longer than I've had that teakettle." She pointed to the battered and tarnished piece of copper that had been a fixture in the kitchen as long as Willa could remember. "That lazy old fool is just counting the days until he can draw his pension."

Willa hid her smile behind the mug of coffee. If she remembered correctly, Sam Pitzer even bore a striking physical resemblance to the squat, bulbous teakettle.

"Last time I called him he laughed at me." Billie's chin lifted. "I even wrote a letter to the editor of the Pinecrest Press. Now everybody thinks I've gone batty out here all alone." She looked at Willa defiantly. "As soon as those boys show up at school with their behinds full of buckshot, they'll see who's crazy."

"I don't think you're crazy, Aunt Billie," Willa said, even though she wondered if all the years living alone had softened her aunt's mind. The Billie she remembered wouldn't have put up with vandals for a few days, let alone several months. "Why didn't you tell me about this sooner?"

"I was afraid you wouldn't come."

Willa was touched by her aunt's words. She didn't have the heart to remind her that her stay was only temporary. "I'm here," she said, reaching across the table to squeeze her aunt's hand.

"I'm so glad you are."

At Billie's trusting smile Willa felt the weight of the world settle on her shoulders. They chatted for a while longer before Willa went up to bed in the room Billie had prepared for her. At 3:00 A.M. she was still wide awake. Her insomnia had nothing to do with the creaks and squeaks of the stairs. It wasn't connected to the sound of the wind rattling the panes, nor the darkness devoid of city street lights, a darkness so heavy that it could almost be touched.

She couldn't sleep because her seventy-six-year-old aunt was bedding down in the pantry with a shotgun next to her cot.

Sighing, she leaned back against the pillows. She'd offered to help Billie make up another bed, but her aunt had insisted that she usually slept downstairs because of her "arthritic" legs. Willa knew better. Billie was afraid. And now, remembering the tire tracks leading from the house, Willa felt a pinprick of fear herself. If the tracks didn't belong to Billie's truck, then where did they come from?

"What have I gotten myself into?" Her whispered question sounded loud in the silence. She'd come to Restless Spirit to say goodbye to the past and regain her equilibrium. Instead she'd *found* a whole new set of problems: an elderly aunt, a run-down resort, and a ghost that wasn't a ghost.

Fortunately, some problems were easier to solve than others. First thing in the morning she would call the sheriff about her aunt's "night visitors." The rest of the day she reserved for looking over the resort and estimating the cost of restoration. And maybe, just maybe, tomorrow night she would convince Billie to sleep upstairs.

While she slept the cold air seeped through the pile of quilts and even into her dreams. When she opened her eyes she saw that the icy whiteness was no dream after all. The window was etched with crystalline frost, and the branches of the oak outside were coated with snow. It all came flooding back—the storm, her aunt, the house, Rod. She groaned and threw off the covers, clenching her teeth against the chill.

As Willa entered the kitchen, wearing most of the contents of her overnight bag, Billie reached to refill the teakettle. Willa returned her "good morning," then demanded, "What happened to the heat? It feels like the inside of a fish house in here."

"The oil burner your grandfather installed has a mind of its own."

"How old is it?" Willa asked, dreading the answer.

"Let me see, that was the year the lake got so high. Was it '67? Or '68?"

"Twenty-five years ago?"

"No, it hasn't been that long, has it?" Billie's brow wrinkled in concentration. "Oh, dear. I guess it has. I suppose we'll be needing a new furnace one of these days. Seems like everything is falling apart at once."

Willa paused in the act of buttering a slice of toast. She decided it would be too pushy to ask for a complete rundown on needed repairs right now—that could wait until later. She shivered. The furnace, however, couldn't wait. "I'll phone a repairman right after breakfast," she told Billie.

"You can't. The storm knocked the phone out."

Willa closed her eyes in resignation. "Then I'll go over to Quinlan's and see if their phone is still working."

"Don't bother."

"Why not? Quinlan's is still there, isn't it?"

Billie snorted. "Of course it is. That old woman is too stubborn to move and too lazy to die."

Willa suppressed a smile. If she remembered correctly Mattie Quinlan was at least five years younger than her aunt. "Then why don't I go and use their phone?"

"That won't be necessary."

"Billie, we'll freeze," she said with as much patience as she could muster. "The fireplace isn't enough to warm the entire house."

"Just be patient. The furnace will be fixed."

"By whom?"

"Ah, if I told you that, I'd ruin the surprise."

Billie's blue eyes twinkled. She stubbornly turned her back, and Willa knew that pressing for more information would be useless. "Is Rod still sleeping?" she asked instead.

"Yes. And if he's anything like you were at that age, he'll sleep till noon."

"You're probably right," Willa said with a rueful laugh. "In that case I'll get started outside. I'd like to take a look at the cottages."

"But it's freezing out there."

"It's freezing in here," Willa pointed out.

Twenty minutes later she was outside, bundled up in Rod's parka. Underneath her jeans she wore leggings, and on her feet were Billie's boots and a pair of snowshoes to help her over the drifts. Even though the icicles that hung from the roof edges were already shrinking in the sun, to Willa—who'd lived in the southwest for her entire adult life—the temperature still felt positively arctic.

She huffed her way to the guest cottage nearest the house, discarding the awkward snowshoes before entering. The electricity had been shut off, but bright morning sunshine reflected off the drifts of snow and made artificial lighting unnecessary. Methodically she checked the cottage's contents, mentally noting what repairs and additions were needed. When she was finished, she refastened the snowshoes and went on to the next cottage.

As she continued going from cottage to cottage, she felt a growing sense of dismay as she realized just how much effort—and money—it would take to get the resort in shape for the summer. She looked at her watch and realized that it was almost noon. Mealtimes at Restless Spirit followed the clock to the minute, and she knew without being told that Billie hadn't changed that custom either. She started for the last cottage, determined to finish.

Willa was almost to the doorway when she stopped and stared. Leading up to the front door were footprints. But whose? Because of the heavy snowfall the island was cut off from the mainland. That left Billie or Rod. Rod was asleep, and she was wearing Billie's only pair of boots. And anyway, the footprints were too large to belong to a woman.

She felt a rush of cold fear even under the heavy parka, but she quickly dismissed it. If Billie was right, the "ghost" was really a teenage hooligan. The owner of the footprints had not only terrorized her aunt, but actually had the gall to show up in broad daylight. She decided to confront him.

But before she could take another step, a hand closed over her shoulder. She muffled a scream and slipped on the icy steps, throwing herself and the other person off balance. The two of them teetered at the edge of the steps for a moment before landing in the snow that had drifted against the cottage.

Willa spit out a mouthful of snow, and a heavy weight settled on top of her. That and the shock of the icy wetness against her skin forced the breath from her lungs. Then the weight moved off her back and a low voice demanded, "Who are you?" as though she were the one trespassing.

She felt the urge to laugh at the ridiculous question. She blinked the snow from her eyes and opened her mouth to speak, but rough hands were already tearing the parka's hood from her face.

"Willow?" The voice was incredulous. It was also much deeper than she remembered, and if it hadn't been for the hated nickname she wouldn't have recognized it at all. He grabbed her arm.

"Christian!"

She used her mitten to rub the last drops of moisture from her lashes and opened her eyes to see him crouching above her. It was Christian Foster all right, but he was certainly not the teenager she remembered. His hair, flecked with snow, had darkened to a rich chestnut shade. His shoulders were broad against the white backdrop, and his face was older, his jaw harder. It looked as though his nose may have been broken once more since the summer when she was ten and he was twelve, when he had defended her honor against Larry Olson. Only his eyes were the same, hazel green and assessing.

And right now they were assessing her. Suddenly the multiple layers of sweaters and Rod's heavy parka felt like the thinnest gossamer. Willa's delight at the reunion altered subtly, until she was simply a woman reacting to a man's undisguised stare. Memories of where they'd left off that last summer, when she was fifteen and Christian seventeen, crowded her mind and caused her chilled skin to heat. But the memories scattered when she saw Christian's grim expression.

His voice was as stinging as his gaze as he said, "I thought you gave up on all us northwoods hicks here in Pinecrest."

2

"*I'm here to visit Billie.*" Willa's voice was as husky as Christian remembered, but now she sounded—and looked—nothing like a tomboyish fifteen-year-old.

He felt his stomach muscles clench at her words, and the old feeling of betrayal crept over him. In his worst dreams, and there had been plenty of bad ones after Rick died, he hadn't expected to see any of Willa's family again—except for Billie, of course. Billie was different. She was the one who didn't run away, the one who stayed behind to carry on the family business. The one who still treated him like family.

One of the reasons he'd returned was the same as Willa's—to see Billie. But Billie hadn't told him that her niece planned to visit. The old woman probably forgot, with all the other problems facing the resort right now. If he'd known Willa Mitterhauser was coming back, he never would have moved into one of the cottages here at Restless Spirit. He would have stayed in the city forever, no matter how much he'd grown to hate it. But he hadn't known, and here he was, face-to-face with the one who'd rejected him when he needed her most.

She was looking up at him, her eyes dark with surprised affront—and something else. He forced himself to relax his grip on her arm.

"I'm sorry I snuck up on you like that," he said. "I thought you were trespassing. From the back you looked like a boy."

"Thanks."

He couldn't stop a fleeting grin at her sarcasm but wisely decided not to acknowledge that she appeared anything but boyish from this angle. The bulky army-green parka was a startling contrast to her translucent skin and reddish-gold hair, which now tumbled around her shoulders like a waterfall of fire. And the layers of clothing couldn't hide the soft curves he'd sensed the moment he'd tackled her, even though it had been too late by then to stop. But now other instincts were taking over, and he realized that little Willow was all grown up.

The direction of his thoughts appalled him. He remembered belatedly that he was still holding lightly on to her arm with one hand while his other imprisoned her against his chest. He released her and moved quickly out of her way.

"Did I hurt you?" he asked, almost as an afterthought.

She grimaced, looking more like the child he had once delighted in teasing. "Not really. But I'm soaked to the skin." She looked toward the main house, and he realized that Billie was calling for them. "It's time for lunch," she said. "We'd better get inside or she'll make us polish the silver."

That was another thing he hadn't forgotten. Polishing the silver flatware had always been their punishment for being late for meals. Since his own mother rarely climbed out of the bottle long enough to cook, he'd eaten nearly every meal at the Mitterhausers' in those days. They'd welcomed the fatherless boy as one of their own. So, along with Willa and Rick, he'd done his share of silver polishing.

Christian pushed the memory aside. The past had haunted him often enough since he'd returned to Pinecrest a month ago. And at this particular moment he had more past right here in front of him than he could handle. He reached out to pull her to her feet.

Willa walked behind Christian, snowshoes under her arm, stepping carefully into the path his steps made. She tried to tell herself that she was imagining the awkwardness between them, but she still burned from Christian's harsh gaze. Why wasn't he happy to see her again?

As they drew closer to the house, she heard a low rumble that her city-attuned ears had dismissed before as background noise. "Who's that?" she asked, gesturing toward the driveway where someone was using a tractor with a front-end blade to scoop snow and add it to an already mountainous pile of white.

"Kevin Quinlan. He gave me a lift across the causeway. I didn't want to take a chance on getting stuck."

She smiled and waved until the man on the tractor finally saw her and waved back, even though it was unlikely that he'd recognize her. She'd known Kevin, Mattie Quinlan's "boy," for as long as she could recall. He would be almost forty now, she realized. Only rarely had he played with Christian, Rick, and her. Most of the time Mattie had had him enrolled in various schools and institutions, never giving up hope that he could be "cured."

"How is he?" she asked.

"He hasn't changed," Christian told her. "He may be slow, but he's steady. Until I got here, Billie counted on him for everything."

Willa felt a pang of guilt. She knew that even though Kevin was physically an adult, he was mentally little more than a child. Mattie had given birth to him when she was in her forties, and Sean Quinlan, unable to bear the thought of fathering a retarded child, left mother and baby. Mattie had given Kevin the best of care, but her husband's desertion had left her filled with bitterness and spite, which she'd taken out mostly on Willa's aunt Billie, who'd once been in love with Sean herself.

Willa thought of Billie here alone, facing the vandals and the resort's disintegration with no one to help her but Kevin and Mattie. And then the other half of Christian's sentence sunk in.

"You mean you haven't lived here in Pinecrest all this time?" she asked, trying to revise the image she'd carried in her mind for eighteen years, the picture of a youthful Christian in faded jeans and a beat-up leather jacket, riding up and down Main Street astride his Harley.

"Nope."

Of course he hadn't stayed the same. Curiosity filled her, but before she could drag another word out of him, he was crossing the front veranda, leaving her to struggle through the snow in his wake. Questions filled her mind as she dutifully followed Christian's example and stamped the snow from her boots before heading inside the house. She had barely managed to hang the wet parka on the hall tree where it could dry when Rod hailed her from the staircase.

"Willa, would you tell Billie I'll be down for dinner in a minute?" Rod asked.

"Sure," she said, then nearly slammed into Christian's back. He stood, motionless as a statue, staring at the spot on the stairs where Rod had been.

"Rick?"

Willa barely heard the softly spoken word, but her heart wrenched. "No. Rick's son. He's named Roderick for his father, but he goes by Rod," she said. "Rod Dane. When Caroline remarried, her husband adopted him." She noted Christian's pale white face. "You knew Rick had a son, didn't you?" she asked.

"No." His answer was curt.

"Caroline—Rick's wife—was pregnant," she said quietly. "She went back to Texas after . . . afterward." Even with all the years in between, she still had a hard time saying it, or even thinking it, for that matter. *Suicide.* The word was sibilant, suggesting peace and serenity. But the reality was harsh and bleak, especially for those left behind.

"Why wasn't there a funeral?"

Christian's question wasn't one she expected, and she struggled for words. She turned to adjust the jackets on the hall tree, hiding her expression from his sharp gaze. She, too, had questioned her parents' decision to bury Rick in the Pinecrest cemetery without ceremony. They'd wanted no one at the gravesite, not even Willa. She'd struggled to understand then, and even now her explanation rang false.

"My parents spent the summer before by his bedside in San Francisco, worrying that he'd never walk again." She was nearly whispering so the sound wouldn't carry to Rod's room at the top of the stairs. "They were proud when he reenlisted, but they were also relieved when he was stationed in Germany. They thought he'd be safe there, far away from Vietnam and his memories of the war."

Her voice caught, and she had to swallow before continuing stiffly, "You can't imagine how they felt when they found out he'd killed himself. They were devastated. Instead of holding a funeral, they just had a quiet graveside service."

"They buried him like they were ashamed of him. Sneaking into town and out again like thieves." His voice was low and tense.

"You don't understand. It wasn't like that," she protested, even though she'd often thought the same thing herself, until realizing her parents' stoic German-Scandinavian upbringing demanded that they deny their grief.

"I didn't even get to say goodbye to him, dammit."

Neither did I! she wanted to shout. His words were an echo of her own. She'd spoken them time and time again, angrily hurling them at her parents before stalking out of the house they'd rented in Scottsdale after leaving Minnesota behind. And every time she rebelled, they responded by polishing the memory of their son a little brighter, holding it up to Willa like a trophy, comparing her to him until she rebelled again. Eventually they'd managed to convince themselves that he'd died a hero on the battlefield. They'd idolized him until Willa thought she'd go crazy. Instead, she'd left.

But that was all in the past, she reminded herself. She had come here to forget the ugliness, to remember the good times. It was time to move on with her life. If only she could share her memories with Christian . . . but something—whether it was the hard line of his jaw or the coldness in his hazel eyes—told her he didn't want to share anything with her at all.

She quickly smothered her pain at his rejection as Billie's voice carried loudly from the dining room. "This is the last call. Dinner's on the table and getting cold."

Willa could hear Rod's footsteps clattering down the back stairs. She remembered nostalgically her own haste when her aunt or grandmother would announce meals. Billie's voice brooked no argument as she warned from the doorway, "You two'd better quit lollygagging and get in here, or you'll suffer the consequences."

She entered the dining room several steps behind Christian, in time to witness the awkward moment as Billie introduced Christian to Rod. Rod looked at Christian with that closed, cautious expression he wore around adults. It disappeared the moment Billie informed him that Rick and Christian were once best friends. At that, interest flashed across the boy's face, but Christian's shuttered expression didn't reveal much.

Willa felt a surge of protectiveness and wondered who it was for: Her nephew, who'd been rebuffed too many times already by the adults in his life? Or Christian, who obviously didn't need or want her concern?

She took the seat Billie indicated, at Christian's left. He was at the head of the table, where her grandfather used to sit, and she wondered why Billie herself didn't take the place reserved for the head of the family. Instead, her aunt sat on Christian's other side. Rod was at Willa's left, and the chair across from Christian, where Willa's grandmother used to sit, remained empty, as though waiting for the lady of the house to claim it.

Billie beamed at Christian before turning to Willa and asking, "How did you like my surprise?"

Willa looked at her aunt stupidly for a moment before realizing that Christian was the surprise Billie had promised the night before. How *did* she feel? Shocked, dismayed, hurt, excited . . . the list went on and on, but she could hardly admit to such a confused tangle of emotions. She caught Christian's glance and realized that he'd read her mind perfectly. His expression challenged her to admit her wildly confused reaction to him.

"Were you surprised?" Billie prompted.

"Why, seeing him knocked the breath right out of me," she said. Christian let out a bark of laughter.

"I knew you'd be pleased," Billie said, looking pleased herself. "You may start passing, Christian," she instructed with a hint of ceremony.

Willa accepted the dish from Christian's hands and felt another wave of nostalgia when she recognized the aroma. "Rouladen," she said, placing two of the rolls of stuffed meat on her plate. "I haven't eaten this in years." She passed the dish to Rod, who looked at it with distaste. She felt like kicking him under the table, but Billie didn't seem to notice.

Christian had. He was staring at Rod with an expression of impatience. "It was your father's favorite," he said evenly. It was the perfect thing to say.

"Yeah?" Interest mingled with skepticism in Rod's voice.

"My mother—Oma, he called her—used to make it for him whenever he did extra chores." Billie followed with a long tale of how Rick would get into mischief and be punished with some disagreeable task, and then lavished with grandmotherly attention and home-cooking.

Listening to Billie speak with perfect ease about Rick reminded Willa of the long talks she and her nephew had had in the car during the journey here. Telling him about the happy times wasn't as difficult as she thought it would be. But what would she or Billie do if Rod's questions turned to Rick's death? No one had told Rod how his father died. His mother, remarried since he had been a toddler, didn't mention Rick at all. And Willa's parents had filled Rod with stories of how his father died a hero's death in Vietnam.

Billie finished her tale and waited expectantly for Rod's reaction to the first bite. Willa felt Rod's discomfort at being the center of attention. She turned to Christian and inquired, "What brings you back to Pinecrest?"

"Work."

Billie expanded on his abrupt answer. "Christian is one of Pinecrest's peace officers."

Before Willa could comment, Rod said, "You mean he's a *cop*?" He pronounced the word with barely concealed disgust, and she forgot her own surprise.

Her parents had told her that Rod was in and out of trouble at school, and now she wondered if the trouble was more serious than they'd let on. She could see the warring expressions on his face as his earlier interest in Christian gave way to distrust.

"I didn't know you'd joined the police force," she said in the silence that followed Rod's comment.

"There's a lot about me you don't know," Christian replied, and for a moment she felt as though the two of them were alone in the room. He hadn't reacted to Rod's insolence at all. His words were strictly for her, and they carried a challenge that she didn't understand. She searched his hazel eyes for an answer until the clatter of china broke the spell.

"This stuff is pretty good," Rod said as he speared the pickle from inside the rouladen and popped it in his mouth. He acted as though nothing had happened. Billie beamed at the boy's words. Willa, who had begun to recognize her nephew's quick mood swings, didn't comment.

The rest of the meal passed in silence—or at least it did for three of them. Billie chattered on, seemingly oblivious of Rod's sullenness and the undercurrents between Willa and Christian.

She waved away Willa's offer to help serve dessert. When the last piece of Black Forest cake was distributed, she looked around the table with a pleased expression lighting her wrinkled face, and said, "Isn't it wonderful to have the family back together again?"

Willa heard the satisfaction in Billie's voice and stifled a sense of dismay. Family? Her parents would never leave Arizona, her grandparents had died several years ago, and Rick was only photographs and memories. Besides, it wouldn't do for Billie to get too used to having "family" at her dinner table. She opened her mouth to remind her aunt that this reunion was only temporary, but before she could speak, Billie dropped a bombshell.

"I'm going into town to see Olaf Johnson this week." At the mention of the family attorney, Willa paused with her fork halfway to her mouth. "I'm changing my will," Billie went on. "I want you to have Restless Spirit now, Willa, not after I'm gone. I'm getting too old to run this place, and I want to see it in the hands of the next generation before I die."

Willa bit into the cake and chewed slowly, not even noticing its taste as she searched for something to say. Billie's announcement was unexpected—and unwanted. Although she had no desire to try to revive her singing career, she knew that as long as she stayed here, the past would anchor her as firmly as concrete and keep her from moving forward. She searched for the words to refuse her aunt's offer without hurting her feelings.

"I'm very grateful, Billie, but . . ." She paused, and something drew her gaze to Christian. The warning in his eyes stopped her. The rest of her answer came without thinking. "I need more time to consider it."

"I'm sure you'll make the right decision," Billie said.

Willa stayed silent. She couldn't bear to erase the happiness on her aunt's face.

"I've had offers to sell, you know," Billie added. "Mayor Nelson wants to bring in some fancy resort, like the ones closer to Minneapolis or Duluth." She looked around the table, her sharp gaze settling on Rod. "But this place has been in the family for over a century now. My grandfather kept it after he went bankrupt, and my parents held on to it through the Depression. Your father couldn't stay away from it, Willa, not even after he got that fancy job in Fargo. Every summer we were all here together." Her glance touched on Christian before returning to Rod.

She continued, "Restless Spirit belongs to our family. And not just to us but to the families that come here year after year for their vacations. Family is the most important thing in the world. And someday, young man, you'll raise your family here, too."

Willa could feel the past pulling her back, threatening to suffocate her. Before she could protest, a hand closed over her shoulder.

"We'll get started on the dishes, Billie," she heard Christian say behind her. His fingers tightened, warning her not to argue.

When they entered the kitchen, she whirled to face him. "What was that all about?"

"I was going to ask you the same thing." His words were quiet but forceful. "This place might not mean much to you, but it's your aunt's entire life. Think twice before you throw it back in her face." He stalked off toward the sink, leaving Willa to stare at his broad back.

She followed and watched him squirt soap into the rushing water. "I don't want it," she said.

"You don't deserve it."

She bit back an angry retort. He made her sound like a spoiled brat, when all she wanted was to be free. "I came here to put the past in its proper perspective," she said, wondering why the words sounded so cold and clinical all of a sudden. She didn't know why she was bothering to make explanations at all. Apparently Christian had already judged her and found her lacking.

But for some reason, she still needed his understanding, if not his blessing, so she went on. "Rick's death troubled me for a long time. I'm over it now, and I want to get on with my life."

"Yeah? Well the past has a funny way of popping up when you least expect it." He looked at her pointedly, and she could feel herself flushing. She refused to look away, and at last he turned back to the dishes. Then she understood.

At age fifteen, all she'd thought about was how the move had affected her—changing schools, having to make new friends, losing Christian. She'd never even questioned the decision to leave the resort in Billie's hands. Her aunt had always seemed so strong and capable. And Christian . . . She paused in the act of drying a coffee cup. She'd been so wrapped up in her own pain that she had ignored his.

Watching him carefully, she said, "I'm going to stay long enough to help Billie get things in order before I leave." Then she added, "Did you know she sleeps downstairs in the pantry with a shotgun?"

Surprise and concern flashed briefly across Christian's face before his expression settled into its neutral lines again. Willa knew then that Christian Foster wasn't as tough as he pretended. He had a weak spot, and it was Billie.

"She's eccentric," he said.

"She's afraid."

"Who's afraid?" Billie demanded as she burst into the kitchen with a stack of dishes. "What are you two arguing about?"

Christian was the first to recover. He grinned and said, "Just picking up where we left off. You remember how we always liked a good debate."

"You two bickered about every little thing," Billie said. Her tone was scolding, but the twinkle in her eye stirred Willa's suspicions.

Could it be possible her aunt was trying to bring them together? If so, she certainly hadn't taken Christian's wishes into consideration. Given his cold disapproval of her, the idea was so preposterous that Willa nearly laughed aloud. As for her, the last thing she wanted was to tie herself to someone who reminded her of the past.

"Rod and I set the rest of the silver out on the dining room table," Billie said. "When you're through in here, you can start on that. You were late to dinner," she reminded them with another twinkle before leaving them.

They finished the rest of the dishes without speaking a word. Willa could feel tension emanating from Christian as he jerkily put the dried dishes into a differ-ent cupboard than she remembered. He was more familiar with her aunt's house than she was, she realized as she watched his strong hands curve around another piece of delicate china. He might pretend to be unaf-fected by everything that had happened since their chilly reunion in the snowbank, but she could tell something was eating at him.

He hung the last cup on the metal hooks inside the cupboard and then strode to the refrigerator and removed a carton of milk. Willa didn't miss the grimace that passed over his face or the hand that briefly massaged his flat abdomen.

"Cold water works better for indigestion," she told him, looking away before she started to think about the muscled flesh hidden by his navy chamois shirt. "The calcium in the milk just stimulates your stomach to produce more acids."

"Are you a doctor now?"

She ignored his sarcastic grin. "No. A singer. But I happen to know a lot about stress."

He opened the carton and drank from it without moving his gaze from her face. She flushed as she realized he was taking note of the way she was following the movement of his throat as he swallowed. He tossed the carton in the wastebasket underneath the sink, brushing against her side as he did. His touch sent shivers up and down her spine.

"Thanks for the advice, but I don't need your help. Neither does Billie." He started for the door.

Willa swallowed back her hurt. She couldn't indulge in self-pity, not now. "Wait."

He stopped but didn't turn around. She hated what she was about to say, but she knew she had no choice. "Rod doesn't know how his father died," she said. "I'd appreciate it if you didn't say anything to him."

Christian turned then, and the bleak expression on his face nearly undid the calm she was trying so hard to maintain. "You must be joking."

"Please, Christian. Don't tell him."

Lying didn't come easily to Willa, but she knew that in this case the truth would hurt Rod far more than the picture her parents had painted of a brave war hero. For once, she agreed with them. She didn't want her nephew to go through the same kind of pain she'd gone through over her brother's suicide. How much worse it would be for Rod to know that his father had deliberately left behind a pregnant wife carrying a son he would never see.

Christian stared at her for a long moment before opening the door and going outside. He left her with nothing but a gust of cold air and the loud slam still ringing in her ears. He hadn't responded to her request, and she worried as she watched him walk from the house to the farthest cottage through the drifts of snow.

His assured gait was so much like that of the boy she used to know, the tough kid who didn't want anyone to see how much he felt. She felt a confused tangle of emotions at the sight, but she smoothed them away with a skill perfected by years of practice.

3

Rod thrust his hands deeper inside the pockets of his parka as he trudged through the snow to the weather-scarred wooden building ahead. Since arriving at the resort nearly a week ago, he'd escaped to this place more than once to get away from his great aunt Billie's sharp blue eyes. The exact same shade of blue as his own, he'd noted with surprise. He, who had never quite fit in anywhere, certainly not among his pretty blonde half sisters, was suddenly finding pieces of himself reflected in others: Billie's eyes, Willa's orange-red hair. He wasn't quite sure he liked it.

He reached out with one bare hand and yanked open the damp-swollen door of the boathouse. Afternoon sunlight filtered through the cracks between the gray boards of the roof and walls. The wide double door that opened onto the lake was falling from its hinges, leaving a gaping opening to the elements and the view. Inside, two rotting rowboats were tied to a short dock with missing boards. The bottoms of the neglected boats were filled with ice.

Rod shut the door behind him, sat down on the low bench next to it, and leaned back against the wall. He patted the pack of cigarettes in his coat pocket and thought about lighting one, but he knew the scent of smoke would never escape Billie's attention. The old woman watched him with that measuring look in her eyes, as if she were trying to decide whether or not he belonged at Restless Spirit.

Wasn't that why he'd come here with Willa? To find out if this was where he belonged? Only now he wasn't sure if he wanted to belong here. The whole resort was ready to fall down, and it was miles from here into town. Not that the town of Pinecrest was much to brag about, either. He'd gone there yesterday with Willa. One video store, a café, and a drugstore with a soda fountain like something out of an old "Andy Griffith Show" rerun.

He wasn't sure what he'd expected, but this wasn't it. He wasn't sure how he felt about his aunt Willa, either. Disappointed, for one thing. When he'd met her at his grandparents' house in Arizona, he could tell she was as impatient with the old folks' stories about his father as he was. That was why he'd cornered her and asked her to take him with her to Minnesota.

Hell, Rod thought, his rebellious bravado almost deserting him, his grandmother and grandfather Mitterhauser certainly hadn't wanted him. His mother had sent him there after he'd been expelled from that stupid military school his stepfather had enrolled him in. Why did Patrick Dane ever bother to adopt him if he didn't want him around? The old man said the school would teach him discipline and respect. Yeah, right.

Adults were big on stuff like that, he'd learned long ago. *Do as I say and not as I do.* Like lying for instance. He kicked at the dirt floor beneath his boots. Everyone lied to him, and Willa was no different. He'd hoped she would be, of course. He'd thought it would be pretty cool to hang out with an aunt who was a rock-and-roll singer. He had both her albums, which he'd kept carefully hidden from his mother.

Caroline never talked about his father, her first husband, at all. Which was probably better than telling him lies, he figured, shifting his weight on the hard bench. She'd barely mentioned his father's family—the Mittenhausers—until it was time to pass him along like a hot potato to his grandparents.

"No one can handle that boy," he'd overheard Patrick Dane saying to his wife one night. "He's been expelled from two schools already. It's time we gave up and let someone else, someone with professional knowledge, take care of him."

But his mother had refused to send him to a foster home. He tried to feel grateful for that, but getting sent to his grandparents in Arizona hadn't turned out to be much better. He ignored the stab of rejection, covering it up with resentment.

He was tired of being treated like a package, getting shipped from one school and home to another. He didn't belong anywhere, not even here, he thought as he stared out the gaping double doors to the snow-covered lake. He'd hoped Willa would be the one who would at last tell him the truth about his father. He couldn't put it into words, but there was something about the way she spoke to her parents that hinted at the same frustration and restlessness that he felt himself. That was why he'd asked her to take him with her.

Some mistake that was. Now she and Billie were talking about putting him in school here in Pinecrest. He couldn't see himself trying to fit in with a bunch of stupid backwoods hicks. But he didn't have anywhere else to go. Willa had talked to his mother on the phone last night, and Caroline told her that if Rod wouldn't stay in Pinecrest until summer, he was going to a foster home.

He kicked again at the dirt beneath his boot. After nearly a week of coming to this run-down shack to think, he'd worn a furrow into the packed earth.

He turned his head at the sound of an engine getting nearer and recognized the rumble of Christian Foster's pickup moving closer along the causeway. He thought about his last run-in with a cop. The jerk had claimed that he'd found shoplifted merchandise in Rod's locker. All the kids knew that it was the cop's son who was stealing, not him. But no one listened to a bunch of kids, and adults could say anything and get away with it.

Christian Foster was probably no different, Rod thought with a cynicism far beyond his seventeen years. Like that other cop, like his stepfather, like his aunt Willa.

He looked out across the lake again, watching the shadows of the pine trees on the shore darken and stretch like bridges across the snow. Maybe he wouldn't fit in here either, but there was nowhere left to go.

Willa walked up the horseshoe-shaped driveway to Quinlan's store. The green-and-white sign outside had been painted recently, but it still said the same thing it had eighteen years ago: Bait, gas, groceries.

She smiled as she thought that the list reflected most visitors' priorities. Ice-fishing season was almost over, but as usual the enthusiasts would refuse to leave the lake until their fish houses started to sink, trying their best to narrow the gap of time between ice-out, which usually happened in early April, and the annual fishing opener in mid-May.

There wasn't much time left for ice-fishing. Five days after the blizzard that marked Willa and Rod's arrival, a thaw blew in from the Dakotas, and here and there patches of wet earth lay in visible contrast to the melting drifts of snow. March was a homely time of year, with its skeletal trees and dirty snow. The causeway was thick with mud, but Willa had insisted on walking to Quinlan's, hoping the exercise and solitude would help her think. As an excuse, she claimed she wanted to buy a can of real coffee. Five days of Billie's instant brew was enough.

She had put off buying ground coffee until now because for some reason the purchase made her stay seem permanent. It was ridiculous to feel that way about something as inconsequential as a can of coffee, especially now that she was practically resigned to staying longer than her original two weeks. What else could she do, with Caroline threatening to send Rod to a foster home? She sighed. Besides, she was no closer to reaching a decision about her future than she was when she arrived.

Things were getting more complicated every day. The amount of repairs required to get the resort fully operational was staggering, her aunt was practically helpless, and Rod needed to have some kind of stability. And then there was Christian. She saw him infrequently—he worked the night shift and slept most of the morning—but his presence was everywhere. Billie spoke of him constantly and glowingly, and Rod reacted visibly every time Christian's name was mentioned. Willa was acutely aware of Christian in a way she'd never experienced with her former husband, Darryl, who'd set legions of teenage hearts on fire.

She opened the door to the small store, barely noticing the jangling bell above her. From this moment, she vowed, she would quit dwelling on Christian Foster. He'd made it pretty clear that he thought of her as a spoiled brat, and it was easier to let him go on thinking so.

"Excuse me," she apologized as she bumped into someone on the way out. A bulky man with a youngish, unlined face and calm brown eyes regarded her. "Kevin!" she exclaimed, smiling. "I was hoping I'd see you soon. I'm Willa Mitterhauser, remember?"

He nodded at her with a shy smile, blushing furiously, and then walked out to the small shed next to the store. Kevin had always been shy around her. Around everyone, she remembered, except Christian, who was in Pinecrest all year and not just summers and holidays like Willa and Rick. Christian had always had the ability to draw Kevin out of his shell. She realized her thoughts had returned to the subject she'd vowed to avoid.

Before she could chastise herself for this, Mattie Quinlan darted from behind the counter with the energy of a small poodle. About five feet tall and all bones, the only soft thing about Mattie was the strawberry shade of blonde that colored her short curls. *From a bottle,* Billie had told Willa with a disdainful sniff.

"I heard you were back," Mattie said, coming to a halt a couple of feet away. "It's about time you stopped by."

"Hello, Mattie. It's good to see you." And it was, Willa realized with surprise. She, Christian, and Rick used to save all their pennies and nickels for trips to Quinlan's, where a glass-fronted freezer case was filled with an enticing array of ice cream novelties. They'd take several minutes to choose between fudge pops and dream bars or ice cream sandwiches and chocolate pies. After making their purchases and savoring them right down to the wooden stick or paper wrapper, they would retreat to the backyard and play with Kevin until it was time to return to Restless Spirit for supper.

"Sure was surprised to hear you came home," Mattie said. "Billie told everyone that you were some kind of famous singer out there in California."

"Hardly that," Willa said. Her closest brush with fame was as the lead singer for Darryl's punk rock band, Natural Disaster. Those were years she'd rather forget, years when she'd tried to bury her memories under an avalanche of wild parties, late nights, and loud music. More people heard her voice now, singing about perfume or cars in commercials. "I've made some TV and radio ads. You've probably heard some of them."

Mattie's wrinkled face showed her disappointment. "Then you've never met Frank Sinatra or Harry Connick, Jr.?"

"Never." More relieved than offended at Mattie's lack of interest, Willa tried to keep a straight face as she added, "But I do like their records."

"Oh, I do, too," Mattie said. "I have every one. That Frankie reminded me so much of my darling Sean." Her blue eyes looked hazy as she was lost in memories.

Willa made a noncommittal murmur that could be taken for agreement or sympathy.

"Billie told me you were a widow," Mattie said.

"We were planning to divorce several months before Darryl died." Willa turned to browse the shelves, not wanting to discuss her disappointing marriage with anyone, particularly the town gossip.

"Well, then you didn't suffer as I did when Sean left," Mattie went on relentlessly. "How lucky for you."

Willa smiled thinly as she reached for a can of coffee. She wasn't even sure which type of grind to buy, since all Billie had ever used was instant. She took the one marked "All Purpose" and continued down the aisle, pausing at the freezer case. This time her smile was genuine. "I don't believe it. You still have ice cream sandwiches and fudge pops."

"I don't sell as many of them anymore," Mattie said. "Pleckner's resort went broke a couple years ago, and Billie doesn't bring much business in these days, either."

"Walt Pleckner closed Whispering Pines?" The resort had been there nearly as long as Restless Spirit.

"His son did. Walter died five years ago. And the Knudsen family is about ready to shut the doors on Sandy Shores. Things have changed since you've been away." Mattie watched as Willa selected a half gallon of ice cream from the freezer. "Your aunt prefers caramel," she said when Willa reached for a jar of chocolate ice cream topping.

Willa absently thanked her and picked up a jar of caramel, too. "I had no idea things were that bad," she said. "Billie never told us anything."

"Too stubborn, probably. She's an old woman, you know. Some people are saying this new hotel Mayor Nelson wants to build would help business around here . . ." Willa listened to Mattie ramble on about time shares and tour groups as she rang up the coffee and ice cream on the old-fashioned cash register.

"Most of the owners on this side of the lake would be glad to sell, all except Billie," Mattie finished. She looked up at Willa as she put the purchases in a paper bag. "That big hotel sure would help my business. Billie hardly gets enough guests to pay her electricity bills."

Which would explain why the resort was in such a state of disrepair, Willa thought, barely hearing the jangle of the bell above the door.

"Maybe you'll be able talk some sense into her," Mattie said. "Help her put a little nest egg together for her retirement."

Willa hadn't even thought of that angle. If Restless Spirit went under as Whispering Pines did, how would Billie live? She turned at the sound of heavy footsteps behind her, her polite expression freezing at the look of disapproval on Christian Foster's face.

"Hi, Mattie." He managed to nod in the older woman's direction without ever taking his steady gaze from Willa's face. "I came to pick up some coffee for Billie," he said. "She knows Willa doesn't like instant, so she asked me to stop on my way home and buy some especially for her."

Willa knew Christian's explanation wasn't for Mattie's benefit. He wanted to make her feel guilty and ungrateful. Well, she didn't need any more of that. Her temper, which she'd learned to control over the last few years, was near to erupting. She reached into the paper sack and held up the can of coffee. "I just saved you the trouble," she said.

She needed to get outside before she could throw the can of coffee at Christian's smug face, so she thanked Mattie and went out the door without a second glance. She didn't slow down until she was at the end of the driveway, where she let out a low sound of frustration.

"Indigestion?"

She whirled around to see Christian right behind her. He'd followed her as silently as a cat. She knew from the heat in her cheeks that her face must be nearly as red as her hair.

"I heard that cold water is the best thing for stomach complaints," he told her. The light in his hazel eyes belied his solemn expression, and Willa's anger and embarrassment fled. Once they'd teased each other easily—until that last summer. Then teasing had taken on a whole new meaning.

"I thought you were a cop, not a doctor," she said quickly, before she started thinking too much about those precious few weeks before Rick died.

"I'm off duty. Or as off duty as a guy can get when he's one of the town's three policemen. And I would definitely be falling down on my responsibilities if I didn't offer one of Pinecrest's citizens a ride home."

Willa silently walked beside him to his pickup, unwilling to remind him that she was hardly a citizen of Pinecrest and had no intentions of becoming one. If Christian was calling a truce, she would honor it. Anything had to be better than the uneasy battle of wills they'd waged during the last week.

"Besides," he added as he opened the passenger door for her, "the sun will be down in a few minutes, and Billie would skin me alive if I let you walk home in the dark. And I'd hate to disappoint her." His voice stressed the last sentence.

End of truce, Willa thought grimly as she waited for Christian to circle the truck to the driver's side. It was cold enough that she could see the puffs of steam from his mouth as he exhaled, like a dragon breathing fire, she thought as she waited for another lecture about her responsibilities.

"Your aunt," he began as he climbed up beside her, "is a remarkable woman. She's managed on her own all these years, trying to keep the family business intact."

"No one asked her to," Willa said tightly. "My father and grandparents washed their hands of the resort. They started new lives for themselves in Arizona. Billie was welcome to go with them, but she chose to hang on to a relic. No one can make a go of a run-down fishing resort."

"And who told you that? Mattie Quinlan?" He shifted gears and turned onto the country road in front of

Quinlan's. "She's a bit biased, in case you didn't notice."

"Maybe," Willa admitted. "But she brought up something I hadn't thought of. If Billie has poured every dime into the resort, she has nothing left for herself. How will she live when she's too old to run it any longer? If she sold it now, she'd have a nest egg in the bank."

Christian pulled the pickup over to the side of the road and parked it. It was difficult to read his expression in the increasing twilight. "Is your concern for Billie, or for yourself?" he asked, turning to her.

Willa didn't want to answer. "I have ice cream in here." She indicated the paper sack of groceries at her feet. "It will melt."

"Then answer my question, and we can be on our way," he said. "What exactly does Willa Mitterhauser Decker have planned for the future?" He must have been able to read the shock on Willa's face through the growing darkness, because he said, "Oh, I know all about Darryl Decker. There was that concert in Minneapolis five years ago, when I worked the security detail. Of course, the real party wasn't at the concert but afterward in the hotel room, hmm? I even had the opportunity to meet your husband and several of his . . . *friends*."

The way he stressed the word told Willa that Christian knew about Darryl's drug use, his continual assignations with groupies and road crew members. She remembered Minneapolis, too. It had been the beginning of the end, the point when she knew that Darryl was hell-bent on self-destruction, and that she couldn't stop him any more than she'd been able to stop Rick.

Her insides churned. She'd never been part of the band's drug scene or rowdy behavior, and it shamed her to think that Christian believed otherwise. She'd wanted to be on stage, to experience the thrill of working in front of an audience. Off stage, she wanted no part of the wild image Darryl and the other band members cultivated.

She looked at Christian sitting next to her. It was dark in the cab now, and she could feel rather than see the intensity of his gaze. Why did it matter so much to her what he thought of her? She wanted to explain, but she suspected that nothing she said would make a difference.

She turned toward her window. "That's in the past," she said.

"What about now, Willow?"

The old nickname drew her gaze to him again. His words had held a hint of tenderness, and she wished she could read his expression. The close intimacy of the cab, the protective darkness—she found herself wanting to tell him everything.

"I don't know," she said. "I haven't performed on stage in awhile." Not since Darryl had died. "I came here to decide what I want for the future, but first I need to finish with the past. Saying goodbye is the last step."

"Which brings us back to Billie." He restarted the engine. "She loves this place." The truck's headlights shone on the sign at the end of the causeway, adding emphasis to his words.

"I have some money saved up," Willa told him. "I was thinking it would help her fix the place up."

"She doesn't want your money," Christian told her. "Look at what she's done for Rod. The two of you haven't even been here a week, and she's already taken him under her wing. She wants a family."

"I am her family."

"Then quit acting like one of the resort guests."

His words stung. "I can't get involved," she said. "Restless

Spirit is Billie's. It's up to her to decide what to do."

"She's already decided. She wants you to have it."

"I already told you that I don't want it. It's part of—"

"The past," he finished for her.

He parked the pickup by the back door of the main house. Willa quickly scrambled down from her seat, but Christian was already there, reaching to take the groceries from her.

"It seems to me," he said, "that you're not quite as done with the past as you claim. You say coming here is the last step. Maybe it's only the first."

The comment caused her to lose her concentration on the icy path. She slipped, and Christian caught her by both elbows, letting the bag of groceries drop to the ground. Her hands came up automatically to grasp his forearms, and as her legs slipped beneath her nearly all her weight was crushed against his chest. For a brief moment his strength supported her. She felt a heady, swirling sensation before she regained her footing, but the sensation only increased when Christian continued to hold her.

"Are you okay?" he asked.

"Sure," she said. The tremor in her voice was due more to the feel of his iron-hard chest against her own soft curves than it was to the near fall, she realized, and immediately broke from his hold. "It's a good thing I didn't buy eggs," she said as she bent to gather up the groceries, which were all intact.

When she stood again, he was still facing her, his gaze dark.

"Willow," he began, and reached out.

She felt an unreasonable thrill of alarm as she stepped out of his range. "I'd better go help Billie with supper," she said and retreated into the house. She was glad her aunt wasn't inside the brightly lit kitchen to see her condition. She set the groceries on the table, then sat down heavily on a chair. Her legs were shaking, and her insides felt as unstable as the melting ice on the lake. Apparently some things hadn't changed. Christian could still make her head spin.

She hadn't felt this way since she was fifteen, when he had kissed her for the first time.

Christian entered the cottage he'd been using since he'd moved back to Pinecrest in January. The doctor had told him then he needed to get away from the stress of being an undercover narcotics cop in his South Minneapolis precinct. His stomach still burned at the memories of the things he'd seen: gangs turning quiet old neighborhoods into battle zones, young kids selling themselves for their next hit, even smaller children playing "cops and dealers" with bags of lawn clippings or powdered sugar.

He liked it here, where powder was something you skiied on, and ice was the stuff that melted from the eaves. Not that there weren't any problems in Pinecrest. A few weeks ago, he and his fellow officer, Skeet Varner, had caught a couple of high school boys fencing stolen goods so they could buy pot. But that was unusual. Most of the time he stopped drunk drivers on their way through town and got cats down from trees.

He'd moved into the cottage at Restless Spirit when Billie told him about the boys who broke windows and tracked mud through the cottages every weekend. The activity had virtually ceased, but Billie had insisted that she felt safer with him around, so he stayed on.

Everything had been moving along peacefully until Willa arrived, he thought, flipping on the light switch by the door. He tossed his keys onto the small table at the end of the sagging sofa bed and walked across the gray-painted wooden floor to the tiny kitchen alcove. An apartment-sized refrigerator and a gas stove were placed on either side of a maple cupboard and sink. He opened the refrigerator and reached in for the milk. But before he drank it, he cursed under his breath, put it back, and turned on the tap. He filled a glass and let the water, icy cold from the underground well, slide down his throat. He imagined he could feel it cooling the insides of his stomach.

If only he could cool everything else. He'd turned down the old-fashioned gas heater before he'd left for town that morning, so the temperature inside the three-room cottage wasn't much warmer than it was outdoors. But he didn't feel the cold air. His skin felt tight and hot, and his arms—which had held Willa only a few minutes before—were heavy.

God help him, he still wanted her.

He wanted her with the same intensity he had eighteen years ago, when he had been almost a man, and torn by the first stabs of desire. He hadn't acted then because she had been too young, even though denial had only increased his wanting. When she'd left, he'd felt as though his soul had been ripped away.

And now she was a woman, a fact that stared him in the face every time he saw that world-weary expression in her deep gray-blue eyes, or noticed the way her casual sweaters and jeans hugged her feminine curves. Feeling her body crushed against his a minute ago was pure torture. It was the same as before, and it was different. No matter how hard he tried, he couldn't make himself forget the evenings they'd spent together, teaching each other what growing up meant.

Nor could he forget the way she'd left him.

It had been almost August when the news came about Rick. She'd spent the summer at Restless Spirit with her grandparents, the first summer since Rick had joined the service two years earlier. He'd seen her on the occasional holiday during those two years, and he'd noticed as she changed from a tomboy to a young woman. And it was that final summer when they'd begun to explore the changes in each other.

He swallowed as he recalled the nights Willa would slip down the stairway and meet him at the boathouse. He could still smell the water, hear it lapping against the dock and echoing around the wooden building, a sound not much louder than their whispers. The sound of the waves matched the feelings that rippled between them as they kissed and touched and tried to control their growing feelings.

They'd almost crossed the line that summer. Maybe they would have, if it hadn't been for the telegram to Willa's parents, the message that their only son had taken his army-issued sidearm and blown his brains out.

Christian had expected Willa's grief to be as passionate as her anger and her love, but she'd responded to the news like a living statue, turning aside his gestures of comfort. Back then he hadn't understood anything. All he knew was that he'd lost his best friend and his best girl all at once.

Now he suspected that Willa hadn't dealt with Rick's death at all.

He heard Billie's voice call him into supper— except for breakfast, he always ate at the big house— and wished that tonight he could beg off. He wished for the hundredth time that Billie hadn't asked Willa here. He was a damn fool for wanting her, but something in him wanted to protect her, to show her how to heal herself and go forward with her life.

The only thing was, going forward meant she would leave again. He swallowed back the aching emptiness that threatened to steal over him. At that moment he realized that he still had his own ghosts to lay to rest.

4

Willa pressed the doorbell of the ranch-style
house on the outskirts of Pinecrest and waited, shivering
in her light fleece jacket. March had come in like a lion
the day before, with fierce winds and pelting sleet that
coated the ground with a hard slippery shell, making the
walk from the end of the car-filled driveway to the
doorstep treacherous.

Nevertheless, she was glad to be out, miles away from
the island and the old house with its creaks and quirks.
Although she'd only spent summers and holidays in
Pinecrest, the Mitterhauser family was well known and she
and Rick had made friends among the year-round residents.
One of them, Brenda Songstad, had called last week to
welcome her to Pinecrest and invite her to this party.

Willa had accepted instantly. She couldn't have borne
another moment of Rod's sulks or Billie's muzzy-headed
approach to the resort's repair. Nor could she stand to
be on the receiving end of another one of Christian's
measuring stares. He expected something from her that

she couldn't give. She couldn't turn back the clock and be happy here, as though those carefree summers had never come to a shattering close.

Yes, she was ready for whatever social life this town of 1,200 could offer on a bitter March night.

She pressed the bell again, wondering if the party noise, audible through the door's heavy oak panels, drowned out the chimes. Hearing the muted laughter, she felt a knot of anticipation and dread in the pit of her stomach. Most of the people here she hadn't seen in eighteen years, and she wondered if any of them had changed as much as she had, if she would be trapped in a roomful of strangers, with nothing to talk about except yesterday's sleet and whether or not the lake would thaw before April. Or worse, if she would have to dodge questions about her faded career all night long.

Before she could press the bell once more, the door opened. At first Willa didn't recognize the very matronly figure that stood in the doorway, but light from a wall sconce shone down on the woman's head, and her curly white-blond hair was unmistakable.

"Hi, Brenda," she said.

Brenda's words were lost in the howl of the wind as it tried to push its way into the house, and the room's occupants added their own howls of protest. "Shut that door before we turn into icicles," she heard someone cry.

Brenda laughed and tugged Willa inside, wrapping her in a comfortable hug that erased most of her nervousness. "Willa Mitterhauser, it's so good to see you."

Willa returned Brenda's hug, deciding she'd better get used to hearing her maiden name again. Here in Pinecrest, she was still Johann's granddaughter, young John's little girl, the tomboy with the carrot-colored hair and freckles. Brenda was at least the fourth person in the past week to call her by her former surname, and she no longer felt a pang when she heard it. She'd left Willa Decker behind in L.A.

"Don't just stand there shivering," Brenda scolded, her expression teasing, although Willa could hardly have moved a step with Brenda hanging tightly on to her arm. The woman's gaze traveled up and down Willa's emerald-colored silk blouse and black stretch pants. "Goodness, look at you," she said, pulling Willa through the foyer, with its line-up of coats and muddy shoes and boots.

Willa paused long enough to hang her jacket in the overstuffed hall closet, already regretting the silk blouse. She'd thought it casual, but had forgotten that rural Minnesota was a long way from L.A. Most of the people crowded around the fireplace and lounging on Brenda's overstuffed sofa were comfortably dressed in blue jeans with sweaters or flannel shirts. Willa felt overdressed and conspicuous, but she forgot her unease when curious expressions changed to smiles.

"Look, everyone, our guest of honor's here," Brenda announced, guiding Willa into the center of the living room with a surprisingly firm grip above her elbow, as though she'd sensed Willa's nervousness and was determined to overcome it. "The whole gang showed up except for my husband, Carl, who's probably somewhere between here and Chicago with a semi-truck full of office supplies, and my daughter, who's staying with a friend."

Willa barely had time to file that information before being surrounded by vaguely familiar faces, and she pasted a smile on her own face. It quickly became genuine as Brenda's guests introduced themselves, each impatiently waiting his or her turn to remind her of some incident of summers past. Their smiles held something of the children and teenagers she'd known, and memories crowded her mind along with new information as she was updated on things that had happened during the intervening years.

She learned that Ron Carter, once the Lumberjacks' star pitcher, now balding and overweight, had taken over the local hardware store from Leo Gullickson, who'd run off to the Twin Cities with the dentist's wife three years ago.

Ron himself told her that Sue Pulaski Johnson, nine months' pregnant and unable to attend the party, had five children, all boys, and that her husband, Steve, had threatened to move back home with his parents if she had another.

And Steve in turn informed her that his cousin in Detroit Lakes had recently divorced and wouldn't mind meeting her. He described the man to her, seeming not to notice as her eyes turned glassy, her smile stiff. Somehow she managed to extricate herself from that conversation and move on to the next cluster of people, but after an hour or two, she started to fade. Trying to keep track of half-remembered names and faces was making her head hurt.

Was it Ted Jackson who had bought out the bakery on the corner or Tom Johnson?

She kept thinking of an old saying, "The more things change, the more things stay the same." Pinecrest might look newer and bigger than when she left, with a fast food hamburger joint on the edge of town and a stoplight on Main Street, but underneath the superficial changes it was still the same hotbed of gossip it had always been.

She found herself adrift from the crowd, standing off to one side and feeling a bit isolated as conversation eddied around her. A tall, golden-haired man approached her, balancing two glasses of beer in his left hand, a cigarette in his right. The crowd parted like magic to let him through. When he smiled, there was something familiar about the way his eyebrows slanted together, but it wasn't until she noted the slightly crooked bent to his nose that Willa was finally able to place him.

"Thor Nelson!" she said triumphantly, her satisfaction at correctly placing him erasing the stinging memories of the time she was eight years old, when he'd teased her mercilessly about her red hair. Christian had finally leaped to her defense, a bit overzealously, resulting in two sets of scraped knuckles, one swollen eye, and a bloody nose— Thor's—which had turned out to be broken.

Thor's parents had complained long and loudly about the "little hooligan" that lived out near the island, and it was John Mitterhauser who'd finally delivered a fatherly lecture to Christian about fighting. Christian's own father had disappeared years before, and his mother barely noticed him, so it had always been Willa's family that stepped in where Christian was concerned.

She dismissed the memory as Thor proffered one of the glasses of beer. "Welcome back, Willa. This town can certainly use some style for a change."

His flattery left her feeling uncomfortable, and she sensed that others in the crowd were listening. She took the beer politely, knowing she would set it down in a hidden corner at the first opportunity. She didn't drink, not since her days on the road with the band. Darryl's substance abuse had made her wary of alcohol used as a social lubricant. Driving those thoughts from her mind she asked, "So, what are you up to these days, Thor?"

Ron Carter whooped with laughter and reached over to slap Thor good-naturedly on the back before saying, "And you thought the whole world knew. I guess not everyone follows the Pinecrest political scene." He turned to Willa and informed her, "Thor is our mayor."

She hid her surprise, remembering that both Billie and Mattie had mentioned *Mayor* Nelson in connection with the proposed hotel complex. Nelson was a common name throughout Minnesota, and it hadn't occurred to her that the mayor might be Thor, who'd been younger than Rod was now the last time she saw him.

"So you're the one who wants to build a new hotel," she said lightly.

Thor's smile was stiff. "I'm just looking out for the community's interests," he said.

Willa wondered if she was simply imagining the tension in the crowd. All week long Christian had appeared every time she tried to discuss the subject of selling the resort with Billie, and she wondered if she wasn't conditioned now to be extra sensitive every time the proposed hotel project was mentioned. People's expressions seemed strained, their eyes watchful.

Conversation resumed after the momentary beat of silence, and Willa joined in. She had almost managed to put Christian's behavior out of her mind in the midst of trying to dredge up the name of the friendly dark blond man seated next to her on the sofa, when a familiar laugh sent a shiver up her spine.

It couldn't be.

She turned and her gaze settled immediately on Christian, standing near the doorway, dressed in jeans, hiking boots, and a navy windbreaker that spelled out in white letters, "Pinecrest Police Department." What was he doing here? She resisted the impulse to glance at her watch and check the time, refusing to acknowledge, even to herself, that she knew Christian's work schedule by heart. Wasn't he on duty tonight at eleven?

Several of the men broke away from the "huddle," as Brenda had laughingly termed the group of males who spent most of the evening by the fireplace, poking at the fire with brass tools that were meant to be mere decoration.

Their voices were loud and jovial as they walked toward the doorway to greet Christian.

Willa watched with growing amazement as Ron Carter, Steve Johnson, and several others milled around Christian, their pleasure at seeing him obvious. Some things *had* changed. Christian had always been the outsider, the boy who didn't fit in. Now he was more comfortable with these people than she was, even though he'd been back in Pinecrest for only three months.

She realized that the years she had been away from Pinecrest made her different. The funny thing was, Christian had been away nearly as long. Maybe she just needed more time for the awkwardness to wear off. Or maybe the fact that she was now a minor celebrity contributed to the difference she felt. She knew that when people thought she wasn't looking, their gazes would settle on her curiously. The sensation of being watched was almost palpable, as though someone was touching her between the shoulder blades.

Christian looked up, and his gaze connected with hers across the room. She swallowed involuntarily, knowing she had to say something, to pretend a casualness she didn't feel in order to allay the speculative glances people were casting at the two of them. Some people had long memories, she thought ruefully. During that last summer, only a few had seen how the relationship between her and Christian had begun to shift. Apparently the grapevine had served to inform several more since then.

She took a couple steps toward him, knowing her actions and words might be witnessed, stored, and repeated over the next few days. As he watched her approach his hazel eyes held a hint of amusement.

"Christian, I didn't expect to see you here," she said, nearly wincing at the inane phrase. "Aren't you on duty later?"

"I traded shifts," he explained, and Willa remembered that she'd seen Skeet Varner, Pinecrest's other full-time officer, leave the party about a half hour earlier.

"Oh." She paused, searching for something else—anything—to say. Ron Carter unwittingly came to her rescue.

"I thought a small-town cop was always on duty," he joked.

"I am," Christian said, his face expressionless.

Willa realized he was teasing before anyone else did. Her grin signaled the rest of the group, and groans met his reply. "Is that a warning," a female voice demanded, "or a promise?"

Willa glanced over at the woman who had spoken, a brunette in a tight red sweater that showed off her generous figure. Ron Carter had pointed her out earlier simply as Madge, because she'd had "too many ex-husbands and last names to keep track of."

The crowd laughed, and Christian said, "I know everyone here will behave responsibly."

Coming from anyone else, the sentence might have sounded preachy, but he had somehow managed to inject just the right note of easiness in his voice. With plenty of good-natured heckling flying back and forth, the party-goers drifted back into the living room. Willa felt she'd done her social duty as far as Christian was concerned, and she spent the next hour or so talking to others, trying to pretend he was miles away.

Unfortunately, she could not help but try to monitor Christian's every move and word. As she smiled and laughed and caught up with old acquaintances, her brain filed away bits and pieces of information. She learned that Christian preferred corn chips to potato chips, that he wore the same pine-scented aftershave as Madge's third husband, and that he told "Ole and Lena" jokes with a Norwegian accent so terrible that listeners groaned. Whenever he refilled someone's glass or brought in more wood for the fire, he whistled in short, tuneless snatches—a sign of the "old" Christian that Willa found almost comforting.

How on earth had she ever thought she could ignore him, she wondered as she tried to concentrate on what Brenda was saying as they stood talking near the sliding glass door that led out to a deck. The little things that signaled Christian's presence—his deep-throated laughter, the scent of his aftershave, the lock of hair that kept falling over his forehead no matter how many times he brushed it back—ran up and down her nerve endings like tiny electric shocks.

When his laugh rang out yet again, she went to the kitchen, hoping to escape. Brenda entered shortly afterward.

"So what do you think?" Brenda asked in a conspiratorial whisper as she refilled a wooden salad bowl with pretzel sticks. "Didn't you just know that Ron Carter would end up bald and paunchy?"

At Brenda's outrageous comment, Willa giggled despite herself. Her amusement faded when Brenda added, "Not like Christian. He certainly improved with age, like a fine wine." She drew out the last two words for emphasis. She darted a glance at Willa and quickly added, "Not that he wasn't always good-looking, in a dangerous kind of way. But he was so wild."

Willa kept her attention fixed on the bag of potato chips she was struggling to open. Brenda had written her a couple letters after her family moved to Arizona, telling how Christian had grown into the role of the town's bad boy, a story she recounted now.

When Sheriff Pitzer had threatened to send Christian to the reformatory, he'd left town suddenly. Willa remembered that part of Brenda's letters, because

Christian had stopped writing to her at about the same time. She herself hadn't responded to any communications from Pinecrest, not even his. She'd been so wrapped up in her pain and rebellion over Rick's death that everything else had seemed like a dream.

"After your family left he got into all kinds of trouble," Brenda was saying. "And then his mother died, and—"

"Corene died?" Willa interrupted, her hands going still. Why hadn't Christian told her? For that matter, why hadn't she inquired after his mother since she'd arrived back in Pinecrest? His comments about her selfishness were uncomfortably close to the mark, and she felt ashamed. "When?"

"About six months after Rick," Brenda said quietly. "She wasn't much of a mother to Christian, everybody knew that, but it seemed like it was just one thing too many for him."

"What happened?"

"Didn't I write you? I guess I must have forgotten. Or maybe I was afraid to tell you . . ."

Willa's attention zoomed in on Brenda's hesitant manner. "Tell me what?"

"Well," Brenda began, "the reason Sam Pitzer threatened Christian with reform school was because he caught him and his daughter Judy in the backseat of Judy's car."

Willa felt a tug of emotion that surprised her. Surely it couldn't be jealousy? "I thought Judy was going out with Thor Nelson," she said casually.

"She was." Brenda's voice was tinged with a note of satisfaction. "You know how Thor and Christian detested each other. Well, Judy apparently preferred Christian. She told everyone she was pregnant with his child."

"Where's Judy now?" Willa asked, trying to keep her voice even.

Brenda smiled wickedly. "According to the grapevine,

she's living in Edina with her third husband. She's got two kids, both of them less than ten years old. I think everyone knew that Judy was only trying to trap Christian. After all, it was pretty obvious that he was in love with you. The summer before, the two of you were like . . ." Her words trailed away.

Willa's hands faltered, sending a couple potato chips scattering into the sink, where they rapidly absorbed water and went soggy. She felt about as limp and boneless herself. She stiffened, sensing the curiosity in Brenda's gaze.

"How does it feel to see him again after all these years?" she asked Willa.

Not used to confiding in people and not prepared to start at this particular moment, Willa said, "Wonderful." Realizing how wooden her response sounded, she added quickly, "I'm so glad things worked out for him. He's been a real help to Billie, too." She changed the subject. "I've heard that Thor is hoping this hotel project will go through."

"You mean PROCOR. Now *that's* old news," Brenda said with a sigh. "I wish it would go away. Unfortunately the subject is about as persistent as mildew."

"It sounds like you're against it."

"I'm not for it or against it. I'm just sick of the people who are. It's all anyone talks about at the café. Hardly a week goes by when I don't have to step in and stop an argument before it gets out of hand, and I'm a waitress, not a referee. It's dividing the town, and I'm tired of it."

"Don't you think it would bring new business to town?"

"Maybe. But for every good thing it does for Pinecrest, there's something bad to balance it. The street congestion, for example. And Carl's concerned about the environmental impact on the lake. Without the lake and the fishing, we wouldn't have any tourists at all." She shook herself. "We'd better go back inside before I start sounding like one of them."

Willa followed Brenda into the living room, balancing a bowl of chips and a smaller container of onion dip. She searched for a place to set them down, and her gaze inexorably settled on Christian, who was standing near the fireplace talking to a group of people. She noted wryly that the fireplace gang was no longer exclusively male. No less than three women, including Madge whatever-her-name-was, stood within the circle.

Willa looked away and headed for the coffee table with her munchies, but the coffee table wasn't there. Someone had moved the table and sofa off to the side and turned up the radio to an oldies station, turning the Indian print area rug into an impromptu dance floor. She grinned at the spectacle of a thirty-pounds-over-weight Ron Carter doing the pony with Brenda.

"Come on, Willa," Ron called. "Grab a partner and get out here."

She laughed and shook her head. "I'll wait for something slower."

When a slow ballad came on only moments later, as if by her command, Willa started discreetly toward the kitchen, only to find her way blocked.

"Dance?" Thor Nelson held out his hand, his gaze running over her before returning to her eyes. For some reason, his obvious look made her feel violated rather than flattered. She hesitated for a moment. If she wanted to know more about the PROCOR hotel development, who better to ask than the town's mayor?

"Sure." She let him lead her onto the floor, where he pulled her into his arms.

"So what's a beautiful woman like you doing without a man by her side?" he asked. He pulled her closer, and she could smell the alcohol on his breath. She wondered if it would be useless to try to get any information out of him at all.

"Thor," she said, waiting until his gray eyes focused on her before continuing. "Tell me more about PROCOR. I was wondering what kind of plans are being discussed."

He straightened, his muzziness gone, leaving Willa to wonder if the genial drunk was some kind of act.

"It's going to make this town economically viable all year round," he told her, "not just in the summer. The downtown area will get a facelift, including a plaza fountain, that will give Pinecrest the atmosphere of an Alpine village. The hotel and convention center will attract businesspeople. We'll be able to compete with bigger towns like Grand Rapids and Brainerd when it comes to fine dining, entertainment, and accommodations."

He sounded like a chamber of commerce speech, she thought. "Don't you think most visitors come here just to fish and be outdoors?"

"That's small-town thinking, Willa. I expected more from you, but I suppose your aunt has influenced your opinion."

Before she had a chance to respond, Thor's expression changed, and his grip on her hand tightened. She followed his gaze over her shoulder to see Christian standing behind her.

"My dance, I believe," he said pleasantly. But Willa heard the edge to his voice, a blend of politeness and tension that was probably missed by Thor and the handful of others nearby who were pretending not to listen. She didn't miss it, not after being subjected to it all week long.

"Hold on, Foster. The lady's with me." Thor sounded belligerent, and Willa thought of the old feud between the two of them. The last thing she wanted was for it to resurface here in the middle of Carl and Brenda Songstad's living room.

"It's all right, Thor," she said. "Christian and I need

to talk about tomorrow's dinner," she said. "Thanks for the dance." She smiled and took Christian's hand, praying for a quick end to the slow song playing on the radio. Her smile vanished the moment Christian led her several feet away.

"What did you do that for?" she whispered in his ear as he pulled her closer to avoid bumping into Ron Carter, who winked knowingly at her before guiding his newest partner, Madge, around the coffee table.

"Me? What about you? *Tomorrow's dinner?*"

"It was the best I could come up with to keep you two from pummeling each other. I'm not so sure you'd win this time."

Christian tipped back his head and guffawed. He was close enough so that Willa could feel the vibrations of his laughter through the thin silk of her shirt. She looked away to mask her reaction. Only two other couples were still dancing. The others had wandered off to slump against a piece of furniture or a wall. The conversation level had dropped several decibels, and someone had turned the radio down. The mood of the party had definitely mellowed.

Christian's hadn't. She felt the tension in his arms as he guided her toward a set of doors standing ajar on the opposite side of the living room. Willa saw the interested glances directed toward them as Christian led her into the room, obviously a study. The walls were lined with oak cabinets, and a rolltop desk stood next to the shuttered window.

As soon as they were inside, he released her, and she stood and watched while he went to close the doors behind them.

"Don't," she warned, her voice pitched low so that the audience outside couldn't hear.

"What's the matter, Willow? Afraid to be alone with me?" He shut the doors and leaned against them, facing her with his arms crossed over his chest. His insolent pose and lazy smile didn't fool her for a minute. She knew that if she tried to walk past, he would stop her.

"Of course not," she said, glad he couldn't know that her heart rate had doubled in the last few moments. "It's just that people are going to get the wrong idea. You know how everyone gossips here. They'll think we're . . ."

"Lovers?"

The word shocked her because it wasn't at all what she'd been about to say. But when she tried to think of a correction, her mind went blank. Or rather, it filled with images of the phrasing Christian had chosen. *Lovers* . . . the scent of his aftershave clinging to her pillow, the feel of him against her skin, his strength, his warmth—

He walked toward her, and she quickly ordered her thoughts.

"What were you and Thor talking about?" he demanded.

"Jealous, Christian? I can't believe the two of you are still acting like teenagers after all these years." The look in his eyes as he approached stopped her from adding to her defensive taunt. She didn't want to battle with him any longer. A wave of tiredness washed over her, and she explained, "I wanted to know more about the hotel complex. All I've heard are rumors and gossip, and I wanted to find out what was really happening."

He stopped about twelve inches from her. "So you asked Thor." He smiled and shook his head. "He's a little biased, don't you think?"

"And you're not?"

They stared, each accusing the other with their eyes. Willa looked away and took a step back, bumping into the edge of the desk. He was so close she could feel the warmth radiating from his skin. Or perhaps the heat came from within herself, she realized, shocked at the idea.

Her words ran together nervously. "I'd like to help Billie make an informed decision regarding the resort. I'm not sure she's thinking clearly, and since my father turned everything over to her when my grandparents died, I believe—"

"Billie's already made her decision," he interrupted. "She wants to keep Restless Spirit. She's deeding it to you so that it stays in the family. If you sell it, you'll break her heart."

Willa felt panic rise up inside her. "Is that her decision or yours? You've probably been trying to influence her ever since you arrived in Pinecrest." She knew she was overreacting, but she couldn't seem to stop the words that came tumbling out of her in angry waves. "Do you think you can keep things the same forever? Or turn back the clock? Some of us want to get on with our lives."

She turned her back on him, resting her hands against the desk's cool surface, knowing she'd said too much. All it took was one disapproving glance from him and her calm disappeared. The sounds of party filled the silence between them as she tried to control her emotions. Through the closed doors she could hear guests saying their good-nights. Embarrassed, she realized that her own raised voice must have carried through even more clearly.

"I was wondering where she'd gone." Christian's comment interrupted her thoughts.

"What?" She spun around in time to see his crooked grin.

"That feisty redhead I remember. I haven't seen her around much lately."

His comment left her speechless. Before she could recover, he added another zinger. "Why didn't you answer my letters?"

Willa stood perfectly still, wishing she could flee

before he turned everything upside down. It was no use pretending she didn't know what he was talking about.

"Didn't your parents give them to you?" he prompted.

"Yes," she admitted, watching the surprised hurt chase briefly across his face.

"I thought maybe . . . never mind."

How could she tell him that she'd pored over every word, longed to see him, to be back at Restless Spirit with him as though nothing had happened? But something *had* happened. She had grown up that summer, in more ways than one, and she'd known even then that she could never go back.

She tried to explain. "Your letters only reminded me of Rick. I guess I couldn't deal with everything all at once—Rick's death, my parents. You." At his implacable stare, she added, "We were just kids, Christian."

"So you decided to make it go away by ignoring it. Just like your parents tried to ignore—"

"Stop!" She tried to leave, but Christian caught her arm as she went past, his fingers like a vise above her elbow.

"What happened to you, Willow?"

"The same thing that happens to every starry-eyed kid. I grew up. Only I did it in one afternoon, when two men in uniform came knocking on the door to tell my parents their son had shot himself in the head with his service revolver."

She'd hoped her blunt words might end this inquisition, but Christian merely loosened his hold on her arm a bit before demanding, "Why did you come back? And don't give me the same line about coming here to help Billie. You don't give a damn about her or the resort."

"That's not true," she whispered, tired of his insults. "I came back to put the past behind me once and for all. To remember the good and forget the bad."

"And what about this?" He pulled her toward him,

never once removing his gaze from hers. "Are you going to try to forget this, too?"

Her heart pounded like a drumbeat as he narrowed the distance between them. She gasped when her body touched his and looked away, much too late to hide her reaction from him. She could feel his warmth through her silk blouse, and it held her more effectively than the light grasp on her arm. She wanted to run, and at the same time, she wanted to throw her arms around him and pull him even closer.

He released her to brush his fingers along the side of her cheek, turning her face until she was looking at him. Instead of the triumph she expected, his expression held only desire. He lowered his mouth to hers with deliberate slowness.

It was nothing like she remembered.

As teenagers discovering physical desire for the first time, their kisses had been exploring, tentative, as though they feared the explosive power between them. But there was nothing tentative about this kiss. Christian's mouth moved over hers with the assurance of a man who knew exactly what he was doing.

It was different. *He* was different. She felt the strength in him, and for a moment she wanted to rest against that strength, to draw it into herself. Her years of self-reliance battled against her impulse to give in.

Somewhere through her warring senses she heard a knock at the door and managed to break away from Christian mere seconds before Brenda poked her head into the room. The rapid rise and fall of her chest and the flush high along Christian's cheekbones should have given them away, but Brenda didn't seem to notice their agitation. Willa felt a sudden chill of foreboding at her friend's serious expression.

"Billie just called," Brenda said. "You'd better get

back to the resort right away. Someone broke into one of the cottages and tried to start a fire. Billie sounds pretty rattled."

Christian was already on his way through the study doors when Brenda added, "She said she can't find Rod anywhere."

Willa felt a stab of panic as she followed Christian through the living room, now nearly empty of guests. "Is she okay?" she asked Brenda, who was two steps behind them. Her question went unanswered as Brenda helped them find their coats. She heard a faint electronic chirp from the beeper Christian wore at his waist.

He barely glanced at the beeper's display before shutting it off. "It's displaying the office number," he told Brenda as she retrieved his windbreaker from the hall closet. "Skeet probably just found out about Billie. Could you call him and tell him I'm on my way to the island?"

"Sure." Brenda held out Willa's fleece jacket, and she shrugged into it. Her fingers were shaking so much she couldn't manage the buttons. She left it open, not even noticing the cold as she stepped out the door.

"We'll leave your car here overnight," Christian said, pulling her toward his pickup. "You're in no condition to drive."

"I didn't even have one beer."

"That's not what I meant and you know it," he said, grabbing her wrist and lifting her hand. She was still shaking. She was about to insist when he added, "I know the road better than you do, and the truck has better traction on this ice."

Needing no further convincing, she let him help her up into the passenger seat as she tried to quell pangs of guilt. Tonight, at the same time she'd been thinking of selling the resort to PROCOR, her Aunt Billie had been fighting to save it.

"Can't you drive any faster?"

"Not without putting us in the lake," Christian replied, aware of her impatience. He was as anxious to get to the island as she was. Already he imagined he could see a faint glow of lights through the trees. He guided the pickup over the narrow causeway, pressing down on the accelerator as hard as he dared. For one moment, the wheels slipped on the soft shoulder, and he heard Willa gasp beside him. Then they were across, the headlights flashing over the faded sign and penetrating the stand of pine trees along the driveway.

"There's someone here," Willa said as they drove into the clearing at the edge of the lake. Her voice was tight with worry.

"It's the sheriff." Christian recognized Pitzer's brown and white sedan among the three cars parked facing the cluster of cottages. The cars' headlights beamed over the faded wooden siding, making an effective searchlight. "And that Chevy belongs to one of the deputies."

He pulled up beside the Chevy, leaving the pickup's headlights on as well. He could see Billie standing at the edge of the clearing, watching Pitzer and two other men trample over the scene like bumbling Keystone cops. He jumped out without pausing to look behind him to see if Willa followed. His anger at the sheriff's incompetence softened as he approached Billie, who was shivering in her nightgown, her hands clutching an afghan tightly around her shoulders and her feet covered incongruously with floppy rubber galoshes.

"Are you all right?"

"I'm fine," she answered, but the tension in her face was all too visible in the headlights' bright beams. Her voice broke as she added bravely, "Those damn kids nearly went and did it this time."

"Did what?" Willa asked as she joined them. The look of concern on her face made Christian reconsider his harsh judgment of her motives toward Billie and the resort.

"They tried setting the mattress on fire. I heard the window breaking and got out here in time to put it out."

"Are you sure you're okay?" Willa asked, reaching out to clasp Billie's hands, turning them over as though searching for burns or scratches. Christian could see the gentleness in her touch and hear the worry in her voice. She cared for Billie. He'd known that somewhere underneath that cool facade she was still his Willow—compassionate, tender, and fierce all at once.

The noises around them faded as he remembered the interrupted kiss. She'd come alive like a flame in his arms, and he'd wanted to scorch away every obstacle between them. He jerked his attention back to the activity surrounding the cottage nearest the trees.

"I'll go talk to Pitzer," he told the women. He drew Willa away. "Get her in the house," he said in an undertone, nodding toward Billie, who was watching the sheriff and his men work.

"Right," Willa said with an ironic smile.

He found himself smiling back. "Use a cattle prod if you have to." Then, sobering, he added, "See if you can find out where Rod is."

He didn't want to say anything now, but he'd spent the week before checking into the boy's background. Although he had little sympathy for parents who tried to unload their problems onto other people, he had to admit that the Danes had certainly had their hands full with Rod.

Christian watched as Willa guided her aunt away from the circle of light, choosing their path carefully out of concern for Billie's flopping galoshes. He shook his head when he saw the older woman reach out to pick up the shotgun from where it rested against the broad trunk of an oak and felt a dart of frustration at his inability to stop the damaging nocturnal visits to the resort.

When Billie had called him in Minneapolis a few months ago to tell him him about the vandalism, he'd dismissed it as teenagers' pranks, remembering his own wildness at that age. But now he suspected there was more to it than just a bunch of boys trying to bully an old woman. He approached the cottage, his gaze taking in the shattered window and scorched bedspread. Before he could go inside for a closer look, the bulky figure of Sam Pitzer ambled toward him.

"Looks like those kids again," Pitzer said, biting down on the end of his ever-present cigar. "I told the old lady to get a watch dog and quit dragging me out here in the middle of the night. My men have got better things to do."

"Like what?"

The sheriff's eyes narrowed. "Maybe you haven't heard, but we got a whole county to look after. Pinecrest is just a little piece of it."

"The island is outside of city limits," Christian pointed out, sensitive to the implied criticism behind Pitzer's words. Pinecrest's tiny police department didn't have jurisdiction here. He wanted to ask the sheriff if PROCOR was one piece of the county they were looking after, but something told him to keep quiet. Pitzer lived in Pinecrest. The town had taken sides on the hotel development, and it was a safe bet that even the sheriff wasn't neutral. Christian swallowed his anger, feeling it burning a hole in his stomach.

He waited until Pitzer and his men left and then started searching the area himself. Or what was left of it, after the three men had stomped all over it. He knelt to examine the ground in front of the broken window, his flashlight's beams catching on glass shards and patches of ice and turning them into mirrors of light. Here and there, the earth was soft and black, and footprints covered the thawed patches. He looked at the mess with disgust. He'd hoped to find the imprint of a certain brand of sneakers, maybe a dropped package of matches. He moved aside a scattered pile of leaves, feeling the dampness in his fingertips. He saw nothing.

"Did they find anything?"

He'd been so intent on looking for some sign of the vandal's identity that he hadn't heard Willa. Her husky voice went right to his gut. He told himself it was because she'd startled him.

"I'm not sure they even looked," he answered, deciding not to mention the possibility that Pitzer and his men deliberately destroyed any traces of evidence. "If we'd gotten here earlier maybe I might have been able to spot something, but all I can see are their footprints."

Before he finished speaking, a rustling sound came from the trees at the edge of the clearing. "Wait here," he told Willa. He started toward the shadowy woods, breaking into a run as he saw a dark form separate from a tree trunk and take off running.

He chased the figure through the underbrush, his growing anger adding speed to his steps, closing the distance between him and the fleeing shadow. He winced as a low branch stung his cheek, but the pain was quickly forgotten when he realized Billie's tormentor was nearly in his grasp.

When the figure stumbled into a small clearing, Christian closed in, reaching out to grab a handful of jacket. The action threw the runner off balance, and both of them fell to the ground. Christian grasped him by the chin and turned his face toward the pale moonlight. His anger disappeared the moment he recognized the boy's pale features.

Rod Dane stared up at him, his expression sullen.

Christian let go in disgust. He stood up and reached out a hand, which Rod ignored. "Get up," he ordered. He heard twigs snapping behind him and realized that Willa had followed.

Rod got to his feet just as Willa caught up to them. "What did you do to him?" she demanded.

Christian could feel his stomach burning as he reminded himself to hold his temper in check. "You saw him running. We both thought he was one of the vandals." He turned to Rod. "Where the hell have you been? It's nearly two in the morning. Billie was worried. Not only that, she was alone. Someone knocked out a window and scared her."

"Are you accusing me?"

Christian stared back at the boy, knowing it wouldn't be fair to voice his suspicions. Why had Rod started running?

"Well, I didn't do it." Christian heard a thread of nervousness in Rod's voice as he added, "I was out."

"With who?"

"Is this an inquisition, or what?" Rod demanded. He made a show of brushing the leaves and dirt from his army parka. "You're supposed to read me my rights first, remember?"

His sarcasm deflated Christian. He sensed that the boy was hiding something, but with Willa looking on like a mother lioness he wasn't about to learn anything else.

"Rod, please go in the house and make sure Billie's managed to get to sleep," Willa said. As soon as Rod was out of earshot, she turned on Christian. "You're not his father. You have no right to speak to him as though he was your responsibility."

"Somebody has to. That kid needs a firm hand. What

makes you so sure he isn't part of the gang who broke
into that cottage?"

"That's ridiculous. He lives here. Why would he do
something like that?"

"I don't know. Maybe because he's done things like
that before?"

"He's had some problems at home."

"And at school. *Three* schools, as a matter of fact."

"His parents would have sent him to a foster home if
Billie and I hadn't arranged for him to go to school here."

"You dumped him on Billie like he was a stray pup.
She's too old to take care of a wild teenager, much less
manage this resort on top of it."

"That's the whole point, isn't it?" Willa's tones were
weary. "I've been trying to tell you that Billie is too old
to take care of the resort. She should sell out and move
into town, or better yet, move down to Arizona with my
parents."

Christian's stomach reacted with a fresh burst of fire
as he fought to ignore the logic behind her words. Was
Willa right? Was he trying to hold on to a past that had
disappeared like a spring snowfall?

No, damn it. He'd left Pinecrest to learn about life outside a small Minnesota lake town, and all he'd learned
was that there was nothing more important than roots.
The thought that the resort might be replaced by an
impersonal multimillion dollar hotel sickened him. "What
are you going to do about Billie's offer?" he asked.

"That's family business. You needn't concern yourself." She dismissed him by turning away and heading
back toward the house.

"Family business? Like lying to Rod about his father?"
He flung the words after her, getting the satisfaction
of seeing her stride falter for a moment before she
disappeared into the darkness.

• • •

After knocking softly, Rod opened the door to Billie's room to check on her as Willa had instructed. His great aunt was asleep under a pile of quilts and afghans. She looked small lying there in the heavy wood bed, not the rawboned, sharp-eyed biddy who seemed to see past his eyes into his brain. He hoped she wouldn't figure out what had happened tonight. He shut the door quietly and felt a wave of guilt.

Christian had looked at him tonight as if he was a pile of dog food, and the truth was, he deserved it. He couldn't defend himself. How could he tell them that he snuck out to be with Kerry Songstad? Kerry was only fifteen, and she was supposed to be staying at her best friend Nancy's house while her mom had some kind of party. No, he couldn't even try to work his way out of this one. Better to let Christian think he was guilty.

He opened the door to his own room and sat down on the side of the bed. He didn't want to blow this. He'd run away before he'd live with strangers. But he didn't want to mess things up at school, either. There was Kerry, for one thing. He didn't want her to know about all the stuff he'd done before, the trouble he'd gotten into. She thought he was pretty cool, and he felt different—better—when he was with her. She was pretty and popular, even with the older kids.

That was where it really got sticky. He knew who was behind the break-in tonight, but if he said anything about it, he'd ruin his chances at fitting into Pinecrest High. And that made him as guilty as the boys who'd broken the window.

Willa sat up in bed, all hope of sleep gone. Every time she closed her eyes she saw Christian's face. Once she'd drifted off, only to dream that she was in his arms again, responding to his kisses. This time there was no interruption from Brenda and no internal warning telling her to stop before it was too late. The surrender was frightening and exciting at the same time.

Her heart pounded. Things were happening too fast, snowballing out of her control. She climbed out of bed, rummaging around in the pitch black closet, moving aside suitcases until she found what she was looking for. She sat cross-legged on a hooked rug, the box full of photographs and letters resting on her thighs.

"What would you do, Rick?" she whispered, pressing her hands on the cardboard lid. "Is Christian right, after all?"

She sat quietly, until her heartbeat slowed and her thoughts settled down. She searched herself, making sure that the answer she came up with was true, and not simply an aftermath of the emotions that had battered her tonight.

She decided Christian had a point. Billie was too old to watch over Rod on her own. Her aunt hadn't been able to keep up the resort, and tonight she'd aged right before Willa's eyes as they stood watching Pitzer and his men sort through the shattered glass.

Willa felt everything closing in on her, making it hard to breathe. She'd promised herself two weeks at Restless Spirit to regain her senses and decide where to go from here. But two weeks had already stretched into three, and she was even further from regaining her balance than she was when she arrived.

And yet she couldn't leave Rick's son behind—not with an old woman who could barely support herself, or with a cop who was ready to believe the worst of him. And she couldn't leave without helping Billie get the resort in working order. She resolved to stay until the summer and do her best to make sure things would practically run themselves. In two months, Rod would graduate, and in August, he'd turn eighteen.

She still had a little money in her savings account, royalties from her work with Darryl and the band. She could help Billie make the necessary repairs so that the resort could open as usual in May. But that was as far as her involvement would go, she assured herself. She was willing to spend her money and her time. But she wouldn't give up her freedom.

She could leave with a clear conscience, her debts paid, her ties finally severed. She would be free of the past and its pain. Her fingers tightened over the box.

There was only one small detail that might stand in her way: *Christian.*

5

Willa woke Sunday morning to the smell of eggs and bacon and glanced at the clock next to the bed—7:00 A.M. Trust Billie not to let little things like a shattered window and arson slow her schedule. She was about to throw back the covers and go downstairs when she heard the back door open and close, followed by the muffled tread of heavy footsteps.

Christian.

Memories of the night before came flooding back: the kiss they'd shared at Brenda's, the argument about Rod. In one night, he'd managed to arouse emotions in her that she had suppressed for years. She felt uncomfortable remembering. She lay back in bed and stared up at the ceiling, waiting for him to leave. She wasn't ready to face him, not when she was feeling so sleepy and vulnerable.

She tried to shut her eyes and fall back asleep, but she was conscious of every sound in the big old house: Rod racing downstairs—in a hurry as usual—the clatter of dishes, Christian's low voice and Billie's answering laughter. The sounds were familiar, almost soothing.

She drifted into a semi-awake state, and the noises shifted and changed until she was once again ten years old, sleeping in the attic room on the third floor with Rick in the room next to hers.

"Last one out of bed's a one-eyed catfish!" he hollered through the accordion divider that separated his half of the attic from hers.

She could smell pancakes and maple syrup, and knew that if she let Rick get a head start the first batch would be gone before she managed to scramble down the back stairs. "Wait!" she cried, searching for her bathrobe among the clothes scattered on the floor. She gave up and grabbed a pair of blue jeans, stuffing the hem of her nightgown inside.

The only response was the sound of Rick's laughter as he raced down the stairs, sounding farther and farther away until only silence remained.

She sat up in bed with a startled cry, confused for a moment to find she was in her grandparents' room and not in hers on the floor above. For a moment she couldn't identify the source of the heavy sadness that shortened her breath. Then her awareness returned completely, and she realized her grandparents were gone, and Rick wasn't waiting downstairs. The sound of the back door closing brought her fully back to the present.

She listened carefully for Christian's voice, but this time when she heard the deep tones, they were coming from outside the house. She got up and went to the window, looking down to see Christian poking around outside the damaged cottage, with Rod standing nearby. For a moment, Rod looked so much like Rick that it hurt. She closed her eyes at the surge of protectiveness that welled up inside her. She hoped Christian wasn't still harboring the notion that Rod had something to do with last night's fire.

A few minutes later, dressed in jeans and a dark blue sweatshirt, she joined Billie in the kitchen.

"I saved you some coffee." Billie pointed toward the pot with a spoon from the sink full of dishes in front of her.

"Thanks. Why don't you leave the rest of those? I'll finish."

"You can wipe." She peered out the window as she spoke. "Things don't look quite as bad this morning."

Willa finished pouring her coffee and joined her aunt at the sink. She set her mug within reach and grabbed one of the flour sack towels her grandmother had embroidered years ago. A pair of kittens cavorted above lettering that said "Wednesday." Since this was Sunday, the dishtowel was four days off. She remembered how she and Rick turned it into an ongoing contest to see who could get the right towel on the right day. She smiled, knowing now what a clever ruse it had been on her grandmother's part to get two children arguing about who got to wipe the dishes that night.

"What's got you looking so cheerful this morning?" Billie asked.

Willa shared the memory with her aunt, who laughed appreciatively and launched into her own childhood reminiscences. Willa only half listened to Billie's chatter as she dried the colorful floral dishes they used for everyday. Her gaze kept straying out the window to the vandalized cottage.

"Christian says he should be able to fix most of the damage," Billie said, and Willa realized guiltily that her aunt had noticed her inattention. "But I'll have to get someone out here to replace the window." She sighed. "Things sure do add up."

There wasn't a hint of anything but resignation in her aunt's voice, nevertheless Willa quickly said, "I thought a lot about it last night, Billie, and I'd like to stay here a bit longer than I planned. I have some money that we can use to get things updated around here. Starting with a dishwasher," she said, putting away the last piece of flatware. "If you're going to continue offering an American plan to the guests, cleaning up after meals will take much less time with a dishwasher."

Willa expected her aunt to show some sign of pleasure at the announcement, but Billie reacted with calm acceptance. Or was there a glint of satisfaction in her blue eyes as she followed Willa's gaze to the windbreaker-clad figure working outside the cottage?

"That would be real nice," she said. "I'll go ahead and call a repairman then. Maybe you'd like to go to town later and help me pick out some material for new curtains? The dime store is open on Sunday afternoons."

"Sure. We might as well get enough for all the cottages. I noticed that the curtains are pretty faded."

They were discussing paint colors and bedspreads when Christian and Rod burst through the back door, their cheeks red with cold. Rod made a beeline for the old gas oven, as if the meager warmth from the pilot light would save him from frostbite. He pressed his hands against the surface, and Willa knew by his reddened fingers that he hadn't worn any gloves.

"I'll put on some more coffee," she said, standing and opening the cupboard next to the refrigerator where the coffee things were stored. She turned to Rod and asked, "How about a cup of hot chocolate?"

He shot Christian a quick glance before answering, "I think I'll have some coffee, too." He looked back at Willa, his expression pleading with her not to comment on his request.

"All right." She hid a smile, making a mental note to add plenty of milk and sugar to one of the chipped mugs. Not once during the three-day drive from Arizona to Pinecrest had she seen Rod drink a cup of coffee, nor had he expressed any interest in doing so. It seemed that today he wanted to impress Christian, and she hoped that meant that they had come to some sort of truce.

She was searching the cupboards for the peanut butter cookies she and Billie had baked the day before when she overheard her aunt.

"Willa is going to help renovate the resort, Christian."

She could feel Christian's sharp gaze on her back, and she slowed her motions, waiting for him to say something. Billie's announcement was a bit ambiguous, and she wondered if her aunt even understood that her intentions were merely to fund the renovations, and not to stay and run the resort. She should have corrected Billie immediately, but she wanted to hear what Christian had to say about her decision.

She waited, but he said nothing. When she finally turned with the plate of cookies, Christian and Billie were discussing who to hire to replace the window. He looked up as Willa set the cookies on the table, his gaze assessing her. She heard the old percolator gurgle its last, and she escaped gratefully to retrieve the coffee.

"Let me help with that." Rod scraped back his chair and moved next to her to reach for the large pot. She tried not to show her surprise at the gesture. There was no sign of the sullen, sarcastic boy Christian had tackled in the woods last night. She watched Rod pour four mugs of coffee, one of them a pale caramel color from the generous dose of half-and-half Billie kept in the refrigerator for her morning oatmeal.

"Here. This one's yours," she said quietly, handing him the mug with the caramel-colored contents.

He gave her a shy half smile before retreating to the

table and putting a mug of steaming black coffee in front of Billie.

Willa handed the other mug to Christian, giving him a startled look when he brushed her fingers deliberately. She held his gaze for a moment, recognizing the challenge in his hazel eyes.

"I guess we'd better sit right here and put together a plan for the repairs, then," he said, and she realized he was trying to pin her down before she had a chance to reconsider her offer.

"That sounds like an excellent idea," Billie seconded. Willa felt cornered again, but she reminded herself how much the resort meant to her aunt. As they went over the bills and receipts for the last year, she saw that Christian had used some of his own money to pay for things such as tools and supplies, and she guessed he'd given Billie some story about needing a new ratchet or T-square anyway.

They planned everything down to the last detail. The discussion took them through morning coffee, dinner, and even dishes, which they cleared away as a team. As they dried and put away the last of the dishes, all agreed that Christian and Rod would do most of the heavy work, repairing roofs and docks, while Willa and her aunt would concentrate on the cottages' interiors, and the business side of the operation. Three of the ten cottages hadn't been used at all in the last five years, and the boathouse had practically fallen into ruin.

All of this had to be complete by the biggest weekend on the resort calendar, the opening of the fishing season in mid-May. Willa calculated quickly. *Eight weeks.* Two months of being near Christian every day. She felt a rush of confusion and looked up to find him watching her. She tried to mask her expression, but she felt completely transparent to his knowing gaze.

Eight weeks just might be an eternity.

Billie cleared the coffee mugs from the table and wiped away the cookie crumbs with a damp cloth. Willa had gone upstairs to change clothes before they left for town, and Christian and Rod were back outside. She was alone at last. She allowed herself a wide smile as she carried the mugs to the sink.

She was glad Willa had decided to help with Restless Spirit. It was a start, at least. How could her niece resist the pull of the lake's quiet beauty, or the majesty of the changing seasons? And if things went according to plan, Willa would be here to see the seasons change, carrying on the rhythm her grandparents had begun: cleaning and planting the garden every spring, hosting guests all summer, harvesting and canning in autumn, and in the winter resting and reflecting on the year to come.

It wasn't that Billie wanted to abandon the place that had been her home all this time. She loved it, every crumbling inch of it. She hadn't complained when the rest of her family had run off to Arizona, nor had she given up when they had tried to persuade her to leave Restless Spirit and join them. But now she was seventy-six years old, and she was tired of making every decision on her own.

She wasn't getting too old by any means. No, she felt as strong and capable as she had at thirty-six, but she knew that it wouldn't be long before she couldn't give Restless Spirit all the attention it needed. And before that time got here, she wanted to go places and do things. All her life, she'd watched other people vacationing and having fun. Now it was her turn. Only she wasn't going to be happy with a weekend jaunt to the lakes, as her guests were.

Oh, no. She wanted adventure and excitement that

far surpassed the thrill of landing a large-mouth bass or catching the limit on walleyes. And she would get it. She heard Willa's footsteps on the stairs and turned, her smile wide with anticipation.

"Ready?" she asked.

Christian stood and began to clear the dining room table. "What do you say we give these two ladies the night off, Rod?"

They'd eaten in there to celebrate "ice out"—the first day the ice melted completely from the lake, and a sure sign of spring. Of course, snowfall was still possible through April and even May, but this year it seemed unlikely. March had gone out like a lamb, and the town's old-timers declared that this year the ice on Spirit Lake had thawed earlier than any year they could remember.

"Sure, now that we have a dishwasher, you men are willing to pitch in with the real work," Billie said. The sparkle in her blue eyes betrayed her plaintive words. She was happy, and Christian felt a stab of worry as he wondered how long it would last. It had been a month since Willa had decided to extend her stay, and he was afraid Billie was getting too used to having her around.

As was he.

His gaze settled on Willa, seated across the dining room table, and he felt an ache around his heart. Her red hair caught the highlights from the chandelier above, its crystals sparkling now after a recent afternoon of dusting away the cobwebs. He'd helped Willa lower it so that she could polish the crystals and replace the burned-out bulbs. They'd worked side by side on other projects, too—painting, sanding the floors, washing windows. He wondered just how long he'd be able to stand having her so close without doing something about it.

She looked up from her coffee and caught him staring. "Are you finished with your dessert?" he asked, reaching for her pie plate, a handy excuse for his attentive gaze.

"Yes." She passed it to him, smiling politely. She'd been acting like this ever since the night they'd kissed at Brenda's party—cool, distant, composed. In other words, nothing like the responsive woman he'd held in his arms, or the spitfire who'd gone to Rod's defense like a mother bear protecting her cub.

And yet, as he'd worked beside her over the last four weeks, he'd grown more and more certain that she was still the same Willa he'd loved since he was old enough to write in longhand. And now her stay was nearly half over. He added her plate to the stack in his hands and headed for the kitchen, cursing the burning feeling in his stomach. Was he worried that *Billie* might get too used to having Willa around? Or himself?

Rod entered the kitchen behind him and carried his handful of plates and cups to the sink. He'd been quiet all evening, leaving most of the celebrating to the others. Christian filled the sink with water and wondered what was on the boy's mind since he'd settled in at school. He'd followed Rod's progress through Willa and Billie, but he'd also consulted his own resources—a friend who taught biology, and Brenda Songstad, who knew more about what was going on in town than any other source, thanks to her customers at the café.

He rinsed the dishes and handed them to Rod, who fitted them into the racks of the commercial-sized dishwasher.

"It's going to be pretty different around here with all those people, isn't it?" Rod asked over the sounds of clinking plates and running water.

Christian hesitated before answering, thinking back to the summers when the resort was at its peak. He, Willa, and Rick had escaped most of the work, giving them plenty of time for lazy afternoons fishing or picking blackberries. He grinned, realizing now that those afternoons weren't as lazy as they'd seemed, with the fish going on the dinner table and the berries baked into pies by Willa's grandmother.

"It's usually only full on the weekends, and remember, it only lasts for about four months."

"Maybe Billie should keep the place open all year, have cross-country ski trails or something, like they do in Ely or some of the other towns north of here. If it costs too much to heat the cottages, we could put the guests up here in the main house, like a bed and breakfast."

Christian looked at Rod in surprise. "You've thought a lot about this, haven't you?"

A flush crept over the boy's cheekbones. "I guess. I just hope Billie can make a go of it."

Christian was about to ask Rod what he was planning on doing after graduation when the boy spoke again. This time, the words seemed to come out of nowhere, catching Christian completely off guard.

"Do you think it's possible to know who you're going to marry when you're seventeen years old?"

The question shocked Christian, and it must have shown on his face because Rod quickly added, "I was just asking, you know? I mean, it's not like I'm really thinking about it or anything . . ."

Rod's mumbled excuses went past his ears as he remembered asking himself the same question eighteen years ago. At age seventeen, he'd been convinced that he and Willa would spend the rest of their lives together.

An array of memories passed through his mind: Hot

summer nights in the boathouse, drive-in movies, picnics in the woods. And each memory had its own special appeal, from the huge backseat of her grandmother's Bel Aire, to the concealing branches of a willow near the edge of the lake. He looked at Rod sharply, wondering what—or who, rather—had brought this question on. Before he could find out, the door to the dining room opened and Billie entered.

"I need some help carrying this box full of supplies down to the root cellar," she said. "Willa and I didn't have time to unload the truck before dinner."

"I'll get it," Rod offered, obviously relieved to have an excuse to disappear before Christian could question him. The pair went out the back door, leaving Christian in the house with Willa.

It wasn't as though they were alone, what with Billie and Rod just outside. But as the days passed he'd grown more and more sensitized to her presence, and tonight he felt as if all his nerve endings had been replaced by a kind of radar that focused only on Willa. He heard her go into the parlor and pull out the bench of the upright piano. This was her evening ritual, to sit at the piano and tinker idly.

When the expected notes sounded through the house, he folded the dishcloth and hung it over the faucet, telling himself to go outside and join Billie and Rod. He could talk to Rod some more, find out what was on his mind. To hell with Willa's warning to stay out of family business.

He started for the back door, pausing when he heard another string of notes from the piano. They seemed to echo around an empty place inside him, and he realized again how little time together they had left. He stood for a moment, indecision keeping him from going out the door.

Everything had been so peaceful, so relaxed before Willa had arrived with Rod in tow. He had a feeling now that things would never be the same. She'd gotten into his blood ages ago, like a tropical fever that kept returning years later to torment its victim, and now he was burning up.

He heard the delicate melody and found himself walking through the house to the arched doorway that separated the living room from the front parlor.

She hadn't heard him enter the room. She was frowning over the keys, her hair falling around the sides of her face. She wasn't really playing, just letting the notes drift and fall like leaves eddying in an autumn breeze, but her skill was unmistakable. He envied her talent, not because he wished to play piano himself, but because he knew it was her talent that would take her away from him again.

He tried pushing away the resentment lurking in the dark corners of his mind, but the effort only stirred up more thoughts and pictures. Five years ago he'd seen Willa in front of a Minneapolis audience, her hair shorn into a spiky crown, blazing red under the stage lights, her body moving lithely to the rhythm set down by the bassist and drummer. Her husband had been standing behind her, playing a guitar riff in counterpoint to her low voice. He'd watched her, searching for the freckled, tomboyish ten-year-old, or the shyly seductive teenager, and not finding a sign of either one of them.

He didn't usually pull extra duty reinforcing the house security at concerts. The noise and hassle wasn't worth the extra pay. But curiosity and a desire to see Willa again had drawn him to that one. Underneath the loud, throbbing music he had recognized real talent. Willa possessed more than a strong, clear voice. She'd displayed a true sense of theater as she entertained the crowd. He had watched her performance and known that she'd grown far beyond this quiet little island.

But she'd come back.

Now, seeing her dressed in a Minnesota Twins T-shirt and a pair of faded jeans, her hair loose around her shoulders, he wondered if she'd ever really left at all. Her face was bare of makeup, and she looked about Rod's age—nothing at all like the seductive vixen who'd danced on stage that night five years ago.

To him, she was every bit as desirable in her jeans and T-shirt. He knew in that moment that he wanted her to stay, not just until summer, but forever. She glanced up as though his thoughts had taken form and startled her somehow.

"Rod's helping Billie move some things from the pickup into the root cellar," he said, hoping she hadn't recognized the desire in his eyes. He crossed the polished pine floor to stand next to the piano.

"He's changed, hasn't he, during the last couple months?" She was obviously pleased. "He doesn't seem as moody."

"I think living here has been good for him," he ventured, judging her reaction. She looked down at her hands, fingering the keys lightly. "It's a good place for a kid to grow up. After all," he continued, "we didn't turn out so bad, did we?"

She hit a discordant note, tapping the offending key several times with her finger, until he had to restrain himself from reaching out and moving her hand away. "This piano needs tuning," she said, and he knew she was deliberately avoiding the subject. He wasn't about to let her run away again.

"Billie's changed, too, since you've been here," he said. "Or haven't you noticed?"

Her hands stilled. "I noticed."

"She likes having you here." He stopped himself before going too far, but he could tell that she knew what he'd been about to say.

"I can't stay. She'll have to get used to the idea."

He sat down next to her on the piano bench. Even though there wasn't much room to move on the small seat, she managed to put more distance between them. Her withdrawal was more emotional than physical, and he told himself to proceed carefully.

"Play something," he said. "You're always in here tinkering around, but I never hear you playing a song or singing."

"I don't sing anymore," she said flatly. "Unless I'm hawking new cars or pushing perfume."

"It's an honest way to make a living," he said lightly.

She turned to face him. "Implying that what I did before wasn't?"

"I didn't say that." Her quick defensiveness told him how sensitive she was about her years with the band. "It just wasn't you. At least not how I remembered you. You were never that hard, Willa."

"I was only a child when you knew me."

"You weren't a child those nights we spent together in the boathouse." His gaze held hers, daring her to escape this time.

She half rose from the piano bench, and he placed a hand on her arm to stay her. He was surprised when she didn't try to resist the light pressure. She sat and turned to him, her eyes a dark slate blue. "It's been eighteen years since that summer. You know nothing about me."

"That was your choice, not mine," he said, deliberately reminding her of the letters she'd never answered. She looked away, and he asked, "What happened to you?"

She pulled down the lid that covered the keyboard. "I already told you. Life happened to me. I grew up.

Maybe you should consider trying it yourself instead of making the rest of us relive ancient history."

"I don't think it's history that's got you all worked up right now." He leaned toward her and took her lips in a brief kiss that wasn't nearly enough to satisfy the hunger that burned inside him. She stared at him, her eyes wide with shock, and he kissed her again until he felt her lips soften and yield against his.

He didn't even hear the back door opening, but Willa did. She tore her mouth from his and nearly tripped over the piano bench in her haste to get away. Her footsteps pounded up the stairs.

If it weren't for Billie and Rod, he would have followed. He stifled a groan. He didn't know whether to feel glad that he'd been rescued from his desires, or frustrated at having them thwarted.

During the days that followed, Willa was grateful for the activity and for the frequent excuses to take Billie's seldom-used truck into town to pick up wallpaper, cans of paint, shingles, and lumber. Even though Christian was still working a full schedule for Pinecrest's three-man police department, his graveyard shift made it seem as though he was at the resort full-time. She welcomed her escapes into town, away from his all-knowing hazel eyes.

If it wasn't for him, she'd actually be able to relax and enjoy what was left of her stay. Billie was content puttering around in the kitchen, cooking for four. Rod seemed to be enjoying school and spent his afternoons at track workout, lending a willing hand whenever he was home, and sticking by Christian's side like a shadow. Having a male role model was good for him, but Willa watched the growing closeness between him and Christian with a sense of ambivalence.

She worried that Rod might become too attached to Christian. But when she examined her feelings closer, she realized that she was envious. She saw the rapport between the two males and wished things were that easy between her and her nephew. For some reason, Rod treated her with a distance that she couldn't seem to breach.

It was for the best, she told herself as she settled into a corner of the broad sofa one evening. It would be even worse if Rod became attached to her. Still, she felt like the outsider, the one who didn't fit into the circle of warmth that seemed to be building as they approached their common goal—restoring Restless Spirit to its former efficiency and charm.

Every evening they would gather in the huge living room after supper. Like the rest of the house, the room was a combination of stately Victorian design and rustic northwoods materials. Antique Oriental rugs softened the pine floors, and the furniture was a comfortable mix of decades, from a walnut and brocade Eastlake loveseat to a worn plaid lounge chair, which was Billie's favorite because the upholstered sides had pockets large enough for her knitting.

Billie sat there now, her head tipped back against the thickly padded cushions, the diamond-patterned afghan she was making forgotten in her lap. Willa smiled as she remembered sitting in this room as a child, surrounded by resort guests and family. Hulbert Mitterhauser may have intended the massive house to be a statement of success and superiority over his neighbors, but his youngest son, Willa's grandfather, had thrown the house open to everyone.

Every evening, Grandfather Johann would perch on the raised hearth of the massive fireplace and tell stories, waving his hands wildly to illustrate some point to the wide-eyed children seated on the floor at his feet.

Willa glanced over at Christian, a smile still lifting the corners of her mouth, to find him watching her. He was seated on the other end of the sofa, his relaxed posture out of keeping with his expression. On the floor, Rod sprawled on the Oriental rug, his attention fixed on the television program he was watching. He was completely unaware of the silent exchange taking place over his head.

Willa's smile faded at Christian's stare. More and more frequently, her thoughts returned to the kisses they'd shared. She knew Christian was thinking about the same thing. His gaze dropped to her lips, and the heat in his eyes wasn't from the fire burning in the fieldstone fireplace. For a moment she allowed herself to imagine what might happen if she was free to reach over and trace the vee of skin revealed by his unbuttoned shirt collar.

"Hey, it's Willa's commercial!" Rod's voice broke into her thoughts. Willa looked at the screen and flushed. She'd been so distracted that even the sound of her own voice, huskily singing about a bewitching perfume, hadn't penetrated.

"That's not you." Christian frowned at the slinky brunette on the screen who was touching perfume to her pulse points and mouthing the words to the song with a sensuous pout.

"The voice is mine," she said.

"She did the one with the electric shaver, too," Rod informed Christian. "And a couple of ads for cars." He turned on his back and looked up at Willa. "Isn't that right?"

She nodded modestly.

"It's very good," Christian said in an expressionless voice.

"She's great. None of the kids at school believe me,

though, when I tell them she was with Natural Disaster," Rod added.

Willa hardly heard Rod's lament. She was still wondering at Christian's weak praise, trying not to let his comment sting. Their gazes met again, hazel clashing with gray, and for a moment it was as though they were alone.

This time the spell was broken by a sputtering snore as Billie awoke from her nap. "Oh dear, I've done it again, haven't I?" she said, reaching a hand up to tidy her white hair.

"It's almost ten. Why don't you go on up to bed?" Willa suggested. "Rod and I did the dishes ages ago."

"I think I will," she said. "I'm certainly sleeping a lot better these days, with you all here. We haven't had a visit from the ghost since that night in March."

Hearing her aunt refer to the vandals as "the ghost" again made Willa uncomfortable. She hoped Billie was just tired, and not slipping back into the mild confusion she'd shown when Willa first arrived.

Billie's sleepy blue gaze took in Willa and Christian at opposite ends of the sofa before resting on Rod. "It's a school day tomorrow, Rod. Why don't you call it a night, too?"

He appeared to be about to form a protest, then glanced up toward Christian, who nodded his agreement with Billie. "All right. I've still got a couple chapters of a book I'm reading for English. I guess I can finish it in bed." He scrambled to his feet.

Willa felt a shock as she realized it was Christian, not her or Billie, to whom Rod had turned for permission. Her fears about them becoming too close seemed to be accurate.

She longed to follow her aunt and nephew up the broad staircase, but that would make it too obvious that she was wary of being alone with Christian. In any case, he would have to leave for work soon, since his shift began at eleven. He stretched his arms over his head before resting them along the back of the sofa, and Willa glanced involuntarily at his hand, only inches away from her shoulder.

"Rod likes you," she said.

"He needs discipline. You and Billie are too easy on him."

Willa wanted to point out that she could hardly take on Rod's discipline when she was leaving so soon, but she knew any protest would give Christian an opening to suggest she stay longer. Instead she said, "He's nearly eighteen. Soon he'll have to be responsible for his own decisions."

"Exactly. But it's hard to grow up if everyone treats you like a child." He straightened, bringing his body closer to hers. "Why won't you tell him about Rick?"

"I can't," she said.

"Why not?"

"Because I'm his aunt, not his mother or stepfather."

"Meaning it's not your place?"

"He never even knew Rick. From the time he was a baby, Patrick Dane has been the only father he's known. If he and Caroline wanted him to know about Rick, they would have told him."

"From what Rod's told me, I get the impression that Caroline hasn't been the most devoted of parents. And it sounds like Patrick Dane resents Rod."

So he felt it, too. That was why she'd been so quick to take Rod with her to Restless Spirit. She'd felt sorry for Rod and empathized with his plight. Her parents had closed themselves off after Rick's death, leaving her to deal with her grief alone. She'd sensed that Rod felt the same alienation within his own family and had reacted by rebelling, as she had.

But somewhere along the journey from Arizona to Minnesota, she'd realized that her impulsive gesture wasn't going to be as simple as it had seemed at first. She couldn't look at Rod without thinking of her brother, and she could feel the bonds tightening, threatening to hold her here to the past. She'd deliberately avoided talking to Rod about his plans after graduation, as if she could make the situation go away simply by ignoring it.

"Maybe Rod is exaggerating," she said, feeling like a traitor.

"I've seen a lot of kids in trouble. Usually it's because they think no one cares what they do. Do you care what happens to Rod when you leave, Willa? Billie is too old to take custody of a teenage boy."

"He'll be eighteen in August. An adult. No one needs to take custody of him then."

"You're talking about legal details when we both know it's much more than that. Do you really think Rod's ready to make adult decisions on his own?"

"I did when I was eighteen," she said, her chin lifting.

"You ran away with a musician on the back of a motorcycle. Some decision." His eyes narrowed, and he moved closer, until Willa caught the faint scent of his aftershave. "What were you running away from, Willa?"

She tensed and made a move to stand up, but his hand stayed her. She knew he'd sit there all night, as patient as a cat stalking a mouse if he had to be. "My parents," she said. "After we moved to Arizona, all I ever heard about was how wonderful Rick was, how brave he'd been to give his life for his country. They didn't notice me or how unhappy I was. If they did, they would have had to admit how their son died. When Darryl came riding along on his Harley, I saw my chance to make them wake up and take notice. But they didn't," she said sadly. "They let me go."

"Did you love him?"

She answered honestly. "I thought I did. He made me forget everything except music. Everything was wonderful for a while. The band clicked, and we started getting national attention. That's when Darryl started to self-destruct, just like Rick, only this time I saw it coming." Her voice broke. "I couldn't watch it."

She tugged at her hand, but he held it fast. "That was years ago, Willa. What are you running from now?"

The question hung between them. She tugged one more time and this time succeeded in pulling away. She stood and headed for the stairs, stopping when she realized that her action only confirmed Christian's belief that she ran at any sign of trouble.

She turned to find him right behind her. Before she could say another word, he reached out and pulled her against him, holding her tightly to his chest. She rested against him for a moment, tempted by the solid feel of his chest, a safe place in the storm of emotions that threatened to overwhelm her. His lips touched her neck, trailing along the neckline of her sweater and making her pulse jump. She realized then that he was the cause of the storm, and not a safe harbor at all. She pushed at his chest, and he released her.

"You left Restless Spirit, but you came back. Like I did, Willa. Why don't you just admit that this is where we belong? That you'll never feel at home anywhere else?"

"No!" She turned and went up the stairs slowly, trying not to break into a run even though she could feel Christian's gaze boring into her back.

Rod quietly shut the door as he heard Willa's steps on the stairs. He stood there, afraid to walk back to the bed in case his aunt might hear him and guess that he'd been listening. Instead, he crouched in the darkened room, waiting while Willa used the bathroom. He heard the water running, the engine of Christian's pickup rumbling toward town, then finally the soft click as Willa's bedroom door closed. Only after everything was quiet did he creep back to bed. He lay there staring up at the quivering shadows the tree branches made on the moonlit ceiling.

He'd been studying when he heard Willa and Christian talking downstairs. He'd gotten up to close his bedroom door, but when he heard his name, he'd frozen with his hand on the doorknob, listening as they argued about him. Half the words were too indistinct to make out, but he caught the gist of it.

They were passing the buck again. Nobody wanted to tell him about his father. And Willa and Christian were already talking about where to send him next, arguing the way his mom had argued with Patrick.

He had heard Willa confide in Christian, telling him about her husband. It didn't take a genius to figure out what they were doing in the long silence that followed. His mind conjured up a picture of them in each other's arms.

Willa and Christian? He felt betrayed. Willa was supposed to be his aunt. She was supposed to be a rocker, someone cool enough to understand a kid. And he thought Christian was his friend. Here all this time they had eyes only for each other, and he was just in the way.

He turned over and pressed his face against the pillow. Just when he thought everything was going to be okay, he was back on the outside again.

6

It was cold enough that night to freeze the whiskers off a catfish, but that didn't stop Christian from rolling down the window of his pickup as he drove across the causeway and headed for town. He welcomed the blast of icy air. For once, he wished Pinecrest wasn't so peaceful. He hoped for some kind of action—a fire, a robbery, even a cat up a tree. Anything to take his mind off Willa.

Immediately he felt guilty. He shouldn't wish misfortune on anyone just because he couldn't control his wayward thoughts. He'd make it through another endlessly routine night, filing paperwork, driving up and down Main Street to check on the local businesses, and trying not to think about how Willa's eyes had turned dark when he kissed her.

God, it was worse than being seventeen again. This time sex wasn't some mysterious delight forbidden to the underaged and unmarried. This time he knew exactly what it was he was wanting—and losing the mystery only made the wanting stronger.

Shortly after he turned onto the highway that led into town, he caught himself humming the refrain of Willa's perfume commercial. He feared that the sensual melody would haunt him for days. Hearing it tonight had only reminded him that her talent put her out of reach of a small-town cop. He knew it, knew that there was no future for them, and yet he couldn't turn off his response to the husky promise in her voice. He wondered how many men had bought their wives or girlfriends that particular brand of perfume because of it.

He laughed shortly, thinking he ought to pull over and dive into the icy waters of Spirit Lake and hope that it would cool him off until she left at the end of May. Then he'd have to content himself with hearing her now and then on TV or radio. He groaned.

He wasn't much better off than Rod. Since that night last week when Rod had started to confide in him about love and marriage, Christian had done a little checking around. According to his friend who taught at Pinecrest High, Rod was seeing Kerry Songstad. He knew Brenda and Carl wouldn't let Kerry date until she turned sixteen, and he wondered if Rod was doing any better than he was when it came to controlling his desires.

When he pulled into the small brick building that served as Pinecrest's town hall and police department, Skeet Varner was sitting on the front steps, smoking a cigarette. Skeet groused constantly about not being able to smoke inside the building, and Christian grabbed this opportunity to razz the younger man and take his own mind off Willa.

"You're going to stunt your growth," Christian warned as usual. At thirty-two, Skeet was barely over five and a half feet tall. In high school his small stature had earned him the nickname "Mosquito." They bantered back and forth for a few minutes before Christian asked him if there'd been any action that evening.

"Nothing but a call down to the Viking Café. The cook locked her keys inside the walk-in refrigerator." He grinned. "I got a preview of tomorrow's rhubarb cobbler. Damn near as good as Billie Mitterhauser's." He glanced sideways. "How's she been doing since that last break-in?"

"Fine," Christian told him. "She pretends to be nervous when it suits her, but she's a pretty tough old bird, you know."

"Yeah. I hear Willa's helping her fix the old place up. Kind of a wasted effort, isn't it, with Thor Nelson so keen on that new resort?"

"Thor doesn't always get what he wants."

"So I've heard. But we're not talking about a girl here. We're talking about a multimillion-dollar deal. A lot of people in town think a big theme hotel would be good for business."

"You've seen the plans. The PROCOR people want to turn Pinecrest into a movie set, some stupid Alpine village."

"Hey, don't shout at me. I'm on your side. I mean, I can see some good in Thor's idea, but all it's gonna mean is another jump in our taxes."

They talked for a while longer before Skeet went home and Christian went inside. He settled behind the desk that had occupied one corner of the paneled office as long as he could remember. He'd parked his butt on the other side of it a few times when he was a kid, getting an earful from the old chief of police.

It was Chief Donovan who had managed to convince Sheriff Pitzer not to send him up just to get him away from his daughter. Those were the dark times, the months after Rick died and Willa's family moved away, when his mother had drunk herself to death. He'd gotten into more trouble during those months than he could count, and all because he was striking out at the pain. Speeding, curfew violations, reckless driving, disturbing the peace—he'd had a whole glove compartment full of warnings and tickets, enough so that Pitzer could have thrown him in jail unless he'd paid them all off.

And now every night he had the whole office to himself. The dispatcher, Sandy, worked only until 6:00 P.M. on weekdays, so he had to answer all incoming calls himself. Come summer, with its influx of part-time residents and tourists, they would hire another officer or two and another dispatcher.

But for the next couple of weeks, it was business as usual, with paperwork and routine drive-bys to occupy him until the end of his shift.

And visions of Willa to drive him to distraction all night long.

The view was great, but that was about the best Willa could say for this latest project. Rod was still at his track workout, so she was helping Christian replace shingles on the roof of one of the cottages. From this vantage point she could see all the way across Spirit Lake to Pinecrest. Today the lake was a deep blue, reflecting the cloud-spotted sky, and shimmering with ripples.

The rest of the view wasn't bad either, Willa admitted as she looked over at Christian, who was kneeling to hammer a shingle into place. He'd rolled up the sleeves of his dark green cotton shirt, baring muscular forearms sprinkled with dark hair. His faded jeans stretched tightly over his thighs and a lock of hair had escaped to hang above his eyebrows, tempting her to reach over and comb it into place with her fingers. It was enough to drive a woman mad, especially a woman whose fingers still remembered the texture of that hair and the smooth warmth of his skin.

But she also remembered his aggressiveness. It had been several days since they had argued about Rod and ever since, they had been needling each other like a pair of bad-tempered children. Somehow they'd managed to work together this afternoon without an explosion.

Willa looked at her watch for what had to be the sixth time in the last fifteen minutes, wondering when Rod was going to get back from the workout and relieve her. Not only was she tired of the monotonous job of handing shingles over, she was just plain tired after a morning helping Billie wax the hardwood floors in the big house. Plus, there was an additional wrinkle, one she didn't like to admit to: high places made her nervous.

The cottages were actually little more than shacks, only a story and a half above ground, but even that was high enough to threaten her equilibrium—as if being near Christian all afternoon hadn't already destroyed it. She'd been afraid of heights ever since he and Rick had dared her to climb to the top of the old oak tree that stood in the front yard and then left her. For years afterward, she didn't climb anything higher than a step stool if she could avoid it.

Not that she would ever admit to vertigo in front of Christian. The way they'd been getting on each other's nerves lately, he'd probably be glad to push her off the edge.

"Think you could hand me a shingle sometime this year?"

Christian's voice broke into her thoughts. She quickly grabbed for a shingle to place into his outstretched hand. He accepted it without another word, and she refrained from answering his sarcasm with a retort of her own.

A puff of wind caught at her hair, pulling it out of the

loose band she'd used to pull it back and sweeping several strands across her eyes. She reached up and dragged them away in time to catch Christian staring at her with unveiled desire. He quickly looked away, but not before she felt an answering tug of need deep inside her.

Was this why they'd been bickering like children all week long? To hide from each other, and from themselves, how much they wanted each other?

She heard the rumble of the bus dropping Rod off at the end of the causeway and exhaled the breath she'd been holding. Christian looked up sharply at the sound, and she pushed another shingle into his hands before he could comment on her obvious relief.

Rod's loping steps crunched on the gravel drive below and then became muffled as he crossed the grassy lawn toward the cottages.

"Hi!" she called down. "It's about time you got home." She smiled to show she was only teasing, knowing how sensitive he could be at times. His mood swings were something she'd learned to accept, along with a voracious appetite for milk and a habit of playing his stereo too loud. It was all part of having a teenager around, she decided, comparing his behavior to her own at his age.

"Gotta catch my breath first," he said, bending over and huffing exaggeratedly. "It's a long way from the causeway to the house."

Willa's grin widened. They had shared this joke every afternoon for the last few days. It was silly, but it made her feel as though he'd finally accepted her. "What, a big athlete like you spends two hours running laps, then you can't even walk to the front door?"

Rod groaned. "You shoulda seen what Coach Davis made us do today. The track was soggy from the rain yesterday, so we had to run around the cafeteria about a thousand times and then do pushups. I sure hope there's something to eat. I'll never make it to supper."

Christian stood, his legs wide apart to brace himself against the roof's sharp pitch. "Why don't you see what Billie's got in the kitchen and then get into your work clothes and take over for Willa?"

"And I thought Coach Davis was a slave driver," Rod said with a shake of his head. "Catch you later." He headed toward the house, his strides long and loose. He was even starting to walk like Christian, Willa realized. She glanced over at him, wondering if he had noticed. But Christian wasn't looking at Rod. His gaze was once again focused on her. She self-consciously crossed her arms over her sweatshirt and sat back on her heels.

He must have mistaken the gesture for tiredness because he suggested, "Why don't you call it quits? I'll take a break for a minute until Rod comes back."

"I can keep going," she insisted, unwilling to show any sign of weakness in front of him. Even as she spoke, she knew the words sounded exactly like those spoken by the ten-year-old tomboy who had tried so hard to keep up with her older brother and his best friend. She was tempted to share the thought with Christian, but his expression was closed.

Since standing up on top of the roof made her dizzy, she backed toward the ladder leaning up against the gutter, crawling on all fours. Relief poured through her when her sneaker found the first rung. More confident now, she placed her other foot on the rung below.

Only the rung wasn't there, and she spent an endless few seconds scrabbling for a foothold.

"Willa!"

She must have made a sound of distress because

Christian was already crossing the peak of the roof toward her. Her nails grabbed at the shingles, and for a moment she thought she would manage to hang on, but the ladder tangled with her legs, pulling her down. Her hands were too damp to get a decent grip, and her fingers slid across the rough surface of the shingles.

The ground wasn't that far away, but it seemed like an eternity before she landed on her back, her teeth banging together as her head hit the ground. She lay there, dazed, staring up at the blue sky, focusing on a fluffy white cloud that reminded her of Billie's hair, noting idly that she couldn't hear or feel a thing.

Then sensation came rushing back, and her senses were crowded with impressions: The screen door slamming, Rod yelling her name as he raced across the lawn, the stinging pain in her shin bone where it pressed against the rung of the ladder, the sharp jab between her shoulder blades, and the warm saltiness of blood in her mouth. Several feet away, Christian dropped down from the edge of the cabin's roof.

"Willa, are you all right?" Christian hovered above her, his eyes dark with concern.

"Oh, God, she's bleeding from the mouth," she heard Rod say. "That means she has brain damage. We learned it in health class last week."

"Willa?" Christian's worried voice was nearly a shout.

"I vit my thongue," she mumbled, avoiding the sore spot.

"What?"

"I'm bleeding because I bit my tongue. The only thing that hurts is my leg. And my back. I must have landed on something."

Christian gently pulled the ladder from her leg, then carefully ran his hands over her limbs before checking her rib cage. His touch was warm against her skin where her sweatshirt had ridden up around her waist. She told herself it was the fall, and not Christian's touch that left her feeling breathless.

"I don't feel anything broken," he said, his voice low and husky as he looked into her eyes. She closed her lids, embarrassed that even in this state, lying flat on her back and bleeding to death from her mouth, she could still react to him.

"How does your head feel?" he asked, reaching up with the tail of his shirt to wipe away the wetness at the corner of her lips.

"Ugh," Rod said, grimacing at the dark stain on Christian's shirt.

Willa found his distaste amusing. She smiled and teased, "You're right. That shirt tasted terrible."

"Sassy woman. Her tongue obviously hasn't suffered permanent damage." She tried sticking it out at him, but started laughing instead, joining Christian and Rod's chuckles.

Billie arrived on the scene, and Willa's smile widened when she saw that her aunt had rushed out of the house without her ever-present galoshes covering her shoes. "I heard you scream," she said, "and I ran all the way here. I'd like to know what the hell's so funny. Just look at you."

"I screamed?" Willa couldn't remember. Her amusement disappeared at Billie's worried expression. All of a sudden she realized how lucky she was not to have broken anything. "I'm fine, Aunt Billie, I just— Ouch." She winced as Christian turned up the hem of her jeans to examine her shin.

"Don't move her until you're sure she's all right," Billie warned.

"I'm fine," Willa insisted again, as Christian pulled

her jeans higher. She watched the top of his dark head. Billie made a startled noise, Rod another expression of disgust. Willa sat up on her elbows and looked down at her shin. The skin was raw and bloody where the ladder had scraped it.

"We'd better clean that," she heard her aunt say. The words faded in and out, and Willa swallowed back a wave of nausea. *So this is what people mean by delayed reaction,* she thought. Christian must have felt her shudder, because he reached underneath her knees and shoulders, swinging her up into his arms. "I can walk," she protested weakly.

"Sure you can. You look like you couldn't even wrestle a field mouse," he said as he carried her toward the house. She could feel his voice rumble in his chest, and it made her feel even weaker. Weak, but sort of pampered and wonderful at the same time.

God, what was she thinking? She must have hit her head too hard because none of the sensations rippling through her made any sense. Nor did she have any control over them. She hid her giddiness behind a wall of sarcasm.

"All this concern when I thought you might just push me off the roof yourself. Christian, I'm touched."

His jaw clenched. "Don't *you* push *me,*" he muttered under his breath.

Billie ran ahead, her brown oxfords covered with mud, calling out instructions on her way. "Rod, you get the door for Christian. I'll call Dr. Sam. And Christian, you take her right up to her room. It's got the highest bed. It will be easiest to set her down there."

"I don't need a doctor," she argued weakly, but her aunt was already tracking mud through the hallway on her way to the phone.

Willa thought of the hours she'd spent that morning

polishing the floors and had to choke back an exasperated laugh as Christian carried her over the threshold. The gleaming staircase, with its wide steps and elaborately carved banisters, stretched out before them. She suppressed another bubble of laughter as Rod looked on, the concern in his face turning to puzzlement as Christian passed by with his burden.

"What's so funny? Or are you going delirious on me?" He spoke into her ear.

His breath tickled, and this time she laughed out loud. "I keep picturing the scene in *Gone with the Wind* where Rhett sweeps Scarlett into his arms and carries her up the stairs." The comparison was incongruous, with her mud-stained work clothes and scraped leg, and Christian joined her quiet laughter as he carried her down the hallway to her room.

No sooner had he set her gently down on her bed and arranged the pillows behind her than Billie appeared, brandishing a bottle of witch hazel. Willa's amusement disappeared.

"That stuff stings."

"Don't be a baby," her aunt said. "Dr. Sam can't get away for a couple hours, so he said we should get you cleaned up." Her brisk demeanor turned to impatience when her gaze went to the bed.

"Christian Foster, couldn't you have waited until I got here before setting her down in those muddy clothes? Look what you've done to that beautiful old quilt. My mother's mother made that on the voyage here from Finland."

They laughed at Billie's shift of attention. "Rod is making you a cup of tea," she told Willa. "Dr. Sam said hot liquids would help soothe you."

"I really don't need the doctor, Billie," Willa insisted. "I'm fine. *Or I was,* she added silently as her aunt dabbed at the scrape on her shin with a washcloth soaked in the astringent liquid. She closed her eyes and tried not to moan.

"Maybe you're fine, but take a look at him."

Willa glanced toward Christian and saw that he was as white as the cotton sheets on her bed. She smiled. "Afraid of a little blood? Not a very professional reaction, Officer Foster."

"Just a bit winded," he returned. "You're not as skinny as you used to be." But his eyes were dark and serious, belying his amusement.

"Can't the two of you stop pecking at each other for one minute? Go help Rod," she ordered Christian as she started to remove Willa's soiled clothing. He escaped downstairs, and Willa wished she could follow.

She suffered through Billie's ministrations, and again through Dr. Sam's later that evening. The elderly physician, who'd delivered half the population of Pinecrest, insisted that she take a tablet for pain before he left, and the next morning Willa slept through the house's usual breakfast bustle. When she woke at noon, she had to resort to wheedling to get Billie to consider letting her out of bed.

They finally reached a compromise. Willa would stay inside the house and work on the resort's books, and Billie would take her place helping Christian. Following Billie's instructions, Christian went to find the ledgers and prepare a makeshift office in the breakfast room, while Billie fussed over a tray of cookies, sandwiches, and a thermos of tea in case Willa got hungry while they were outside working on the cottages.

They left her ensconced in a flannel nightgown and a fleecy pink robe—both too hot for the lovely mid-April weather—and surrounded by pillows on the Queen Anne chair Christian had carried in from its usual spot next to the fireplace. After all the commotion, the small breakfast room with its view of the cottages and woods seemed blessedly quiet. Willa poured some tea into a delicate pink-and-white china cup and wondered why invalids couldn't drink coffee.

Then she smiled and admitted to herself that she had actually enjoyed being fussed over. Billie had not only used the good china, she'd covered the round oak table with a lace cloth, adding to the breakfast room's feminine atmosphere. The room was filled with her grandmother's presence. It had always been too small for the family's use, and it had therefore become Oma's private retreat.

The walls were papered in a burgundy-and-cream floral pattern, and the oak breakfront was crowded with glass bowls and vases. She wondered how Oma could have left the pieces she'd been collecting for years, the Mary Gregory and carnival glass, and the sparkling cut-glass vases she'd used to hold lilacs from the bush at the side of the veranda.

They'd all had to leave something behind, she realized. Her grandmother left her treasures, her grandfather the wide hearth with its circle of listening children. And she'd had to leave Christian. She stared sightlessly at the ledgers in front of her for a few moments before opening the top one.

The records went back to when Restless Spirit had first opened, during the Great Depression. Her grandparents had needed to take in boarders and guests in order to survive. They'd opened up the house to strangers and finally built the cottages to handle the overflow as the island became a popular getaway for people who loved the outdoors.

After awhile Willa got caught up in the figures in front of her. She recalculated last year's revenues, but the results were the same. They needed to do twice as much business this year just to pay for the repairs. She felt the cloak of responsibility settling over her shoulders and wished she could throw it off and run outside, to be a child again, carefree and happy.

She was back to poring over names, dates, and figures when a sound from outside caught her attention. Through the lacy Priscilla curtains, she could see that Christian had used Billie's truck to haul the brush he had collected from the woods a few days earlier to the woodpile at the back of the house. He pulled the dead branches from the truck bed and dropped them to the ground, where he began to trim them and stack them.

She was still staring out the window when she heard Billie clear her throat. She turned around guiltily, feeling a bit like she had when her aunt used to catch her daydreaming instead of practicing the piano.

"I told Christian to bring the brush back here. Anything too small for firewood can go into piles for bonfires this summer. The guests will like that." She looked at Willa. "He's a handsome man, isn't he?"

Billie had phrased the question innocently, but Willa detected a speculative gleam in her blue eyes.

"If you like the bossy type," she answered. Then she spoiled her indifferent response by taking another glance out the window. Christian was lopping off branches with an ax, graceful power evident in every swing. His shirt was open in front, and she could see sweat darkening the edges of the blue cotton.

"I was in love with a man like him long ago," said Billie. "Handsome and strong."

"Sean Quinlan?" Willa asked, trying to fit the memory of a younger Billie, tall and rawboned, with the idea of romance. The rivalry between Mattie and her aunt over the same man was one of those tales that still continued to circulate in the small town.

"Don't look so skeptical," her aunt said. "Unfortunately, he preferred the sweet, retiring sort of lady." She sniffed, and Willa smiled in commiseration. Then she tacked on, "I bet Christian likes independent, feisty women."

"Then I wouldn't fit the bill," Willa said flatly. Seeing the argument in her aunt's eyes, she abruptly changed the subject. "Did you come in to tell me something?"

"Yes, I did. Someone just called to book a cottage for opening weekend. I wrote it all down so you could copy it into the records."

Willa accepted the scrap of paper Billie handed her and flushed. So much for her show of being indifferent to Christian. She hadn't even heard the phone ringing. Billie must have had to run in from outside to answer it. She glanced at her aunt's cramped handwriting and read the name with surprise.

"James Roth. Didn't he come here with his parents when he was a little boy? I think I even baby-sat him a couple times."

"And now he's bringing his wife and their two children. Maybe you'll get to baby-sit again," Billie said, as she backed toward the doorway. "By the way, I told Rod I would drive into town and pick him up after school. He'll help me with the groceries. I ordered an Easter ham from the locker plant."

"For the three of us? I thought we could just have chicken."

"Four. It's Christian's weekend off," she reminded her. "And it wouldn't be Easter, would it, without the traditional ham? I thought we could all decorate eggs the night before, just like old times."

"Just like old times," Willa echoed, her smile tight.

Billie seemed to be catching Christian's fascination for the past. Not only that, her aunt seemed to be under the impression that Willa and Christian could continue their childhood romance. Willa's gaze bored into her aunt's back as she left the room, humming an old show tune. Billie hadn't shown a bit of tiredness or confusion since Willa's accident, taking over the extra workload and Easter preparations with the precision of a drill sergeant.

Willa remembered the slip of paper in her hand and opened the reservations book, trying to imagine little Jimmy Roth with a family. And here she was with nothing or no one to show for all the years that had passed.

Now where did that maudlin thought spring from? she wondered, deciding she'd spent too much time reminiscing herself. She didn't want anyone's children. There was too much involved in raising a family, too many heartaches and disappointments. But even as the thought formed in her mind, she glanced out the window again to where Christian worked.

"Well, I'm off to town," Billie announced, untying her ruffled blue gingham apron.

Christian looked up from the kitchen sink, where he was washing the grime off his hands. He'd finished stacking brush a few minutes ago and had returned to the house to see where Billie would direct his efforts next. She was back in her old form.

"I'll drive you," he offered.

"No need. I'm perfectly capable. And Rod will help me after I pick him up from school. I think one of us should stay here in case Willa needs something."

Alone with Willa. Christian's mind started to work

in high gear as Billie chattered on about Easter ham and daffodil cakes, cookies and hard-boiled eggs. He only half listened. Willa had been in Pinecrest two months now, and this was the first time they would be alone. Until now, Billie or Rod had always been in the background.

Not that anything could happen while Billie was gone to town for an hour. Not that he *wanted* anything to happen.

He'd stay out here in the kitchen, where he could hear Willa call if she needed anything, concentrating on— *What?* He couldn't very well sit out here and twiddle his thumbs.

Billie gave the apron strings one last tug before stepping away and eyeing him critically. "There. Now you just remember to take out those cookies."

"Cookies?"

"The ones I've been telling you about," she said patiently. "The last pan of ginger creams. They'll be done in about five minutes. Let them cool a bit before you put on the icing."

"Sure," he agreed, wondering what the hell she was talking about and hoping he'd figure it out as soon as she left him to the stacks of dirty dishes and an oven full of cookies. He spotted an old yellowed recipe card on the kitchen counter and breathed easier.

She paused in the doorway, pulling her galoshes over her sturdy brown shoes. "They're Willa's favorite. You might take her in some."

"Sure," he said again, feeling a bit hoodwinked as he heard the coy note in Billie's voice. He wondered how much more complicated his duties were going to get.

A little more than twenty minutes and a half dozen dirty dishes later, he carried a tray of iced cookies and coffee into the breakfast room to find Willa with her head tilted back against the chair, her eyes closed, and a ledger book lying open on her lap. The late afternoon sun deepened the color of her hair, turning it to a rich reddish gold against her creamy skin.

Her eyes snapped open. "Do I smell coffee?"

"I thought you might like a few cookies before Rod gets home and devours them all. Billie just left to pick him up."

Her eyes fixed greedily on the mugs of steaming coffee. "I've been craving coffee all day." He set the tray down on the small oak table, and she helped herself before he had a chance to hand her the mug. The she stared speculatively at a cookie in her hand. "Ginger creams. This was Billie's idea, wasn't it?"

"How did you know?"

She laughed, and the husky sound tripped over his nerve endings, making him feel as weightless as a helium balloon. He pulled out one of the press back oak chairs and quickly sat down, grateful for the anchoring feel of the hard wooden seat.

"Can't you see what she's up to?" Willa asked, reaching for another cookie. She took a bite and followed it with a long swallow of coffee, sighing pleasurably.

"Tell me."

"I think she's matchmaking—sending you in here with cookies, leaving us alone."

"I've had the same suspicions myself," he admitted, enjoying the light blush that settled over her cheekbones.

"So what are we going to do about it? We can't let her go on thinking that we're going to pick up where we left off eighteen years ago."

"Why not?" he heard himself asking, staring at the deepening red of her cheeks.

She didn't answer right away, and when she did, her

words were an echo of his own thoughts. "I'm beginning to believe she's much craftier than she pretends to be."

He grinned and reached for another cookie. "It's taken you awhile to notice."

"You mean you already guessed that she's been faking her—her old lady weakness?"

Christian sobered. "I don't know if I'd call it that. Her fears about the vandalism were genuine. When she called me last winter she sounded pretty desperate. I think our being here has helped bring her back in touch."

Willa nodded. "At first, Billie kept talking about Hulbert out wandering again. That's when I thought her mind was starting to go. But she hasn't mentioned the ghost for a while. And she's certainly taken over my share of chores, plus organized Easter dinner right down to the last detail. Nice apron, by the way," she added.

Christian looked down to see he was still wearing Billie's blue gingham apron. He reached back and untied it, pulling it off as though it were strangling him. "I only hope she manages to hold up after you leave."

Willa's expression revealed a mixture of hurt and anger. "No fair, Christian. That's blackmail. Or are you in on this with her? Sacrificing yourself for the cause?"

"No, I'm not." *But maybe I should be,* he thought. Maybe Billie had the right idea after all. Would enough coffee and ginger creams, along with a little persuasion from him, keep Willa here at Restless Spirit? He smiled to himself, then quickly lifted his coffee mug to hide his expression. He'd been fighting to keep from showing her how good it could be between them, knowing she needed to reconcile her other feelings first. Billie saw it in simpler terms, and maybe he should, too. Between the two of them, Willa didn't stand a chance.

He quickly changed the subject before she could

guess what he was plotting. "But I think you're right about Billie being in fine form this weekend. She's been helping me since noon. We're almost finished repairing the roofs. She's a real trooper."

Willa smiled. "Did she let you get any sleep today after your shift?"

Her concern warmed him. "A hour or two. I thought I'd take a nap after supper tonight. I don't need a routine like most people do. When I was in Minneapolis I used to work rotating shifts before I got promoted to detective."

"I still can't see you as a policeman," she said. "You were always such a rebel. I lo—" She broke off suddenly. "If I don't get my eight hours in, I'm miserable," she admitted.

He knew that wasn't what she'd been about to say, but decided not to push it. He set down his mug and teased, "When I came in a few minutes ago, it looked like you were trying to get a few extra."

She smiled sheepishly. "I usually don't nap in the middle of the day like that. It must have been those pills Dr. Sam gave me last night," she said and wrinkled her nose. "I tried to tell all of you that I didn't need fussing over."

Her words reminded him of something he'd planned on saving until she was feeling better. Now seemed as good a time as any. "Do you ever smoke?" he asked. She looked startled by the abrupt question.

"No, why?"

He reached into the pocket of his jeans and pulled out the object he'd found earlier that day.

"A cigarette lighter?"

"It was near the spot where you fell. I think this might be what was poking into your back."

"It doesn't look like it's been sitting outside for very

long." She took it from him, her fingers brushing his lightly before rubbing at the bright silvery finish.

From any other woman, he might have thought the touch was deliberate. He dismissed the possibility before responding, "No, but it's an old lighter. Most people today use the disposable kind. See how the engraving has worn off? You can't even read it."

She took the lighter from his hand, examining it for herself. "Maybe one of the guests . . . " Her words trailed off.

"This lighter hasn't been outside all winter. I'd say it hasn't been there for more than a few weeks."

"The night of Brenda's party was a few weeks ago." Her voice rose in excitement. "The night someone tried to set a fire."

"Yep. I think our culprit left this behind."

"Maybe Pitzer or one of his men dropped it."

"I called as soon as I found it. None of the deputies smoke. Pitzer quit about five years ago. He said it didn't belong to anyone from his department. Of course, someone could have dropped it out there since the night of the party."

She looked from the lighter to him, her expression startled. "That would mean that someone's been hanging around watching us."

"That's right." He took the lighter from her relaxed fingers and pocketed it again.

"Then it isn't just Billie."

It was his turn to look startled. "What?"

She shrugged. "Now that I've finally figured out she's sharp as a tack, I was wondering if she might have created the ghost herself."

"No way." Christian shook his head. "She wouldn't do anything to hurt the resort. You know that."

"Of course. I wasn't thinking."

"There's still one person I haven't talked to."

"Who?"

"Rod. It could belong to him."

"He doesn't smoke."

Christian gave her a pitying look. "What do you think he does when he disappears every evening? Although I haven't noticed any hint of smoke around since he's been in track." She looked surprised, and he added, "Believe me, if that's the most trouble he's gotten into since he's been here, there's no reason to get upset about it."

"I don't think he tried to set that fire. He wouldn't do that to Billie. Or me. And the vandalism started long before he got here."

"Yes, but he might have gotten tangled up with the kids who did. I have a feeling he's hiding something."

"You've said that before, but you've never offered any evidence."

As she spoke the back door opened, and Christian could hear Billie telling Rod where to set the groceries. Willa sent him a warning glance, indicating that the discussion was over.

"You leave him alone, Christian Foster. I mean it," she said quietly. "Let Billie have her Easter holiday without anything to spoil it."

"Three and a half days," Rod complained, knowing that in the past he would have been overjoyed at the extended weekend. It was noon on Friday, and Pinecrest High had just recessed for the Easter weekend. The students were excused the rest of Good Friday and the Monday following Easter. He and Kerry stood near the foot of the broad central staircase, stretching out their goodbyes as long as they dared before Rod missed his bus.

"We'll see each other Tuesday," Kerry said. "And I'll call you tomorrow, I promise."

"I wish your folks would let you go out with me," Rod said, even though he knew that without a license or a car there wasn't anywhere he could take her. Thanks to Patrick Dane, he was the only senior boy in school who hadn't taken his behind-the-wheel test. He knew how to drive, thanks to a friend at the military academy whose parents had given him a new car for his sixteenth birthday. But a fat lot of good knowing how did him when he didn't have a license.

He and Kerry were stuck with after-school "dates" under her mom's supervision. She wouldn't turn sixteen until September, and if he didn't have his license by then, he vowed as he gazed into her sparkling green eyes, he'd slit his throat.

"Cootchy-coo, look at the love birds," a voice taunted from the stairs above. Rod looked up to see Jerry Miller and and Dean Roberts, both on the track team and two of the school's most popular students. He stepped forward protectively and blocked Kerry from their view.

"Oh, look at the tough guy," Jerry mocked. "Hey, Kerry, why don't you go out with a real man? I'll drive you into Grand Rapids or Duluth and we can go to a movie."

"No, thank you," she replied politely. Rod would have preferred her to blow Jerry off or spit in his face. He itched to smash Jerry's face in, but that would not only land him in a whole lot of trouble with his parents, who might decide to snatch him away, it would also seal his fate at Pinecrest High. Being the new kid was sort of like being on probation. One slip-up and he'd be an outsider for sure.

He was beginning to like being in. Kerry was one of the cutest girls in school, and popular enough with the upper classes to make the cheerleading squad for fall. As long as he kept his nose clean, he'd be the one taking her to the movies.

If only he hadn't seen Jerry, Dean, and the rest of their clique at the island the night the cottage was set on fire.

Willa hid a grimace as she swallowed the last of her morning coffee. They'd all overslept, even Billie. Even worse, they'd run out of coffee again, and Billie had tried sneaking instant into the old coffeepot. Willa wasn't fooled.

Rod looked about as grumpy as she felt. When Billie asked him cheerfully, "Glad to have a long weekend, Rod?" he merely grunted and asked to be excused, leaving only the two of them at the kitchen table. Christian had decided to skip breakfast altogether, poking his head in through the back door long enough to mumble something about a lousy night and sleep before heading off to his cottage.

Willa exchanged a look with her aunt. "I vote we go to Mattie's for coffee and start the morning over." Within minutes they pulled into Quinlan's parking lot, Billie complaining that they should have walked the short distance, Willa knowing that she couldn't walk anywhere until she had some real coffee in her system. "Hello, anyone here?" she called out as the chimes above the green-painted door of Quinlan's announced their presence. "Mattie must be in back," she told Billie, who was at her heels.

"It's after nine," Billie said testily, her narrowed eyes searching the wide open doorway between the store and the rear apartment where Mattie lived alone with Kevin. "She must not want any business."

"I heard that," Mattie said, appearing in the short

hallway. "Good morning, Willa. Billie," she greeted with a nod of her head. Out of the corner of her eye, Willa saw her aunt return the nod briefly before turning and making her way down the middle aisle.

"We ran out of coffee this morning," Willa confided to Mattie. "We're all kind of grumpy, I guess."

"That woman was born grumpy."

Willa decided to let Mattie's comment pass. "That can't be Shamrock?" She nodded toward the Irish setter watching alertly from its position on a rag rug in the hallway.

"Her granddaughter. But Kevin calls this one Shamrock, too." Mattie turned toward the counter behind her. "How about some hot coffee, then? I think there's still some left in the kitchen."

"That sounds wonderful," Willa said, glancing toward her aunt, who was reading labels she couldn't possibly have seen without using a pair of the horn-rimmed magnifiers she bought at the drugstore in town.

"You, too, Billie," Mattie added over her shoulder in a louder voice. As Willa followed her down the hallway to the living quarters, she said in a more normal tone, "Sad when their hearing starts to go, isn't it?" even though she knew very well there was nothing wrong with Billie's hearing.

Willa tried to not laugh as Billie set the can down with a loud thump and followed. As they passed by the open screen door at the end of the hall, Willa caught a brief glimpse of Kevin working out in the garage.

"So," Mattie began as she set a pair of coffee mugs on the laminated kitchen table and gestured for Willa to sit. "I hear you and Billie are fixing the old place up. Hoping to get more business this summer?"

"We've already had a couple bookings. Now that all

the cottages are in working condition, we should have a good year."

"Well, I still can't believe a young thing like you would want to spend the rest of her life changing other people's bed linens and talking about whether the walleyes are biting or not." Mattie shook her head. "Pinecrest is enough of a backwater, but you're nearly ten miles from town. And that's when the causeway's open. If we get as much rain as we did the summer two years ago, you might as well be on the other side of the moon."

"That's just what some people are looking for." Billie's voice carried clearly from the hallway, and Mattie and Willa turned to see her enter the room. "Christian says that he knows lots of policemen and workers in the Twin Cities who want to get away from it all for a few days. We'll do just fine this summer."

"I hope so," Mattie said with a sniff, "because I need to make a living, too, and since Whispering Pines closed, there hasn't been enough business on this side of the lake to make it worthwhile to open in the mornings." She sent Billie a sharp look.

Willa was about to put an end to the battle, when Billie said quietly, "Why don't you move into town, Mattie? You've got a son to support, and you'll need to see he's taken care of after you're gone."

"I intend to hold on to what I've got, just like you," Mattie said, "but it's been home to Kevin and me, and I still have fond memories of our years together here."

Mattie turned back to Willa. "I heard you had a little accident day before yesterday."

"Yes. I fell off the roof of one of the cottages." Willa explained what had happened while Mattie clicked her tongue.

"Repairing that old place is a losing battle."

Billie stood stiffly to one side of Willa's chair. "Restless Spirit will be better than ever. You'll see, Mattie."

"I'd like to see that. Truly I would," Mattie said, her wide smile showing off her too-white dentures.

"We've already taken several reservations, haven't we, Willa?"

Willa nodded. "With any luck, your door chimes will be ringing constantly this summer, Mattie."

"As Billie says, we'll see."

Willa barely managed to hide her surprise as Billie suggested, "Why don't you and Kevin come for Easter dinner tomorrow? That way you can judge for yourself."

Willa quickly added her own support to Billie's invitation. "Please do. We have plenty of food."

Mattie glanced out the window at Kevin before accepting. After a few more minutes of conversation, Willa and her aunt paid for their coffee and left. As they walked toward the old truck, Billie said, "Mattie doesn't know when to let go of the past."

Willa kept silent, though she couldn't help thinking that quite a few people around here suffered from the same affliction. Then she said aloud, "She and Sean lived together at the store for nearly twenty years before he left. She must have some happy memories."

"You can't live on memories," Billie said stubbornly. "It's fine to appreciate what you had, but there's a time for moving on and making new memories."

Billie was hardly being subtle, Willa thought. She wanted to argue that that was exactly what she intended to do. She'd returned to Restless Spirit to refresh her happiest memories before moving on with her life, wherever it would lead her. She had no intention of spending the rest of her life here, nor of falling for the wrong man, something both Mattie and Billie were guilty of.

She could learn from other people's mistakes without making her own, she thought as she put the old truck noisily into gear.

7

Billie's daffodil cake was as big as a porcupine, and she held it away from her sagging bosom about as carefully. Rod half rose from his chair to help her carry it into the dining room, but Christian beat him to it. From the lace tablecloth to the sparkling crystal, they had celebrated Easter in style.

The oohs and ahs that greeted the cake's appearance were mixed with uncomfortable groans. Willa complained, "I can't eat another bite," and Mattie murmured her agreement.

"I can," Rod said, his gaze traveling around the table before returning to the cake with its garland of white frosting. "It looks great, Billie."

"Thank you, Rod. I know that you and Kevin will do it justice, even if the rest of these wimps can't keep up."

Among the laughter that followed her comment, Kevin announced, "This is my favorite kind of cake."

"Kevin, darling, chocolate is your favorite," Mattie corrected from across the table.

"Nope. This is my *new* favorite," he insisted.

"Mine, too," Rod said, giving Kevin a sympathetic smile. At first he'd felt awkward, not knowing how to talk to someone in his parents' generation who still thought and acted like a kid, but then he realized that Kevin knew a lot about some things. Like cars, for instance. It bugged Rod the way Mattie kept treating her son like a baby. Kevin was all right, but Mattie was an old witch. He sort of wished Billie hadn't invited them, but then he thought of Kevin eating alone with his mother in the apartment behind their store, and he was glad.

Knowing Billie was watching, he crammed a huge fork full of cake in his mouth. He smiled, getting a big kick out of the way she seemed to puff up with pride. He couldn't believe he'd actually dreaded this day. Holidays at his house had been strained, with his mother tired and bad-tempered from cooking and Patrick Dane snapping at the kids. This was actually kind of neat, and Billie's cooking was sure a lot better than his mom's, too.

The only thing missing was Kerry.

Last night, after everybody was sleeping, he'd crept downstairs and called her. They had already talked on the phone earlier, but he had to hear her voice just one more time before he went to sleep. As if he'd conjured it up with his thoughts, the hallway phone rang now. Willa left the table to answer it while he strained to listen, every muscle poised to leap up and run to the phone.

"Rod, it's for you," Willa called. A surge of joy rose in his chest before Willa continued, "It's your mother."

Joy was replaced by panic. Had Caroline and Patrick Dane had another one of their arguments about him? Afterward, she usually went through a period of motherly guilt—just long and deep enough to get him back until Patrick Dane drove him out again. The memory of his adoptive father's cool sarcasm made his insides curl. He bunched up his linen napkin and set it next to his plate.

"I don't want to talk to her," he said. He could feel Billie's blue eyes piercing him with a stare from across the table. "Aunt Willa didn't talk to her dad when he called. I don't see why I have to talk to my mother."

"She probably wants to wish you a happy Easter." Christian's voice was quiet and even, but Rod could hear the command behind it, and his will asserted itself.

"I don't want to talk to her," he repeated, feeling the panic closing over him. "I don't want to go back there."

"Roderick!" Billie's tone was of mild shock.

He felt as if he was on display, with everyone's eyes on him, even Kevin's. It was Christian's unyielding stare that did it. Maybe Christian was perfect, being a cop and everything, but Rod wasn't. He pushed back his chair and stood.

"May I be excused?" He didn't wait for an answer before storming through the hallway, pausing long enough to grab his jacket from the coat tree.

"Rod?" Willa held the phone toward him, her hand covering the mouthpiece. She looked sad, and for a minute he felt almost guilty enough to relent. Then he turned and headed outside to the boathouse.

"Maybe I should go after him," Billie said. "He's probably in the boathouse."

Willa shot a quick glance toward Christian, feeling partly responsible for the blowup and knowing that she should be the one to talk to Rod. After all, he'd only been following her example. She hadn't even spoken to her father this morning when he called to wish them a happy Easter, using the excuse that her hands were covered with sticky bread dough. The truth was, she'd been enjoying herself so much helping Billie in the kitchen and reliving happier times that she hadn't wanted the bad times to intrude.

"I'll go talk to him," she said quietly.

Silence followed her words. She couldn't tell what Billie was thinking, but Christian was watching her thoughtfully.

"No, leave him alone for a while," he said. "He'll probably come back in a half hour."

She'd resisted his advice regarding Rod before, but this time she was only too glad to listen. Feeling responsible for ruining Billie's dinner, she was all too aware of Mattie and Kevin's stares. She tried to restore the sense of peace and contentment she had felt earlier. "I think I'll have a piece of cake after all," she said with a smile for her aunt.

The front door opened and closed quietly, and Billie stirred underneath the unfinished afghan she'd been working on as she rested in her chair. It couldn't be Mattie or Kevin. They'd left an hour ago, after Kevin had eaten a second helping of his "new favorite" cake.

She smiled. Rod had finally had enough of that old boathouse and decided to rejoin them. She wondered what it was about that place that seemed to attract teenagers so.

She lifted her head and glanced toward the old regulator clock next to the fireplace. Christian's estimate had been off by a couple hours. He and Willa were in the kitchen doing dishes, and she heard Rod join them.

She felt herself relax against the cushions and was surprised. She hadn't realized how tense she'd gotten. For a moment there at the dinner table it had seemed her beautiful dream world was about to crumble like the piece of cake she'd served Mattie, who'd wasted no time pointing out how dry it was.

Why, if the old biddy had eaten her cake the same time as the others, it would have been perfectly moist. Billie's fingers fumbled with the knitting needles, and she bit back a curse. Sweet, helpless little old ladies didn't cuss. And she sure as hell wasn't going to let on that she was anything but sweet and helpless. Not when she was so close to getting what she wanted.

Billie let the needles and yarn slip from her fingers as she leaned her head back against the cushion. She and Willa had spent the last two days cooking, and she was tired. But now that Rod was back, she could enjoy her little rest while the others clattered around with the dishes.

She closed her eyes and let herself dream of faraway places, managing to conceal a smile when she heard the others enter the living room.

"Shh. She's asleep," Willa whispered. "If you're going to watch TV, keep it down."

Billie felt secure knowing they were all gathered around her, and she went back to her pleasant imaginings. Where would she go first? Europe, maybe. No, it was too old, too civilized. She wanted to go some place wild, somewhere that would make her feel young.

Ah, to be young again. Would she have spent her youth at the resort if she'd known it was going to tie her there for most of her life? She knew the answer, and she felt a bit guilty for hoping Willa would take her place.

She opened her eyes a crack and saw the glance Willa sent Christian. She wondered if her niece had any idea how much passion there was in her eyes. Now that was what youth was all about. It didn't matter where you spent it, as long as you spent it with passion.

Only these two were too damned stubborn to get on with it.

Swallowing another smile, she closed her eyes again and envisioned the outback of Australia, the red earth contrasting with jewel blue sky and dotted with kangaroo, wombats, and wallabies.

"Billie?" Willa looked over the seat at her aunt, who'd fallen asleep on the way back from town. She'd been napping even more frequently than usual, and Willa guessed that the weekend had taken more out of her than she let on.

She straightened, blinking her blue eyes. "We're almost home," Willa told her gently. "When we get back, why don't you go upstairs and lie down awhile before lunch?"

"I'm fine," Billie said, and indeed, she looked completely alert as Willa steered the old truck across the causeway to the island. As they neared the house, Willa spotted a dark figure in front of one of the farthest cottages.

"Is that Christian?" she asked. "He certainly hasn't been getting much rest after his shifts lately."

Billie put her hand over Willa's. The same moment her aunt made the warning gesture, Willa realized that the figure near the cabin wasn't nearly large enough for Christian's six-foot-plus height.

"It's one of them. Get him!" Billie hollered, her booted foot coming down on top of Willa's on the accelerator. The truck's engine roared in protest, and Willa quickly jabbed at the clutch to shift into a higher gear, steering the old Ford toward the clearing where the cottages stood. The figure turned toward them, half hidden in the shadows from a nearby oak, then broke into a run for the trees.

"Let up, Billie, or I'm going to drive this thing right into a tree," Willa said as she pushed in the clutch to slow them down. Any other time, her aunt's bloodthirsty enthusiasm might have been amusing, but not while sitting inside a half ton of metal, hurtling toward a stand of pine.

Billie removed her foot, and Willa braked to a halt at the edge of the woods and leaped down from the truck just in time to see Christian racing toward them. The commotion had obviously gotten him out of bed— shirtless and barefoot, he was zipping his jeans on the run.

"What the hell's going on? Did you lose control of the truck?"

"No, when we drove up we saw someone standing outside one of the cottages. He took off toward the trees, and Billie—" Willa shot her aunt an exasperated glance "—decided we should tackle him with the truck."

"Quit talking and go after him before he gets away," Billie said, already heading toward the woods, her galoshes flapping open with every step.

Willa shrugged and followed, and after a glance down at his bare feet, Christian was right behind her. They combed the woods from the clearing to the water's edge, but didn't see or hear anything larger than a chattering squirrel.

"How could he get on and off the island without using the causeway?" Billie wondered aloud.

"With a boat." Christian was kneeling in the grass, looking down at the soft ground at the edge of the lake.

He pointed out the evidence—crushed grass and foot-prints marking the spot where someone had stashed a small boat.

"We would have heard him," Billie argued.

"He probably rowed out past the point before he started the engine," Christian said. "The ground is higher there, and it would have blocked the engine noise."

"Then he might still be on the lake somewhere," Billie returned. "I'm going to the house to call the sheriff."

Willa watched her aunt stomp away. She turned to Christian as soon as Billie was out of earshot, and the doubt on his face was easy to read. "You don't think the sheriff's going to do anything about it, do you?"

"Nope," he said, rising to his feet. "At best, Pitzer thinks she's nutty. At worst"—he paused significantly—"he's part of the problem."

"What?"

"I'm beginning to think our vandals have been getting a little cooperation from the sheriff's department. Pitzer should have found something by now."

"First you suspected Rod was in on it, now the sheriff. You're making it sound like a conspiracy."

"Maybe it is. A lot of people in town would like to see PROCOR go through. A group of them might be getting desperate now that the resort is being refurbished."

"Desperate enough to show up in broad daylight?"

"Maybe he was looking for something."

The words made Willa pause in the middle of the path. "The lighter?"

"Yep. He probably watched the house and waited for you and Billie to leave. He knew I'd be heading back to the cottage to sleep."

Willa felt a chill creep over her skin, leaving goosebumps. "I can't stand the thought of someone watching us that closely."

"Did you recognize him?"

"No. We couldn't see him in the shadows. But he wasn't dressed like a high school kid."

"Too bad." Christian started walking again, taking the lead along the narrow dirt path. "We could have called the school and found out which students were absent or late this morning. Can you remember what he was wearing?"

She shook her head. "Dark slacks and a jacket. That's all I could see."

Christian nodded and held a branch out of her way. "The footprints looked like they came from men's dress shoes. This winter, when Billie first told me about what was going on, it sounded like something a bunch of kids would do—rattling chains, digging holes, moaning. But attempted arson is pretty serious business."

"This theory of yours is getting complicated," she said. "I can't imagine anyone actually wanting to hurt Billie. Besides, won't the hotel project have to come up for a vote sooner or later?"

"The land's outside city limits, and the project doesn't require any public funds. There won't need to be a zoning hearing, and the county planning commission will listen to whoever they think best represents Pinecrest's interests. And we both know who that will be."

"Thor Nelson, of course."

"You got it. The town is split right down the middle, with Thor and his faction on one side, and everybody else on the other side."

"I know. I could feel it that night at Brenda's."

He stopped to regard her intently. "Which side are you on, Willa?"

She felt a flash of anger. "You know which side I'm on."

"Sometimes I'm not sure. You're helping Billie now, but you're going to run away again in a few weeks, just when it's going to start hitting the fan."

Willa remembered how tired Billie had appeared during their expedition to town that morning and felt a stab of guilt. She started to walk faster, and he followed suit.

"Wait up a minute, would you?" he called, then stopped abruptly and cursed. She looked back suspiciously. He was bending forward, his hands resting on his knees, a grimace on his face.

"What's the matter?"

"I stepped on something." Her gaze went from Christian's shoeless feet to his bare chest before meeting his eyes. "Can you give me a hand on the way to that log over there?" he asked.

Suspecting a trap, she approached cautiously before holding out an arm to help him keep his balance as he hobbled toward the fallen tree. As much as possible, she tried to avoid contact with his bare skin.

"Gee, thanks," he said at her meager support. He sat and propped his bare foot up on his opposite knee, examining it closely. "I don't see anything, do you?"

From this distance, he could have had a thorn the size of a toothpick stuck in his foot, and she wouldn't have been able to spot it. Letting out an impatient sigh, she sat down next to him on the moss-covered old wood. When she brushed her hand over the sole of his foot, he jerked suddenly, nearly setting her back on her heels.

"That tickles." His voice was accusing.

"I'd almost forgotten how ticklish you were," she said, a smile in her voice as she probed the skin more carefully. "I remember . . ."

"Remember what, Willa?" His voice was low.

"Nothing." She concentrated on her task, finally spotting a small dark splinter of wood poking out of the skin of his instep. She squeezed gently until it came out. "There. You should be fine now."

She looked and found him watching her, his eyes filled with the same desire she'd been struggling to keep at bay. He moved closer, and she reached out to stop him. When her palms landed flat against his chest, the contact with his skin made her gasp.

"Are you remembering what I am?" he asked, capturing her hands by the wrist and holding them against him. His skin was warm and slightly damp from exertion, and the feel of his hair against her fingertips made her want to turn the contact into a caress. "The night we took a boat and a blanket out past the point?"

She closed her eyes, fighting the dual onslaught of memory and sensation. But it was useless to try to ignore the feel of his skin against her fingers and the vivid pictures the memory of that night invoked. Her mind filled with images of them exploring each other's bodies in the moonlight, hearing the sound of the waves lapping gently against the bottom of the boat.

She opened her eyes to remind herself where she was.

"You do remember," he said. His intense gaze dared her to deny it.

"Yes."

With her admission, he bent toward her and took her lips in a slow, sweet kiss. Beneath her fingertips, she could feel his heart beating. Her hands clenched, and the kiss grew wild. In an instant, they were both on the verge of losing control. Then, just as quickly as it happened, she ended it by rising abruptly to her feet.

"No," she managed to choke out.

It was as though a part of her had been torn away, and Christian looked as dazed as she felt. She darted out of his reach and ran through the trees, avoiding the worn dirt path, knowing he couldn't follow her in his bare feet.

Billie welcomed the feel of the warm spring sunshine on her arms, bare now that she'd tossed her cardigan over a nearby bush. What a lovely day. Seeing that lurking figure had given her the starts, but no more. She would be ready for him the next time. She looked up to see Willa crossing the yard toward the house.

She poked at the flowerbed she'd been pretending to dig up and smiled when she heard the door slam behind her niece. Willa had rushed toward the house as though demons were chasing her. Or maybe one demon in particular.

She smiled again when Christian limped into the clearing, heading for the cottage he'd been staying in since midwinter. She glanced at his strong chest, glistening with sweat from exertion. Or from something else?

If only they would get down to business and let her get on with her own.

She glanced toward the cottage again, and her eyes grew thoughtful. Surely Christian realized they couldn't turn away paying guests? In a few short weeks, the resort would be full, and they would need every single cottage.

Why, he'd just have to move into the big house, she decided, wondering how she was going to convince Willa. Billie would have to play this right or Christian would end up staying in town, probably in some scrubby little apartment over a shop. She watched out of the corner of her eye as he left the cottage. He was fully clothed now, but that didn't make him look any less dangerous as he got into his pickup.

Her chuckle was lost in the sound of engine as he roared away.

"I'll have another cup, Brenda." Christian smiled up at the blond-haired waitress as she refilled his mug with black coffee. He'd spent a couple hours driving along the lake and looking for a boat, a futile quest he'd assigned himself because it gave him time to cool off after the encounter in the woods with Willa. He'd stared at dozens of boats, almost any one of which could have been on the island this morning. Now, after taking care of some things at the station and enjoying the Viking Café's Tuesday special, he was finally beginning to wind down.

"I hear you've all been busy out at the resort," Brenda said as she removed dishes scraped clean of hot turkey sandwich and mashed potatoes, green beans, and salad. Her comment brought his mind back to Willa.

"Word gets around," he said with a smile that belied his inner tension. He waited for her to move on to the next table, where a pair of local businessmen sat over afternoon coffee. They'd gone quiet at the mention of the resort, and Christian found himself looking to see if either man was wearing dark slacks and dress shoes. He caught himself in disgust. Pretty soon he'd be suspecting everyone, from Brenda to Pinecrest High's principal.

And maybe he should. He could feel it, a tension in the air. Out of the corner of his eye, he saw the surreptitious glances in his direction. Long ago, this town had been built—literally—from lumber. But when the market for white pine went bust, lumber barons like Hulbert Mitterhauser had gone bankrupt, and people who worked for him had lost their jobs.

Jobs were hard to come by this far from the Twin Cities, and the whole town relied on the summer lake crowd to bring in cash. Times were hard, and people were restless.

He took another swallow of black coffee and wondered if he was imagining the resentment behind the stares. He hated what PROCOR and the promise of money was doing to this town. He tipped back his head and finished off the coffee, catching Brenda's eye as he set the empty mug down on the table.

His ulcer protested at the acidic brew, and he unconsciously ran a hand over his flat stomach. A small pitcher of cream appeared next to his plate, and he looked up to see Brenda's knowing grin. "You know you're not supposed to drink it black," she said as she refilled his mug.

"Thanks for reminding me," he said dryly.

"I have a fifteen-year-old daughter," she said. "I can't stop the mother impulse, even with big, tough guys like you."

Deciding to trust her, he reached into his pocket and pulled out the lighter he'd found, holding it in his palm so only she could see. "Any of your customers use this?"

She examined it carefully. "It looks familiar. Want me to keep it here and ask around?"

"No. As a matter of fact, I wish you wouldn't say anything about it. But if something comes to mind, talk to me first, okay?"

"Sure. Is everything all right at the resort?" she asked, her concern showing. "Rod told me Willa had an accident last week."

"She fell off the roof of one of the cottages and ended up with some bruises. She's fine now," he said, remembering how quickly she'd managed to elude him in the woods.

"Great. I thought maybe the four of us could get together the next time Carl's back in town. Maybe go to the tavern for some steaks."

"That's kind of a busman's holiday, isn't it?"

"Are you kidding? There's nothing I like better than to have someone wait on me for a change. You'd better watch that coffee," she added as she left. "It isn't good for you."

He took one long, hot swallow—black, the way he liked it—before diluting it with cream. Hell, nothing he wanted was good for him.

Like Willa. God, he wanted her. His mind flipped back to the kiss they'd shared in the woods, and he knew he'd be back for more. The lady had said *no,* he reminded himself. Only a caveman would push her any further.

But they were so good together, a voice inside him argued. If only it wasn't for that mysterious barrier between them that he just couldn't breach. Nothing he said seemed to get through that shell of hers. In fact, the only time she responded to him was when she was in his arms.

So maybe it was time to forget about words—like the word *no,* for instance.

As soon as she stepped through the Viking's wide glass door, Willa spotted Christian sitting by himself in a booth, scowling out the window. She felt equally unenthusiastic about this errand Billie had sent her on. When she was halfway across the checkerboard vinyl floor to his booth, he looked up. His scowl deepened.

She sat down across from him, dispensing with pleasantries. "Billie sent me to find you."

"What?"

"She's worried because you didn't come home for dinner at noon, and she wants to make sure you'll be back for supper tonight. She's planning some kind of celebration." He looked so pained that she couldn't help chuckling. "Believe me, I don't feel like celebrating either." A cup of coffee magically appeared at her elbow. "Hi, Brenda. I'll have a piece of pie with this."

"You're in luck. We've got one slice of rhubarb cobbler left." She glanced over her shoulder. "If you want it, you'd better speak up now. Old man Lindquist just came in, and rhubarb is his favorite."

"By all means, bring on the rhubarb," Willa said. As soon as Brenda left, she picked up her mug and glanced over the rim at Christian. "Billie's been wondering where you've been."

She knew by the glint in his hazel eyes that she hadn't fooled him. She was as curious as Billie to know what he'd been doing the last half day.

"I spent a couple hours looking along the shore for a hidden boat, then stopped at the office to call Pitzer and see if he found anything. Afterward, I stayed to help interview a couple of the applicants for temporary officers. I took a nap on the sofa in the dispatcher's office, and I had a late dinner here." He glanced at his watch. "I just finished about fifteen minutes ago. Want to know what I ordered, too?"

She ignored his sarcasm. "Did Pitzer or his men see anything?"

"What do you think?"

She sighed, then put on a smile when Brenda delivered the rhubarb custard pie. Brenda removed her white cotton apron with a flourish and sat down next to Christian, putting her feet up on the vinyl bench seat next to Willa. "I haven't had a break since morning," she said, groaning and reaching to rub her plump ankles.

Willa checked the clock above the old-fashioned lunch counter. "It's almost three." She looked at Christian. "I can't remember if Rod has track this afternoon or not. We may as well pick him up at school."

"He won't be there."

Willa looked questioningly at Brenda.

"Didn't you know? He's been seeing Kerry," Brenda explained. "Oh, don't look so worried. Kerry's too young to date, so they come here after school two or three afternoons a week. That way I can keep an eye on them until my shift ends at four. Not that they haven't tried breaking the rules," she said with a grin. "You can't fool someone who's been there. Remember sneaking out after your parents were asleep?"

Willa shot Christian a sideways glance, feeling her face turn a bright red. How could she forget with everyone reminding her?

"Oops. There's Mr. Odegard. I'd better get back to work or he'll fire me."

She left, tying her apron on the way to the kitchen. Willa glanced at Christian to find him looking over her shoulder toward the door. She turned to see Rod and Kerry sitting down several booths away. When Rod spotted them, a startled expression crossed his face. He leaned over and said something to Kerry before coming toward them, reluctance evident in every step.

"I thought you had track," Willa said as he joined them.

"No, that's tomorrow afternoon," he said, staring at

his shoes. Willa tried not to mind that he hadn't told her about Kerry or asked for permission to spend every afternoon in town. She realized that she felt hurt because he hadn't confided in her.

"Next time," Christian said mildly, "it would be a good idea to let Willa or Billie know where you are."

"Sure. Am I excused now?" There was more than a hint of sarcasm in Rod's words. Willa shot Christian a quick glance.

"Billie's planning a special supper tonight. Be sure you don't miss the activity bus," she told Rod, knowing he wouldn't appreciate it if either she or Christian offered to take him home.

"Anything else?"

"Yes, as a matter of fact, there is." Christian quickly described what had happened that morning on the island, and Willa watched as Rod's expression changed to dismay. "So I think she'd feel better if we were all home for tonight's meal," Christian finished.

"I'll be there," Rod promised, and Willa hoped he would keep his word.

He couldn't do anything right, Rod thought as he sat down across from Kerry. He'd screwed up everything from the very beginning. He should have told Christian about Jerry Miller. Now it was too late, and he was getting in deeper all the time.

Kerry's voice reassured him a bit as she told him about something funny that had happened in her third period English class. He listened, thinking how lucky he was to be with one of the prettiest girls in school. Her hair was white-blond like her mother's, and she had eyes the color of the sage plant Billie grew in the windowsill above the sink.

He relaxed a bit more after Willa and Christian left the café. If it wasn't for Kerry's mother glancing over at them every few minutes, he could pretend that they were all alone on a real date.

"I could go watch your workout tomorrow," Kerry said. "I'll tell my mom that I went home with Nancy Olson after school."

"No," he said quickly. Realizing she was staring at him, her green eyes wide with hurt surprise, he added, "I couldn't keep my mind on intervals if you were sitting there. I'd be too busy looking at you." The words were convincing, even to him. Sports were a measure of popularity at Pinecrest High, and if Kerry found out he'd dropped out of track . . .

"Hey, there's the two sweethearts," he overheard a loud voice say. He looked up to see Jerry Miller and the other boys from the senior clique of athletes standing by their table. He straightened and tried to feel like he belonged there with Kerry, but he was afraid Jerry and the other guys saw right through him.

"Hey, Jerry," he said, nodding casually at the rest of the group and leaning back against the booth.

"How are things out on the island, Gilligan?" a blond basketball player asked, to the amusement of the others.

"Okay," he said, trying to ignore the flash of anger and humiliation that went through him.

"I don't know," Jerry said. "It sounds pretty boring to me. Betcha could use a little excitement out there, huh, Dane?"

Rod saw the knowing glint in Jerry's eyes, and he gripped the edge of the table to keep from swinging up with his fist as he and Jerry stared at each other.

Kerry's mother appeared next to the table, a pot of coffee in one hand, menus in the other. "If you boys are looking for a place to sit," she said, gesturing with the coffee, "there's another booth down the way a bit."

Rod felt relieved when the group took her suggestion and left. He also felt like the biggest wimp in the world for needing to be rescued by his girlfriend's mother.

Christian sniffed and smiled as he entered the kitchen about a half hour later. Ginger cookies, cabbage, and vinegar—three seemingly incompatible items that made up German ambrosia.

"Is that really sauerbraten I smell, Billie?" he asked, hanging his windbreaker over the back of a chair and sparing a brief glance for Willa, who was stirring something in a large Dutch oven on the stove. "You know that's my favorite."

"Good. Then you won't mind taking the gingersnaps out of the oven. I have to go upstairs and fix my hair."

He held his arms out at the sides, resigned, while she tied her apron around his waist.

"Wouldn't want to get those jeans dirty, would we?"

Willa snickered as Christian looked down at his favorite pair of denims and pretended to be offended at the sarcasm in Billie's voice. It was his turn to laugh as Billie ordered, "You can make the spaetzle, Willa. Unless you've forgotten how?"

"Of course not."

"We'll eat at six. And make sure Rod doesn't eat too many cookies," she added over her shoulder as she started up the stairs.

"Her hair looks fine to me," he heard Willa mumble. He glanced over to see her scanning the counter helplessly. "There's got to be a recipe around here somewhere."

"For spaetzle? Don't kid yourself. The Mitterhauser women are born knowing how to make dumplings," he joshed. After helping Billie finish the cookies and clean up last week, Christian knew exactly where to find the small tin box full of yellowing recipe cards, but he decided to let Willa panic for a while. Although her wide grin could hardly be called an expression of panic. "What are you smiling at?" he asked.

She nodded toward his apron, and he crossed the kitchen to the drawer where Billie kept the linens. He pulled out another apron—red gingham this time—reached into the cupboard above for the recipe cards, then presented them both to Willa. "Go to it, kiddo."

"She certainly had this all planned, didn't she?"

"Let her have her fun," Christian said, tightening the apron strings around her waist. "Just don't ruin the dumplings."

"I can make spaetzle as good as Billie's or Oma's," she said defensively. He looked at her skeptically and she added, "What do you think I did whenever you and Rick went off on one of your boys-only excursions? If you two hadn't managed to dump me occasionally, I never would have learned to cook. Or play piano."

As she spoke, she retrieved eggs and milk from the refrigerator and got down a mixing bowl and colander from the cupboard. She moved the flour canister over, too, until everything she needed was neatly lined up on the counter. Then she stared at the items helplessly.

"Try finding the recipe," he suggested.

She shot him a glance that was half gratitude, half resentment. While she flipped through the recipe cards, he stood guard over the cookies in the oven. Not for the first time, Christian found himself thinking that the kitchen was the heart of this house. It seemed to exert a soothing, comforting influence on everyone who entered. For now anyway, he and Willa were working side by side despite their earlier clash.

Why couldn't it be like this always? He closed his eyes at his feelings. Sensitive, nineties guy be damned, he had to find a way to get her to stay with him. He had an incongruous picture of her waiting for him at home every night, with a half dozen kids and supper on the table, and nearly laughed aloud. No, it wouldn't have to be like that at all.

He wouldn't mind a couple of kids, but he'd settle for Rod. He'd like to see Rick's son grow into a man and start his own family. Which reminded him . . .

"One of us needs to have a talk with Rod," he said.

She whirled on him, a sticky, batter-covered spoon in one hand. "I told you not to say anything to him about Rick."

"That's not what I meant. One of us has to talk to him about safe, responsible sex."

"He's only seventeen. And Kerry's just fif—" A look of shock passed over her face. "Oh, God, that's exactly how old . . ."

"We were," he finished.

She turned and replaced the mixing spoon, staring down at the bowl. He went over to stand behind her. "But we didn't go through with it," she whispered.

He wondered if she regretted that as much as he did. *If Rick hadn't died . . .* He pulled his mind away from the thought. "No, but we came close. Remember that night in the boathouse, Willa?" She leaned back against his chest, and he sighed with pleasure. Before he could wrap his arms around her, the back door opened, and she quickly moved away.

Rod entered the kitchen with a perfunctory greeting. He reached out to grab a handful of cookies from the cooling rack, and Christian slapped his hand playfully with a spatula. But Rod didn't respond to the teasing with his usual bantering reply.

"Sorry, man," he said, with a cool lift of his eyebrow. Christian stared after him as he went upstairs, wondering if Kerry was the only thing that had Rod in this state. Apparently, not everyone found the kitchen's influence calming.

When he turned around again, the kitchen was empty. Willa had disappeared, and he was alone.

8

Willa wondered how Billie could be so oblivious to the undercurrents marring her celebration dinner. Rod hadn't said more than two words since he sat down, Christian concentrated on his food as though someone might take his plate away when he wasn't looking, and the spaetzle tasted like erasers in her mouth. But Billie chattered for all of them, telling stories about how her mother used to make sauerbraten for a family of seven and a resort full of guests, until her cooking attracted nearly as many people to the island as the fishing.

"I'll do the dishes." Rod leaped up from the table and began stacking plates, obviously eager to escape. Willa wished she'd thought of it first.

Christian and Billie headed for the living room, but Willa continued through the wide archway to the front parlor. She lifted the lid that covered the piano keys and stared at them until black and white started to blur.

Once, music was her escape. After Rick's death she had played piano until her fingers were sore. She'd also used music to escape from Darryl, and from her own growing knowledge that their marriage was in trouble. She'd even written quite a few of the songs on the band's two albums—a fact few people knew, since she'd published them under her married name.

Sometime during the last couple years, between recording commercials and picking up extra jobs—singing backup in a studio session, doing voice-overs for radio, even waiting on tables, for God's sake—her desire to create had evaporated. She had been surviving, she realized. Living from day to day and from one bill to the next. If she hadn't tired of that aimless existence, she never would have accepted Billie's invitation to come to the resort. Whether her impulsive decision to come to Restless Spirit was good or bad remained to be seen.

She ran her fingers over the keys lightly, picking out bars of songs she remembered. Her playing reflected her disjointed thoughts, never continuing with one melody long enough for it to be recognizable.

"Play something for us, Willa," her aunt called from the next room. "You never finish a song. It's quite frustrating."

Willa's fingers stilled on the keys. "I can't remember anything."

"I'll help you." Christian entered the parlor and sat down next to her, his thigh brushing hers, and sending even the shortest memorized piece of music completely out of her head. "There's some music here," he said, reaching underneath the fern sitting on top of the piano to the old pages of sheet music that Billie apparently used to protect the piano's walnut finish.

"I think this used to be one of Billie's favorites." He pulled out a yellowed and water-stained folder for the song "A Fine Romance."

"I can't," she said quietly, so that Billie wouldn't overhear. She stared at the keys, refusing to look up even when she knew he was waiting for her to respond.

"Sure you can," he said. "It goes like this."

He pounded at the keys, wincing exaggeratedly when he hit a sour note. She couldn't help smiling at his comical efforts, then broke into laughter when he started singing along.

"A fine romance, with no kisses . . ."

His left hand kept missing the bass line, and she filled in, playing the lower keys while he played the higher chords. Through her giggles, she managed to hum loudly enough to keep his singing on key.

When his left hand brushed hers, her fingers faltered, and the tune dissolved into discord.

"Oops, sorry. I guess I didn't spend as much time in here as you and Rick did," he said.

"Boy, you guys really stink," Rod said. Willa looked up to see him leaning in the doorway. "I guess if I'm going to get any studying done tonight, I'd better go upstairs."

He turned to leave, and Willa and Christian exchanged glances.

"Are you going to talk to him?"

She didn't answer right away but peered through the archway into the living room and saw that Billie was in her favorite chair, her eyes closed and her knitting needles fallen from slack fingers. How could she have slept through all this? Willa wondered. At least this conversation with Christian would be relatively private.

"Don't you think he knows?" she asked, focusing her

attention on closing the piano and straightening the sheets of music. "Surely Caroline and her husband have talked to him about safe sex before now."

"I wouldn't gamble on it, would you? Before you answer that, remember that Kerry is only fifteen."

Willa stared at a sheet of music until the black notations danced before her eyes, remembering her own fifteenth summer. God, she'd been so young, so innocent. And yet so . . . *ready* to know what physical love was all about.

She looked up and met Christian's gaze, knowing his thoughts must be a near reflection of hers. They hadn't considered anything those nights except learning what made each other happy. They certainly hadn't discussed protection.

She stood reluctantly. "I'll talk to him." She'd made the decision, but her steps were slow as she climbed the staircase, trailing her hand along the polished banister. She knocked quietly on Rod's door, then more loudly as she realized he couldn't hear her while he was listening to his portable stereo.

"Come in."

She winced as she entered. Even from across the room she could hear the tinny buzz from his headphones. She bit her tongue on a lecture about ruining his hearing, knowing it had taken her a year of standing in front of a five-piece band and a sound system bigger than this bedroom before she started to believe the well-meaning advice others had given her. The screeching coming from Rod's earphones made the most raucous dance tune Natural Disaster had ever recorded sound like a romantic ballad by comparison. She felt a million years old.

"Could you turn that down? Or maybe find some Badfinger or Santana?"

"Badfinger? Never heard of 'em," Rod said as he pushed the off button and went back to his open book. "I've heard Santana on the oldies station, though. He's cool."

She didn't comment, unsure if "cool" was an expression whose meaning had changed since she'd used it. She sat down gingerly on the side chair that he had pressed into service as a laundry hamper. Then she decided to join Rod on the hooked rug that covered the wood floor from the bed to the doorway. He paged idly through a textbook.

"Your dad used to think Carlos Santana was the greatest guitar player ever."

"Oh, yeah?" He looked up from the book, his attention captured.

He never failed to brighten at the mention of Rick. Even though she felt a little stab whenever she talked about her brother, it was worth it to see Rod's expression change. And it made her more determined than ever not to challenge his beliefs by telling him how Rick died.

Her gaze went past Rod's shoulder to the framed photograph sitting on the walnut nightstand. With surprise, she recognized it as a family portrait of his mother, Patrick Dane, and Molly and Melinda, Rod's half sisters. Rod was standing to the far left, and he looked out of place among the varying shades of blonde.

Rod's gaze followed her own, and he colored. "He was pretty good-looking, huh?"

For a moment she thought he was referring to his adoptive father, then she realized that a worn photograph of Rick in his army uniform was stuck in the corner of the family picture.

"Yes, he was. Although I never would have told him that when we were kids."

Rod's smile faded quickly. "Not like me. I don't know who I look like." He flushed a bit when he glanced at Willa's hair. "I mean, if I'd been a girl . . ."

She laughed. "Stop before you dig yourself any deeper." Her grin faded, and she added seriously, "Except for your hair, you're the picture of Rick. When Christian first saw you . . . . " She stopped, unable to go on. There was an awkward moment of silence, then Willa took a deep breath and started over. "I bet Kerry Songstad thinks you're pretty good-looking."

He flushed all the way to the neckline of his oversized T-shirt.

"Brenda says you two have gotten quite close. I thought, ah, that is . . ." Her words trailed off again. She cursed herself and stumbled on, knowing that her cheeks were turning as red as Rod's. "I just wanted to make sure that you two are being careful about expressing your feelings for each other."

He looked at her blankly for a moment, as though his brain needed time to process the adult euphemism and translate it into standard teenage English. Then an expression of understanding crossed his features. "I've already got enough problems without doing something stupid that would hurt Kerry," he told her. "She's the first person that ever cared about me. I mean, I've always made a couple friends wherever I was, but I've never been anywhere long enough to feel like I belonged with someone."

Willa's heart twisted at his open admission. Before she could find the words to tell him that she cared for him, he looked at her and asked, "Did my dad have to marry my mom because she was pregnant?"

The question startled her. The fact was, she didn't know. Rick had never told her in his letters, but she knew her brother well enough to answer. "Rick loved your mom. They met when he was in helicopter school in Fort Worth, but they waited to get married until he was—"

Willa caught herself just in time. She'd almost said *out of Vietnam*, but remembered that as far as Rod knew, Rick had died in Nam. She felt a surge of resentment at the lies her parents had told. Lies that she was protecting, as though they were as precious as the pieces of glass displayed in Oma's breakfront.

Was Christian right? That it was better for Rod to know the truth, no matter how awful?

No, she decided as she looked into her nephew's clear blue eyes. Rod was the one person who could remember Rick without any bitterness to mar the memories. And right now he was staring at her, waiting for her to tell him more about the father he'd never known.

She began awkwardly. "He wrote and told me how much he wanted to marry Caroline. He said she was fun to be around, always laughing and doing things."

Rod nodded. "Yeah, she played games and stuff with me when I was little, like my sisters are now." He paused before asking, "What was he like?"

"Your father was a good man, Rod. He would have been a caring father."

"No, what was he really like?"

She dug deeper, trying to satisfy Rod's hunger to know. "He was the best big brother a girl could have. We fished and swam and climbed trees. Even though he was so much older than I was, he always let me hang around—except when he and Christian would sneak off together and leave me in the kitchen, helping my grandmother or Billie." She grinned and shook her head.

"You like Christian, don't you?" he asked.

She felt her smile slip. "Sure. He's been very kind and helpful toward Billie."

"No, you know what I mean," he insisted. "You *like* him, don't you?"

She remembered that *like* was a teenage code word. While young people often exaggerated—a killer exam, a bitchin' car—they still used the mildest word to explain the strongest feelings. She would sooner run out of the room than bare her heart to her nephew, but he'd been honest with her, and he deserved the same openness. She finally said, "He's a good-looking man, and he's good inside, too. And I'm very lucky to be his friend."

Rod groaned and rolled his eyes upward. "How come you two don't get together? I know you like each other more than friends. Friends don't kiss like that."

He turned bright red again, and Willa resisted the temptation to ask him how he knew she and Christian had kissed. She gave him the same explanation she'd used again and again on herself. "It isn't fair for two people to start a relationship unless they both want the same thing. I'm going to be leaving soon, and Christian's life is here in Pinecrest."

"You're still going?" He picked at the laces of his black high top sneakers. "What if I want to stay?"

"Well, if it's all right with your parents—"

"Come off it, Willa. They don't care what I do."

"That's not true."

Rod remained stubbornly silent, and Willa realized she'd said the wrong thing. Instead of offering a sympathetic ear, she'd done what every other adult in Rod's life had done—get upset, then talk at him instead of listening to him. She told him, "Your mother calls Billie and me every week to see how you're doing. I know she'd rather have you there with her, but she thinks that you might be happier here."

"I am," he said gruffly, staring at the cover of his book.

"Good." She sensed that the conversation was over, at least as far as Rod was concerned. But she couldn't stop herself from adding, "I know you and I don't talk much. But if you ever have a problem, or if you're ever feeling bad about something, I hope you'll tell me about it. Or Christian, if you feel more comfortable talking with him," she tacked on reluctantly.

"Sure," he said, without taking his gaze from the book.

I've just been dismissed, she thought wryly, as she got to her feet and left Rod to his music and his studies. She paused at the head of the stairs. Down below she could hear someone playing piano, probably Billie, judging by the absence of off-key notes. She and Christian were half singing, half shouting "Ramblin' Rose," a song Oma used to hum when she was doing dishes or laundry.

For a moment, she wished she could walk down and join them, to laugh freely and sing with a whole heart. But her talk with Rod reminded her that she didn't belong here, not the way Christian did. He was more a Mitterhauser than she was, she realized.

He wanted her to stay, and not just for Billie's or Rod's sake. She knew he didn't just want to get her into his bed for a night or two. That was what made any hint of romance between them impossible, no matter what arguments he raised or what type of persuasion he used: when she left Restless Spirit this time, she didn't want to leave her heart behind.

The last few bars of the song—turned into a rousing finale by Billie's crashing chords and Christian's laughter-threaded baritone—drifted up the staircase.

"*. . . who can cling to a Ramblin' Rose?*"

Willa's hand tightened on the banister for a moment before she turned and went to her room.

Christian hesitated on the back steps. He was taking a big chance, and he knew it. For two and a half months now he'd tried one way or another to get Willa to stay at the resort. He'd tried talking to her and arguing with her, and neither worked. For the past couple days, he'd taken advantage of every opportunity to touch her fingers as he handed her a paintbrush or screwdriver, brush against her as he passed her in the hall, send her steamy looks over the mashed potatoes at every meal. Still she had remained immune.

Now it was time to bring out the big guns.

He shoved his bundle a little further underneath his windbreaker. The jacket was unnecessary except as a hiding place, since it was an unusually warm May morning. He had finished his shift forty-five minutes ago. Most days he was home by this time, comfortably settled in Billie's kitchen and starting his second cup of coffee, but today he'd made a slight detour, stopping at Skeet's parents' farm.

So far Willa had managed to resist every one of his efforts to keep her there. He hoped she wouldn't be able to resist this pair of pleading brown eyes.

He opened the back door quietly and slipped inside. Willa was alone, just finishing her coffee. The bundle under his jacket wriggled, and she glanced at the badly disguised surprise but said nothing.

"Sorry I'm late," he said. "Where's Rod? And Billie?"

"He left for school about five minutes ago. You must have just missed meeting the bus. Billie's in the cellar rearranging her canning shelves. *Again.*"

Christian chuckled. Now that opening weekend was drawing closer, Billie had entered a state of constant movement, like a hummingbird trying to get every flower before they wilted.

"Did you need to talk to them for some reason?" Judging from Willa's suspicious expression, she'd already figured out that something was up.

"No. Not exactly." He was a little disappointed that Rod wouldn't be here to share in the surprise. The bundle hidden under his jacket was more for Rod than Willa, really, although he hoped it would bring a smile to her face and a tenderness to her heart. "In that case, I guess there's no point in making a production out of this."

He reached inside his coat and pulled out his secret weapon, a fifteen-pound bundle of cute, quivering canine. He set the puppy on the floor, and after wagging its black tail briefly, it sniffed at the recently waxed linoleum and squatted.

"Nice," Willa said, staring with a stony expression at the months-old black Lab and the rapidly spreading puddle. Oblivious to the sarcasm in her voice and the lack of welcome on her face, the puppy shuffled over to her legs. "Just what do you think you're doing?"

Christian realized the question was directed at him, and not at the animal sniffing Willa's jeans and sneakers. He had his excuse ready. "I've been thinking of getting a watchdog ever since the morning you and Billie surprised that guy hanging around the cottages."

"Watchdog? This *puppy* isn't even old enough to watch its bladder. And the incident you're referring to happened nearly a week ago." Her eyes narrowed. "Why did you bring home a dog now?"

He shrugged and moved on to his back-up excuse. "I

kept thinking of Rod. I bet his parents didn't let him have anything bigger than a hamster. A boy should have a dog. They can tramp through the woods together, go hunting—"

"Hunting season isn't until fall. Rod might be gone." Her voice was expressionless. "You know what's going to happen. Billie's too busy with the resort to fuss over a puppy, Rod will lose interest, and I'll be the one who ends up taking care of it." She glared at the puppy pulling at her shoelaces as though it were a cockroach.

"That won't happen. Not for more than a few weeks anyway. Unless, of course, you decide to stay?"

She turned her glare onto him, and Christian felt his plan beginning to backfire. What had happened to the big-eyed little girl who wanted to bring home every lost or injured creature she found in the woods or along the road? The one who had cried for hours when her grandmother said she couldn't keep the baby raccoon because it would get into the garden?

Luckily, providence intervened.

"Oh, what a sweet little puppy," Billie said as she came up from the cellar, carrying an armful of glass jars. "What's his name?"

"Fred. It's short for Winifred. He's actually a she."

Billie bent down and patted the Labrador on the head with her free hand. "A girl with a boy's name—we already have something in common." She straightened. "Rod will love her. I'll go and see if we have a box for her to sleep in."

The minute Billie left the room, Willa turned on Christian. "This is emotional blackmail."

She was weakening.

"You might be able to fool Billie, but I know what you're up to."

It was only a matter of time.

"And if you think I'm going to fall for this . . . this transparent attempt to get me to stay here—"

He grinned. His grin faded instantly when he saw Willa's slate blue eyes fill up with tears. *What the hell was going on?*

Billie's footsteps approached from the hallway. Willa quickly wiped a hand across her eyes and pushed past Christian. She escaped into the pantry, and he followed, closing the door behind them and turning on the light. "Willa, what's the matter?" His gaze searched her face, trying to figure out what he'd done that was so terrible.

"Take her back," she insisted, backing up until she bumped into the shelves that lined one wall.

"Why are you so upset over a little puppy?" he asked, stepping closer.

"It's not just a puppy, and you know it," she accused as he advanced another step. He reached out and took her into his arms. "Don't," she whispered. "Billie's in the kitchen."

He could hear the old woman crooning soft words to the puppy. If only Willa had reacted with the same love and acceptance. He pitched his voice low and brought his lips close to Willa's ear. "Don't you like animals?" he asked, raising his arms to encircle her.

"Christian . . ." she said, turning her face aside as he dipped his head toward hers. The quick turn of her head made her hair brush against his lips, and he responded by nuzzling at her ear. He heard her sharp intake of breath. She turned back, opening her mouth to scold him, and he took the opportunity to close his lips over hers.

The past few days he'd intended to drive her crazy with little accidental touches, but all he'd managed to

do was set his own blood on fire. He nibbled at her ear-
lobe, hoping to kindle a few flames in her.

"Stop teasing, Christian," she said between nibbles,
her voice strangled.

"Whatever you say." He'd stop teasing, all right. He
pressed his mouth fully against hers to show her he
meant business. For a moment she froze; then she
began to shudder, waves of reaction he could feel
through their clothing all the way to his bones. He held
her tighter, and she clung to him as though she was
about to fall off a high ledge.

The door clicked open, and they both turned.

"Don't mind me, I just need to get the lima beans,"
Billie said. A smirk lifted the corners of her mouth as
she selected a can from the shelves covering one wall of
the pantry. She retreated, closing the door behind her.

"Your aunt approves," Christian said, lightly rubbing
his hands over her back, taking heart from the fact that
she was still in his arms.

"She needed lima beans."

"At eight o'clock in the morning? That was only an
excuse so she could check and see if we were getting
along."

"Well, we're not," she said, shoving him away. Her
move caught him by surprise, and he stumbled back
against the shelves. Cans and jars banged together,
threatening to fall.

He recovered quickly and went after her. But when
he entered the kitchen, she'd already disappeared. The
room's only occupant looked up at him sweetly and
wagged her tail.

Predictably, Rod loved Freddie. Boy and dog disappeared for over two hours after he got home from

school, and they still hadn't returned by the time the sun disappeared behind the horizon, turning the lake to a rosy pink as it sank.

Willa watched with amusement as Billie prepared a plate of food for Rod and put it in the oven to stay warm, then made up a second plate of leftovers for Freddie. If either she or Christian had been this late for supper, they would have ended up with the silver polish and an old rag.

When the pair finally returned, the puppy fell into its box with exhaustion. Rod, on the other hand, was abuzz with nervous energy, swallowing his supper without chewing and talking faster than an auctioneer. Later, as the four of them sat in the living room, he related everything the puppy had done, from chasing birds' shadows to yipping at her reflection in the lake.

Christian shot Willa a victorious glance, and she knew Freddie was part of the family. Nothing could have induced her to spoil Rod's pleasure.

"I can't wait to train her," Rod was saying. "Think she'll learn to point?"

"Her mother's a top-notch bird dog. Skeet says he takes her out hunting grouse and pheasant every fall," Christian said.

"I haven't had pheasant in years," Billie said with a smile. "Mother used to fix it with wild rice stuffing."

Christian groaned with delight. "I remember. Rod, wait until you taste it. Your dad and I used to eat ourselves sick every time Oma served it."

"I bet the guests would really like it, huh? We should stay open in the fall. Winter, too. We could have ski tours, and . . ." Rod rattled off a list of activities that would tire a triathlete, and Billie and Christian added ideas and objections of their own.

Willa felt a sense of detachment as she listened to their brainstorming session. She wondered where she would be this fall when they were enjoying their pheasant feast. She had never imagined her life without music, but the thought of going back to L.A. and recording more commercials or trying to make it again on stage somewhere simply didn't appeal to her anymore.

She tried to remember what it was that she'd liked about her career. Even though performing had often exhausted her physically and mentally, it was being on stage that she enjoyed the most. She could do without the traveling, but nothing else had ever come close to making people smile and laugh and move to the music. Communicating with the audience, she guessed it was called.

Well, she certainly wasn't communicating now. She stood and stretched. "I guess I'll call it a night," she said.

"Oh, but I was just going to make some popcorn," Billie protested. "You hardly ate a thing for supper."

"I'm tired. You all go ahead."

But long afterward she lay in bed staring up at the ceiling and listening to the laughter below.

Billie reached up to turn out the hurricane lamp next to her bed. Her hand paused halfway before moving down to touch the silver filigree ring box that rested on the lace doily covering her nightstand. She picked it up and lifted the lid, staring at the dark blue velvet lining.

The box was empty.

The sight still managed to move her after all these years. She sighed and lay back against the pillows, remembering. Sean Quinlan had given her the box, promising her a ring to go inside. But Mattie had received the ring instead, a square-cut emerald with three seed pearls on each side.

It was an ugly ring, she assured herself. And Sean Quinlan was no prize either. Unfortunately, the story hadn't ended there. Years after he'd married Mattie he had come back to Billie, begging her to run away with him. He'd promised her adventures—travel to the corners of the earth. If she'd wanted him, he could have been hers. But she had been too stubborn to accept anything less than a decent man with honorable intentions. Besides, he'd already broken one promise. She set the ring box back on the nightstand.

She'd done the right thing by refusing him. She knew that now, but there were still times, like tonight, when she wondered what it was like to know a man's arms around her as she fell asleep.

She turned out the light and smoothed the quilt over her chest. She hoped her niece wouldn't throw away her chances. It had hurt tonight to watch her, silent and thoughtful, sitting outside the circle instead of accepting the love that was hers to receive. Would Willa ever heal?

It was so hard to be patient when you were old. Billie knew better than Willa or Christian that the years could slip away before you even realized what was happening. Time was too precious to waste.

She sighed and turned her mind away from the young people and their problems and the resort and its demands. Instead she filled her mind with scenes of mountains and oceans, cactus-studded deserts and lush green forests.

Imagination was her escape. It was fine to picture exotic places, but she wanted to set her foot on foreign soil, to breathe the scent of jungle flowers into her lungs, to touch the fur of a kangaroo or a sloth. She wanted the real thing, not pictures. She wanted to escape.

Christian tipped back in the rickety chair that sat on the small porch, leaning it against the side of the cottage, and stared into the darkness. He'd unbuttoned his shirt and left it hanging out of the waistband of his jeans, trying to beat the warmth and humidity so unusual for this early in May. A few flashes of sheet lightning occasionally lit the clouds in the distance, but that was the only relief from the darkness.

The light in Billie's window had gone out long ago. He didn't know why he was keeping watch. There hadn't been a sign of any suspicious activity since the morning Willa and Billie had surprised the mysterious figure outside the cottage.

But tonight was his night off, and he couldn't sleep. Every time he closed his eyes, he saw Willa. And it wasn't just his visions that tormented him. He could still smell her spicy perfume, feel the texture of her hair as it cascaded down her back and over his hands—and he could still hear her husky voice telling him *no*.

So here he was sitting on the porch of his cottage, wishing that his memory wasn't so damned good. He needed his brain for other things tonight. Something was going to happen. The burning sensation in his stomach was like a premonition.

It happened even sooner than Christian expected. A dark shape moved across the front lawn, and he was instantly alert. He sat up straight, ready to move. He knew Rod made a habit of going to the boathouse for hours at a time, but something told him that this stealthy figure wasn't Rod. He waited for the dark form to open and close the boathouse door, then, silent as a shadow, he crossed the lawn.

Willa sat on the bench at the rear of the boathouse, letting the sound of the gentle waves lapping against the dock soothe away her tension. She couldn't have stayed in her room, pretending to be asleep, for another moment. The house was pressing in on her, like one of those rooms in horror movies where the walls started to collapse inward.

Ironically, as the time neared for her to leave Restless Spirit, she felt more and more trapped. It didn't make sense because there wasn't much left to do. It was only a week before the opening, and the cottages were clean and tidy, the house ready to welcome the guests who'd chosen the American plan for meals. A new refrigerator large enough to hold food for a crowd stood in the kitchen, and a chest-style freezer filled with goodies took up a corner of the cellar. Fortunately, Billie's permit for food service had been renewed before the situation with PROCOR had heated up. With a little yard work and some last-minute cooking and shopping, the resort would be almost the same as when she and Rick used to spend their summers and holidays there.

Except for the boathouse, everything was nearly ready. Christian was looking for a couple more used boats to replace the old and rotting rowboats and canoes, and the materials for the dock were piled up outside. Many guests brought their own boats, but the resort had always provided extras. Rod and Christian would take care of the outdoor projects, and Billie could always hire someone to help her with the cooking and housecleaning.

They didn't need her. She saw past the darkness, picturing the boathouse as it was those nights years ago when she and Christian used to meet there, long after the guests had settled into their cottages for the night and the house had turned silent and dark. The shack he and his mother lived in over a half mile away had since crumbled into rotted boards. But back then she could see its lights through her third floor window, and she knew when she saw the flashlight bobbing along the ditches toward the causeway that Christian was on his way. She'd sneak down the back stairs and wait for him inside the boathouse.

She remembered one July night in particular. It was the last night she'd come out here to meet Christian, although neither of them knew it at the time. The night was warm and humid, like tonight, with flashes of sheet lightning silently brightening the sky in the distance. Christian had opened the wide double doors for relief from the airless heat of the boathouse, and they watched the lightning from one of the docks. Boats tied up on either side sheltered them, although the darkness and the lateness of the hour already kept their presence secret.

The boats bumped softly against the dock, no louder than Willa and Christian's heartbeats as they slowly undressed each other. They lay back against the wooden dock, mindless to any discomfort. All Willa knew was the exquisite and unfamiliar feel of Christian's nude body pressed fully against her own. That night, they came within inches of consummating their growing feelings for each other.

Her mind filled with remembered sensations: the sound of the water rippling under the dock, the heavy air and distant lightning, Christian's voice telling her, "Oh, God, baby, we have to stop," even as his fingers were strong against her skin, imprinting her with longing.

The images fled when the door swung open.

She gasped to see a dark figure standing in the doorway, silhouetted by moonlight. She thought of the man she and Billie had seen standing by the cottage and her heart froze in her chest.

"Willa?"

She sagged with relief at Christian's voice.

"What are you doing here?" he asked, moving toward her.

"I couldn't sleep, so I came out here to think. There's so much I need to do before I leave."

"Then you're going back to L.A.?" He stared past the sagging doors to the lake's dark surface. The quiet acceptance in his voice caught her by surprise.

"I haven't decided." She felt his quick sidelong glance and braced herself for an argument.

"You can walk away, just like that?"

"I have a life, Christian. And it doesn't include this." Her gesture indicated the rotting boats and dilapidated building.

"What about Billie and Rod?" When she didn't answer, he went on. "When you first arrived, I thought you were a selfish brat. You were ready to sell out to PROCOR and leave. Instead, you've stayed long enough to raise Billie's hopes. That's even worse."

The accusation hurt her. "You don't understand," she said.

"Make me." When she didn't respond, he asked, "Do you have any idea what it was like when Rick died?"

"Of course. He was my brother, remember?"

"And you had your parents and grandparents to fall

back on. I had no one, Willa, no one. My mother wasn't sober long enough to give a damn, and no one else knew we were closer than brothers. Except you, and you weren't here." He sat down next to her on the splintered bench. "I thought I'd go crazy. Hell, I guess I did, a little. And none of you had a clue. You deserted me. And now you're going to do it again."

"I'm sorry," she said quietly, not even daring to breathe for fear she would burst into tears. What else was there to say? Perhaps she could have offered comfort to the boy Christian had been then, but now he was a man, harder and tougher, with a pain that went deep below the surface. She knew there weren't words that could erase it.

God, how he must have resented her family. And her. How could they ever cut through his anger? Christian didn't realize that she'd felt deserted, too, ripped away from all that was familiar, closed off from her parents, and lost to everything but her own storm of emotions. She'd weathered it, but the experience had changed her. How could she ever go back?

A flicker of compassion showed on his face, or maybe it was just the lightning that softened his granite-hard features momentarily. "I swore I'd never come back to Pinecrest," he said.

"It's true what they say, isn't it? That you almost got sent to reform school. That you were—" the words caught in her throat "—sleeping with Judy Pitzer?"

"Of all the stupid, thoughtless things I did, that was the worst. I tried using Judy to forget about you. It was always you, Willow, from the very first time I saw you. Remember?"

She responded to the smile in his voice. "You and your mother had just moved here. You were walking in the woods. *Our* woods."

"And you and Rick attacked me from the treetops. I looked up to see who was throwing acorns and rocks at me, and I saw a monkey with red pigtails. From that moment on, you two were the center of my life."

Emotion made her voice husky. "Rick's death wasn't easy for me either, Christian. I watched my grandparents turn old overnight. Every time my dad looked at me I wanted to apologize for not being his son. And Mother . . . all she did was cry, day after day." She closed her eyes at the memories. "When Grandpa Johann died, and then Oma, it felt as though Rick had left me all over again. My parents wouldn't talk about what had happened. I used to play the piano for hours and hours, trying to cover up the silence."

Christian touched her shoulder lightly, sending a shiver over her skin. "We could have helped each other, Willa."

Maybe we still can. She was afraid to say the words aloud. Instead, she rose to her feet. "Come with me. I want to show you something."

She led the way across the lawn to the house, opening the back door quietly so as not to awaken Freddie and set off a flurry of barking. She led the way up the stairs to her room and turned on the bedside lamp, conscious of his dark stare as she opened the closet and lifted down the shoe box from the shelf above.

"I've never showed this to anyone," she said as she untied the ribbon that held the lid shut. She hesitated, and Christian took the box from her and lifted away the lid. He stared for a long time at the photo on top, the picture of the three of them on the veranda. She could see the emotions playing across his face, settling finally on a smile. He began to flip through the envelopes below.

"Those are from Rick," she said unnecessarily, wanting to fill the silence.

"And these?"

"Those are the letters you wrote me. I saved them, too."

He closed his eyes momentarily before taking out the envelopes from Rick. Then he sat down on the bed, the box on his lap. Willa sat next to him, watching him shuffle through the letters. The last one was dated July 16, 1975. Willa knew the letter by heart. *Hi, Sis*, it began. *I looked at the calendar today and thought of you picking blackberries on the island.*

Her breath caught deep in her chest at Christian's expression as he read. When he finished, he looked at her, his hazel eyes shining with unshed tears. Without removing his eyes from hers, he carefully set the box down on the dresser next to him. Then he reached out and slowly pulled her toward him.

This time she didn't feel like running, not when they both needed this so much. When only centimeters separated them, and the emptiness still hadn't gone away, she lifted her face toward his. He understood her need and rested his lips against hers.

The kiss began as comfort and apology, tender and warm, but it quickly grew into something more. Willa felt heat flash through her like the lightning that still marked the sky. When he traced the cupid's bow of her upper lip with his tongue, she barely hesitated before opening her mouth to welcome him. The symbolism in the gesture didn't escape her. She was ready to finish what they'd begun eighteen years ago.

Her heart pounded. She was half afraid, half eager, like the fifteen-year-old girl she thought she'd left behind forever. He nuzzled her neck, and his tenderness both soothed and thrilled her.

She made a small cry and tightened her fingers on his shoulders. In response, Christian circled her waist with his hands and leaned back until they were lying on the old quilt, their legs tangled together. Her hand slipped to his chest, bared by his open shirt. He was warm against her palm, and she traced her fingers over his ribs.

Slowly, deliberately, his eyes never leaving hers, he began to unbutton her shirt. The cotton felt almost rough against her sensitive skin, and she sighed with pleasure when his hands smoothed over her shoulders and arms, sliding off the offending garment.

"You're beautiful," he whispered, as he stared at her lacy bra and pale skin.

She smiled and spoke her thoughts. "I wish we had made love that night."

He didn't have to ask which night she referred to. "I'm glad we didn't. You still would have left, and I would have gone out of my mind missing you. Besides, we were too young to appreciate this."

She would have argued, but the words flew from her mind as he moved his hand from the side of her face across her neck, lightly exploring the shadow between her breasts. She decided he was right after all. They never would have been able to build each other's pleasure with this exquisite slowness.

She reached out, slipping open his unbuttoned shirt and pressing her fingertips against his nipples. He groaned.

"Shh," she whispered, wishing they were all alone in the big old house, free to call out their pleasure.

She traced the angles and planes of his face, etched sharply with shadows from the light coming in through the window. She'd left it open to let in the clean spring air, but now a familiar smell teased her nostrils. Before her mind could identify the odor or explain why the darkness outside flickered with an unusual shade of yellow, a pounding at the door interrupted.

It was Rod, his voice cracking from excitement as he yelled "Fire! Wake up, Willa. One of the cottages is on fire!"

9

Adrenaline carried Christian down the stairs. He ran out the back door, the open ends of his shirt flapping. Freddie barked excitedly as Rod followed. Through the commotion behind them he heard Willa hurrying Billie down the narrow back staircase. He paused long enough to shout for Willa to call the fire department, then hurried on toward the clearing, where yellow flames danced behind the window of one of the cottages. *His*. If he hadn't been with Willa . . . He pushed the thought away. There was no time for "what ifs" now.

With his blood pulsing loudly in his ears, he headed directly for the water faucet at the side of the house and unfurled the garden hose, running with it toward the clearing. He cursed when he realized the hose was about twenty feet too short.

His curses ended abruptly when he saw a shadow dart into the trees. He spun around searching for Rod, who was standing by the faucet waiting for his instructions.

"Go to the boathouse and see if you can find some bait buckets. Bring back as many as you can carry," he ordered before taking off after the figure.

It was like waking up from one nightmare only to find that you'd slipped into yet another. He raced through the woods, but his legs moved unbearably slow, as though they were attached to a ball and chain, and his quarry's lead seemed to be growing. The cloudy night sky made the darkness almost impenetrable, and he tripped over rocks and branches, scratching his bare chest on a scourge of thorns. The pain and the bitter odor of smoke made it all too clear that this wasn't some kind of dream.

He stopped as soon as he realized that the figure was no longer in sight and that he'd left two women and a boy to fight a rapidly growing fire by themselves. He listened for any sound that would tell him what direction his quarry had taken, trying to catch his breath by drawing in lungfuls of smoke-tinged air. When he heard a footfall behind him he spun around, poised to end the chase here and now, until he recognized the man standing underneath the shadows of a large pine.

"Kevin?" he asked, disbelief freezing him to the spot. The man stepped further out of the shadows, his moon-shaped face filled with fear. Before Christian could ask him if he'd been near the cottages, Kevin took off running with the ease of someone familiar with the area. He was probably the only person in Pinecrest who knew these woods better than Christian.

He didn't bother to follow. He knew where to find Kevin. But was this man with the mind of a child the shadowy figure he had seen earlier? Questions crowded his mind as he loped back to the clearing.

Why would Kevin do anything to harm Billie's interests? Unless he felt his mother's were being threatened. Kevin was fiercely protective of Mattie. But was that enough to cause a gentle man to commit a crime?

He knew it was possible, although his mind balked at the thought. Then, as he spotted the orange glow through the trees, he had no time to think about anything except the fire.

"Go make sure the faucet's wide open," Willa shouted at Rod as he dumped an armful of buckets on the ground by the garden hose. "Billie, you take the buckets after Rod fills them and hand them to me," she ordered. "I'll throw the water on the fire."

"You can't go in there," Billie protested, her eyes narrowed against the smoke that swirled malevolently around the clearing.

"All Christian's things are in there," Willa said. She realized that was a stupid excuse for risking smoke inhalation or burns, and quickly added, "If it flares up, it might take every single cottage with it."

Billie faltered and reached out to steady herself by grasping Willa's arm. Her eyes were wide and shining with tears. "We could lose Restless Spirit."

"It'll be fine," Willa assured her aunt. "It hasn't even caught the mattress yet. Here comes Rod with the first bucket. Go bring it to me." Billie stood frozen to the spot, still holding on to her arm. "Come on. Are you just going to stand there and let the place burn down?"

Billie turned and silently went to meet Rod.

Tears stung the corners of Willa's eyes. It was the smoke, she told herself. She didn't have time to feel guilty at the way she'd spoken to her aunt. Seconds later, Billie returned with the first buckets of water.

She took them from her aunt's hands and ran up the cottage steps into the smoky interior.

"Holy shit," Rod said as he watched Willa go inside the burning cottage. His aunt was going to die, and it was all his fault. He could have stopped this weeks ago, if only he hadn't been so worried about how he looked to the other kids at school.

He swore again, rooted to the spot. Billie ran toward him, shouting for more water, while Rod stared at the cottage where Willa had disappeared. "Is she crazy?" he asked. Guilt and fear kept him from action.

"Get moving," his great aunt ordered. His stunned gaze took in her white hair, which was sticking out wildly, and her bare feet. For the first time since he'd arrived at Restless Spirit, he realized that his great aunt was tougher than the hide on a football. "Yes, ma'am," he mumbled, already bending down to pick up the buckets.

When Christian neared the cottages he could see that the others had organized a slapdash fire line from the end of the garden hose to the burning cabin, passing the pitifully small buckets as quickly as they could fill them up with water from the hose. Flames still licked and curled behind the cottage's window, but somehow they'd managed to keep the fire at bay. He realized he'd been gone only moments, though it had seemed like hours. Urgency added speed to his steps.

He knew now why some of the firefighters he'd worked with had insisted on referring to flame as though it possessed some kind of demonic intelligence. This fire was simply waiting. They couldn't let up for even a moment, or the flames would take the opportunity to flare up and burn out of control.

He'd been on the scene at countless arsons, even a bomb blast. This was a weenie roast by comparison. And yet none of those fires had scared him so much. Never had the tongues of flame curled quite so devilishly, nor had the heat seemed like the very fires of hell. He knew why this fire was different. He'd never had anything to lose before.

When he saw Willa disappear inside the burning cottage, he felt his heart jump within his chest. He raced for the open doorway, catching her in his arms as she stumbled out with the empty buckets. He picked her up, buckets and all, and practically hurled himself down the steps.

The orange glow from the fire was reflected in the droplets of perspiration running down her temples and soaking the collar of her blouse. Her hair was a wild mass the color of the fire itself, and her eyes were wide as Christian took the empty buckets from her hand.

"Are you crazy? You can't go in there!" he said as he rested her on her feet.

"I can't hear the sirens," she said, a desperate note to her voice. "They should be here by now."

"Maybe they're on another call." He doubted the excuse even as he uttered it. He looked at the cottage, assessing the flames with a professional eye. The fire was limited to one side of the building, near the window. He figured whoever had started the fire had used the curtains to set it. His gaze returned to Willa, who was taking another pair of buckets from Billie.

"Think you and Billie can keep this up for a while longer? I'm going to take Rod and see if we can rig up something to pump water out of the lake. Just don't go inside," he warned her. "Try to water down the roof to keep it from catching."

"Quit gabbing and go! We'll stay here until the fire trucks get here," Billie said as she snatched the empty bucket from Christian's hand. "Go!" She waved her arm toward the lake, and Rod relinquished the hose and followed Christian.

Everything seemed to take longer with the acrid smell of smoke filling the air. Christian and Rod didn't speak as they rummaged around the dim interior of the boathouse, raising dust and fighting cobwebs as they sorted through piles of junk that hadn't been disturbed in years.

"I don't even know what we're looking for," Rod said, his voice hoarse from shouting.

"A pump. It looks like a small engine. Dammit, I know there's one around here somewhere." His mind kept leaping back to the clearing, hoping Willa and her aunt were keeping away from the flames and smoke.

Hell, the whole damn place could burn down as long as they were okay, he decided. Restless Spirit wasn't important enough to risk their lives. He was ready to give up and tell everyone to get into the pickup and drive off when he heard the noise.

Rod looked up at the same moment, his expression puzzled. "What's that?"

Christian managed a tired grin, wanting to shout with laughter but lacking the energy. "That's the cavalry," he said, grinning wider when Rod stared at him as though he'd gone insane. He did feel a little crazy, he decided, heading toward the door. "It's raining!"

They burst out of the boathouse and into the deluge that pounded like horses' hooves against the galvanized steel roof. Rod let out a whoop and took off for the cottages. Christian followed more slowly, letting the water stream down his face.

When he joined the others, the rain had already weakened the flames. He laughed at the sight of Willa and Billie doing a lurching polka on the sodden grass, with Freddie barking excitedly and getting tangled in their feet. Billie pulled Rod into the dance, while Christian grabbed Willa and spun her around, resisting the impulse to kiss her senseless in the middle of the clearing.

"This boy doesn't even know how to schottische," Billie complained, as Rod awkwardly tried to match his great aunt's mincing steps.

Christian's heart swelled as he watched. Then he turned his head to catch Willa's quietly spoken words.

"Button up your shirt."

He looked down and remembered exactly what they'd been doing when Rod sounded the alarm. His gaze trapped hers, letting her know that he intended to pick up where they left off. She looked away, and his stomach burned in warning.

The sound of a wailing siren distracted him. Through the sheets of rain a flashing red light was visible as it threaded across the causeway.

"Well, it's about time," Billie said, her cantankerous words sending them all back into crazy laughter.

Willa hesitated in the doorway, not quite ready to face Christian in front of an audience. Rod was seated at the kitchen table half asleep, with his head resting on his arms. Freddie was at his feet, snoring softly. Nearby, Billie made coffee, while Christian leaned against a counter and watched.

"I'll get a cot ready for you in Rod's room," she overheard her aunt say. "I'm afraid I've been using the third floor as storage. We can clear it out tomorrow and put you up there. I meant to do it before, but we've been so busy."

Willa tried to hide her feelings as she entered the kitchen. Since arriving at Restless Spirit, she'd done no

more than walk by the door leading to the large room
upstairs. The converted attic was where she and Rick
had stayed, with a collapsible wall separating her half of
the room from his. She poured herself a cup of coffee,
congratulating herself on keeping her hands steady
under Christian's gaze.

"I can stay in town," he told Billie.

"I won't hear of it. We need you here more than ever
now."

Billie's voice held a quavering note, and Willa didn't
have the heart to accuse her aunt of shamming. This
time the hint of weakness had to be genuine. Willa felt
much the same way, ready to let someone else take over
the problems surrounding the resort.

But she refused to give in to the temptation. It would
be all too easy to start relying on Christian for everything. She had to stop now, before it went any further.
Tonight hadn't changed a thing, except that it showed
her it was more imperative than ever to get away from
Restless Spirit.

"Why don't you and Rod go on upstairs?" she suggested
to her aunt. "I'll find the witch hazel for Christian's
scratches."

He groaned exaggeratedly. "Anything but that."

She tried not to respond to the light of laughter in his
hazel eyes. For Billie's and Rod's benefit, she said,
"Serves you right for laughing at me when Billie fixed up
my scratches when I fell from the roof."

Billie gave them an approving smile before steering
Rod up the back stairway. Willa escaped into the pantry
and searched the mirrored cabinet above the sink for
the bottle of witch hazel, delaying the moment when
she'd have to face Christian again.

How was she going to tell him that what had almost
happened between them tonight was a mistake? That

she had decided that she didn't want to be tempted again? She pressed a hand to her stomach. Her decision was so painful she could feel it, a tearing deep inside her midsection. She steeled herself, knowing that making love with Christian would only make it harder to leave.

When she reentered the kitchen she saw that he had removed his shirt. The bulb above the sink was the only light left on, and the low wattage turned his skin to gold, marred by a score of angry scratches.

"Oh." Her sound of distress was automatic. She took a deep breath and began to cleanse the scratches with the witch hazel and a square of gauze, striving for a teasing note as she commented, "You look like something the cat dragged in."

"You're starting to talk like your aunt," Christian said. "Ow!" he exclaimed as she dabbed at one of the deeper scratches. "Can you take it a bit easier? You're not polishing a piece of woodwork, you know."

"Sorry," she mumbled, though she hardly needed the reminder. She had to bite her lip to keep from reacting every time her fingers slipped from the edge of the gauze to come in contact with the same skin she'd caressed only a few hours ago. His flesh was cool from the rain, and she wanted nothing more than to put aside the gauze and warm him with her hands.

"I think we should tell him, Willa." Her hand stilled as she panicked. "I think we should tell Rod that his father committed suicide."

"No." Anger replaced panic when she realized that Christian had mistaken the closeness they'd shared earlier as an invitation to take over her family.

"No," she repeated, more firmly this time. Her ministrations turned brisk, and Christian grabbed her wrist before she could add more witch hazel to the gauze pad.

"That hurts," he said, his voice a warning.

"Not nearly as much as the truth would hurt Rod."

"You told me tonight what your parents had done, shutting you away from grieving for Rick. Can't you see that you're doing the same thing to Rod?" His fingers tightened. "What is this, some twisted family tradition?"

"Let me go."

He released her instantly. Not expecting the sudden release, she splashed witch hazel on the floor. She stared at the puddle of liquid and mumbled, "I'd better clean it up before Freddie drinks it."

"Freddie's upstairs in Rod's room."

"It still needs to be mopped up," she insisted, searching the kitchen for something to wipe up the mess. Her gaze passed over the washcloth and dishtowel, not seeing them at all.

"Quit running away."

"I'm not running away," she said fiercely, though she was unable to meet his eyes. "But I'm not running into your arms, either. We shouldn't have started something we can't finish." She looked up, and her breath caught in her chest. "Tonight was a mistake," she whispered.

"A mistake?"

He stared at her, his jaw tense with suppressed emotion. She saw his gaze drop to her lips before deliberately continuing down her chest where her rain-soaked blouse still clung damply to her breasts. Her nipples hardened instantly, and she closed her eyes, afraid she'd see triumph in his gaze. If he reached out and touched her now, he'd prove how weak her words were. But the expected touch never came.

"Look at me, Willa."

Reluctantly she opened her eyes.

"This barrier you keep putting between us is more than you let on. Tonight I think I finally figured out what's the matter."

At last he reached out to touch her, but his fingers smoothed her hair gently, as though she were a child in need of comfort. "Your parents took you away before you had a chance to come to terms with Rick's death. Maybe that's what brought you back to Restless Spirit, I don't know."

He lightly brushed the side of her face with his fingers and then shoved both hands into the pockets of his jeans. "You call it putting the past behind you. Just make sure it isn't your future that you're setting aside."

She turned away and headed for the stairs on shaking legs. His tenderness frightened her much more than his passion.

Only one set of footsteps clattered up the stairs. Billie waited for the second, heavier tread, but it never came. She turned over on her side, feeling every one of her seventy-six years and harboring a growing doubt that things were going to work out as she'd hoped.

She saw her mistakes clearly now. Her eyes had been opened when she had witnessed her niece risking her life tonight in the fire. That's when she'd begun to realize that the resort was expendable. Restless Spirit was important only because of the people—the generations of Mitterhausers who'd lived inside these walls. If the cottages and house had all burned to the ground, her memories would still be there. But if Willa had—

Her heart fluttered at the horrible thought.

Playing God, that's what she had been doing, and tonight had taught her that a little old lady didn't have the power to control her own life, let alone the lives of others. Things happened in their own good time, and she'd damn well better be prepared to wait.

She pulled the old quilt up to her chin and squeezed

her eyes shut. For once, dreams of mountains and beaches didn't soothe her as she drifted off to sleep.

Rod lay quietly in bed, his head turned toward the window, listening as the old house and its occupants settled down for what was left of the night. Billie and Willa were both in their rooms, and Freddie was fast asleep at his feet, but Christian hadn't come upstairs yet. Rod closed his eyes—he wasn't taking any chances on being found awake.

Not that he was about to fall asleep just by wishing it. He'd be lucky to get a wink of sleep tonight. But he kept his head turned resolutely away from the door and strained to keep his breathing regular. When Christian finally bedded down on the cot Billie had made up on the other side of the room, Rod wanted him to think his roommate for the night was lost in dreamland.

Yeah, he was lost all right. He was wandering in a forest of trouble, and he didn't know which way to turn.

A creak on the stairs made him tense up. His breathing quickened until he realized it was just the wooden staircase contracting after the day. Willa had explained all that to him not long after they got here. He'd never lived in an old house like this before, but he'd grown used to the creaky sounds, and even found them kind of comforting. *But not tonight.*

He was jumpier than a cricket, and he knew he'd better settle down before Christian came in. He didn't want that astute gaze turned on him tonight, not until he figured out what he was going to do.

He'd like to punch Jerry out for what happened tonight, only he knew that would land him in deeper trouble. He flopped onto his back.

"Stupid, stupid," he whispered up at the ceiling. God, he was an ass sometimes. Why hadn't he said something right away, before things got so mixed up? Now there was Kerry, and she probably wouldn't like him anymore if everyone else at school hated him for narking on Jerry. No, he didn't dare get Jerry and the other guys into trouble.

For a minute he considered talking to Christian about it anyway, but then he remembered Christian was a cop. It was his job to make Rod tell who did it. There was only a couple more weeks of school left, though. Maybe after that—

His thoughts broke off when he heard heavy footsteps—Christian's—coming up the back stairs. Quickly, he turned over again and started breathing slowly. But the steps stopped before they got to his room. He listened as a door somewhere down the hall opened stealthily.

Something he'd almost forgotten in all the excitement popped into his mind at the sound. When he'd gone pounding on doors to wake everybody up because of the fire, Christian had come out of Willa's room. *Christian and Willa.*

The idea didn't bother him as much as it had at first, when he'd been kind of jealous at having to share their attentions. But now he was beginning to see that if Christian and Willa got together, it might just be the answer to everything.

Christian stood just inside the doorway and watched Willa sleep. He didn't know how it was possible after a night like this one. Certainly he wasn't going to be able to manage to sleep at all. His body ached with sheer physical exhaustion, but his mind leaped from one thought to another. In just one night he had chased a man through the woods and battled two fires—the one that burned the cottage, and the one that had nearly consumed him and Willa on this bed.

She, on the other hand, looked as though she were enjoying blissful slumber. With her hair spread over the pillow in rippling waves, and her full mouth slightly parted, she appeared innocent and sensuous at the same time, like a Renaissance angel. He ached at the sight, wanting nothing so much as to ravish those lips with his own, kissing her awake and then climbing into the carved walnut bed beside her and doing his best to keep her awake until the sun rose.

He fought back the automatic arousal his thoughts caused, took a deep breath, and willed his body to relax. He forced his gaze away from the tempting sight and glanced around the darkened room until he spotted what he had come here to find.

There, still on the nightstand, was the box full of letters Willa had saved. Apparently she'd fallen into bed without bothering to hide them away again, the secret treasure she'd kept to herself for so many years.

This family had too many secrets, and he'd like to do something about it, he thought as he walked toward the bed. But he was no more a part of this family now than he'd been eighteen years ago, and his intervention wasn't welcome. Willa had put him firmly in his place again tonight.

This time, however, he saw through her to the fear that lay hidden underneath. She'd done a good job of concealing her pain behind layers of prickly independence and self-centered concern, but he had known the girl long before he'd met the woman. He stood there, box in hand, and let his gaze move over her once more, the way he wished his hands could.

She looked so fragile and pale, as though only in sleep could she let her vulnerability show. She was afraid of the past, afraid of the future, afraid of her own emotions.

And she was afraid of him. He backed away toward

the door, as silent as a shadow. It was going to be a long
night, and he intended to make use of every minute.
Somewhere in these letters was the key to reaching the
woman, and he meant to find it.

He crept down the front staircase like a thief, not
turning on a light until he reached the living room. He
thought about taking the letters to one of the cottages,
but he didn't feel like seeing the charred building he'd
called home for the last few months. He'd have a hard
enough time erasing his mind of the sight of Willa
entering the building filled with flames.

He sprawled out on the sofa and opened the box.
He hesitated over the half dozen or so envelopes that
bore his own familiar scrawl, half tempted to relive his
adolescent longings and half certain that they would all
too clearly echo what he was feeling right now. He'd
rather go on deluding himself that he had matured since
seventeen.

He set those letters aside and started with the very
first letter Rick sent Willa from helicopter school in
Texas. Three years' worth of letters were packed into
the small box, and he planned to read every single one.

During the next few hours, he read words that made
him laugh, remembering Rick's love for stupid jokes
despite his inability to tell them. He read parts that
scared him, stories about combat, and he questioned
the impulse that had made Rick share such horrors with
his sister. It was obvious that Willa was the one he'd
trusted to share his deepest fears with, and for a
moment Christian felt a stab of jealousy—Rick had
been *his* best friend. Then he wondered if he could
have understood Rick's fears. At seventeen, he'd been
blindly patriotic and frustrated that he couldn't go off to
war with Rick. By the time he was old enough to enlist,
the war was over.

He felt tears trailing down his cheeks as he read Rick's anxiety about not measuring up to the courage of his buddies. At that point Christian wanted more than anything to tell Rod about his father. To show him the letters and tell him that Rick had been a hero all right— not some red-white-and-blue toy soldier that died fighting in one glorious battle, but a man who had died a little every time he saw a friend hurt or killed.

The letters broke off for the six-month period that Rick spent recuperating in the VA hospital in San Francisco. That was the summer that Willa and her parents hadn't stayed at the resort. And it was the following summer when Christian finally noticed just how much Willa had grown up during their separation.

Rick's letters picked up again, but this time the postmarks were from West Germany, where he'd been stationed next. The gossip in Pinecrest at the time was that Rick's doctors advised against reenlistment, but he was adamant. Rick never even came back for a visit, spending his furlough in Texas with Caroline's family before heading for Europe with his pregnant wife. Christian remembered wanting to hitch to Texas to see Rick before he left, but by that time his mother had been drinking constantly, and he was afraid to leave her alone, even for a few days.

The tone of these later missives was often rambling. He felt a cold sense of shock steal over him as he realized the pain and confusion Rick had been going through.

God, no wonder Willa felt so confused. She was only fifteen when she read these letters, too young to read between the lines and see that her brother needed help. He tried to match the dates of the letters with the things he remembered about that summer, knowing that Willa had probably done the same. Like Billie, she'd been crazy about celebrations and anniversaries, and she never forgot a date.

He glanced at the postmarks again. May 25 he and Willa had rowed out onto the lake to watch the sunset and kissed for the very first time, and Rick had been assigned to guard duty. On the Fourth of July, when he and Willa had necked on a blanket on the public beach, pretending to watch fireworks, Rick had spent a homesick holiday on base.

And then there was the night that they had almost made love, a night that would stay clear in his mind forever. He and Willa had met in the boathouse, as usual, but this time their gentle exploration had nearly turned into a conflagration. On that very same evening, Rick had locked himself in his room and cleaned his service-issued revolver before shooting himself in the head.

10

Willa woke slowly, wondering why her arms felt so sore. When her nostrils caught the faintest hint of smoke in the air, blowing in the window with the morning breeze, the events of the night before flooded her mind—the boathouse, the letters, the fire.

She and Christian had been about to make love on this very bed while outside, part of Billie's dreams burned.

She knew that the fire hadn't started with lightning, as the late-arriving firefighters had suggested. It was arson. Someone was trying to destroy everything they had worked to rebuild. The idea that anyone could be that malicious frightened her.

She closed her eyes and wished she could stay in bed and sleep until she forgot all about it. But the strong sunlight and the sounds of activity outside—the puppy barking and the noises of someone already digging through the charred cottage—told her that she'd already overslept. And today of all days, when Billie must be half frantic with worry.

She wrinkled her nose at the stale smell of the clothes she'd been wearing last night and shoved them into a pile. Then she took a quick shower to cleanse her hair and skin of the same odor. With all traces of the night before gone, at least on the surface, she dressed in a clean pair of jeans and a pale pink shirt.

Downstairs, she learned that Christian and Billie had already been outside to assess the damage first thing that morning. Now they were just finishing their breakfast. Willa entered the kitchen in time to claim the last cup of coffee.

"Rod left for school about ten minutes ago," Billie told her. "Why don't you fix yourself something to eat while Christian and I finish going through the cottage? We're going to try to salvage what we can of his things."

Willa glanced across the table at Christian. He looked tired. A shadow of beard darkened his jaw, and his eyelids were heavy from lack of sleep. She hadn't heard him come upstairs last night, but then she'd fallen into an exhausted sleep the moment her head touched the pillow.

"I'm not hungry. I'll help." She was about to suggest that Billie get started upstairs preparing a room for Christian, but realized that would leave the two of them alone in his cottage. On the other hand, she had no intention of going into the attic bedrooms herself. She was debating over which was the lesser of two evils when Billie solved her dilemma.

"You eat," Billie ordered. "We've got a long day ahead of us."

Her aunt hardly sounded like someone who'd nearly lost the most important fixture of her life, but Willa's eyes expressed her concern as she looked at Christian. She didn't want Billie rooting around through the remnants of the fire, where she might be reminded of what she'd almost lost.

He must have understood her silent message because he said, "Why don't you go upstairs, Billie? I thought Willa could help me later this morning." He turned toward her. "We already called a contractor to come out and rebuild the wall that was burned. We'll need to get everything cleaned out so they can work, and after that, we'll have to paint again."

"You're on duty tonight?" Willa asked.

"Yes, but I'll be working days now and then while we're getting the new officers trained. I juggled my schedule and asked for some time off next week, so I could be on hand when the guests start arriving."

"How thoughtful of you, Christian. I'll go get started." Billie left the two of them sitting at the kitchen table.

"We need to talk about something," Christian said, his voice low.

She looked at him, wondering if he could read the apprehension in her eyes as easily as he had read her concern for Billie. She didn't have the strength this morning to resist his arguments, let alone his kisses, but if he thought he was going to pick up where he left off last night, he was sorely mistaken.

"It's about the fire," he said. "I'll be clearing out the cottage. Make Billie happy by eating something, then come outside."

Breakfast food didn't appeal to her, so she fixed herself a cheese sandwich, thinking her system must be all turned around from the late night. She ate mechanically, wondering what Christian would tell her. She'd found the box of letters missing this morning and guessed that he'd taken it and read them. That would explain the tiredness around his eyes. For a moment she wished that he would show the letters to Rod, taking the entire decision out of her hands.

But it was her decision, she realized. Rod was right. Caroline and Patrick Dane seemed all too ready to wash their hands of responsibility for him. Whenever Caroline called, her questions about Rod's progress were perfunctory, and sometimes it sounded as if guilt was the only thing that motivated her to keep track of her son.

He was Rick's son, too, Willa thought, and her nephew. If Caroline didn't want him, then— She stopped, horrified at where her thoughts were beginning to lead. Rod was almost eighteen and an adult. He didn't need her.

She brought her mind back to the problems at hand. Christian wanted to talk to her about the fire. Had he found something this morning while he and Billie were outside? Some clue the arsonist left behind? The possibility made her rush through the morning dishes.

She was putting away the last piece of flatware when she heard a scraping sound from the upper floor. She guessed her aunt must be moving furniture or boxes, and knew she should offer to help, but the thought of entering Rick's old room stopped her cold.

Instead she went outside, where the scent of smoke was stronger. Once again the flames flickered before her eyes, this time in imagination only, but for a moment her stomach threatened to reject the breakfast Billie had insisted she eat. She collected herself and walked to the cottage, unable to suppress a horrified exclamation when she saw the destruction inside.

Christian didn't notice her at first, as he concentrated on sorting the water- and smoke-stained furnishings into two piles. The former looked salvageable, but the latter pile's blackened contents were barely recognizable as clothing, books, or bedding. Freddie ran between the piles sniffing at each as though she, and not Christian, was the arbiter of whether something was salvageable or not. Her bark alerted Christian the moment Willa stepped inside the doorway.

She was supposed to do that last night, before the fire started," Willa pointed out. "Some watchdog she turned out to be."

"It's not as bad as it looks," he assured her. "The fire didn't get very far, but there was a lot of smoke damage. I called the insurance agent. Luckily, your aunt had updated the policy."

"I'm sorry about your things," she said numbly as she picked her way through the mess. The curtains she and Billie had sewn up on the old Singer were blackened rags, the front window was shattered, and the hooked rug was soaking wet and covered with mud and sooty footprints. Wallpaper and paint were soiled with streaks that looked like dark reflections of the flames themselves. But Christian was right. There was little real destruction. Except for one wall that had burned through, revealing blackened two-by-fours and a patch of outdoors, most of the damage was cosmetic.

"I didn't have much here besides clothing," he said with a shrug. "I spent most of my time up at the house anyway."

She bent down to pick up a charred book, smiling sadly when she realized it was an Audubon. Most of the beautiful colored illustrations had been damaged by water. She remembered how Christian used to spend hours in the woods, sketching birds and plants. The book must have been a prized possession.

"Did you leave most of your things in Minneapolis?" she asked, thinking of the furniture and boxes of clothing she'd left behind in Los Angeles.

"I never collected a lot of possessions," he told her. "Even though I lived there for over fifteen years, I guess I never put down roots."

Because his roots were here. She heard the unspoken words and felt defensive as though he'd criticized her directly. Before he could try to convince her that her roots were here, too, she changed the subject. "You said you wanted to talk to me about the fire."

He looked around. "Let's get out of here for a minute. How about a walk? We won't go far. I'm tired of looking at this mess."

"All right." They followed the path into the woods just far enough so that the trees screened the fire's damage. Christian gestured toward a broad stump, which was covered on one side with bright green moss. "How about this?"

Willa sat, taking care not to crush the delicate maidenhair ferns that clustered around the stump's base. She waited for him to speak.

"I saw someone last night," Christian said. "When I came out of the house, someone started running for the woods, and I followed. I lost his trail and nearly turned back when I looked up and saw Kevin Quinlan."

Willa was shocked. "Kevin? He couldn't have—" She broke off. "What if Kevin wanted to help his mother by making sure the new hotel complex would go through?"

She didn't realize that she'd spoken aloud until Christian said, "My thoughts exactly. I didn't say anything to the fire captain. They seemed ready to believe that the fire started from lightning, and I let them think I agreed with their explanation."

"Is it possible that lightning did start the fire?"

"No, not the kind of lightning we had last night. It wasn't close enough. I found a half-burned, kerosene-soaked rag when I was digging around this morning.

It was obvious that someone used it to set that fire. And one of the fire crew must have noticed."

"You don't think—"

"Oh, yes. I do. It's this thing with PROCOR and the hotel. Somebody obviously wants Billie to go out of business or give up. I'm even beginning to wonder if it might be for the best if she sells out."

"*What?*" Willa couldn't believe she'd heard him correctly.

Her surprise at his sudden change in position must have been obvious because he grinned crookedly and said, "When I realized last night that you could have gotten hurt trying to save a run-down old shack, I decided the whole place could burn to ashes and it wouldn't matter."

She looked away from the intensity in his eyes. His announcement turned everything upside down. *No Restless Spirit?*

"It's just a bunch of buildings, Willa. Without you here to help, I'm not sure Billie can keep up with all the work, let alone fend off someone who wants to destroy her business. And what if they get desperate enough to hurt her?"

The possibility chilled her, as Christian must have known it would. Had he switched positions in order to convince her to stay? She looked at him suspiciously.

"There's something else, Willa." She braced herself for another attack, but this one came from an unexpected direction.

"I read the letters last night. The date . . ." His words trailed off awkwardly, and Willa wondered when she'd ever seen him this uncertain. Uneasiness grew inside her, and she turned and stared into the trees.

He ignored her discomfort. "I should have figured out the thing with the date before. You think Rick's death is your fault, don't you? Maybe mine, too, because you were with me that night. And that's why you won't let me—or anyone—too close." He reached for her hand, which was resting limply on her lap, and his touch made her jump. "Look at me."

She complied reluctantly, knowing that if she didn't, he might very well keep her out here in the middle of the woods until she relented. Her breath caught in her chest when she saw the knowledge in his eyes.

This was intimacy. It frightened her even more than his lovemaking. He saw too much, and if he ever realized the truth—*No.* How could he realize something she wouldn't even admit to herself?

"We couldn't have saved him, Willa. Just like you couldn't stop Darryl from destroying himself. We all have to make our own mistakes."

"You think you've got it all figured out, don't you?" she said in a ragged voice.

"It's why you didn't answer my letters. You felt guilty. Just like you felt guilty this morning because we were together last night when the fire started." He reached for her other hand, and she pushed him away.

"You've got it all wrong," she said. "You don't know anything." Oh, but he was close, too close. She stood slowly, hoping he couldn't see that her knees were shaking underneath her jeans. She started walking away, but his next words nearly made her stumble.

"It's not fair to keep those letters from Rod."

"They're mine," she said. "Rick sent them to me."

"They would help Rod understand why Rick killed himself."

"No." She whirled to face him. The determination in his expression scared her. "Promise me you won't tell Rod."

"I can't promise that."

She felt her control slipping away, as surely as if the ground was dropping away from her feet. She gathered her strength and said calmly, "If you ever cared for me at all, Christian, you would know how important this is to me. Promise me that you won't tell him."

"All right, I won't tell him." She relaxed, but not for long. Her relief ended when he said, "As long as you will."

Long after Willa had left, Christian sat and let the silence wash over him, remembering the times he'd escaped to this side of the island as a boy. The woods had always been a special place, somewhere he could get away from his mother. And even though he loved the rambling old Mitterhauser home and its hodgepodge of cottages, now and then he had needed to be by himself, away from people, even from Willa and Rick.

His best friend.

He ached whenever he thought of the letters, but his ache was only a small echo of how much Rick must have hurt to write them, and the pain Willa must have felt as she read them. She'd never shared the letters with him when they were teenagers, and she still carried them around like a penance. Had he misunderstood about her feelings of guilt, as she'd claimed? It seemed so obvious. Why else would she act the way she had—avoiding family responsibility, hiding her emotions behind a wall of indifference, running every time someone got too close?

He didn't have time today to sit here and debate the issue. Billie needed him at the resort.

But Christian didn't move, and eventually the silence turned into the song he remembered, the whisper of pines and aspen in the breeze, the melody of birds calling to one another. He hadn't been back there since he'd come back to Pinecrest. Hell, the only times he'd entered the woods was to chase after somebody. He'd nearly forgotten about the silence, how it changed and swelled until it was a symphony of insects and birds and trees.

A squirrel scolded him from a tree branch nearby, and the corner of his mouth lifted in a smile. Why hadn't he let himself enjoy this peaceful place before now? To be alone with his thoughts?

With a flash of insight, he realized that he hadn't wanted to think. All he'd been doing was reacting: moving here to help Billie, trying to stay one step ahead of the vandals. He was nearly as bad as Willa, only she was trying to keep herself from feeling.

He was a little shocked to realize that he didn't have everything all figured out. He thought he'd gotten over Rick's death years ago, but Willa, Rod, the resort, the letters—all these—dredged up feelings he thought he'd dealt with.

Could he and Willa have resolved their feelings about Rick and about each other if they'd been able to mourn him together all those years ago? But an even bigger question was, could they resolve them now, when she wouldn't even discuss Rick's death with his own son?

He had promised silence, and he would try to keep his word, but he knew it was time for the secret to come out. The resort was scheduled to open in less than two weeks, and afterward Willa would leave. If she was ever going to heal enough to love again, the truth would have to come out soon.

His mind began to retreat from the dilemma, but he forced it back. It was up to him. If Willa didn't give Rod the letters by the time the resort's Grand Opening was over, he'd do it himself.

Rod's sleepless night had convinced him that he had to do something. In the crowd of kids surging down the stairway in front of him, Jerry Miller was easy to spot. He had a habit of wearing practice shirts and uniforms, depending on which sport happened to be in season at the moment. Today, his name and the number "1" were emblazoned on the back of a red and white pinstriped baseball shirt.

Rod pushed his way through the herd of students on their way to fourth period until he got close enough to shout, "Hey, Jerry. Can I talk to you for a minute?"

The other boy slowed down and looked at Rod coolly. "I guess. I gotta go to biology now, though. How about after lunch?"

"No, now." Rod caught up to him at the base of the steps and grabbed him by the shoulder.

Jerry gave him another cool look, but Rod could feel how his muscles bunched underneath the baseball shirt. "You got a problem, Dane?" he sneered.

"No, you do," Rod said quietly. He didn't want anyone to hear him argue with the most popular boy in school. "I want to know why you keep bothering my great aunt."

"I don't know what you're talking about," he said, jerking his shoulder out of Rod's grasp after checking to see who was watching. "The old bat must be seeing ghosts again."

Rod ignored the insult to Billie, though his blood heated and he wished he could take Jerry outside. "One of the cottages burned last night. It wasn't a ghost that started the fire."

The students eddying around them started moving faster as the second bell rang.

"I don't have to listen to this." Jerry made a move to follow the stragglers to class, but Rod caught him by the tail of his shirt, which was hanging loose over his jeans.

"You haven't answered my question yet. Why won't you leave Billie alone?"

"You don't know what you're talking about," Jerry said, his voice low and urgent.

"Oh, yes, I do. I overheard you in the locker room when you were talking about breaking windows and stuff. Somebody broke a window to start that fire last night."

By now, their raised voices had attracted a few onlookers, who gathered in classroom doorways or pretended to be getting something from a locker nearby. Jerry shoved Rod against the wall. The impact rattled a whole row of steel lockers and slammed Rod's teeth together.

Through the buzzing in his ears, he heard a girl's voice shout, "Get the principal!"

Rod charged forward, grabbing hold of Jerry before he could get away. Off balance, they stumbled, and their books and papers scattered to the floor. In the resulting confusion, Rod felt a pair of arms lock around his waist like steel bands. He turned his head and recognized Dean Roberts' bony face leering at him over his shoulder. Another member of the senior jock clique helped Jerry to his feet while Rod twisted and struggled to free himself. Before he could loosen Dean's iron hold, he felt Jerry's fist connect with his right eye.

"All right, everybody calm down," Rod heard an authoritative voice order. It was Principal Adams. "Let go of him, Dean."

Rod caught himself from falling as Dean released him. He straightened to find himself staring into the principal's stern countenance. "What happened here? Who started it?"

The half dozen students clustered around them spoke all at once.

"He did." A finger pointed at Rod.

"Jerry hit him while Dean and Stewart held him."

"Dane threw the first punch."

Apparently the principal heard only the latter response, which belonged to another one of Jerry Miller's friends, the co-captain of the baseball team. "Is that true, Mr. Dane?"

His eye was swelling already. If he tried hard enough, he could just make out Principal Adams' scowl. He wanted to argue that it had been Jerry who threw the first punch, but then he'd have to explain how the fight started. And that was between him and Jerry. He remained silent.

"Well, Mr. Dane. I had a feeling it was only a matter of time before you showed us your true colors. You boys go to the nurse's office. She'll give you hall passes to get to your next class. Dane, you're coming with me."

Rod followed behind the principal, keeping his gaze resolutely fixed on the worn terrazzo floor. Even so, he could feel the curious eyes watching him from doorways and lockers. A lot of students were late for fourth period. The school secretary was going to have to order a whole new batch of tardy slips, he thought with wry humor.

He felt something wet on his face and realized his nose was bleeding. He sniffed and stopped to wipe away the blood with his torn sleeve. Principal Adams turned around to see what was keeping him, and his grim look softened momentarily.

"Here." He handed Rod a handkerchief.

"Thanks," Rod mumbled.

They continued down the hall toward Principal Adams's office. Rod couldn't ever remember the east hall being this long before. He wondered what was going to happen next, if Adams was going to call Willa . . . or his parents.

He nearly stumbled as an unwelcome thought entered his mind. Patrick Dane might try to send him away again. Oh, hell, he was almost eighteen, wasn't he? They couldn't do anything to him now. Could they?

He swallowed, realizing how much he'd miss out on—the summer at the lake, training Freddie, learning how to fish. And Kerry. If she still liked him after she heard about what happened with Jerry.

One thing was for sure, he thought as he stepped through the glass doorway into the reception area, his good eye fixing on the principal's door as though it were an execution chamber. If Jerry did anything else to Billie or the resort, he was going to flatten him.

Willa entered the kitchen before lunch to find her aunt staring out the window at the men fixing the cottage. She joined Billie at the window, her gaze automatically seeking a familiar figure.

"Where's Christian?" she asked.

"I saw him walking across the causeway a little while ago. He must have needed something at Quinlan's. I've been moving his things inside. They were getting in the way of the workers. I guess he must not have known how soon the men would be here."

Willa's brows came together in a frown. It wasn't like Christian to disappear when there was work to be done. What was he up to now?

". . . and I thought you might help me."

"Sure," Willa said absently, then wondered what

she'd agreed to do. She followed Billie to the back door, where Christian's things were packed into a large box. She stared, already guessing what Billie wanted.

"You might see some of your old things that you'd like to keep. The rest you can put into this box after Christian has unpacked. We'll store them or give them to the thrift shop."

Understanding dawned. "Christian is moving into *my* old room?" At least she wouldn't have to cross the dividing wall.

Billie shook her head exasperatedly. "Why, yes. That's what I said before. Weren't you listening?"

Willa answered with a muffled grunt as she hefted the cardboard box and headed for the back stairs. It wouldn't be easy getting the bulky shape around the turns in the narrow staircase, but the main stairs didn't go all the way to the third floor. Old Hulbert Mitterhauser had obviously intended to use the attic as servants' quarters.

Unfortunately for Hulbert, the family had barely moved in when the market for white pine had gone bust. He'd died a broken man, leaving behind a white elephant of a house and a family that had no means of support. Willa had heard the tale of Hulbert's ghost and the beginning of Restless Spirit a hundred times. She retold it to herself as she climbed the stairs, using it to keep her from thinking about her destination.

She reached the top of the stairs and paused by the doorway. With relief she saw that the divider was still there, pulled across the long room, hiding the half that had been Rick's domain. She walked through the side of the room that had been hers, shocked to see some of Christian's things already piled in a corner next to the remnants of her stuffed animal collection. He'd be sleeping in the very bed in which she used to dream of him, just one floor above where she was sleeping now.

Two more weeks. They stretched ahead of her like a jail sentence, and once more she considered leaving sooner. But last night's fire had removed that option. She couldn't leave with a clear conscience until the cottage was repaired and the resort was whole again.

She busied herself emptying out the pine dresser, amazed to realize that some of the items of clothing were back in style again. She set them aside, thinking Kerry might be interested. But most of her old summer clothes were barely suitable for rags, and she tossed them into a pile.

Inside the closet she found a treasure: Packed in tissue was a heavy wool sweater that Oma had knitted in a Scandinavian design of snowflakes. She held it against her and looked in the mirror above the dresser. It still fit, and the dark navy and white contrasted nicely with her hair.

She was about to set it aside to take with her when she realized she would never need it in Los Angeles. She reluctantly added it to the pile she was giving to Kerry, before moving on to the rest of the room.

She managed to keep her gaze from straying to the accordion divider until she was through. Then she sat on the bed, facing the fold-away wall that had separated her room from Rick's. She felt the breath constrict in her chest. What if she could pull back the divider to find Rick there, lying on his bed, reading a comic book or listening to his favorite Doors album? What would she say to him if she could see him just one more time?

She began to feel lightheaded and fought to breathe past the heaviness in her chest.

"Willa?"

She spun around at the sound of her aunt's voice, her breath returning in a gasp.

"I didn't mean to startle you," Billie said from the doorway. "I only wanted to see if you could—" She stopped, then exclaimed, "Why, you look as though you've seen a ghost."

"No." Willa shook her head, partly in denial, partly in an attempt to clear it. "I was about to, though." And she felt her eyes fill with tears. She pushed past Billie and hurried ahead of her down the stairs, continuing on through the kitchen and out the back door.

As if by instinct, she ran to the boathouse. It wasn't until she was inside, looking around numbly at the gaping door and splintered docks, that she realized the boathouse would provide little escape. There was no escape anywhere on the island. Everywhere she went, she was assaulted by memories.

She turned and walked slowly back to the house. When she entered the kitchen, Billie glanced up from the pie crust she was rolling out on the scarred counter. Her blue eyes didn't miss a thing.

"I've got some pie dough left over. Want some cinnamon crust?"

"Sure." Willa smiled. Oma used to roll out the leftover scraps of dough, rub them with butter, and then sprinkle the pieces with cinnamon and sugar. For Willa, Rick, and Christian, it was always a game to see who could discover the crust before the others found out it was in the oven baking alongside whatever kind of pie Oma happened to have made that day. It was the ultimate in comfort food.

"Just don't spoil your appetite," Billie warned as she scattered cinnamon and sugar over the top of the dough. She glanced through the window. "Here comes Christian. I'll just put it in the oven before he sees it, hmm?"

"Thanks, Billie." She smiled gratefully at her aunt,

wanting to say more, but knowing she didn't need to. There was understanding in Billie's blue eyes and a spark of compassion.

Christian entered the kitched carrying the wriggling puppy in his arms, explaining that Freddie had followed him to Quinlan's but was too tired to make the return trip. Willa waited until he and Billie had gone outside to check the progress on the cottage before removing the crust from the oven.

Too impatient to wait for it to cool, she burned her fingers and tongue on the first bite. She quickly took a swallow of cold milk. She was breaking off her second piece when Christian's voice startled her.

"Holding out on me?"

She jumped, dropping the crust onto the tabletop. Quick as a flash, he snatched up several pieces.

"Got any coffee to go with this?"

"If you make it."

"Oh sure, and when I turn around again, you'll have snarfed up every last crumb."

"Here," Willa told him, holding out a flaky triangle. "This one has your name on it." He grinned and busied himself filling the coffeepot with water while she looked on. She searched for feelings of awkwardness after all they'd shared the last twenty-four hours, but there weren't any. She took that as a sign that her decision not to rekindle the past was the right one.

Her good spirits weren't destined to last, however, not with Christian so obviously determined to change her mind. He set two mugs of coffee on the table and sat down across from her, eating his pastry with relish.

"Billie must have made this. I bet you don't even remember how to mix pie crust."

His teasing got to her, seeming like one more push toward an intimacy she'd decided she didn't want.

"You're right. I don't." Her chin lifted. "That particular skill isn't exactly in great demand among touring musicians."

"Didn't the rock star like to eat?"

"We had a cook who traveled with the band," she said, her mood rapidly becoming unsettled. "Look, if you're going to start digging at me because I turned you down . . ."

He lifted an eyebrow, and she left the threat unspoken, afraid he might point out that she hadn't exactly turned him down last night, when it had counted. Instead, she asked, "What happened at Quinlan's?"

"I tried to talk to Kevin, but he wouldn't say a word. Literally. He was in the kitchen fixing Mattie's range when I got there, and he simply pretended I wasn't there. I asked the questions, but he ignored me."

"Was Mattie there?"

"No, she was waiting on customers out in the store."

Willa sighed. "I thought we might be getting somewhere for a change. Every time we find some little bit of evidence, it turns out to be nothing. And just when we start to forget they're around, they strike again."

Christian reached out and covered her hand with his. "How about if we get away from it all for a while tonight? Drive into Brainerd for dinner, just the two of us?"

She pulled her hand from beneath his. "I thought we discussed this."

"I don't think so."

"Too bad." She rose from the table. "The matter is settled."

His gaze held hers. "Oh, yes. We'll settle it, Willa. One way or the other."

The ring of the telephone was a welcome respite. Willa answered it and listened to the voice on the other end of the line. Her distress must have showed on her face because Christian got to his feet and stood by her side.

"What's the matter?"

"It's the school calling. Rod's being sent home. He got into a fight."

He took the receiver from her numb fingers before she could protest. "This is Officer Christian Foster," he told the principal's assistant on the other end. "When can we pick him up?"

Willa sat down, her legs too weak to hold her. She listened as Christian made arrangements to get Rod. When he hung up the phone, she bombarded him with questions.

"Is he all right? How did it happen? What should we tell Billie?"

"Why don't we let Rod explain the first two," he said. "He's waiting for us in the principal's office. I'll drive you. If you want to go, that is."

She should rail at him for interfering again. Already today he'd called the contractor to arrange for work on the cottage, talked to Billie's insurance agent, and tracked down a possible witness to the fire. If she let him creep into her family's life this way, she'd have to fight him for control of her very soul. But right now she was just so damned grateful that she didn't have to deal with this on her own that she didn't care.

She stood. "I'm going with you. But first, give me a few minutes to talk to Billie."

Christian glanced over at Rod, seated between him and Willa in the pickup's cab. His black eye was a beaut, Christian decided, and he considered himself an expert. But he'd learned that getting into a fight at school was a lot more complicated than it used to be.

By the time he and Willa had gone over the papers formalizing Rod's half day of suspension, spoken with the principal, heard warnings about custody arrangements, and so on, Christian's head was pounding, his stomach burning, and his temper about to crack. Willa had broken the news to Billie before they left the island and told her they would miss dinner. But that was hours earlier, and Christian added *starving* to the list of uncomfortable adjectives that described the way he felt as they had faced Principal Adams across his oak veneer desk.

"I'll have to report this to the boy's *real* parents, of course," the principal had said, steepling his fingers and looking stern. "I've left a message on their answering machine, and on Mr. Dane's office voice mail. I'm sure they'll return my call soon."

"Don't count on it," Christian mumbled.

"Pardon me?"

"We'll inform Rod's parents," Willa said quickly, before Christian could voice his cynicism again.

"I'm sure you will," Nick Adams said with a cool smile. "But I have to do that myself. Regulations, you understand."

Christian grinned now and glanced over the top of Rod's head to Willa as he remembered what she had told Adams to do with his regulations. Up until that point, she'd been the calm one during the difficult interview. Not calm, he corrected himself as he turned onto the gravel county road that led toward the island, but unemotional, contained. Then she'd acted like a mother bear who just spotted someone trying to pick up her cub, and Christian had almost cheered aloud right there in the principal's office. No matter how Willa protested or fought against it, her heart had already chosen.

Now, as they sat in the pickup, she was silent again,

as was her nephew. They'd heard the principal's version of what happened, but Rod had yet to say a word in his defense. The silence continued until they reached Restless Spirit.

Billie greeted them at the door and ushered them into the kitchen, where supper waited. Talk was delayed further while the four of them helped themselves to pot roast, potatoes and gravy, corn, and rhubarb pie.

God forbid anyone should ruin one of Billie Mitterhauser's meals, Christian thought. Across the table from him, Rod concentrated fiercely on his potatoes, mashing them with a fork and stirring gravy into the mass until it looked like baby food. He hadn't eaten a bite. At least no one was jumping down the kid's throat or telling him he should have known better. But this silence and waiting had to be almost as hard to take as a lecture or hysterics.

Christian wanted to start the ball rolling, but he knew Willa would only accuse him of interfering again. But when the plates were cleared and rhubarb pie set in front of him, he decided he'd had enough silence.

"How about telling us what happened today, Rod?"

"You know what happened. I got in a fight." Tension showed in every line of Rod's lanky body, although he was trying to look casual, with one arm draped over the back of his chair.

"Why?" Willa's question was mild, almost timid.

"Because this guy, Jerry Miller, said something stupid." He shrugged. "I shoved him. He hit me back, and then a bunch of other guys started in. It was no big deal."

"It was a big enough deal to get you suspended from school and banned from the prom," Willa pointed out.

Rod leaned back and grinned. "I wasn't going anyway."

Christian wasn't fooled by his apparent unconcern, and he wasn't about to let Rod off the hook without finding out what happened today. "What did Jerry Miller say?"

"Just some stuff."

"Like what?"

Rod shrugged and shot Billie a quick glance. She had sat quietly throughout the conversation, although Christian noticed that she hadn't touched a bite of her pie.

"He said some mean things about Billie," he said in a rush, before Christian could question him further. "They're just a bunch of dumb hicks anyway. I don't even know why I'm going to school when I could join the service like my dad."

"No." From the stricken look on her face, Christian knew that Willa had spoken involuntarily.

"Your father finished school first, young man," Billie said sternly. It was the first time she'd spoken, and everyone turned to listen. "I'm proud of him, just like I'm proud of my brothers. But they're all dead except your grandfather, and sometimes I wish they'd been teachers or mechanics or doctors instead of soldiers."

Silence reigned again. Christian could see that Willa was trying to hide her emotion. Rod stared down at his plate.

"You only have a couple more weeks of school left," Christian said. "Sticking it out could make a lot of difference, whether you decide to join the service or not. Your dad wasn't a quitter."

He felt Willa's sharp gaze on him. Was that it? Did she think Rick had quit by killing himself?

"Your grades have improved so much, dear," Billie added gently. "It would be a shame if you didn't finish when you're doing so well."

"All right," Rod said. "Two more weeks. Then I'm outta here." His expression challenged them all to object. "May I be excused?"

Billie nodded. After Rod closed the back door behind him, silence reigned again.

A sense of urgency pressed against Willa, suffocating her. She was inside the cottage again, seeing the flames twist and dance only inches away. She knew Christian was in here somewhere, and she had to find him. She couldn't believe he could be so careless.

She reached out, feeling the heat . . . but the figure standing before her had Rick's face.

She bolted awake, opening her eyes to see that she'd taken a page out of Billie's book and fallen asleep in the living room after dinner. She looked around, disoriented.

"If you're looking for Billie, she's gone up to bed." Christian said. She turned to see him seated on the other end of the sofa. "Nightmare?" he asked.

She hated being this vulnerable with Christian only a couple feet away. "Yes. I don't want to talk about it."

"Surprise, surprise," he murmured.

"What's that supposed to mean?"

"You don't like to talk about much of anything, do you? I watched you and Billie sit through nearly the entire meal without saying a word to Rod about what happened today at school."

She looked at him helplessly. Why was he picking on her this way when she was so tired?

"Just like you won't tell him about his father." He paused. "Willa, those letters would show Rod what it was really like to be a soldier. You're only compounding the problem by not telling him about Rick."

"No. Don't you understand? The truth will hurt him, and he's had a hard enough time."

"Give the kid a little credit. He's had to be tough to make it in new schools and new homes every few months. He'll get through this, too."

When had Christian moved closer? she wondered. A moment ago, he'd been on the other end of the sofa, and now she was pressed into a corner, both literally and figuratively.

"Please don't," she said, but his mouth had already trapped hers, and the last half of her command was lost. Half asleep, still vulnerable from her bad dream, she wasn't prepared for his onslaught, and feelings from the night before came rushing back.

With her rising excitement came awareness. She nearly shoved him off the end of the sofa before heading for the staircase. She knew he wouldn't come after her with Billie and Rod on the same floor. He'd probably accuse her of running away again, but she didn't care.

11

Christian stood in the driveway of Quinlan's store and stared at the shamrock-shaped sign. It had been two days since the fire. Since then, none of his efforts had brought him any closer to finding out what had taken place that night. And he wasn't just referring to the fire.

His efforts weren't working with Willa either. He thought he had it all figured out, that he'd made some kind of breakthrough, but for two days she'd treated him as merely a pleasant acquaintance. If they were in L.A., she might have asked him to "do lunch." Here in Pinecrest, she barely gave him the time of day.

He told himself to be patient, but patience had never been his long suit, as a man or as a cop. He decided it was a hell of a lot easier to concentrate on being a cop. He couldn't seem to get to the bottom of Willa's behavior, but he knew that if he dug deep enough, he could get to the bottom of the incidents plaguing the resort.

He felt guilty for pressing Kevin. It was like fighting dirty, but he sensed that it was only a matter of time and the right kind of persuasion before he would talk. And he needed to find out just what Kevin had been doing in the woods that night.

The bells above the door rang as he entered, and Mattie stepped out from behind the counter with a smile that could only be described as coquettish, even on a seventy-year-old woman.

"Hello, Christian. Tired of Billie's cooking? I've got chicken and dumplings in the oven right this very moment."

"Thanks, Mattie, but I've already eaten. I'm here to talk to Kevin. Is he around?"

Her demeanor changed instantly. Or maybe he was starting to get paranoid, seeing guilt everywhere. "He's in the garage, working on the old Falcon. Is there something around the resort that needs fixing?"

"Not today. We've pretty much got things under control. We'll be ready for business in time for opening weekend."

"So I've heard. Sure hasn't been much work for Kevin since you came back to town. What is it you want to see him about?"

Christian was silent for a moment. He hadn't even considered that Mattie and Kevin might be depending on the small amounts of cash Billie paid him for fixing this and that around the resort. He wondered how much Kevin had told her about that night, and how much Mattie had put together herself after his visit a couple days ago.

He watched her expression carefully as he answered, "There's some details I need to clear up with him. If everything works out, we might hire him to do some things next week. The boathouse is still a mess, and

Willa could use some help with the lawn and garden."

She said nothing, but gave him a sharp look before nodding her head toward the back, indicating that Christian could walk through their living quarters to get to the garage behind the store. He could feel Mattie's gaze on him as he passed through the narrow hallway to the living room, but he still managed a surreptitious appraisal of his surroundings.

Only the TV set was new. The furniture—a sagging sofa and chairs covered in avocado-colored plaid—must have been the same set Mattie had bought from the local furniture store almost twenty years ago. He still remembered it from the times he had come by with Willa and Rick to see if Kevin wanted to join their play.

A short breezeway led to the garage. Here in back of the building, paint peeled from the narrow siding, and the door sagged on its hinges. Mattie had kept up the part of the store visible from the dirt road, but this side showed neglect. He wondered if Mattie was under the delusion that PROCOR's hotel would bring more business to Quinlan's. Didn't she realize that PROCOR would close down her run-down little store so it wouldn't detract from their groomed, planned neighborhood?

He found Kevin with his head stuck inside the engine compartment of the aging Falcon Mattie used on her infrequent trips into town. The Irish setter, Shamrock, was curled up near his booted feet.

"Hi, Kevin."

Shoulders so powerful they seemed to fill the engine compartment stilled for a moment before Kevin backed out from the car, a ready smile lighting his round face. But the smile disappeared when he saw Christian's serious expression. He stood there, wrench in one hand, his eyes downcast.

The picture of guilt. Christian dismissed the involuntary thought before speaking, his voice gentle. "Kevin, I came to ask you again about the other night when I saw you in the woods. Do you remember?"

The other man shrugged, glancing away through the half-opened garage door to the large shade tree outside. "We used to play in that sandpile when we were kids, remember that?"

Kevin nodded, a hint of a smile chasing across his bland features. "I remember," he said, and Christian felt about two inches high for resorting to this kind of questioning. "My ma, she said that you were nice to play with me."

"You know I wouldn't do anything to hurt you or your mother, don't you? I just want to ask you a couple more questions, that's all."

Kevin nodded again.

"Do you remember seeing a fire that night, Kevin? One of the cottages?"

This time he shrugged and said, "It was burning."

"Did you start the fire?"

He shook his head rapidly. "No. I never done nothing like that, even when—" The flow of words stopped abruptly, and Christian felt a flat kind of victory.

"Have you ever done anything else to the cottages?"

Kevin looked down at the garage's oil-stained dirt floor. Christian repeated the question.

"A couple times I took some chains and made noises. And I used a shovel to dig holes." His voice was barely a whisper.

"Anything else?"

Kevin shook his head vigorously, and Christian knew he was telling the truth.

"You wouldn't do anything like that again, would you?"

"No." Kevin looked up, his expression as earnest as a

child's. "I promise, Christian. I won't hurt the cottages again. I know you work hard on them. I seen you all the time."

"From the woods? Do you spend a lot of time in the woods?"

"Yeah, I like it there. I see a squirrel and a—" he hesitated, as though he had to pull the word out of a hat "—hedgehog. I like animals."

"So do I. I used to go into the woods and draw pictures of them."

"Maybe I can come with you sometime?"

Christian felt an ache of compassion. Was Kevin lonely? He knew that Rod had stopped by Quinlan's to visit once or twice, but the rest of the time, it was just Kevin and Mattie. "That sounds good," he said, intending to follow through with an invitation sometime. "But I don't have much time now. We're almost finished fixing up the resort for Billie. All we've got left are the boathouse and the yard."

"I could help."

Christian nodded. "We'll need someone to plow up the garden next week. Billie's going to have a big garden this year, with lots of sweet corn and tomatoes for the guests. She's going to need a gardener. But first, I need to ask another question. Now this is very important, Kevin. Did you see anyone else at the cottage that night?"

"Nnnno." He drew out the word, just enough so that Christian suspected he was lying. He sighed, knowing he'd try again another time, but he just couldn't bring himself to push Kevin any harder than this, even if someone else had. Kevin wouldn't have hurt the resort on his own, so someone, possibly Mattie, must have pushed him into it. But neither Mattie nor Kevin wore men's dress shoes, and the person Willa and Billie had seen by the cabin that day did.

When he got back to the island, a dark blue BMW was parked in front of the house. He didn't think Billie was expecting any guests until the weekend. Judging by the vehicle, this wasn't a typical visitor to Restless Spirit resort.

He nearly headed for his cottage before remembering he'd been living in the big house since the fire. He and Willa had finished painting the new siding and Sheetrock yesterday. Next week the cottage would be ready for guests.

He climbed the back steps to the usual accompaniment of Freddie's frantic barking. She'd be a good watchdog as soon as she learned to quit barking at every person she saw. And every bird, cat, squirrel, bug, shadow . . . the list went on. For once, when he opened the door, he didn't find Willa trying to discipline the puppy.

She met him at the foot of the staircase, her eyes darker than usual, her face pale. He was instantly on alert.

"It's Caroline and Patrick Dane. They've come to take Rod back to Minneapolis with them."

"He'll be back in school on Monday. He'll have missed only half a day of classes," Willa told the couple sitting side by side on the antique brocade sofa. All of them—the Danes, Christian, Billie, Rod, and Willa—were seated around the large living room, which no longer seemed as comfortable as it usually did. Rod looked as though he were sitting on a bed of nails, and she herself would have preferred a form of ancient torture to this conversation.

"I'm talking to the school counselor this evening," she added, "and I'm sure she'll help monitor his performance during the next couple weeks."

"What about the prom?" Caroline pointed out. "The most important memory of a young person's life, and he has to stay at home."

Willa swallowed a frustrated groan. Perhaps the prom had been that important to Caroline, but if she thought Rod was devastated because he was missing a dance, she didn't know her son very well at all. "His girlfriend's only a sophomore. Since she wouldn't be allowed to attend the Junior-Senior Prom anyway, Rod had already decided not to go," she explained.

Caroline's pretty china blue eyes looked unconvinced, and Patrick Dane took up the argument. "We think it might be better if he went back to the military academy to finish up and get his diploma. Of course, he'll have to take this last quarter over again, but with summer sessions, he should be ready to start college in the fall." He nodded his dark blond head, as though approving his own suggestion.

"He'd be living with you?" Christian asked. So far he'd left it up to Willa to talk to these two, and she breathed a silent prayer of thanks at his intervention. She might have been able to win an outright argument with the Danes, but they were so calm and so unemotional, that she couldn't begin to reach them. With that thought came a stab of knowledge that she quickly shoved away.

"Well, not exactly. We're leaving for Europe the first of June," Caroline said. "The girls are coming with us, of course. They're so young, but—"

"Rod needs to be in a more disciplined environment. This latest episode proves it," Patrick Dane finished for his wife. "We know what's best for him."

Billie's querulous voice carried loudly. "You mean to tell me that you're here to take him home with you although you don't even want him home?"

Christian smoothed over the outburst by saying he

knew everyone wanted what was best for Rod. Underneath his calming exterior, Willa could tell that Christian didn't like Patrick Dane. Even though both men were self-assured, confident, they were a study in opposites. Whereas Christian appeared relaxed, almost indolent, Dane wore his confidence on his sleeve like a military decoration.

He'd been Rick's CO in Germany, and he was already a lieutenant colonel at forty-eight. She wondered if part of the reason Caroline hadn't told Rod about his father was because his suicide violated some kind of macho code practiced by her father, a two-star general, and Patrick Dane. Caroline might have been ashamed at what military types probably regarded as the ultimate weakness.

Willa felt a flash of resentment that quickly died. She was being unfair. None of her family had told Rod the truth, either, and this was the mess that had resulted. It was no wonder that Rod wanted to join the service when all the males in his family history had been military men.

With one exception. She glanced at Christian, who continued to try to mediate the awkward conversation. As a cop, he'd had to play the role of negotiator and psychologist, and he'd learned to control his temper. She was forced to admit that he was the very best influence for Rod.

But these were Rod's parents. And hadn't she wanted to see an end to her responsibilities? They were offering her a way out, and certainly no one could blame her for returning Rod to the family he grew up with.

No one, that is, except Christian.

"We're talking about uprooting him when he's only two weeks from graduation," Willa said. "And he's been doing very well in his classes here. Why don't you let him finish at Pinecrest High, and then let him decide about college this summer?"

"He'd have a hard time getting into a good school at this date. West Point is out of the question, of course—" Patrick Dane shot Rod a glance that was almost accusing "—but we want him to have a good education."

"I think Rod's the one who should decide what he wants," Christian said. "Why don't we put the question to him?"

Rod sank back into his chair as though he wished he could disappear. He looked around at all their faces, a small grin catching at the corners of his mouth when he met Billie's eyes.

"I'd like to stay here, if it's okay with Billie," he said, sitting up straighter in his chair. Willa's hand clutched Christian's without her even realizing it.

"Restless Spirit is your home as long as you want it, Rod," Billie said firmly.

"Rod's home is where we say it is," said Patrick Dane. "Until he turns eighteen, we'll be the ones to decide if this is the right place for him or not."

Billie's wrinkled face fell, and Willa could barely restrain herself from ordering Patrick Dane out of their home. But before anyone had a chance to say another word, Billie stood up. "Restless Spirit is the right place. Rod knows it, and so do we."

She glanced at the clock. "Now, if you'll excuse me, it's time to start making supper." She marched out of the room, her head held high, and the discussion was over.

Billie felt ancient as she slowly climbed the grand old staircase to her room. She picked up the pace a bit and made it to all the way to the top of the staircase without having to pause and catch her breath.

But there was no one to share the victory with. Willa had taken her car to town for her appointment with the school counselor, Rod had disappeared into the woods with Freddie, and Christian had been summoned away by his beeper. None of them had returned yet, although it was fast getting dark. She'd missed the usual after-supper gathering in the living room, although after this afternoon, she didn't blame anyone for wanting to avoid that room for a while.

Caroline and her husband had left for Duluth hours ago, saying they needed to relieve the hotel nanny they'd left watching their daughters. Apparently, Pinecrest didn't offer enough to keep them amused. That pair would probably be all for the PROCOR's new hotel complex, Billie thought grimly.

She turned on the light next to her bed, scowling at the book she'd started reading a few weeks ago. It was a travelogue on Australia, but she was getting tired of making do with words on a page. Her dream of traveling seemed further away than ever.

But at least one battle was won, albeit a temporary one. Rod was staying until school was out.

Now, if he would just come to his senses and stay out of the army. Or, in this case, the Marines. Let him spend a summer here, fishing and chasing Freddie through the woods. If he still wanted to join the service in the fall, well, then at least he would have taken the time to decide.

One should never, ever decide one's future under pressure, she thought sadly as she dressed in her summer cotton nightgown, which was identical to her high-necked, long-sleeved winter gown except for the fabric. In winters, she wore striped flannel. As soon as the weather turned warm, she changed to batiste. It had been that way as long as she could remember, long before Willa and Rick had been born. It wasn't so much that she feared change as that she honored tradition.

There had been a lot of pressure on her when Rick died. No one had known, of course, wrapped up as they were with their own miseries. She'd felt the weight of generations coming down to her. Would it be because of her that the family home went to strangers?

No, she'd decided then, but all she'd done was buy an eighteen-year delay. The future of Restless Spirit was in more jeopardy now than it had been when Hulbert died and left his family penniless.

Was it fair to expect Willa to make the same sacrifice she had? Maybe her niece didn't realize it yet, but the place was in her blood, just as it was in Billie's. Willa had at least had her chance to see the outside, to be somebody and do things. Other people didn't need to get away—people like Mattie Quinlan, for instance. But she wasn't going to molder here like her, Billie vowed.

Oh, no, she was going to go places and do things.

It wasn't as if she'd never had the opportunity. She'd had her chance, once, when Sean asked her to run away with him. By then, she had realized what a shallow man he was, a man who would leave his wife and son rather than face the fact that he'd fathered a less-than-perfect child. And yet she'd still been tempted to go.

However, she'd come to her senses and turned Sean down, and a few days later Pinecrest's trusty grapevine had informed her that Sean had ended up in Cuernavaca, Mexico, with the postmistress from Nashwauk. That decision—to let Sean Quinlan go without her—wasn't made under pressure. But, oh, to be in Mexico.

Willa stood outside the door marked Heidi Walker, Counselor, for some reason reluctant to go inside. She knew Rod's attitude and grades had improved since he had come to Pinecrest, and yet she feared this stranger's judgment.

Christian had offered to accompany her, but that would have been even worse than coming here alone. She could see what he was doing—trying to make himself indispensable, to work his way into her life until she relied on him for everything. And in the guise of helpfulness and support, he would take away her freedom.

She rapped lightly on the door and entered at the cheerfully spoken invitation. The woman seated behind the metal, school district–issued desk was pretty and blond and looked young enough to be in high school herself. She was giving these kids guidance?

"Sit down. I'm glad you could come in tonight," Heidi Walker said, after rising from her seat to shake Willa's hand. "I have a full schedule with graduation coming up, but I didn't think we should put this off."

"Thank you for taking the time to see me," Willa said as she took the seat across the desk, knowing the other woman must have given up some of her personal time in order to make this evening appointment.

Her skepticism changed to growing respect as the counselor started talking about Rod, only occasionally referring to the file filled with papers on the desk in front of her. After several minutes of conversation, she said, "Rod's had problems developing attachments in the past."

"That's hardly surprising. His parents sent him in turn to her family in Texas and a military boarding school. His adoptive father told him that the next time he got into trouble, they would put him in a foster home. But he seems very much at home with us." Willa realized she was talking rapidly, trying to present as much evidence as she could. "He has a girlfriend, Kerry, and a puppy that he adores."

"But you say he's lived in—" the counselor glanced down at a file "—five different places in the last three years?" Her brow furrowed. "No wonder he doesn't stick with anything very long. Track, for example."

"I'm sorry?"

"His coach informed me that Rod hasn't been at workouts the last few days."

"Oh, yes, well . . ." Willa stammered, unwilling to let the counselor know she had no idea Rod had been cutting workouts. Or worse, no idea where he spent those afternoons when he came home from school on the late bus, the one reserved for students with activities and athletics. Brenda would have told her if he and Kerry were seeing each other more frequently. Thankfully, before she had to come up with an explanation, Heidi Walker continued.

"It says here that Rod's father died before Rod was born. Is there a family history of illness that we should be aware of?"

"My brother committed suicide," Willa said quietly.

"Oh." Heidi Walker's gray eyes transmitted sympathy. "How did your family react?"

Willa winced inwardly. *And how do you feel about that?* The line was a standard joke in L.A. among those who'd sought therapy. But Heidi Walker's concern was genuine, and Willa found herself responding.

"Rick's death was difficult for all of us. My parents especially. They wanted their son to be a hero. They were shocked by Rick's suicide. They even managed to convince themselves that he died in battle."

"Denial is a common reaction among survivors of a family member's suicide. I've noticed that Rod sometimes acts as though he hasn't dealt with his father's death."

"Rod doesn't know Rick committed suicide," she admitted reluctantly. "His mother never told him, and neither did my parents when he lived with them."

A look of confusion passed over the other woman's face. "You mean no one in the family has discussed his father with him?"

"We've talked about Rick, or at least Christian and Billie and I have told him what Rick was like when he was younger. But we haven't told him how Rick died."

"Why not?"

Willa glanced out the window, before admitting, "We just don't talk about those kinds of things, I guess. I wanted Rod to think of Rick in a good light." She relaxed when she saw no sign of judgment in Heidi Walker's eyes.

"Did the family seek counseling after your brother's death?"

"No. My parents moved to Arizona shortly afterward, and I guess in all the confusion, it was something that simply got shoved aside." Her discomfort grew as she offered the excuse, and she quickly corrected herself. "No, that's not true. My parents aren't the type to believe a stranger could help them with their family problems."

"What about you? How do you feel about Rick taking his own life?"

Willa hardly even noticed how the conversation's focus had drifted to her. "Sad. Unhappy. Upset that I couldn't see him one more time." She swallowed back the lump that rose in her throat. "I also felt deserted," she added. "I'd been dating a boy at the time, and we . . . we were becoming physically intimate. It was a very confusing and emotional time for me, and I knew the only one who would understand, the only one I felt like talking to, was Rick. We talked about everything.

Even after he left for Nam, he sent me letters, telling me about it. He was the one I wanted to talk to. And he left me."

"I understand," the counselor said. "Suicide survivors experience many emotions—guilt, grief, abandonment. It's also very common for survivors to feel anger toward the loved one who committed suicide. And since feeling angry toward someone who died seems inappropriate, that emotion often gets buried."

"Angry? How could I be angry at my brother?" Willa set down the paperweight that had somehow found its way into her hands. She looked at her watch, saw that she'd been there nearly two hours, and said, "Is there anything more we need to discuss concerning my nephew?"

Heidi Walker leaned back in her chair. "Only that you might want to think seriously about talking to him sometime about his father. Ask him how he feels. He could surprise you," she said with an encouraging smile. "And let's make this a weekly visit. That way we can keep each other informed about Rod's progress."

"Of course." Willa smiled back. "That sounds like a good idea."

Rod walked past the crumbling granite monument, hardly even seeing it. The first few times he'd been here, it had given him the creeps. It marked a baby's grave, and the inscription below the statue of an angel read: *Our Darling*.

It was pretty disturbing, especially during twilight like now. He'd had to wait until his parents left and supper was over before going up to his room, then climbing out the window. He'd walked out to the highway, then hitched a ride into town with a farmer. It was a lot easier coming here after school and taking the bus home. Kerry always refused to come with him, but that was okay. He wasn't sure he wanted to share this with anyone, even her. He hadn't heard from her since the fight at school anyway, he thought glumly.

"Be quiet," he instructed Freddie, using her leash to tie her to a low hanging branch. They'd hitched all the way to town, and if Freddie started barking now, they'd get caught for sure. "Stay," he ordered, and headed for his destination.

The first time he caught sight of the plain marker engraved Roderick Mitterhauser, 1954-1975, he'd felt a chill. This square of granite set into the ground was all that was left of his father.

Now he sat down beside it with a comfortable familiarity, as though he were sitting down on the living room sofa, about to have a talk with a real live person. Usually he asked questions or told him about Kerry, how pretty she was and how she'd helped him straighten himself out at school. He talked about living at the resort, knowing his dad would probably like to hear all the old stories as much as Christian or Billie seemed to. Today he just needed to be around someone who might understand.

Rick never lied to him, not like the rest. He knew it as soon as he'd seen the date marking his father's grave. He stared at the carved numerals on the stone.

Two years ago, when the rest of his classmates were sleeping through the last weeks of their sophomore U.S. history class, he'd listened with rapt attention to the teacher, a Vietnam vet himself, talk about the war in southeast Asia. For the first time in his academic career, Rod hadn't needed to concentrate or study to remember dates or places. It was as if they were being inscribed into his mind the way the date had been engraved on this stone. Dienbienphu, 1954; Gulf of Tonkin, 1964; Hue, 1968.

His enthusiasm brought him closer to his father, who for the first sixteen years of his life had been nothing more than a black-and-white snapshot, a youthful face with a grin that matched his own.

His mother and grandfather had been vague about which battle Rick had fought and died in. And now he could guess why. The date on the stone said July 16, 1975. The last American troops had left Saigon in April 1973.

So what was the big secret?

That was the one thing this stone couldn't tell him. And it was the one thing he was afraid to ask Willa, or Christian, or his mother, or anyone else. He didn't know what he feared the most, hearing another lie. Or hearing the truth.

Chicken. That's what Rick would have called her.

She stared at the photograph in her hand, the picture of her brother on the veranda of Restless Spirit. At twelve, he'd jumped off the banks along the point into Spirit Lake where the water was so deep it was black. She and Christian had watched, their hearts in their mouths until Rick's head popped out of the dark water. He'd challenged them to come in after him, and when they'd hesitated, he'd hollered, "Chicken!"

She never did jump—although she remembered that Christian had done it, once, after a few days of Rick's relentless teasing. She wasn't sure she was ready to jump in deep waters now, either.

Chicken, chicken!

When she'd gotten home after her appointment with Heidi Walker, the house was empty and dark, and she'd assumed everyone had gone to bed until she'd heard Rod's footsteps sneaking up the stairs over an hour ago. Now she sat here in the low light of her bedside lamp, going through the box that Christian had returned sometime the day before. It had sat accusingly on her nightstand, the first thing she saw when she entered the door.

She tried to imagine telling Rod about his father, picturing the scene a million ways. Sometimes he was furious with her for lying, other times he was shattered by the truth. She didn't know if she had the strength to deal with her own feelings, let alone her nephew's. Would she ever be ready to tell him the truth about Rick?

She still hadn't decided when she was interrupted by a noise downstairs. She thought it must be Christian, until she glanced at the clock to see it was nearly two in the morning. He would have left for his shift hours ago. She listened for the noise again, or for Freddie to start barking.

Rod must have taken her to bed with him again. Some watchdog. Of course, that wasn't why Christian had—

She froze. The sound came again, stealthy footsteps coming from the direction of the back stairs. She turned out her lamp and tiptoed to the doorway, straining to listen. Then she crept down the back stairs to the kitchen, wishing she would have thought of rousing Rod to accompany her.

She stood in the doorway, her eyes searching the darkness. She took a step forward and brushed against another body. Her instinctive scream was silenced by a hand covering her mouth.

"Shh. You want to wake the whole house and everyone on this side of Pinecrest besides?" It was a familiar whisper. The hand moved away.

"*Christian*. What are you doing here? I thought you were working," she said when he finally withdrew his hand.

"Not really. I'm taking Skeet's shift tomorrow morning. I got called in to help with an accident out on the highway."

"You nearly scared me to death. I didn't even hear you come downstairs. Why are you lurking around down here?" She saw that he was dressed in jeans and nothing else, his chest bare. She snapped her gaze back to his face.

"I was hungry." He grinned and lifted an eyebrow. "Did you know that Billie has a whole freezer full of food ready for next weekend?"

She tried to look stern. "That's inventory."

"There's strawberry ice cream," he said, still grinning. "Sure I can't tempt you?" He reached into the silverware drawer and waved a spoon in front of her face.

"Maybe," she said, wishing it were only the ice cream she found so tempting. "I'll try some tonight, but only because I'll be too busy next weekend to even think about strawberry ice cream."

"That's the spirit." He reached into the cupboard above the dishwasher and grabbed two bowls while Willa tried not to notice how nicely his jeans fit his behind or how his muscles stretched and bunched as he took the bowls from the shelf.

She followed him down the steps to the cellar where the new freezer stood next to a second refrigerator and a shelf filled with canned goods. Willa hoped that the resort would stay as busy all summer as it was going to be opening weekend. Between the cellar, the pantry, and the root cellar, there was enough food to feed the entire population of Pinecrest.

Christian opened the lid to reveal a horde of goodies,

from muffins and cakes to steaks and roasts. While she and Christian and Rod had concentrated their efforts on getting the cottages into shape, Billie had been shopping and baking. Willa sank down onto a step.

"I'd forgotten how much work this place is during the summer."

"Don't tell me—you thought it would all be over when we finished painting the last cottage?"

"It will be for me," she reminded him, keeping her voice light as he handed her a bowl of ice cream.

All hints of his earlier teasing mood disappeared. "You can really walk away just like that? Without knowing if Billie will be able to handle it all by herself?"

She took a spoonful of ice cream, letting it melt in her mouth before answering, "Sure." She waved her spoon toward the freezer. "Look how organized we are now. Billie will do just fine." She tried to appear unconcerned, but the ice cream treat wasn't as wickedly fun as it had sounded a few minutes ago.

"And you've figured out what you're going to do? Where you're going to live?"

"I can always go back to California, continue my career in music."

"Since you've been here, you haven't even sung 'Mary Had a Little Lamb.'"

"Maybe I just don't feel like singing while I'm here." She heard the defensive note in her voice and continued, "I'm not sure I even want to sing. I'd rather do something behind the scenes, like write music." She swallowed the last of her ice cream, all her pleasure in the post-midnight snack gone.

Christian shook his head. "You have the gift of bringing happiness to others, Willa. And not only with your voice, but with yourself."

She dropped the spoon back into the empty bowl

with a clatter. "You're pushing too hard, Christian. When are you going to realize that I don't want the same things you do?"

She stood and started back up the steps, moving quickly when she heard Christian one step behind her. The hurrying was her undoing. She stumbled on the hem of her nightgown, and a drop to the cement floor below flashed through her mind. Then she felt the solid warmth of Christian's arms around her and landed instead against his chest. The force of her fall should have knocked him off his feet, but somehow he managed to brace himself against the handrail and regain his balance.

"Thanks," she said, the word muffled against his bare skin.

"Don't mention it." His voice was strangled, and she glanced up.

"What's the matter? Did you hurt something?" she asked, thinking it was a miracle they hadn't crashed through the wooden handrail and fallen to the cement floor. Her gaze met his, and when she saw the tortured expression in his hazel eyes, understanding swept through her like a fire storm. The pain reflected in his eyes wasn't due to physical injury. He was hurting, all right, and she felt it, too.

"Willow—"

She could feel the heat of his skin through her cotton nightgown, and she could see the same heat burning in his gaze. He shifted her weight more comfortably, until she was standing on the step above him, resting against his hard chest, their eyes on an even level. There was no way she could dissemble anymore, not when his gaze seemed to see right through her.

The eyes are the window of the soul, she thought, a cliché she'd always considered silly and sappy. Tonight, she was ready to believe anything—clichés, fairy tales, even happy endings.

She was thirty-three years old and no other man had ever made her feel this way. Was she really going to throw this bliss away, ending up no better than her aunt, a dried-up old woman with no one to share her life? How many women were blessed, even for one night, with a lover this perfect?

She raised her hands to his shoulders, feeling his muscles tense and flex as he reached down to lift her into his arms. He carried her—*actually carried her*—up to his room. She held back a delighted giggle at the chivalrous gesture, marveling at his strength, running her fingers avidly over the hard muscles of his arms. He wasn't just the guy next door; he was exceptional.

And tonight, if she wanted him, he was hers.

Lord, how she wanted him. Enough to drive away all thoughts of tomorrow, enough to make eighteen years disappear. How many people had a chance to act on all the "if onlys" they thought they'd left behind? He set her gently down on the narrow bed she'd slept in as a girl.

"I used to dream of you in this bed." Her voice was little more than a whisper. She waited for him to take her back into his arms, but he sat perfectly still and watched the emotions play on her face.

He was making her decide, she realized. She wanted to be swept away, to have the choice taken out of her hands, to leave the responsibility for what happened next up to him. And he was having none of it.

He waited with the patience of a monk, with his gaze fixed on the bared skin of her shoulder where the cotton nightgown had slipped away.

Even that small gesture was enough to make her respond. She felt a flash of humiliated anger, which disappeared rapidly when he said in a voice so low she had to strain to hear, "I've wondered nearly every day for eighteen years what it would have been like."

"Yes," she admitted. "Me, too."

He reached for her hand, tracing the palm with one fingertip before lacing his fingers through hers. Her jolt of reaction surprised her. She smiled, remembering the code teenagers used to employ when talking about sex—coming up to bat, first base, and so on. She'd forgotten the power of simply touching hands, the gesture of trust, the beginning of a journey.

"I wanted you to be the first," she told him solemnly.

"I don't mind not being first," he said, "as long as I'm the last."

She swallowed, afraid to speak. He wasn't even leaving her with the illusion that this could be a simple, mutual, *temporary* distraction.

With their hands still clasped together, she leaned forward and touched her lips to his, trying to coax him out of his firm control. *First base.* The kisses became harder and deeper, until at last, he groaned and opened his mouth, letting her inside.

She'd never seduced a man before. She had always considered herself too shy, too inhibited. But there was nothing inhibited about the way she stroked the inside of his mouth with her tongue.

And still they sat on the edge of the narrow bed, inches apart, relying on clasped fingers and joined lips to carry the messages of need and desire. She had to know that he wanted her as much as she wanted him. She pleaded with her lips and tongue, making small sounds until he reached out and slipped his hand inside the gaping neckline of her gown. *Second base.*

"Make love to me," she whispered and lost all count

of bases as he answered her plea by leaning her into the pillows. The softness against her back helped her cushion his weight as he pressed himself to her, using his lips and hands to show her how much he wanted her. She responded without hesitation, as though her body remembered his from all those years ago. Yet he was different than she remembered—harder, surer, greedier.

His hands explored places where he'd touched her before, and they found new ways of touching that left her shivering with stunned reaction. It was discovery and familiarity all at once, and she didn't need to be shy of his increasingly intimate caress.

She touched him, too, stroking her hands over the smooth skin of his shoulders and back, slipping inside the waistband at the back of his jeans to press him even more tightly to her. He groaned in reaction. In moments they'd stripped away each other's clothing until they were lying inches apart on top of the narrow bed, the window above washing their bodies in pale moonlight.

The unsteady rise and fall of her rib cage gave away her sudden nervousness. How was she supposed to bring this up now? "After that talk I had with Rod . . ." she began uncertainly.

He grinned and touched a finger to her lips. "Shhh." He rolled to his side and reached into the drawer of the nightstand, the muscles of his back rippling in the moonlight.

"You're beautiful," she told him when he was facing her once again. Her gaze traveled over his powerful shoulders, the shadowy vee of hair on his chest, lower . . . She snapped her gaze back to his eyes to find him grinning at her.

"I'm supposed to say that," he told her.

"Then say it," she whispered and reached out to guide him to her.

"You're beautiful." He ended the sentence with a thrust of his hips, and she cried out with joy.

12

Willa frowned and squinted against the sunshine. It couldn't be time to get up yet—she hadn't heard a sound from downstairs, and she was still sleepy. It wasn't until she rolled over to hide from the persistent beam of light and her foot slipped from the too-small mattress that she realized she wasn't in her usual room.

She opened her eyes slowly, noticing the east window above the bed. The sun was stronger up here. She turned, searching for a clock, and her gaze settled on the digital alarm clock. It was seven-thirty. She hadn't heard breakfast sounds from downstairs because the hall doorway was closed, and an additional floor insulated her from the kitchen.

Christian must have left for his shift an hour ago at least, and she'd been sleeping so soundly she hadn't heard him. She blushed when she realized how little sleep she'd gotten. They'd made love again in the early hours of the morning, even more slowly than before. Her body was slightly sore, her skin extra-sensitive. The cotton sheets felt pleasantly rough against her bare breasts.

She reached for her nightgown, hoping no one had opened the door of her room on the second floor to see why she was so late to the breakfast table. She was still a little awed by what had happened, and she certainly wasn't ready to let everyone know she and Christian had entered a physical relationship.

She smiled secretly as she slipped the gown over her head, tossing back her hair as the nightgown settled over her shoulders. Then she looked up and saw it.

The wall.

Her breath caught as she remembered the arguments it had caused. Before her grandparents had divided it, the attic had been one large room, like a dormitory, with a small bathroom by the back staircase. The accordion divider was added for her and Rick when they grew too old to share a room. Because his half of the room was farthest from the stairs, he'd had to cross her half to get to it.

The divider was supposed to give each of them some privacy, but it seemed to Willa as she got a little older that they had even less than before—especially when she turned twelve, with all her adolescent modesty protesting at the thin wall that might be pulled open at any moment. She'd insisted every night that Rick be showered, changed, brushed, and in bed before she would even begin getting ready to go to sleep.

As she sat on the edge of the bed she wondered why Billie had never bothered to redo these rooms. With the dormer ceilings and the bright east-facing windows, this would be a perfect playroom for kids.

But there'd been no children at Restless Spirit for years. Rod hardly counted as a child. Willa thought of the big empty house and wondered how it must have felt to live here all alone, with no sounds of laughter or footsteps chasing up the stairs. How had Billie managed all this time?

She continued to stare at the divider, wondering what was on the other side. Billie had told her she was using it for storage, and she pictured rows of impersonal boxes stacked along the walls. She got to her feet and walked to the end with the latch and handle that opened the divider, pulling just far enough so she could step in. She gasped and clutched a hand to her chest. There were boxes, but only a few. The rest of the room looked exactly the way it had the day Rick left.

On one wall was a Twins pennant and a picture of Rod Carew. On another was a bulletin board covered with pictures cut out from magazines of Rick's favorite musicians: Carlos Santana, Jim Morrison, the Moody Blues. Then there were the things her parents had added while they had waited for Rick to come home—letters of commendation, newspaper articles, and a formal, unsmiling photograph of Rick in uniform.

So much of who Rick was, and it was all right here in this room, the issues of *Mad* and comic books stacked in one corner, a pair of binoculars, a shelf full of books by Jack London, even a pair of jeans folded neatly on the seat of the wooden chair by his bed. It was as though he could walk in at any moment and make himself at home.

As she continued to stare, she realized that the island had always been "home" even though they'd only spent summers and holidays here. The three houses that they'd lived in in Fargo, North Dakota, over the years were already indistinct in her memory. She and Rick used to mark the days until summer when they could come to the lake and run wild, as though they'd been raised by a pack of gray wolves instead of decent middle-class parents.

And her parents had been every bit as anxious to get here, even her mother, who hadn't grown up in this house. How could they have left it? she wondered as she sat down on the twin-sized bed with its blue corduroy spread, her legs too weak to support her any longer.

She tried to hold on to her sense of reality. The room was like a time capsule. She could almost believe that Billie had left everything as it was so that Willa would find it like this someday. But her aunt probably hadn't had the strength to put away Rick's things any more than she would have.

Why hadn't anyone taken care of this? she thought, a little angrily. It wasn't right to go off and leave everything like this. How could they have left? she asked again. This time she knew the answer.

It had taken an act of stupid violence to drive them from their home. They left because of Rick. *Damn him for ruining everything.*

She gasped, and then covered her mouth with her hand, horrified at her thoughts. A tightness settled around her rib cage, and she recognized it as suppressed tears. She felt the tightness growing until she couldn't breathe, until all she could do was take in great ragged gasps of air that turned to sobs.

She cried for what seemed like hours, until she fell asleep from sheer exhaustion. When she awoke, she knew that Billie must be looking for her. She dragged a hand through her mass of tangled hair and stood, walking through the room with her head down, trying not to look at the faces on the posters and photos, afraid they might be staring back with accusing eyes.

She stepped back through the divider into her old room, breathing easier. But her relief was short-lived. Her gaze landed on the tousled sheets of the bed she'd shared with Christian the night before.

Lord, what had she done?

Christian caught up to the activity bus just as it slowed down to drop Rod off at the end of the causeway. He waited for the bus to pull in its red stop sign before pulling up to the side of the gravel road.

"Hop in—I'll give you a ride across the causeway." Rod opened the door and clambered in. "How was the workout?"

"Okay." Rod didn't make his usual joke about how hard Coach Davis had made them run or how many pushups they'd had to do. He stared out the windshield instead.

Even this sudden moodiness couldn't deflate Christian. He had spent the day with one of the new men they'd hired for the summer, showing him around the small town, describing the routine patrol routes and warning him about the heavy summer traffic to come. But nothing had seemed routine or dull, not writing out warning tickets for moving violations or even completing the paperwork at the end of the shift he'd traded with Skeet.

He liked working days, he decided, knowing his good humor had nothing to do with the brief change in schedule. He'd thought about asking for days permanently.

Because he wanted to spend his nights with Willa.

He hid a satisfied grin and asked, "Ready to start on the boathouse this afternoon?"

"I guess. Hey, ouch." Rod swiped at his cheek, brushing away a thorny branch. He turned to look at the rose bush sitting on the small bench seat behind them, its branches heavy with deep red blooms. "What's this for?" Rod asked. "Some kind of occasion?"

"Nope." Christian hoped he wasn't as transparent as he felt. He wanted to keep this new turn of events to himself for a little while longer before shouting it from the rooftops. "Just something for a pretty lady," he said.

He could feel Rod staring, and he turned to find the boy sprouting a slow, wide grin. "Maybe I oughta try that sometime."

"Still seeing Kerry Songstad?"

"Yeah. Sort of. She's still a little mad about the fight with Jerry Miller. I might have to get her roses or something." He was silent again, hunched back into the corner of the cab. Christian smiled inwardly as they pulled into the sweeping drive.

By the time he'd unloaded the rose bush, taking care not to knock off any buds or petals, Rod was already in the kitchen, with Freddie barking excitedly, and Billie taking cookies off a baking sheet to cool. He hesitated in the doorway, doing what he could to shield the rose bush from view until he spotted Willa.

She walked through the doorway from the hall, and the look on her face froze his smile in place.

He'd lost.

It was an achingly public moment, with Rod's gaze going from Christian to Willa and back, and Billie looking on sympathetically. Even the dog ceased barking for a few seconds. Willa fled from the room, her expression telling him clearly that she wasn't at all happy about what happened the night before.

Then Christian recovered, pasted a grin on his face, and stepped inside the kitchen, going over to give Billie a peck on the cheek.

"This is for fixing my favorite dinner," he said, presenting her with the rose bush.

"Oh my." She stopped and wiped her hands on a dish-towel before reaching out and brushing one of the rich blooms with her bent finger. She smiled up at him, her blue eyes watery. "No one's given me roses in over forty years. Thank you, my dear."

Christian was grateful for the way Billie pretended not to know the rose bush wasn't meant for her. "I don't know if it'll live through the winter," he said apologetically.

"We'll plant it on the south side of the veranda. It's warmer there." She reached out and covered his hand with hers. "Don't worry, once something is planted here, it takes root."

The final week before opening day had started off with a frantic blur of activity. Willa needn't have wasted so much time worrying about facing Christian again—they were never alone. He and Rod spent most of their spare time working on the boathouse, and she really only saw him at mealtimes. The odd thing was, as much as she dreaded their next encounter, she wanted to get it over with. There were too many loose ends holding her here at Restless Spirit.

Every time the phone rang, like it did this Tuesday morning, she expected it to be another last-minute guest, or Heidi Walker calling to ask about her "talk" with Rod—something she still hadn't found the nerve to do.

The last thing she expected as she picked up the receiver was a job offer.

The voice on the other end of the line belonged to Cal Smith, her agent, who'd called to tell her that he had a possible contract for her. Willa didn't know how to react. A cosmetics company had listened to her perfume ad and loved it. Would she consider becoming their "voice" for a series of television commercials introducing a new product line?

The front door opened and closed, and she turned to see Christian standing there watching her. Her gaze met his with a jolt of awareness, and as impossible as it might be, she felt he'd already guessed who she was talking to. She heard herself telling Cal, "It sounds like a terrific opportunity, but I'll need some time to think about it. I'm not sure that's what I want to do anymore."

"Honey, you're lucky they're not asking you to audition. I can't sit on this forever. I've got other clients, you know. And you haven't done any work in months."

"I know, I know. I promise I'll call you next week." She hung up the receiver, staring at Christian. Was the man a mind reader? Before he could comment on her indecision about working, Rod tromped into the hallway, balancing a bag of groceries in either arm.

"Hey, somebody give me a hand, will ya?"

Christian turned to help him, and the spell was broken. Somehow, between his unpredictable working schedule and all the last-minute efforts on the resort, she made it through the remainder of the week without being alone with him again.

Thursday night, some of the guests began to arrive. Willa watched from her bedroom window as carload after carload pulled into the driveway, people hoping to get an early start on one of the most important dates on the Minnesota calendar. Next weekend the rest of the country celebrated the Memorial Day holiday with an extra day off, but no one who'd sat through a long northern winter wanted to wait that long.

After the phone call from Cal she'd been too agitated to concentrate on anything but the most menial of tasks. Even Rod seemed to be filled with nervous energy. He was moody and excitable, and Willa used his unsettled mood as an excuse to avoid telling him about Rick. She'd wait until all the excitement was over before showing him the letters.

They made it through Friday night without incident, serving supper family-style in the dining room and inviting any guests who were interested to join the family afterward in the living room. Willa sat and observed, thinking it was almost as she remembered: the small table by the window offered guests a quiet spot to play checkers or chess, and extra chairs in the living room provided plenty of space for television-watching or chatting. But something didn't seem quite right, and she realized she missed Grandpa Johann sitting by the fireplace telling his tales. Before she lapsed into melancholy nostalgia, one of the guests—a middle-aged woman whose husband had gone to bed early so that he could wake up at dawn to fish—engaged her in pleasant conversation.

Saturday morning, as Willa came downstairs to help Billie serve breakfast, she heard Christian's teasing voice.

"He said he came here to look at birds, Billie, but I think he was looking at you."

"Oh, stop it now. Weldon McNeil is an old man, not a teenager."

"Didn't you say he was two years younger than you?" Rod asked.

Billie looked relieved to see Willa walk in, and quickly filled her in on their vacancy status.

"The last car rolled in at seven this morning. You must have been in the shower," Billie told her. "We've only got two cottages left empty, and chances are someone will come along to rent another one by supper tonight."

"That's a great start to the summer," Willa said, trying to share in her aunt's pleasure. But she couldn't seem to shake the sadness that had stolen over her during the last few days. She felt detached from all the excitement over the resort's first weekend, as though she'd already said goodbye.

She joined the others at the kitchen table, where the family ate their breakfast. There was a buffet in the dining room for the guests, so they could eat whenever they wanted. All Billie or Willa needed to do was check the large coffee urn occasionally, keep the platters and baskets filled with food, and clear away dirty dishes. For those who stayed at Restless Spirit, breakfast was a leisurely meal, but here inside the kitchen it was like a chief-of-staff briefing, with everyone speaking at once.

"I saw another ad for a boat in the classifieds. I thought we should call and see what they're asking."

"Brenda's taking time off from the café to come in and help with meals."

"There's a soft spot off the edge of the causeway. I'm going out later to bolster it up with some rocks."

So when Rod looked up from his corn flakes and asked innocently, "What's a lunker?" it was a moment before anyone reacted.

Christian hooted with laughter, Billie chuckled, and Willa wanted to hug her nephew for unintentionally defusing the nervous tension that surrounded them all.

"A lunker's a great catch," Christian said. "You must have overheard some of the guests talking at supper last night."

"Nope. I heard one screaming 'lunker' from somewhere out in the middle of the lake. I thought it meant 'abandon ship.'"

They laughed again, and Christian's gaze settled on Willa. Her breath caught in her throat at his expression. When he smiled like that, only a department store mannequin could keep from reacting. She looked away.

"I think we'd better take this boy fishing. What do you say, Willa?"

"There's too much to do. You go. I'll stay and help Billie with the breakfast dishes and dinner."

"Nonsense," Billie argued. "We did most of the cooking yesterday, and only a couple of the guests will take the time to eat in here. The rest of them asked for sandwiches to carry out on the lake with them. You go ahead and take this afternoon off and enjoy yourself before—"

Before leaving for Los Angeles. Billie didn't finish her sentence, but they all knew what she'd been about to say. Tension once again gripped the small group.

Willa broke the silence. "You're the one who should take some time off, Billie. It's going to be a long summer."

"I've got Brenda to help me," she replied staunchly. "She'll be here until after dinner. Besides, I'm used to it."

"And isn't Weldon McNeil one of the guests who's staying in for lunch?" Christian inquired, his eyebrows lifting.

This was the second time she'd heard them talking about this man in connection with Billie. Willa stared at her aunt in puzzlement. "Who's Weldon McNeil?"

"Oh, just some old man," Billie said. "He brought his great-grandson with him so the boy could see the place where he used to visit every summer. The McNeils have been coming here ever since Johann opened the resort in '37. Maybe you remember them?"

"No. I don't." She looked at Christian for an explanation, but he was concentrating on his coffee mug. Once again, she felt like an outsider, but she could hardly complain. After all, it was what she wanted. "I'm afraid I don't have a fishing license," she said as a final excuse.

"I took care of all that," Christian countered. "We've all got licenses." He grinned at her over the rim of his mug. "We can't very well run a fishing resort if we can't fish, right?"

"Come on, Willa," Rod pleaded. "Let's go. I've never even been out on the lake." His blue eyes were wide and earnest, with no trace of the sullen look she'd seen off and on during the past week.

"All right," she agreed, a small bubble of excitement

building inside her despite her misgivings. She herself hadn't been out on the lake since she was fifteen.

She immediately regretted thinking of it, for it reminded her of the first time that summer when she'd been on the water. She and Christian had met in the boathouse after supper and taken one of the rowboats out to the middle of the lake to watch the sun set. It was one of her first days back at Pinecrest since Rick was released from the VA hospital in San Francisco, and it was the first inkling she'd had that things were going to be different between her and her childhood pal from then on. They'd spent the evening talking and filling each other in on the months they'd spent apart, pointing out falling stars and leaping fish, and when they'd returned to the boathouse, Christian had kissed her for the first time.

Oh, they'd kissed before, but those were childhood games. That night was the first time he'd kissed her as though she was grown up, and the memory of it still had the power to move her.

She shoved back her chair, afraid to look at him. Surely he couldn't remember an incident that occurred so long ago. "I'll just go change into my old cutoffs," she said before escaping upstairs.

She decided that her white shirt would be cool enough if she rolled up the sleeves and tied it at the waist. She still had plenty of time, and she delayed by pulling her suitcases out from the back of the closet. She may as well start deciding what she was going to take with her and what she was going to leave behind.

When she heard Rod and Christian crossing the lawn to the boathouse, she went outside to meet them. The moment she opened the door of the boathouse and saw Christian standing by the dock waiting for her, she knew he remembered their first kiss every bit as well as she did. His gaze scanned her legs, lingering on the strip of bare skin revealed by the bottom edges of her blouse. Rod could have been invisible, for all his clattering and banging around as he loaded the boat with tackle.

"Shouldn't we leave the boat for the guests?" she asked, her voice husky despite her determination to control her reactions when he was around.

Christian shook his head. "Everyone who was planning to go out fishing this morning is already on the lake. We can take this one."

He helped her into the small boat, and her hand reached out to grab his shoulder for support as the boat bobbed gently at her weight. She tried to forget the brief touch as Christian and Rod climbed in.

The loud roar of the outboard motor disturbed the peaceful morning, and she winced as they skimmed through the open doors onto the lake.

The noise was forgotten as they headed farther out. The slightly fishy, gassy odor of the boathouse was replaced by cool, fresh air, and the wind pulled her hair back from her face. The lake was a pure deep blue dotted with colorful boats of all sizes from one shore to the other.

"Wow, I've never seen so many boats. It looks like a convention," Rod shouted over the noisy motor. "Where are we going?" he asked as Christian headed around to the rear of the island, where it almost touched the mainland, where he cut back on the throttle.

"Our secret walleye hole. Remember?" He looked at Willa.

Oh, yes, she remembered. As children they used to anchor there for hours at a time, and it was still vivid in her mind—the sound of the waves lapping against the sides of the boat, the feel of sunshine against her bare skin, the smell of water and fish and wild grass.

As they put-putted into the sheltered area and found it deserted, as usual, all those old sensations returned. She could almost hear childish laughter carrying on the breeze, only to be drowned out by one of Rick's shouted dares.

She stared into the thickly wooded State Forest, her eyes suddenly damp from more than the breeze coming off the water. Rod was too excited to notice her efforts to compose herself, and if Christian witnessed her struggle with her emotions, he didn't say anything. His attention seemed to be focused on letting out the anchor and unpacking their equipment.

She watched out of the corner of her eye as he helped Rod with the fishing gear, showing him how to bait a hook and cast before turning to his own preparations. Her pensiveness disappeared, and she reached for the rod and reel she'd borrowed from her aunt. Christian's elaborate preparations were like a ritual, and it was all she could do to keep from laughing out loud at his concentration.

"Hey, how'd you do it so fast, Willa?" Rod asked in amazement. Her line was already over the edge of the boat and into the water, the red-and-white bobber marking her place.

Christian guffawed, and a warm flush that had nothing to do with the sun crept from her neckline to her cheeks. "She never baits her hook," he told Rod.

"But how do you catch anything that way?"

"That's the whole point. She doesn't *want* to catch anything."

Rod looked at her as though she was crazy. Willa felt a smile steal over her lips, and soon she was laughing, too.

"It's because of your father," Christian explained once the laughter had died down. "One time when the three of us were out here—I suppose Rick was about thirteen and Willa eight—he landed the ugliest, slimiest Northern I've ever seen."

Rod's expression was comic as he glanced toward the line stretching into the water in front of him, and Willa had to hold back another laugh at his obvious distaste.

"Rick tried to get it off the hook," Christian continued, "but it kept sliding out of his hands. He finally got a grip on it and reached for the hook, but his hand slipped, and he sliced his thumb open on one of the gills."

"Ugh. Did it bleed?"

"Everywhere. Willa hasn't caught a fish since, although she sometimes pretends to be fishing."

"That's not true," she protested.

"Yeah, but whenever you caught one, who had to take it off the hook for you?" he teased, his eyes sparkling with laughter. For a moment she was filled with the sense of belonging she'd been missing. Rod's voice took it away again.

"My father was pretty fun to be around, huh?"

"He was the best," Christian replied. He launched into a series of tales about the escapades Rick had gotten them into, from the dive off the banks nearby, to the time he'd taken them out for a drive—at age ten. It had taken the sheriff's department all afternoon to find her grandmother's car. "The A&W drive-in was the *first* place they should have looked," Christian said, shaking his head.

Willa laughed, reliving the good times through Rod's obvious delight. It wasn't often that she could think of her brother without feeling a pang, and she was grateful to Christian for reminding her of all the fun and laughter they'd had as children. *This* was why she came back.

Hours later, with an ice chest half full of crappies and one prized walleye, they headed back to the island, sunburned, windblown, and pleasantly tired. Willa helped Christian pull up the anchor, but she nearly let the rope slip from her fingers when Rod asked out of the blue, "Why did my father stay in Vietnam after the war?"

Willa felt as though the bottom had dropped out of the boat, leaving her sinking helplessly. She shot a desperate look at Christian, trying to tell him with her eyes that she couldn't talk about this. Not now, not after the morning had passed so pleasantly. "I guess he felt he was doing his duty for his country, Rod," she said, trying not to see the disappointment that crossed Christian's features.

Rod looked as though he wanted to ask another question, but she forestalled him. "Look." She pointed as the house came into view around the curve of the island. "Billie's walking with someone."

"It's that Weldon McNeil guy. Do you really think he's got the hots for her?" Rod asked Christian as the elderly pair disappeared through the front door.

Willa held her breath, hoping the question would occupy Rod until they'd moored the boat at its place inside the boathouse. Christian handed the fishing tackle to Rod and said, "Get this stuff into the house."

The three of them stepped outside together, but Christian placed a hand over her arm to delay her as her nephew walked ahead. As soon as Rod was out of earshot, he turned to Willa. "Why didn't you tell him? It was the perfect opportunity."

"I couldn't do it."

He ran an impatient hand through his dark hair. "Willa, if you don't tell that boy, I will."

"You promised."

"I never promised. I said I would try. Besides, what are promises to you anyway?"

She wrenched her arm from Christian's grasp, knowing

she should simply walk away now that she was free. But she couldn't let his comment go by. "I never made you any promises. On the contrary."

"What we did a week ago *was* a promise, Willa. We just didn't say the words." She felt panic building inside her until he added, "We could be a family together— you, me, Billie, and Rod."

She was tempted in spite of herself by the picture his words brought up. Stay here at Restless Spirit? No, the responsibility was too much, the chance of failure too high. She'd lost one marriage already; she couldn't bear to lose again. She understood completely what Rick had written in his last letter about it being easier not to make friends anymore. He'd surrendered.

"Stay with us, Willa."

It was like hearing a voice from an opposite shore. Christian pulled her unresistingly toward him, and she felt his arms go round her. She didn't pull away, not even when he lowered his head and covered her mouth with his. The kiss was another taste of the tender passion he'd shown the night they made love, and she could feel her will slipping.

"No." She pulled away, afraid to slip any further. "I can't. I'm sorry."

She walked up the dock toward the house, thankful that for the moment, at least, all the guests seemed to be out on the lake and that Billie was inside the house. No one had witnessed that little scene.

Her footsteps slowed as she saw a figure hunched over a shovel at the far end of Billie's huge garden. She relaxed when she recognized Kevin. He looked at her curiously, and she waved, keeping her back straight and chin high as she walked toward the house.

Billie dropped the curtain before Willa could look up and spot her standing by the front parlor window. It had been easy enough to figure out what had occurred between Willa and Christian a few moments ago as they stood near the boathouse. She had refused him. Billie's attention wandered, and for a minute, she couldn't hear what her guest was saying.

". . . and I thought you might want to join us. If you're not busy, that is?"

She turned to stare at Weldon McNeil. The seventy-four-year-old gentleman and his great-grandson, the only guests who hadn't taken to the lake to fish, had joined her in the parlor for midmorning coffee and stayed while she packed picnic lunches and arranged the cold buffet in the dining room. Afterward Weldon had stuck to her like a burr while she did her chores and his great-grandson played a handheld electronic game that made the most annoying bleeps and beeps.

A retired high school biology teacher, Weldon hadn't come here to fish, as he repeatedly reminded Billie whenever she suggested that he borrow one of the cane poles they kept on hand for those who had come to the resort unprepared. He was here to bird-watch. Or at least that's what he'd told her, even though the light in his gray eyes seemed to dance and twinkle every time he looked her way, making her feel like a snowy white egret or a giant crane.

"I'm sorry. What did you say?" she asked, feeling a bit faint. It had been a busy week, and now this.

"I asked if you'd like to go with us on a little nature hike in the woods. We could take our lunch like everyone else and have a picnic. Unless you have too much work to do?"

Billie considered Weldon's invitation. She'd finished with everything she needed to do here, and Willa and

Brenda would help with supper when the time came. Right now, she felt unaccountably tired, a bit depressed even. Perhaps a trek through the woods would do her some good. She might be two years older than Weldon's seventy-four, but she could still walk like a seventeen-year-old. The great-grandson, Mickey or Mitchell or something like that, ten years old last week according to Weldon, eyed her doubtfully, as though he didn't believe anyone so old could manage to totter over to her favorite chair.

"I'd be delighted to join you," she said.

But her attention was briefly diverted once again as Willa slammed through the front door and ran up the staircase. She stared after her niece helplessly.

You catch 'em, you clean 'em had been the rule at Restless Spirit for long as Christian could remember. So why, he wondered, had he ended up out here behind the boathouse all by himself when at least half these fish were Rod's?

He knew better than to expect Willa to come out of the house and give him a hand. Hell, she was probably halfway to Los Angeles by now. Once again, he'd pushed her too hard, and she'd reacted by running.

"Excuse me." Christian looked up to see a heavy-set middle-aged man. He recognized him as one of the guests from Number Three. The man was red with exertion, and sweat soaked the collar of his polo shirt.

Christian leaned over to rinse his hands in a nearby bucket of water, then stood. "Can I help you?"

"You sure can. I ran out of gas and had to walk back here." He bent to scratch a red swollen mosquito bite inches below the hem of his plaid Bermuda shorts. "I left my boat on shore. If I had a gas can . . ." His plea trailed off as he reached to scratch again.

Christian tried not to grin at the man's predicament. After all, this guy had just provided him with a surefire way to forget about Willa for the next hour at least. Not to mention a hand with the rest of the fish.

"I'll go get a gas can and fill it." He headed for the boathouse, then turned back to the man. "You can finish up with those fish while you're waiting."

"Sure." He agreed eagerly enough, but as Christian ducked into the boathouse door, he caught a grimace on the man's red face.

While the guest—who'd introduced himself as Bob Johnson—scaled the fish, Christian filled a gallon-sized can with fuel from the tank sitting by the boathouse and loaded it onto the bed of his pickup. He could have just handed Bob the fuel and let him walk back to his boat, but he decided that wouldn't be at all neighborly. And maybe, if he drove slowly enough, he could stretch out the task for another hour or so.

He was counting in hours now, he thought grimly as he negotiated the causeway. Bob kept up a steady stream of chatter that Christian barely listened to, his thoughts taking up most of his attention. When Willa first arrived, he'd measured time in terms of months. Three months and she would be gone. Then he'd started counting by weeks, then days. Now he was counting hours.

His time had almost run out. She'd told Billie that she'd stay through Memorial Day weekend and the resort's Grand Opening, but he knew she'd flee if he pressed her any harder.

He'd already pressed for physical intimacy without waiting for her emotions to catch up. He was a fool to think that making love would change anything for her, even though it sure as hell changed things for him. He couldn't let her walk out of his life one more time, he knew that now. But he also knew that if he succeeded in holding her here, she would resent him for the rest of her life.

But giving up just wasn't an option. How could he get through to her, get her to realize for herself that she belonged here with him?

Bob pointed through the window, successfully capturing Christian's attention at last. "It's right up ahead, around that corner and through the trees down toward the lake."

Christian turned where indicated and drove as far as he could on the dirt track. "This is the end of the line."

Bob's face was crestfallen. "The boat's at least another half a mile from here. Can't you go any further?"

"Nope." His duty done, he could turn the truck around and head back to Restless Spirit. Or he could find a way to kill some more time. He looked over at the guest, who was staring morosely out the window at the narrow dirt track beyond the truck's front wheels. "I'll go with you," Christian offered.

This should take another thirty minutes at least.

Rod lay sprawled across the bed in front of his second-floor window, scratching idly at a mosquito bite and watching everyone leave. Billie took off for the woods with some old man and a kid, Willa disappeared somewhere in her car, and Kerry's mother got into her blue Firebird and drove back to town. Before that, he'd seen Christian load a gas can onto a truck and head off with one of the guests from North Dakota. He almost ran down the stairs and asked if he could go along, but he suspected the outing might entail more mosquitoes.

The truth was, he didn't feel like doing anything. He

wondered how long he could loaf before someone asked him to carry a box up from the cellar or wash a sink full of pots and pans. But he started to get hungry, and remembered he hadn't eaten since breakfast. Too embarrassed to admit to Willa and Christian that the smell of fish had made him slightly sick, he'd headed straight for his room before Christian offered to show him how to gut and clean their catch. *Ugh.* He hoped Billie had fixed something to eat besides fish.

He got up and wandered downstairs, relieved at the sight of the sandwiches in the refrigerator. He grabbed two. Carrying a sandwich in each hand and gripping a can of soda pop under his arm, he headed for the veranda to eat. No sense in getting any dishes dirty, he thought, watching the crumbs drop to the floorboards. He used the toe of his sneaker to shove them down between the cracks, watching an ant go after the ones he missed.

He had just finished eating and was thinking about wandering into the woods himself, when he heard the loud thump-thump of a car stereo's woofers. He looked toward the causeway, shading his eyes to see who was disturbing the peaceful afternoon. The sandwiches turned to lumps in his stomach when he recognized Jerry Miller's convertible. The top was down, and the backseat spilled over with Jerry's cohorts. The car came to a noisy halt in front of the house.

"What are you guys doing here?" he asked, standing and crossing his arms in front of his chest.

"We've been driving around all morning, checking it out," Dean said. "The town's pretty lively today."

Jerry leaned back in his seat, his arms folded behind his head. "We thought you might want to come with us. There's a party tonight in the old gravel pit east of town. How about it?"

"Maybe." Rod mistrusted Jerry's sudden friendliness. No doubt the invitation was some kind of setup. Still, he hated to admit that he was going to be here at the resort, probably carrying dirty dishes back into the kitchen or refilling water glasses. "I thought I told you not to come around here anymore."

"Hey, man. We're only looking around." Jerry grinned and got out of the car, and Rod could see a baseball bat resting against the front seat. "Kerry's gonna be there. Her old lady's working here tonight, so I'm giving her and Nancy a ride."

A shaft of jealousy pierced him. Kerry had hardly spoken to him since the fight. He shrugged, as if it was no big deal. "I think you guys better leave."

Jerry's eyes narrowed. "Want to have another round, Dane? Maybe you'll get expelled this time or sent up for violating parole."

"I'm not on parole," Rod said. "And school's done in a week. They can't do anything to me after that."

"Whooo, I'm scared. How about you guys?" The group of boys laughed on cue and, one by one, hopped out of the car, scattering in different directions. Rod tried not to let his alarm show. He was thinking fast, hoping for a way out of this one when he heard the rumble of Christian's pickup returning across the causeway.

"You guys better leave now," he said again.

Jerry looked over his shoulder and spotted Christian's advancing truck. "It's the cop," he said, and the boys scrambled back into the Mustang. They pulled away with a spray of gravel just as Christian pulled up.

He parked the pickup and climbed out, watching the car drive away before joining Rod on the veranda.

"Trouble?"

"Nah, nothing I can't handle," Rod said. *Tell him,* an

inner voice insisted. He glanced at Christian's forbidding expression, and the words stuck in his throat. He could handle it on his own, he assured himself. After all, he owed his loyalty to no one.

Willa stayed away as long as she dared. She spent the afternoon in her car, driving around the lakes and through other small towns like Pinecrest—La Prairie, Cohasset, Deer River. But the sense of freedom she was longing for didn't come.

She felt like a frightened animal watching the jaws of a trap closing over her . The suitcases were still sitting in her room, but she couldn't leave yet, not while Rod was still in school and the Grand Opening still lay ahead. Rod needed her, Billie needed her, and Christian . . . Oh, God, Christian. *She* needed *him.*

She pushed the thought from her mind, even as she turned the car around and headed back to Pinecrest. When she arrived at the house, the kitchen was bustling with supper preparations. Billie was in and out of the kitchen with plates and bowls of food, and Brenda had organized an assembly line with Rod in the middle, refilling platters of fried fish. He looked up at Willa accusingly. If she hadn't felt so guilty, she might have started laughing. She dropped her purse in a corner of the pantry and touched Rod on the arm.

"I'll take over," she told him quietly.

There wasn't time for discussion as they kept the food moving from kitchen to dining room: fried fish, baked potatoes, green beans, corn, salad. Finally, they switched over to cutting large wedges of rhubarb pie, and the pace slowed.

While Willa made another huge pot of coffee, Billie

herded everyone who didn't want to return to their cottages into the living room or parlor. Willa could hear the piano as she gathered up the dirty linen from the dining room. She dropped it in a pile inside the cellar door and made her way for the staircase, hoping to slip upstairs undisturbed, but Billie spotted her through the open doorway and gestured her inside the parlor.

"Take over for me, would you, while I go refill the coffee."

"Oh, but—" Her aunt slipped away before she could complete the protest. She entered the parlor, seeing the expectant faces scattered throughout the two large downstairs rooms. She supposed she could have made some sort of excuse, but a half-remembered sense of confidence and excitement stole over her, and she sat down at the piano.

"Do you know 'Stardust'?" one of the guests called out. Willa searched her memory, playing the first few chords haltingly until the song came back to her. Scattered applause greeted the last note. Willa looked around, wondering what was taking Billie so long, before starting another Hoagy Carmichael tune. She followed that one with another, the notes coming easier now. She barely noticed her aunt come and sit at her elbow until Billie's strong contralto began singing the verses.

After the applause died down, Billie asked Willa to play another ballad from the forties, and this time Weldon McNeil harmonized with Billie. Some of the other guests added their voices, reluctantly at first, but with growing enthusiasm. Rod came down the stairs, curious, with Freddie at his heels. When the dog joined in the chorus with a discordant howl, everyone broke into laughter, then sang even louder, the last of their inhibitions gone.

Willa forgot her reluctance and joined in a rollicking version of Billie's favorite, "A Fine Romance," her clear voice carrying above the others. One by one, the other singers dropped away, until the last notes were hers alone. For a moment, silence filled the room. Then Weldon McNeil pronounced a hearty "Brava," his schoolteacher's voice resounding throughout the adjoining rooms. Willa smiled at him, her joy spilling over. She'd found her music again, and in the least expected place—a living room and parlor full of fishing enthusiasts and a bird-watcher.

"Sing another one," a dark-haired woman said.

"Hey, Billie," someone teased, "How about playing some Billie Holiday?"

Billie played the first notes of "Them There Eyes," and Willa sang, hamming up the lyrics and enjoying the guests' reaction. The feeling of freedom that Willa had been searching for all afternoon hit her now full force as she lost herself in the music.

She turned and saw Christian leaning in the doorway. For a moment, her voice faltered. Then, with a wicked smile and a toss of her red hair, she spun around on the piano bench and sang to him while Billie played with a flourish.

The guests loved it, their giggles and smiles egging her on, and she had the immense satisfaction of seeing Christian's features color with a faint hint of red. Then everyone else faded into the background until it was only the two of them. The song ended and her audience showed their appreciation by clapping and calling for more.

"Enough," she said, laughing, her gaze going to Christian, who was walking toward her with a deliber-ate tread. She felt a thrill of anticipation and won-dered if she should have played with fire that way. He looked dangerously aroused and amused at the same time, and she waited breathlessly for him to reach her side.

But whatever he'd intended to do would remain a mystery, as an unearthly shriek split the air.

13

Several of the guests rushed to the windows to see where the eerie noise was coming from, while others sat frozen in their chairs, their expressions horrified. Christian ran for the door, voices behind him rising in excitement as old hands filled in first-timers with snatches of Johann's ghost tales. Rod was close at his heels, turning to look as one of the guests shouted.

"Look!" Bob Johnson—the man Christian had helped earlier—pointed out the living room window.

"Oh, my! It's a ghost," an older woman exclaimed.

The voices grew fainter as Christian ran around the broad veranda that circled the house, heading toward the glowing light coming from the edge of the trees. "Stay close," he told Rod.

The boy's face was white and still, and Christian felt a flicker of surprise at Rod's fearful reaction to this obvious hoax. Although he had to admit that the sound effects *were* convincing—horrible, pulsing noises that seemed to come from every direction. In the distance, underneath a broad-trunked oak, a pale white figure stood hunched over a shovel.

A female voice from inside the house carried clearly through the screen window to Christian's ears. "It's him. It's Hulbert!"

Christian leaped over the veranda rail and headed for the apparition, which seemed unaware of his approach. Then, as he crashed through the underbrush, the apparition disappeared, its wails cut off abruptly. But not before he'd spotted a dark shadow—this time definitely not a ghost—running through the trees.

"We're not going to follow, are we?" Rod was still pale, although the sickly shade of white could have been a trick of the moonlight.

"No. I have a feeling we'll find our ghost right here."

He headed deeper into the brush, holding branches out of the way so that Rod could follow. At last he found what he was looking for—a small generator tucked underneath a leafy bush. A cord led from the contraption, and he ran his hands down its length, using it to guide him to a vee in a tree trunk about five feet above the ground.

"It's a movie camera," Rod said, his voice awed.

"A projector," Christian corrected. "And our ghost. Apparently the person operating it left in such a hurry that he didn't have time to take his equipment along. We'll probably find a couple speakers in the morning, when it's easier to see."

They retrieved the things they could find and headed back for the house. Christian could see the guests milling around on the veranda, craning their necks to see.

He walked into the clearing holding up the generator and gesturing toward the projector in Rod's hands. "Here's our ghost," he said.

Embarrassed laughter and scattered applause greeted

his announcement. "Very clever," someone said. "Quite something," another agreed.

The guests wandered off, some of them disappointed that they hadn't seen a real ghost, others laughing and congratulating Billie on a fine end to an entertaining evening. She took the compliments in stride, a smug smile lingering about the corners of her mouth.

"You didn't, did you?" Christian overheard Willa ask her aunt as he joined the informal receiving line.

"No, but don't tell anyone," Billie said through her smile, accepting another compliment on the "interesting" entertainment. "It was a damned fine idea."

When the last guest had gone, Christian turned to Billie and explained how the ghost had appeared. "The projector was hooked up to a small generator near the garden. The culprit used the trunk of the oak tree as a screen."

"But who would have—"

"I think I know," Christian said. "Mattie Quinlan."

"*Mattie?*" Billie's voice was shocked.

"Kevin admitted to me that he had helped Mattie try to frighten you away before. But not with the fires," he added quickly. "We still don't know who is responsible for those."

"The ghost was Kevin," Willa said, her voice rising with excitement. "I saw him standing by the garden with a shovel earlier today, and he looked just like that."

"But surely he couldn't have set up this electronic marvel on his own, and goodness knows Mattie can't do much more than plug in a toaster," Billie objected.

"Kevin is pretty good with mechanical things," Rod said, breaking his long silence. "He could probably figure out electronic equipment, too."

"He might have had some help," Christian said, staring at Rod, who looked away at the scrutiny. "What do you think, Rod? Ever set up something like this in school?"

Rod shrugged. "Film class is for jokers." He turned to Billie and said, "I'm tired. If you don't need any help, I'm going to bed."

"Brenda did most of the cleaning up before she went home, but we still have a few things to do," Willa said.

"I've got a half hour before my shift starts," Christian told her. "Let Rod recover. There will be plenty of cleaning to do tomorrow after the guests start going home."

Rod wished them a hasty goodnight, as though he couldn't wait to get away. Christian stared after him, wondering what was eating at the boy until Billie pulled him into the kitchen and put him to work wrapping silverware in napkins in preparation for Sunday breakfast.

"I suppose Mattie thought the guests would go running for home," Willa said as she arranged the coffee cart so the large-capacity urn would be ready to plug in at 6:00 A.M.

"It certainly didn't have quite the effect she hoped for, did it?" Billie said with a satisfied smile.

Christian paused and stared at her, wondering for a moment if Willa's suspicions had been on target, and if Billie, not her nemesis, had planned this whole thing. After all it was the vandalism—Billie's "hauntings"—that had lured him here, and Willa, too.

He watched Billie descend the cellar steps, the picture of elderly innocence with her white cloud of hair and sensible shoes. A harmless little old lady? Hell, no, he thought. Billie was as feisty as a young mule. But would she stoop to tricks to get what she wanted?

"The ghost was quite a hit," Willa said. He turned, his speculations forgotten at the sight of her bending to reach into the linens drawer, her hair falling around her face.

"So were you," he said. She glanced up and colored, and he felt avenged for the torment she'd put him through in front of that crowd tonight. "You really had the crowd going." He added silently, *me too.* A vivid picture of her singing to him replayed in his mind. He'd been about to jump out of his skin, hearing her husky voice tease him that way.

"I can't resist a live audience, I guess," she said with a lightness he knew was forced.

"You resisted for three years. Ever since Darryl Decker drove his Porsche into that brick wall." She stared at him, her eyes wide with shock. "Oh, I knew," he said softly.

They turned at Billie's footsteps. She appeared in the doorway to the cellar and warned him, "You'd better keep an eye on the time. You're going to be late."

He glanced at his watch. "So I am. I'll call Skeet and warn him."

Willa caught up with him as he reached the hall phone. "Are you going to tell him about Mattie and Kevin?" Concern showed in her eyes, and he wondered how he could have ever believed she was a selfish, spoiled brat.

"I don't think so. This latest prank was pretty harmless. I'm not even sure it's connected to the other incidents, but I'll have a talk with Kevin myself," he promised, his gaze running over her hair, remembering how it felt in his hands. He wanted nothing more than to kiss her senseless and carry her up to bed.

Stop pushing, he reminded himself. His voice was harsh when he said, "We'd still better be prepared for something worse." He said an abrupt goodnight and strode out the door before all his good intentions disappeared.

When Rod finally heard Christian's pickup leave the island, he let out the breath he'd been holding. Could Kevin have put together that contraption by himself? If not, he knew who had helped him. While the generator might have been something anyone around the lake kept in case of a power outage, the projector looked suspiciously like some of the school's AV equipment.

Damn it, he'd warned those guys to lay off. He felt a frustrated dampness around his eyes, which he quickly wiped away. Should he talk to Jerry again? Or should he tell Christian, which would mean admitting that he'd known all this time who the guilty parties were?

The prank hadn't hurt anyone. In fact, Billie had seemed kind of tickled. The guests sure got a kick out of it, and he probably would have, too, if it weren't for the secret he'd been keeping for months now. At first it hadn't mattered because he'd learned not to care what happened to anybody else. He'd always had enough to worry about just trying to look out for himself. But he cared now, and he wasn't going to stand around and watch while Jerry and his buddies got pleasure out of hurting Billie.

Jerry Miller needed a lesson. He stared at the glowing red numbers on his digital alarm clock. It was after eleven. He wondered if the party was still going on at the old gravel pit. He could sneak out. He'd done it before—the night he and Kerry had gone out for the first time, and the time he'd had to wait until after his parents left before he could visit the cemetery. A spreading maple tree stood less than ten feet away from his window, and one of its branches came within inches of the veranda roof.

He turned and looked out the window, trying to see beyond the darkness. The gravel pit was a long way from school property. No one could bust him for fighting there.

Except Christian.

His bravado slowly ebbed. What if somebody called the cops? There was a housing development less than a half mile from the old pit—someone was bound to hear them. He lay back against the pillows, paralyzed with indecision and doubt.

Wimp, he said to himself, wondering what his father would have done in this situation. Probably smash Jerry Miller into the next century. He turned over and stared at the photo tucked into the frame by his bed. He couldn't make it out in the darkness, but his mind recalled perfectly the close-fitting uniform and broad shoulders. His dad was a fucking hero, and he was just another wimp.

Billie Mitterhauser watched her niece rub absently at a sunburned shoulder before she turned back to the dishwasher. Brenda had taken care of most of the dishes before leaving tonight, but the clean ones were still inside that contraption. Between rinsing and loading, then unloading and putting away, she often felt that the new dishwasher was more trouble than it was worth.

"I'll finish putting these away," Willa told her, taking a plate from Billie's hand. "You go on up to bed."

Billie decided not to put up a fuss. She could tell by her niece's nervous energy that Willa was as agitated as she was, although perhaps not for the same reason. She'd caught that look between Willa and Christian during the song. But then who hadn't? There'd been a whole room full of witnesses.

And then there was the tête à tête she'd so clumsily interrupted by coming up from the cellar. She'd lingered down there as long as she dared. Not that Christian or Willa would have noticed how long she'd been gone, but any longer and one of the spiders might have decided to start spinning webs around her.

Otherwise, the evening had gone tremendously well.

Still, she worried. What if she ran out of coffee? Or forgot to turn on the oven after putting a batch of muffins in? It was relaxing to work alongside Willa, knowing her niece was there to back her up if she forgot something. If only she could be sure Willa would always be there.

"Mr. McNeil seems like a nice man." The comment interrupted Billie's thoughts. As distracted as she was, she heard the overly casual note in Willa's voice and barely refrained from a coy smile. A woman her age shouldn't be coy—it wasn't at all flattering.

"I remember when he used to bring his family," Billie said. "He and his wife—Rita, I think her name was— always seemed so in love, like newlyweds. I felt old whenever I saw them together." She wasn't even aware of the wistful rise to her voice.

"Even now, he seems rather young at heart," Willa said.

"Yes, he does, doesn't he?" She couldn't hold back the smile any longer as she told Willa, "Today we went for a walk and showed his grandson how to find morel mushrooms. They're hard to spot, you know. Like looking for camouflage."

"I remember." Willa paused, her smile mirroring Billie's own. "But I don't remember seeing them on the supper table tonight."

"I'm saving them for Mickey and Weldon's breakfast. They're eating with the family tomorrow." She could feel Willa looking at her, grinning. "We didn't find enough for all the guests," she added, feeling a flush rise to her cheeks. Blushing like a schoolgirl she was, and over a handful of mushrooms.

"I hope you're going to sing again next weekend for the Grand Opening," she said, knowing the change of subject would capture Willa's attention. When Willa's smile disappeared, Billie immediately regretted her ploy. She felt a pang of sympathy at her niece's obvious distress. "Everyone enjoyed it," Billie said gently. "Me, especially. It's been so long since we've played and sang together. I had a marvelous time."

"I enjoyed it, too. I just don't know if I can do it again."

"Why not?" She watched as her niece struggled for an answer, and said gently, "You know, there's an old saying. 'If you can walk, you can dance; if you can talk, you can sing.'"

Willa stared at the cup in her hands, almost as though she'd forgotten where it belonged. "I'm not even sure I can talk yet. Nothing is happening the way I hoped."

"Life is like that," Billie said. She realized Willa's hopes were probably opposite of her own and felt guilty. "Well, when you decide you want to talk, I'm always here to listen." She dared to add, "So is Christian, you know."

"Yes. I know." Willa's expression was unreadable as she put the cup away in the cupboard. Billie was caught by surprise when Willa turned and reached out to pat her hand wordlessly.

"Well, goodnight, my dear." Billie, halfway to the back stairs, hesitated before turning to find Willa staring out the window toward the woods. She added quietly, "I want to tell you how much it has meant to me to have you here."

She waited for a response, some small sign that Willa had heard, but her niece continued to look through the window, as though she could see beyond the darkness outside. Billie wanted to tell Willa that it was the darkness inside she had yet to penetrate, but she kept silent. That was one lesson her niece would have to learn on her own.

Willa squinted at the hands of her clock in the gray predawn light. It was 5:30 A.M. She groaned. Billie was already up—the scent of freshly baked bread wafted enticingly from the kitchen. Willa wanted nothing more than to pull the covers back over her head, but no one ever slept in at a fishing resort. Half the guests were probably already out on the lake.

She dragged herself out of bed. At least she was getting up to a fragrant kitchen and a hot cup of coffee, and not a fishy-smelling boat and a bucket of worms or leeches.

She dressed quickly and went down the front staircase, her gaze traveling critically over the polished wood and the sparkling leaded glass inset in the front door. These would be the first things the guests saw when they entered. She bent to straighten the hall runner, then continued the inspection, walking through the parlor toward the dining room, where the buffet breakfast would await both early- and late-risers. Her footsteps were muffled by the Oriental rug, and she caught Rod in the act of filching goodies from the table.

"Aha!"

He spun around guiltily, a slice of nut bread in one hand and a blueberry muffin in the other. He relaxed when he realized it was Willa.

"Gee, I thought you were Billie. She nearly took my hand off when I tried to taste the fruit salad she's making for us. She said we can eat at seven and not a minute before. A guy could starve."

Willa smiled at his earnest expression. "She's expecting a guest for breakfast."

Rod looked around pointedly. "We've got guests for breakfast, dinner, and supper. This place is crawling with guests."

"This one's eating with us in the kitchen."

Understanding dawned in his blue eyes, and a slow smile spread over his face. "That old guy? Is that why she's fixing steak and biscuits and gravy for breakfast?"

Willa smiled back. "It sounds like she wants to impress him. And don't call him old."

"Who's old?" Both Willa and Rod looked up, but Billie saw the food in Rod's hand and forgot her question. "You're not going to spoil your breakfast, are you?" she asked, going to the table and rearranging the basket of muffins.

"No, ma'am."

"Look at this big hole you left when you took the bread."

Rod looked at Willa and rolled his eyes.

Without turning, Billie groused, "I don't know what you're doing up so early. Either get out of my way or make yourself useful."

"Yes, ma'am." He started backing toward the doorway, nibbling at his blueberry muffin.

Willa nearly choked on her laughter when Billie said, "You, too."

"I thought I'd get a head start on the dishes," Willa defended mildly. "That way the kitchen will look tidy for Weldon."

Rod snickered through cheeks stuffed with bread. Billie shot him a warning glance, and he said, "I think I'll go take Freddie for a walk." He shoved the bread into his mouth and headed for the front door, disregarding the crumbs that scattered in his wake, while Billie tsk-tsked over the sight.

"Nervous?" Willa asked as her aunt joined her in the kitchen.

"I guess I still haven't settled into the routine yet."

Willa watched her aunt set the kitchen table with the good china. "Are you sure that's the only reason?" she asked and was rewarded with a hint of blush along Billie's wrinkled cheeks.

There was no more time to tease as they got down to work doing dishes, refilling bread baskets, and honoring special requests: herbal tea for Mrs. Goodwin, crackers for the Baylors' baby, margarine instead of butter for a man on a low-cholesterol diet. By seven, the rush seemed a bit more manageable, and they sat down to their own breakfast.

"'Morning."

Willa was in the process of pouring more coffee for Weldon, and she looked up when she was done. Christian's greeting was meant for everyone at the table, but his gaze had singled her out, and it was her turn to blush as he looked from her hair down to her legs, bare beneath her cutoffs.

Her hand shook, and she nearly spilled coffee in Weldon's lap, but he politely pretended not to notice. She was relieved at the shift in everyone's attention when Rod asked, "What are these things floating in the gravy? They look like little sponges."

"Those, young man, are morel mushrooms," Weldon said, the ex-biology teacher in him taking over. "They are members of the saprophytic species of fungi." At Rod's grimace, he added, "No need to be worried. They're quite edible. A delicacy, in fact, especially when prepared by your great aunt."

Rod's cautious expression changed to intrigue, then surprise when he worked up enough courage to taste one. "Hey, these *are* good." He held out his plate. "I'll take some more."

"Me, too," echoed Mickey McNeil, who seemed to have developed a case of hero worship. Rod handled the attention gracefully, helping Mickey pour more mushroom gravy over his biscuits.

Willa's eyes met Christian's in a silent smile. When she realized how automatically her gaze had sought his to share the moment, she felt a flicker of fear inside her and quickly looked away. She longed to leave the table and disappear, but she had to stay and help Billie clean up and start dinner.

She concentrated on the work at hand, trying to keep busy so she wouldn't have a chance to think or feel. When the phone rang shrilly that afternoon, she was elbow-deep in wet laundry. She paused in the middle of pulling a tangle of sheets out of the washer, listening to it ring unanswered, before starting up the steps. Apparently Billie and Rod hadn't yet returned from their walk in the woods with the McNeils.

Her "hello" was a bit breathless, and she tucked the receiver under her chin so she could rummage through her pockets in search of a pen to take down reservation information. When she heard the familiar voice on the other end of the line, she nearly dropped the receiver.

"Hello, daughter."

"*Dad?*" Hoping he hadn't heard the dismay in her voice, she quickly continued. "How are things in Arizona?"

"Getting warm. One hundred five today." He hesitated before asking, "How are things there?"

"Busy. In fact, I can't talk very long. I'm in the middle of doing the linens right now, and we have to start supper soon."

"But it's Sunday afternoon," he said, and she realized he remembered the routine as well as she or Billie. "Half the guests must be on their way home by now."

"It is a bit more peaceful around here," she admitted.

"I'm surprised you're still there. Is something wrong?"

"No, of course not. We're all fine."

"What about your work? Can you take this much time off?"

"I'm between jobs right now," she said evasively. "Actually, I have an offer waiting for me in L.A."

"Good." His voice was hearty. "We were worried about you wasting opportunities because of that old place. Billie won't be able to hold on to it much longer, you know. I've told her she should sell out to this development company. Take the money and run, while they're still interested, that's what I think."

She felt a flash of resentment so strong that it shocked her. "You told her that?" At his affirmation, she echoed a sentiment she'd heard Christian voice many times. "Maybe people want to go somewhere simple and old-fashioned. They can relax here."

"Not like they can at the resorts here."

Willa thought of the glitzy resorts in Scottsdale, where she'd lived as a teenager with her parents. They were beautifully constructed and landscaped, with every amenity from golf to hot tubs. But Restless Spirit's guests didn't want luxury. They wanted a slower pace. She knew it wouldn't do any good to argue with her father, who was still complaining about Billie.

". . . but the stubborn old woman wouldn't listen. I think she's getting senile. Your mother and I wanted to talk to you about that. We don't think it's a good idea for you to stay there. You can come and stay with us."

The suggestion caught her by surprise. Fortunately, before she was forced to come up with an answer, her father said, "Here's your mother. She wants to talk for a while."

Willa could hear a muffled exchange as her father handed the phone over to her mother. They exchanged small talk for a few minutes before her mother said, "You plan on stopping in Arizona on your way back to California, don't you?"

"Maybe. I don't know. I'm not even sure if I'll take

the job," Willa surprised herself by saying. Her heart was pounding hard when she finally hung up the phone. She pressed a hand to her temple and turned to find Christian standing in the doorway to the kitchen, watching her carefully.

How much had he overheard?

"Excuse me." She brushed past him without meeting his eyes, returning to the cellar to finish the baskets overflowing with sheets, towels, and tablecloths. She half expected him to follow her and told herself that she was glad he didn't.

"Thanks for staying after school to help put these up," Willa told Rod as they left the hardware store Wednesday afternoon. He and his aunt were walking along Main Street, stopping to ask shopkeepers' permission to post flyers in windows for the Grand Opening. "I thought you and Kerry might be doing something together."

Rod stared at the bright sheet of paper advertising Restless Spirit's Grand Opening until the letters blurred. "Kerry and I aren't seeing much of each other anymore."

He glanced over to check Willa's reaction. She had stopped in the process of stapling a flyer to a telephone pole and stared at him as if she were about to say something. Before she could get all philosophical on him, he continued, "She went to a party with some other guy."

He turned away from the sympathy in Willa's eyes and froze as his gaze landed on Jerry Miller. *Speak of the devil*, he thought grimly. Jerry was standing there, talking to the town's mayor a few yards down the sidewalk from Rod and Willa. He wanted to wipe the smug smile off Jerry's face, but he guessed it probably wouldn't be a good idea to start a fight on Main Street with Mayor Thor Nelson looking on.

When he realized Willa was waving her hand to return the mayor's shout of hello, he wanted to dive right into the cement sidewalk as Thor and Jerry walked toward them. Wearing a smile smarmy enough to charm a snake, Thor reached up and pulled away the flyer that Willa had just finished stapling to the telephone pole.

Rod fought the instinct to step closer to his aunt as Thor said, "I was hoping that as mayor I might get a personal invitation, at least."

"Of course you're invited, Thor," Willa said. But her expression didn't look inviting in the least, and Rod relaxed. His aunt could apparently hold her own. "Billie wants everyone in Pinecrest to know that Restless Spirit is back and better than ever," she added.

Thor's smile stiffened a bit. "I heard you had a little problem last weekend. Something about a ghost?" he asked, while Jerry snickered. This time Rod could barely restrain himself. Willa touched his hand lightly in warning.

"Yes, we did have some excitement. And it's been great for business. The phone's been ringing off the hook." Willa gave Thor a wide smile. "In fact, the Minneapolis paper called yesterday and asked if they could take pictures of the resort and interview Billie for an article they're doing on Minnesota traditions."

"How nice," Thor said, his smile more of a grimace now. Rod shot a triumphant look at Jerry, who was standing at Thor's elbow like a shadow.

After a couple more minutes Willa wished Thor a polite, but chilly goodbye, and Rod breathed a sigh of relief.

As they crossed the street to Willa's car he could feel her gaze on him. He wasn't going to say anything, but when she crawled into the driver's seat, he said, "Kerry went to a party Saturday night with Jerry Miller. He's got a red Mustang."

He heard the whine in his voice and winced. Willa must have heard it, too, because she glanced over at him. "His eyes are too small and dark. He looks like a weasel."

Rod grinned and waited for her to start the engine. When she didn't turn the key right away, he looked over to see her regarding him thoughtfully. "Have you got your learner's permit?" she asked.

"Yeah, before I left the military high school and went to Arizona. But your folks didn't want me driving their new Cadillac."

Willa pulled the car keys out and dangled them in front of his face. "Here," she said, dropping them into his palm. "You'll need to get in some practice before you take your road test."

They got out and circled the car, and Rod felt like leaping up and clicking his heels together before he got in the driver's side. It wasn't just being able to drive, although that was pretty terrific. *Willa trusted him.*

When he turned off the highway onto the gravel road he saw that she was resting her head back against the seat, her eyes half closed. She couldn't be as relaxed as she looked—who would be with a seventeen-year-old behind the wheel of her almost-new car?—but he appreciated her effort.

He slowed down over the causeway but pulled up to the house with a flourish. Christian was walking up from the boathouse, and Rod hailed him as he got out of the car. But Christian's gaze was all for Willa. Rod should have put two and two together sooner when he saw how Christian had managed to make himself scarce since the weekend. Now, only a fool could miss what was going on as these two stared at each other. A guy could get burned just standing in between them like this.

He cleared his throat and said loudly, "Thanks again for letting me drive, Willa. I guess I'll go in and see if Billie needs any help." He waited, but neither of them seemed to have heard him.

He gave up and headed for the house, shaking his head. And he thought he and Kerry had problems.

"Hi."

Willa managed to drag her feet forward until they were facing each other at the bottom of the veranda steps.

"Hi, yourself. Tough week?" She nearly groaned aloud at the impersonal small talk. They were acting like two strangers, awkward and unsure.

"It's been busy. Quite a few of the motels are already filling up for the big weekend. Are you and Billie managing to keep up with everything?"

She nodded. "We rented only two of the cottages for the whole week. It's a bit early in the season yet. But the weekend is booked solid, and we're hiring caterers to help Saturday night."

"Ah, the big Grand Opening dinner. I'm taking both nights off to help Billie. There's going to be a lot of people here Saturday night now that she's invited the whole town."

They may have been talking like strangers, but their eyes told another story. Christian's gaze burned her where it traveled over each of the places her navy cotton sundress didn't cover—neck, shoulders, arms, legs. When he looked back up, his gaze locked with hers, and she knew he recognized the awareness in her eyes.

They stared at each other silently, and Willa couldn't even remember when or where the conversation had drifted off. When Christian spoke again, his voice was lower, huskier.

"Billie says you're all packed?"

"Just about."

They fell into silence again. Somewhere in the back of her mind, Willa could hear a telephone ringing. She vaguely remembered Rod going into the house a few minutes ago, but he wasn't answering the insistent rings. She mumbled an "excuse me" and ran into the house to pick up the hall phone.

"Could I speak to Miss Mitterhauser, please?"

"Speaking," she answered, before remembering that she technically wasn't a Mitterhauser, or even a miss, anymore.

"Wilhelmina?" The voice was puzzled, and Willa realized the caller wanted Billie.

"You must mean my aunt. She's not here at the moment, but I'd be happy to take a message."

"This is Weldon McNeil. I was hoping I could stay at Restless Spirit this weekend. Is Number Eight available again?"

Willa flipped through the reservation cards, stored in the small secretary desk in the hall. She knew all the cottages were full, thanks to the news articles the "ghost" had inspired, but hoped that Billie might have recorded a cancellation while she and Rod were in town.

"If not," he continued in a rush, "I could take something smaller. My grandson won't be accompanying me this time."

"I'm sorry, but we're all booked up." She knew Billie would be disappointed, and she was, too. Then an idea occurred to her. "You could stay in the main house with the family. We'd be happy to have you, as long as you wouldn't mind putting up with a little inconvenience, such as sharing a bathroom and trying to sleep through our early morning routine. We wouldn't charge you cottage rates, of course."

His voice held an eagerness that was touching. "I wouldn't mind a bit. I get up with the early birds, you might say. And I'm quite handy with a dishtowel if you need help."

"Wonderful. Billie, er, *Wilhelmina*—" the name rolled strangely off her tongue "—will be so glad you could stay with us again," Willa said, wondering as she hung up where she would put him.

Once, the house had had five bedrooms. But one room had been converted to an office, another a storage room for linens and bathroom supplies. She, Billie, and Rod, occupied the others. The only room not in use was the other half of the attic—Rick's room.

She quickly dismissed the idea. She couldn't put a guest there, not when it meant putting up with the divider and having to cross through Christian's room. But she knew that Rod probably wouldn't mind using his father's room.

Was there any other solution?

She heard someone enter the kitchen and went in to find her aunt rinsing a huge bunch of rhubarb in the sink, which explained why she hadn't heard the telephone. Billie was wearing a cotton sundress, too, more modest than Willa's, but still quite feminine compared to her usual dungarees and brown oxfords. Was it her imagination, or had her aunt been dressing up more since Weldon McNeil's last visit?

"Mr. McNeil just called," she told her aunt. "He wanted to stay with us over the weekend."

"Oh, dear. We've been booked since yesterday afternoon," Billie said, her distress obvious. "All those newspaper articles . . ."

Willa couldn't bear to tease her a moment longer. "I told him he could stay here in the house, as long as he didn't mind the noise and confusion."

"But we don't have room for him."

"I thought Rod might agree to staying in Rick's old room," Willa said casually. "I'll clear it out a bit tomorrow morning and get rid of some of the junk."

Billie's gaze was sharp. "That would be a neat solution. I saw Rod head for the woods with Freddie a few minutes ago. When they get back, I'll warn him that he needs to clean his room before he moves upstairs. Not that we won't have to clean it a second time ourselves," she added in a mutter as she shook the water from the rose-and-green rhubarb stalks.

Willa stifled a smile as she headed for the back stairs. She climbed two steps, then paused and turned back to her aunt. "If Rod's room is unsuitable I have a feeling that Mr. McNeil wouldn't mind sharing yours."

"Why, Wilhelmina Mitterhauser!" Even from this distance Willa could see that Billie's pretended outrage didn't match the sparkle in her blue eyes.

"Maybe he'll propose this weekend."

Billie sniffed. "I certainly hope not. I don't want to be tied down, you know."

Willa's teasing mood ended. Her aunt had been tied down for years and always would be. Restless Spirit was more demanding than any husband, requiring commitment and hard work. Or was Billie still deluding herself that Willa might take over the resort?

She was about to remind her aunt that she would be leaving soon, but a pensive expression settled over Billie's face, making her look young and vulnerable in the flowered sundress. Willa went upstairs, assuring herself that by morning, she'd feel up to going into Rick's old room again.

But when Thursday morning came, she held an

empty cardboard box to her chest and stared helplessly at Rick's things. This wasn't going to be easy, after all. She sank down onto the floor next to the heavy oak chest of drawers, deciding it was as good a place to start as any. She shivered. The floorboards were cool against her bare legs, and goosebumps rose on her thighs below the edge of her cutoffs.

She yanked at the brass pull of the bottom drawer, but it refused to budge. After a second try, it finally slid toward her. She sat back with surprise, leaning against the twin bed for support, when she saw that the drawer was filled with toys and junk, from a handful of agates to a metal erector set to a headless doll—hers—that Rick had "operated" on when he was eight and wanted to be a doctor.

She started to laugh at the thought of him saving all this junk over the years, but the familiar band of tightness squeezed her rib cage, and she realized she was on the edge of tears.

She felt a surge of denial. She'd already cried enough—for Rick, for her grandparents, for her Darryl. Why couldn't she ever seem to control this well of sadness, this grief that bubbled up periodically like an unpredictable geyser?

Was this how Rick had felt after seeing his friends die in combat? As though there was an open wound somewhere inside him that never seemed to heal, but festered until it started to ooze again? Rick was the only one who would understand what she was going through.

And, *by his own hand*, he wasn't here.

The anger she'd only glimpsed the last time she was in this room came bursting forth now. She began to claw at the drawer full of junk, throwing it into the cardboard box, missing her target several times. A half-dozen marbles skittered noisily across the wooden floor, and shredded foam from a ripped teddy bear littered the pine boards. A glow-in-the-dark ball rolled under the bed, and a bean bag came apart in her hands, covering her lap with little white beans.

She tore open the next drawer and pulled out T-shirts and bathing trunks and socks, wanting to rip them into shreds.

Damn him, how could he have done it? He'd had a wife, a baby on the way.

A sister. One great, wracking sob welled up from inside her chest, and she pressed her face against the side of the bed, waiting for the storm to pass, using the mattress to drown out her cries.

The rage inside her was shocking, embarrassing, but she couldn't stop it any more than she could stop a rushing train. She could only be grateful for the fact that she was on the third floor of the house, where no one could hear her. She could scream and rant all she liked, and no one would know. The tightness in her chest loosened as if by magic, and eventually her tears ceased.

She lay there, half sprawled against the side of the bed, feeling utterly empty. *Nothing.* She felt nothing as she slowly straightened and began to clean up the mess she'd made. She stared at the rest of Rick's things— posters, magazines, record albums—and realized they didn't make her feel guilty anymore.

Was this why she'd come to Restless Spirit? The empty feeling was almost as disconcerting as that unnamed heaviness she'd carried around for years without even realizing it.

She looked at the box, then at the room once more, and realized that Rod would probably like being surrounded by his father's things. It might help to satisfy his curiosity about Rick. On the other hand, it could make him ask more questions. She waited for the panicky feeling, but only a mild pang disturbed her. She felt the way an amnesiac must feel at having to relearn everything that was once familiar—activities, places, people.

She thought of Christian, then, and felt her emotions returning in a confusing rush.

14

Christian straightened, wiping his brow with the back of his forearm and glancing at his watch at the same time. He had at least an hour to go before Rod got home from school. Yesterday, buying this old pontoon boat had seemed like a good idea, but that was before he'd spent a hot afternoon trying to repair everything that was wrong with it. And Billie wanted it "seaworthy" by Saturday morning—tomorrow.

He saw her heading toward him across the lawn and stood straight and tall, as ready to take his lumps now as when he, Rick, and Willa were kids getting into trouble. Then they'd taken their punishment standing tall and always together, like the Three Musketeers.

But Billie was all smiles as she handed him glass of ice water. "Looks like you're almost done."

"Almost," he said with false optimism, after letting half the contents of the glass slide down his parched throat. It was unusually hot and dry for this time of year, and he ran the bottom of the glass over his sunburned shoulders before taking another swallow. "I'll need a hand from Rod or Kevin to get it into the water, but it should be ready to float tomorrow."

"You and Rod work together well," she said with a glance toward the new dock they'd finished the week before. Christian watched her carefully, wondering what she was getting at. He didn't have long to wait before finding out.

"I'm tired of all this tiptoeing around," Billie announced. "I want Rod and Willa to stay."

"I do too. You know that."

"Can't you make her—" She broke off and stared out at the lake, its waves sparkling with late afternoon sunlight. She sighed. "No, I suppose you can't."

"I've tried, Billie," he said gently.

"What about Rod? Do you think Caroline and what's his name will let him stay here?"

"I hope so."

"Will you help me, Christian? They might think I'm too old or too . . . *something* to take care of him without Willa here. If they knew you'd be here with me . . ."

"Sure," he said through the tightness in his throat. He didn't feel like making plans for after Willa's departure, even though it was only a matter of days now. She intended to leave following Rod's graduation ceremony, which would be on Monday night, and she still hadn't talked to Rod about his father. He swallowed the last of the water, hoping it would put out the fire building in his stomach.

"You'll keep trying, won't you?" she asked as he handed over the empty glass.

"Yeah." He watched her walk back to the house before he turned his attention to the boat.

An hour later, dripping with sweat, he headed toward the house himself, hoping for a shower before supper.

Guests had been coming and going all afternoon long, and he'd been interrupted several times with well-meaning advice on pontoon repair, offered by middle-aged men with skin so pale they looked as though they'd never been outdoors on a boat. Now, if they'd only offered him a hand instead . . .

He was crossing through the backyard when he spotted Willa carrying something. He grinned when he saw the garden hose trailing behind her. She was moving the sprinkler toward the grass between the house and garden and was unaware of him standing in the shadows next to the house.

He glanced over at the faucet only a few feet away. She'd be furious. He tiptoed over and turned it as far as it would go, then waited for the water to reach her. It was glorious—a spitting, twisting cascade that caught her full in the chest and ran in rivulets down her legs, bare beneath her shorts. She shrieked in outrage, and he laughed, giving away his position.

"Christian Foster, I'll get you for this!" she shouted as she raced toward him, water flying in every direction from the sprinkler in her hand.

He saw her intentions and tried to run, but laughter made his legs weak. Soon he was caught in a spray of ice water, streaming over his bare chest and back. After a few feints and dodges, slipping on the wet grass, he managed to catch her by the wrist. He tried to wrench the sprinkler away, but his legs tangled in the garden hose, and he fell on the ground.

The air rushed out of him when Willa landed on his chest. She was breathing hard, her shirt clinging to her and her hair a wet tangle. He was seized by instant desire—and her wriggling didn't help matters any.

"You—" She stopped when she saw the look in his eyes.

His hands worked their way up her back, holding her to him, and he only needed a little pressure to bring her mouth down on his. Water still sprayed them whenever the sprinkler made its pass, but he hardly noticed. All he could feel was burning heat, and all the cold water in the world couldn't put it out.

Willa thrust herself away from Christian and scrambled to her feet. "Stop it," she said, hoping her ragged breathing wouldn't betray her.

"Stop what? You were the one on top. I thought that was the dominant position." He lazily folded his hands behind his head as he looked up at her. Nearby a bird twittered, as if it were impatiently waiting its turn to dance underneath the sprinkle of water.

He might look the picture of relaxed amusement, but every time the water turned back toward them, it sprayed him from the soles of his boots up to the middle of his shins. She quelled an impulse to giggle. This was serious. She had to make him understand.

"Stop trying to make me change my mind about leaving," she said clearly and slowly, as if she were speaking to someone who hadn't quite grasped the English language.

"All I did was kiss you, Willa. I can't stop you from responding. Now that we know what it's like between us—"

"Stop," she said again. She wanted to hold her hands over her ears and squeeze her eyes shut, but nothing would erase the images racing through her mind of the night they'd had together. Those images would stay with her forever, and she realized that instead of being upset, she should be glad to always have the memories of that night. Behind her, she heard tires crunch over the drive. She turned, relieved. "That must be the people in Number Six. They're the only ones who haven't arrived yet.

I'd better go get the keys to their cottage and help them settle in."

"Like that?"

She looked down at her grass-stained, muddy legs and then headed for the back door instead, ignoring the ring of Christian's laughter as it followed her.

The car turned out to be a couple from the Twin Cities area without reservations. They waylaid Willa halfway, and she tried not to laugh as they politely pretended not to notice her bedraggled appearance.

After assisting them she let the screen door slam behind her, and Billie called out in response, "Rod, is that you?"

Willa followed the sound of her aunt's voice to the open cellar door. "No, Billie, it's me," she called down the steps. "I haven't seen Rod all afternoon. Wasn't the senior class supposed to stay late for graduation rehearsal?"

Rod's commencement ceremony was Monday night, and Willa wondered how many of the seniors would come back from the holiday weekend with sunburn-bright noses under their mortarboards. She could hear her aunt's footsteps on the stairs and smiled when Billie appeared in the doorway, cobwebs clinging to her white hair.

"He said he'd be home as soon as they finished. I thought he'd be back by now. I need help moving the canning shelf over a few inches to make room for another box of supplies."

"Christian's outside on the lawn. I'm sure he'd move it for you."

"*On* the lawn?" Billie's gaze took in Willa's tousled hair and the grass stains on her legs. "It looks like the lawn's on you. What have you been doing, or shouldn't I ask?"

Willa could feel the heat rising to her cheeks, while a half-dozen unbelievable explanations crossed her mind. "We had a water fight," she said at last.

"At your age?" She tsk-tsked. "Remember when the three of you used to lay on the grass and roll down the hill behind Quinlan's? Your mother was sure you'd end up in the middle of the road someday and get hit by a car."

Willa smiled. "She always worried, but you and Dad never said anything about the stuff we did."

"That's because we'd all done the same terrible things when we were kids—climbing trees, jumping off the banks into the lake. In the winter, we'd take the toboggan out and slide down that same hill. Sometimes, if we got going fast enough, we'd slide all the way to the lake."

"I fell through the ice once," Willa confessed. "We were here for Christmas vacation. Christian and Rick pulled me out. We never told my parents what happened."

"Neither did I." Billie's grin was wicked.

"What?"

"I found your snow suit hanging in the basement near the furnace, soaked and dripping. I figured it must have been enough to scare some sense into you for a while."

"It did. For about a week," she added with a grin. "Then I was right back on top of the hill, daring Christian and Rick to see who could go the farthest on our sleds. It was the one activity where I managed to keep up with them. I used to wish we could stay all winter, like we did the summers. I hardly even remember living in Fargo."

"It's too bad Rod's all grown up. He missed all those things."

They heard a frenzy of barking out on the lawn and ran to the window to see Freddie defending her territory from an Airedale belonging to the people in Number Ten.

"He hasn't missed everything," Willa pointed out as they watched Rod drop his book bag in order to grab Freddie and try to keep the two dogs apart. If nothing else, Willa thought, at least this trip back to Restless Spirit had brought some moments of happiness for Rod. Happiness she might destroy by telling him about Rick.

Rod quietly let himself into the hallway. He hadn't meant to get home so late, but he'd stopped at the cemetery. He'd felt like talking before coming back here. Seeing the rows and rows of kids assembled in the school gym for graduation rehearsal made him realize for the first time that this was it. No more books. No more teachers. No more school. He'd be eighteen in August, and he still hadn't figured out where he was supposed to go, or what he was supposed to do. He was as bad as his aunt Willa. And this was the only time talking to Rick hadn't helped him see the answers.

He started up the staircase, then remembered that he was sharing the attic room with Christian. He'd packed his things up last night, though it seemed kind of a waste of time when he might be packing again for real in a few days. His parents had yet to approve his wishes to stay at Restless Spirit for the summer. They were treating him as if he was still a little kid, unable to know what he wanted.

He backtracked and snuck through the kitchen to the back stairs, seeing the bustle of supper preparations and doing his best to avoid bumping into anyone, like Kerry's mother or Billie, who might tie an apron on him.

"There you are," Billie said from the cellar doorway. Christian was behind her on the descending steps. "It's about time you got home. Supper's about ready to start."

"I'll be down in a few minutes, okay?" Rod said.

"That's fine. Willa's still in the shower. Everyone's eating in the dining room tonight. We're having rouladen," she added.

"Sounds great." He tried to act enthusiastic and hoped Billie didn't notice the forced note in his voice. He didn't feel like sitting around a table full of strangers and trying to make conversation. Even helping out in the kitchen was more appealing. He started up the steps. Maybe he could talk to Kerry's mom and find out why Kerry had been avoiding him.

He threw his books on the bed and looked around at the old posters and stuff that had belonged to his father. It had been weird the first time he saw this room to realize his father was once just a kid like him, but then he'd started to get excited about sleeping here. It felt comfortable. Too comfortable. He could imagine spending the rest of the summer up here, a haven from the busy operation below, and he hoped his parents would let him stay. He dreaded the evening ahead and changed into a different pair of jeans just to delay going downstairs for a while longer.

But he dreaded the next night even more. Jerry Miller and his buddies had spent the afternoon jabbing each other with their elbows and laughing and pointing at Rod. He'd overheard one of them say something about Saturday night's Grand Opening celebration. What were they going to do? And how was he going to stop them?

He went downstairs to the dining room to find he was seated across from Billie. Willa sat at the head of the other table, acting as hostess. She looked pale in a dark sleeveless blouse, and he wondered if she was nervous about singing tonight. Christian sat at the smaller table they'd set up to make more room for guests, listening to an elderly couple who finished each other's sentences like a relay team, a habit that allowed them to keep up a constant stream of chatter without much input from Christian.

Only Billie seemed to be having a good time, laughing with her guests and smiling a lot at a white-haired man seated to her right. It was the bird man, Mr. McNeil.

"Hey, you were here last weekend," Rod said. All conversation at the table had ceased, and he realized he'd sounded rude, like a kid.

"Why, yes, I was. I enjoyed myself so much that I decided to return."

"Oh." He saw the man glance at Billie, who was staring down at her plate, her cheeks pink. *Blushing?* Oh, ho, so that was how it was, Rod thought with surprise. God, they were pushing eighty, at least.

He listened idly to the conversation around him, feeling satisfied at the guests' compliments on Billie's cooking and their accommodations. When there was an electronic beep he saw Christian rise to his feet.

"Skeet must need a hand. I'll use the phone in the hall," he said. He smiled at Billie. "Thank you for a wonderful dinner."

"Oh, but can't you stay for dessert? Willa and I baked a Black Forest cake."

"Rod can eat my piece," he said, and patted him on the shoulder. Rod felt like a kid again and wondered when people would start treating him like an adult. He was graduating from high school in three days, for Pete's sake.

"You said I could go with you sometime—how about tonight?" he heard himself asking. Christian had made the offer months ago, and Rod had turned him down then, certain that it was some kind of ploy. No wonder Christian looked surprised now that he'd brought it up again. He waited for an answer. Maybe, once he and Christian were alone, he'd tell him about Jerry.

Christian didn't meet his eyes. "It's going to be a busy night with all the visitors in town for the weekend. That's probably why Skeet needs me to go in. How about some night next week?"

"Sure," Rod said, trying not to show his disappointment. *If I'm here,* he added silently, watching Christian disappear into the hall. The thought of leaving made him lose his appetite. "May I be excused, too?" he asked Billie.

"Of course," she said, but her blue eyes were quizzical. "I'll leave some cake in the refrigerator for you."

Rod stopped at the side of the house to check on Freddie, who now had her own doghouse. He certainly wouldn't be sneaking her upstairs to sleep with him anymore, not with Christian on the other side of the divider. Then he headed for the boathouse, which wasn't the quiet haven it once was. These days the building was a hive of activity, with guests storing their boats near those belonging to the resort, or using the landing next to the building to lower them into the water. The track that had once been covered with weeds was now a well-worn path down to the water's edge.

With his hand on the door, he changed his mind and headed for the long dock he'd helped Christian build the week before. He walked out to the edge and sat down, taking off his sneakers so they wouldn't get wet when he hung his legs over the side. He heard Christian's pickup truck leave for town, and now and then he caught a snatch of laughter or conversation from the main house when the breeze carried it his way.

There was only a hint of orange left on the horizon, and the sky turned a deeper and deeper blue. He lay back on the dock and stared up at the stars, making a wish, knowing only kids believed in stupid things like that. He wished he could stay at Restless Spirit as long as he wanted to, with Kerry, Billie, and Christian. And Willa. He wished she wouldn't leave, either, even though he was supposed to get only one chance for a wish.

When he heard a crashing noise through the woods, he assumed it was one of the guests. He hadn't heard anyone leaving the house, but some made their own dinner in the cottages with kitchenettes. The sounds were stealthy, though, and the hairs on the back of his neck rose as he turned his head to peer into the darkness. He quietly rose and tiptoed back across the dock, his sneakers in hand.

He paused to slip them over his feet, not bothering to tie them before heading for the source of the noises.

Christian parked the pickup about a half mile beyond the causeway, concealing it in a brushy approach off State Forest land. The phone call from Skeet had been a decoy, which was overdoing it a bit, he supposed, even though they had to consider the possibility that Pitzer and his men were monitoring their radios.

He'd felt like a jerk telling Rod he couldn't come along, but this was the only way he'd find out for certain if the boy was involved. Rod still acted guilty, as if he knew something. Christian hoped to God he was wrong as he got out of the truck and walked back across the causeway to the island.

He took the long route, staying to the woods and listening for anything that sounded bigger than a skunk out looking for grubs or a raccoon making plans for Billie's garden. When he heard something large moving slowly through the brush near the cottages, he headed in that direction.

By now his eyes had adapted to the darkness, and the nearly full moon made it even easier to see. But what he saw confused him. There, only twenty feet away, someone was lifting something heavy onto the branch of a tree. It looked like the movie projector that he and Rod had confiscated the week before.

He froze, watching the broad-shouldered figure that bore a striking resemblance to Kevin Quinlan. But he'd already talked to Kevin and gotten his promise that he wouldn't do anything else to harm the resort. He was about to step out of the brush and show himself when a rustle off to his left alerted him. He crouched lower and waited.

He didn't have to wait long. The rustle turned into a loud crashing, as if an elephant was charging its way through the woods. A second, smaller figure leaped on top of Kevin and pulled him to the ground. Christian recognized Rod's voice and hurried over to break up the struggle.

He pulled Rod and Kevin apart, trying to ignore the feeling of betrayal he felt as he looked down at them. A cop was supposed to be neutral and calm at all times. But this was one time he'd like to shake a pair of perps until their teeth rattled.

"What are you doing here?" he asked, not directing the question to either of them in particular. Rod, who'd done most of the struggling, was breathing too heavily to answer. Kevin looked scared, and the whites of his eyes practically glowed in the moonlight. "Well?"

"Billie asked me to do it," Kevin said finally, his voice quivering. He looked about to cry.

Christian looked around and spotted the generator and a cord that snaked up into the tree. "She asked you to set up this contraption again?"

Kevin nodded. "She wanted the ghost to come tomorrow night. A surprise. She said people liked it. I didn't know you wouldn't like it."

Christian repressed his laughter. Trust Billie to take advantage of every opportunity. He turned to Rod, all traces of amusement gone. "What about you? What do you have to say for yourself?"

"I heard Kevin and thought he was . . ." He hesitated, then continued, his words running together. "I thought he was Jerry Miller and those guys. I heard them planning to do something this weekend, and I wanted to stop them."

"Jerry Miller? The captain of the baseball team?"

"Yeah. I should've figured you wouldn't believe me," Rod muttered as he brushed himself off and stood up, then reached down to give Kevin a hand. "Just because he's friends with people like Thor Nelson—"

Christian felt a stab of excitement. "Hold on there. What's this about Thor?"

Rod told him that he'd seen Jerry and Thor together. Christian glanced at Kevin thoughtfully, who was staring at his boots. "Do you know anything about this, Kevin?" he asked.

"I don't like Thor anymore."

"Why?"

"He wanted me to do bad things. He—" Kevin broke off, and Christian and Rod exchanged concerned looks.

"Hey, Kevin," Rod said, "didn't you tell me there was a squirrel around here that was tame?"

Kevin looked up, his distress half forgotten. Christian smiled while Rod talked Kevin into joining him in a squirrel watch. The three of them leaned back against a log, waiting for the squirrel to appear, and as Kevin relaxed, the story eventually came out. One night,

Kevin told them, when he had been following Mattie's instructions, standing near the cottages rattling chains and moaning to scare Billie, he'd spotted Thor in the shadows. Thor had asked him to break a window, and he had refused. But he'd kept watch after that, he assured Christian.

The way Christian figured it, Kevin's and Mattie's shenanigans had given Thor the idea to ask Jerry and his friends to start plaguing Billie with broken windows and vandalism. But the fires . . .

"Did you see who set the fire?" he asked Kevin, who was a willing witness now that he knew he wasn't going to get into trouble.

"Thor."

Christian thought grimly of the lighter, and an idea was born. "Are you sure Jerry and Thor are plotting something for tomorrow night?" he asked Rod as the three of them started back across the causeway toward Quinlan's.

"Pretty sure. I just don't know what."

"Well, we'll just have to stop them, won't we?" They paused at the side of the store, where a light burned in the window. "Don't forget that Billie needs your help tomorrow, Kevin."

He was rewarded with a look of relief and a wave before Kevin headed for the breezeway entrance between the store and garage. They walked on toward the pickup, and Christian shook his head.

"That's one crazy old woman, your great-aunt." He heard muffled noises beside him as Rod tried to stifle his laughter. He reached out to drape an arm across Rod's shoulders. "Don't tell her I said that, okay?"

"Nah, I can keep a secret," Rod said as they continued toward the pickup.

"No kidding. You kept quiet about Jerry long enough." He felt Rod stiffen.

"I'm sorry. I was afraid I'd get into trouble. I screw up a lot so people always think the worst about me."

Christian laughed. "Boy, do I remember what that's like."

"You?"

"Hell, yes. I was the biggest troublemaker this town ever saw."

Rod was silent until they reached the pickup, as though he needed time to digest Christian's words. "Why'd you decide to be a cop?" he asked finally.

"Because it was a cop who kept me out of jail. He gave me a break."

"That sounds cool. I guess the only cops I knew tried to put me in jail. One of them was covering up for his own kid."

"Cops are people just like everyone else, Rod. Some are good, some are bad." He unlocked the passenger-side door of the pickup. "Ready to head back to Restless Spirit? I think there's some cake with our names on it in the refrigerator. What do you say?"

"Sounds good to me." Rod's smile grew even wider when Christian tossed him the keys.

"I think it's about time you learned how to drive a truck, isn't it?"

Willa woke up Saturday morning and saw the suitcases standing at the foot of her bed. Their presence accused her.

There simply hadn't been time this past week to start packing, she told herself. Last night she'd tried to excuse herself after dinner, intending to come up here and get started, but Billie had steered her into the front parlor.

She'd ended up playing the piano and singing until

Rod and Christian had walked through the door, whispering like a pair of conspirators. Shortly afterward, the guests returned to their cottages, and she'd wandered into the kitchen to find Christian and Rod stuffing their faces with Black Forest cake. She'd avoided meeting Christian's eyes, knowing he would send her *that* look, the one that told her time was running out. He might have given up on persuading her to stay, but he was still determined that she talk to Rod.

She pulled back the covers, dressing mechanically in jeans and a T-shirt. After the big party that night, she would be all out of excuses. Sometime by Tuesday morning, she would have to find the words to tell Rod about how Rick died.

She sank down onto the bed and stared at the empty suitcases. She hadn't even bothered to call Cal Smith about the cosmetics company's offer. She'd probably blown her chance at the job by now. She just didn't care, one way or the other. What on earth was wrong with her?

Christian hung up the hall phone and grinned. Thanks to Skeet and Brenda, they should be able to keep Thor and his boys from doing anything to rain on Billie's plans for tonight. She'd invited everyone in town to this pig roast of hers, and every refrigerator, freezer, and cooler in the house was stuffed with salads, desserts, and side dishes. Outside, the caterers were setting up a huge grill, made from an old oil barrel, where they would roast the pig slowly all day. Rod was helping Billie and Willa arrange long tables on the back lawn. Off to one side, old Iver Lindquist and Al Odegard rehearsed on their stand-up bass and electric guitar. Billie had hired them to accompany Willa, though old man Lindquist probably would have happily played all night just for a piece of Billie's rhubarb pie.

Yes, it was going to be quite a party, all right, Christian thought as he joined the others. He'd made his own plans, too. He glanced toward Willa, who looked no older than Rod in her jeans and bright blue T-shirt, and felt a stab of nervousness. He laughed at himself. He'd spent the afternoon confidently plotting a trap for Thor and Jerry, but all it took was one look at Willa to send him into a state of uncertainty. He had a lot riding on tonight.

Somehow, as he got caught up in the flurry of preparations, he managed to put his fears at the back of his mind. The hours passed quickly, and all too soon the backyard was crowded with people. Laughter flowed beside food and beer, and Christian found himself relaxing—until he spotted Thor Nelson lounging on the veranda's glider, his legs stretched out in front of him, a beer in one hand and a cigarette in the other, looking as though he'd moved in to stay.

"What's he doing?" Christian asked, glaring in Thor's direction.

"Campaigning, probably," Billie murmured as she rearranged a relish tray. "The next election is only five months and one year away."

"Yeah, well, I'm not voting for him," Christian said as he helped her carry some dirty serving trays and bowls toward the house.

"He'll be crushed." He looked up to see Willa standing in the doorway, balancing a huge bowl of potato salad in her arms. She'd changed into a red jumpsuit that zipped up the front and a pair of gold sandals. The outfit was pure California, as out of place here at a Minnesota picnic as a swarm of mosquitoes in the Mojave Desert. But it was perfect.

Apparently Thor thought so, too. Like a bear in pursuit of honey, he stood up and crossed the veranda to take the bowl from Willa's arms.

"Allow me," he said with a slight bow.

Christian felt a hot wave of jealousy pour through him. Face it, he told himself, *you're no sensitive nineties guy. You're a caveman, and it's stupid to pretend otherwise.* Satisfied amusement eased his jealous heat when Willa handed the bowl to Thor and pointed him in the direction of the tables.

"You can put it down anywhere over there," she said, before turning her back on him and going back into the house.

Christian waited only moments before following her into the kitchen. He saw her enter the pantry and knew there wouldn't be a better opportunity for hours. He followed, shutting the door behind them. She spun around to face him, a jar of pickles in her hand, her eyes wide with surprise.

He reached out and took the jar, his movements slow and deliberate as he set it back on the shelf. "We have something to discuss," he told her.

"Here?" She looked around, one eyebrow arched in amusement. "This is getting old, Christian."

Her teasing irritated him. He was tired of this dance too. "Want me to call your secretary and make an appointment for your office Monday morning? Or do you make house calls?"

She stared at him silently, and he could almost feel the resentment rolling off her in waves, like the ripples seen on hot summer days reflecting off roads and dark surfaces.

"Stay away from Thor," he warned.

"*What?*" She tried to move away, but he stood in front of the door, blocking her escape. This wasn't only about his reaction to seeing Thor flirt with Willa. This was about Restless Spirit, too, and he had to warn her so she wouldn't unconsciously ruin their plans.

"He's part of it, Willa. Kevin admitted it last night. He said Thor got Jerry Miller and some other high school boys to vandalize the property. He also coerced Kevin into helping with the film of the ghost. But Thor was the one who started the fires." He saw the change come over her expression. "They're planning something for tonight."

"What? How will we stop them?"

"We've already got Jerry. Skeet and a bunch of the guys are waiting in the woods for them. And we're going to let Thor dig his own grave, so to speak. Just try and avoid him tonight, okay?"

She smiled. "And miss seeing your eyes turn green?"

"Willow, didn't anyone ever tell you not to play with little green monsters?" He reached out quickly, catching her by the wrist before she had time to react. "They bite."

He nipped at her thumb and pulled her toward him. For a brief moment, she didn't resist. He forgot about teasing as his lips found hers. She kissed him back, and he relaxed into the embrace.

When she finally pulled back he expected a smart reply, a teasing jab. But Willa stared at him, her eyes huge. He felt almost guilty for pushing her, but someone had to make her see sense.

"We're going to drive each other crazy, Willa, if we don't do something about this."

She looked away. "There's nothing we can do because I'm leaving. I have a contract."

"Do you? Or did you even bother to call your agent back?"

She flushed nearly as red as her jumpsuit, and he felt

a surge of triumph at hitting on the truth. He knew then that things just might work out before Tuesday, if he could only find the key between now and then. Why was she still hesitating? It must have something to do with Rick. Maybe once she'd talked to Rod—

"After Monday night, there's nothing keeping me here." Her announcement interrupted his thoughts.

"What about Rod? Are you going to tell him about his father? Or shall I?"

"I'll do it."

"When?"

"Tomorrow."

"How about right now? He's outside with Kerry, probably hoping he won't have to say goodbye to her.

"I'm sure Caroline and Patrick will relent and let him stay here."

"I wish I could be that sure. Patrick Dane is a controller. He wants to direct Rod's life. Who do you think is going to stop him? Billie?"

She shrugged, but her show of unconcern didn't convince him. "I have to go back outside now. Billie's no doubt looking for me." She moved past him to open the pantry door, surprising her aunt who was at that moment reaching for the door handle from the outside.

"Excuse me," said Willa, brushing past Billie and nearly running through the kitchen.

Billie looked at Christian. He shrugged and handed her the jar of pickles. "She says she's leaving."

Billie sighed. "I was hoping . . ."

"I know." He headed in the opposite direction Willa had taken but Billie's voice stopped him, the words echoing in his heart.

"Are you going to give up that easily, Christian Foster?"

When she stepped back onto the veranda a few minutes later with the jar of pickles in her hand, Billie felt a deep sense of satisfaction. She looked over all the people crowding her lawn. Nearly half the town was there to show their support. Her gaze caught Weldon McNeil's, and he smiled and waved as he bent to the brush pile they'd stacked near the lake's edge.

She felt a trifle of worry as he lit a stick of kindling and held it to the pile. She wasn't worried about the fire. Willa had soaked the lawn with the sprinkler during the last couple days, and there was no chance the bonfire would get out of control. It was Weldon she worried about. She hadn't been able to find Christian earlier when it was time to start lighting the bonfire, and Weldon had offered to help instead. She relaxed a bit now when she saw how capably he handled the task. He was quite a man, she decided.

Satisfied that he could cope without her watching him, she hurried toward one of the tables with her jar of homemade pickles, secure in the knowledge they would be better than the ones the caterers had brought. She'd no sooner finished emptying the jar into a tray when she felt a pinprick on her arm.

Billie scowled and swatted. She'd sprayed bug fog up and down in every direction, hoping to annihilate every last mosquito, but the little pests were invincible. At least they were better than the big pests, she thought as she spotted Thor Nelson talking to Sam Pitzer. Those two were definitely flies in the ointment.

The only other thing keeping her evening from being perfect was the thought of her niece leaving Tuesday morning.

Willa was easy to spot in the bright red jumpsuit, looking slim as a candle with her hair like a flame. Billie caught her attention and held up her wrist, pointing to her watch to signal that it was time. She hoped Willa wouldn't back out, although Iver and Al could probably manage to entertain the crowd themselves.

Willa nodded and a few minutes later, her clear voice carried across the night.

Rod leaned against the porch railing and listened to his aunt. The slow stuff she was singing tonight was nothing like the music she used to sing with Natural Disaster. He was a bit disappointed, especially with so many of his classmates here tonight watching, but he supposed it was pretty hard to get a rock and roll band together in the middle of the woods. He winced at old man Lindquist's off-key bass playing.

But it seemed as though everyone else liked it all right. A few couples were even dancing on the lawn in the flickering light from the bonfire, and he spotted Billie and Weldon among them.

"Hi, Rod. Thanks for waiting while I finished helping Mom."

He straightened up and smiled down into Kerry Songstad's green eyes. Willa had suggested seeing if Kerry wanted to help Brenda tonight. What a great idea that had been. He felt a rush of gratitude for his aunt, who was singing something slow and romantic in that husky voice of hers.

"Do you want to dance?" he heard himself ask, thanking God the military high school he had briefly attended considered social comportment important.

"Sure, but I don't know how."

"I'll teach you. It's easy." He took Kerry into his arms

and caught a whiff of her sweet perfume. This kind of music was all right, after all.

He was glad he and Kerry had had a chance to clear up their misunderstanding. Earlier she had told him that Jerry had taken Nancy's older sister to the party last week, and Kerry and Nancy were along just for the ride. Jerry had exaggerated the incident just to get Rod's goat.

He looked over Kerry's shoulder, remembering belatedly that he should be on the lookout for trouble. He spotted Christian standing at the side of the "dance floor" watching Willa, wearing an expression that Rod was beginning to recognize. Rod sympathized, feeling pretty superior now that he had his own woman wrapped in his arms.

Christian looked over, and Rod saw him lift a hand, circling his thumb and forefinger to signal that everything was okay. Rod smiled over Kerry's head and pulled her as close as he dared.

He wished this night would never end.

Willa checked her watch, thankful that Christian and Rod had forced Billie to confess her plans regarding the ghost. Otherwise her aunt probably wouldn't have told a soul. Willa preferred to be prepared, and when the haunting hour approached, she launched into a tongue-in-cheek version of "Ghost of a Chance."

She'd enjoyed herself tonight, never realizing she could have so much fun singing in this kind of casual setting. She idly considered getting work in a club, then remembered how the smoke had bothered her throat.

She looked toward the edge of the crowd, where

she'd seen Christian earlier, and her pleasure faded. As she finished the song the tremor in her voice was genuine when she sang, "*I don't stand a ghost of a chance with you.*"

The last note hadn't quite faded when "Hulbert" made his perfectly timed appearance at the edge of the trees, sending a thrill of reaction through the crowd.

While people screamed or giggled delightedly and craned their necks for a better look, Willa slipped away from center stage. She saw Christian moving toward her, fighting the swell of the crowd, and a minute later his fingers closed over her arm.

"Come with me," he urged. "Let's get away from here for a while."

The chance to escape the noisy crowd with Christian was too tempting to resist, even though she knew that giving in would only make things harder. But it might be her last chance to be alone with him. Tomorrow Billie wanted them all to attend the local Memorial Day services, and Monday was Rod's graduation ceremony. She hesitated only a moment longer before nodding her agreement.

They slipped away, unnoticed but Willa halted as soon as they were free. "Billie is expecting me to lead the guests in a sing-along," she said.

"She won't mind," he assured her. He led her to the boathouse, and she nearly lost her courage again when he opened the door. Moonlight streamed in and illuminated the end of the dock, where a rowboat bobbed gently up and down.

She was struck by a sudden thought. "What about Thor?" she asked. "Don't you need to stay and make sure he or those kids can't make any trouble?"

Christian shook his head, bending down to untie the boat as he said, "I got a call from Skeet about thirty minutes ago. He and another off-duty cop, plus a couple friends, had been sitting in the woods just waiting for Jerry and his gang to show up. Skeet already nabbed them."

He straightened up and held out his arm for her to use to steady herself as she climbed on board in her high-heeled gold sandals. "Since this isn't their jurisdiction, they had to make a citizen's arrest, of course."

As he pushed the boat away from the dock, she caught a glimpse of the devilment in his expression. "And?"

"There's nothing to hold them on, so Skeet's friends intend to take their time finding the county sheriff's department. They'll probably make it in, oh, a couple more hours." His grin grew wider as he settled on the bench seat next to Willa.

"So as long as Skeet's friends are baby-sitting, the kids can't warn Thor?" she asked, dipping her oar into the water.

"Exactly." He glanced down at his watch as they rowed out of the boathouse onto the lake. "Right around now, Brenda is lighting a cigarette for Thor. With his own lighter."

"The one we found, of course." Willa laughed delightedly. "Thor's too stupid not to react in some way."

"And Skeet plans to be standing nearby with Pitzer when that happens. Even if it doesn't all fall into place as planned, Pitzer can hardly ignore the evidence once those boys start talking. I think we've got 'em."

She felt relieved that one problem, at least, had been solved. "Then Billie's going to be all right," she said.

"You can leave with a clear conscience."

"Don't," she warned him. "Let's just enjoy what's left of tonight, okay? I don't want to argue with you anymore."

He fell silent beside her. They rowed past the point toward their special fishing spot, the full moon lighting their way. A cool breeze carried the faint sound of singing from the resort, while tree frogs made their own music from the nearby banks. As they drew closer to the protected area, the wild sounds took over. A turtle jumped off a submerged log as they passed, landing with a soft plop into the water. Frogs sang, the breeze rustled through the treetops, and a pair of startled loons flew up in front of them, laughing eerily.

It was magical, and Willa was so enchanted by the sights and sounds of the night that she forgot to row.

"Hey, how come I'm doing all the work all of a sudden?" Christian complained. The boat drifted sideways, and she stuck her oar in and pulled until it straightened. "Let's stop here for a while," he said.

He dropped anchor and reached behind her for the lidded compartment in the stern. He opened it and pulled out an old plaid stadium blanket and a bottle of wine.

"You planned this," she said, feeling an unreasonable sense of disappointment that this perfect night wasn't a happy accident.

"Yep. Sorry I didn't bring two glasses. I thought we could share."

"Christian, if you think—"

"Shut up." He leaned over and kissed her, stopping her protest. "Like you said, let's just enjoy it. Who knows when you'll do anything like this again?"

His words silenced her. He spread out the blanket on

the bottom of the boat, and she settled onto it, leaning back comfortably against the bench seat.

She looked at his profile as he poured the wine, trying to memorize this moment. They sat quietly, passing the glass back and forth, listening to the night sounds. Now and then Christian would identify something for her—a fox's bark, the flapping of an owl's wings.

She didn't protest when he put his arm around her, but leaned into his strength and allowed the comforting feeling to wash over her. She had always trusted him. Unable to stop herself, she reached out and traced her fingers along his jaw.

"Willow?" He turned his head slightly and pressed his lips to her palm. When she would have pulled away, he held her wrist gently and kissed each one of her fingers in turn. How did someone who'd always been a fighter, a loner, a cop who had seen violence, turn out to be so gentle? she wondered.

They kissed, and the slow rocking of the boat heightened her sensation. It was like falling, Willa thought, only she knew that she didn't have to worry about landing. Christian would always be there to catch her.

Their caresses grew bolder. Christian unzipped her jumpsuit and slipped a hand underneath the fabric. She tightened her fingers on his shoulders in response to the delicious warmth of his fingers as they stroked the side of her rib cage.

When he withdrew his hand and pulled up her zipper, she nearly cried out in disappointment.

"What's wrong?" she asked, confused by his withdrawal.

"I didn't plan for this to get so out of hand. I had something else in mind for tonight."

She stared at him, suddenly unsure. Was it possible he didn't want her anymore?

He must have read the insecurity in her eyes. He swallowed and said quickly, "I want you so much it hurts, Willa. I've never loved any other woman." He reached out for her hands.

"I'm only going to ask this once. Will you marry me?"

15

Willa stared at him, her eyes dark with shock. Not shock, Christian thought, *horror*. He felt his heart sink faster than a heavy anchor. He'd been crazy to think that there was any chance. It seemed as though she was beginning to vacillate about leaving Restless Spirit, but apparently he'd read all the signs wrong. For a moment, he hated the resort, hated Rick. If it weren't for them, she might have wanted him.

He tried to keep the anger from his voice. "Just say it, Willa. Yes or no. I want to hear you give me an answer."

"You know I plan to leave on Tuesday."

"Willa—"

"No." She stared at him, unblinking. "The answer is no."

He had to ask. "Is it the resort—or is it just me?"

As she continued to look at him, he understood every nuance of the word *rejection*. "If it wasn't for the past," he pressed, "how would you feel about me?"

"I don't know," she told him quietly. "That's just it. I

can't separate you from this place or . . . or from Rick. You've always been at the back of my mind, even when we were apart, like—" She broke off and shook her head. "I can't begin to describe it."

"Try. *Please.*"

"All I know is that it wouldn't matter even if you left everything here behind and came to L.A. with me. Even then I couldn't see you without remembering."

"Isn't that why you came back? To remember?"

"Partly," she admitted. "I guess I thought remembering the good times might make it easier to forget the bad. That sounds pretty stupid, doesn't it?" She stared off toward the wide swath of moonlight reflected across the water. "But I don't feel much of anything lately. It's this place." Her voice gained strength. "I have to get away."

"Well, then, I guess that's all there is to it." He reached for the oars, but she held out her hand to stay him.

"I don't want to leave with things between us like this," she told him. "Why don't we stay out here a little while longer?"

"What?" Confused, he stared at her fingers grasping his forearm.

"I told you that I can't feel anything. I lied. There is one thing I can still feel," she said, squeezing his arm. He pulled from her touch as if it burned him.

"What are you asking, Willa? For a memory to put in your shoe box along with the other bits and pieces of the past?" Let *her* feel rejection, he thought as the lining of his stomach began to burn.

Who was he kidding? Every muscle in his body strained to act, to reach out and take what she was offering, to lose himself so deep inside her that he could forget all of this. He grabbed both oars to keep from grabbing her, and started to row, pulling deep and hard.

He didn't let up until he could see the boathouse perched on the edge of the island. His angry strokes had built up such a momentum that they practically coasted in.

"There's just one more thing," he said, breathing hard. "I said I would tell Rod about Rick if you didn't. You have until Tuesday to give that boy his father back. He needs to know, Willa."

The boat hit the dock with a loud thump. She scrambled out on her own, gripping the ridiculous gold sandals in her hand. Before he had a chance to finish tying up the boat, she turned on him.

"I'll tell Rod. But if he's hurt, I hope you remember that we'll all lose."

With one foot Billie set the glider in motion, rocking back and forth and watching the cottage lights go out one by one. The lawn was littered with folding chairs and paper plates, and she was so tired her bones ached. But watching everyone have fun had made her feel young again. She hummed and leaned her head back against the weathered pine, seeing past the mess, past the days ahead to the end of the summer. Maybe for Labor Day they could have a dance, a polka band outdoors. Of course, Willa wouldn't be here to sing.

She stopped pushing against the veranda with her sensible brown shoe and let the glider's motions slow. She didn't want to see that far ahead, after all.

"A penny for your thoughts?"

Her eyes snapped open, and there was Weldon standing next to the glider, a teacup in each hand. He'd loosened his plaid tie and she could see the edge of his white undershirt peeking out above the button. She smiled. "Couldn't you sleep either?"

Before he could answer, she caught hold of herself. What kind of hostess was she, lounging around and letting a guest wait on her? She straightened. "If you find your room uncomfortable, I can—"

He shook his head. "It's not uncomfortable. Just a bit lonely tonight. I thought you might like a little company and a cup." She took the cup and moved aside a bit so that he could sit down next to her on the glider.

She sipped, and her hand went to her throat in surprise. "Oh, my," she said. "This is whiskey."

"I should have warned you." He fussed over her, taking the cup from her hands while she dabbed at her eyes with a handkerchief. "I often have a short nip before I retire. A nasty habit, I suppose."

"A very bracing habit." She reached out her hand, silently demanding that he return the drink. "And just what I need tonight. A shot of reality."

"Is something the matter?"

"No, of course not," she said, feeling his gaze on her in the darkness. She stared at her fingers, so bony and old against the delicate china, then looked into Weldon's gentle gray eyes.

The eyes, she thought, *that's* how you tell how old someone really is. Weldon's held a spark of gold and a hint of laughter, and she knew he would understand her dreams for adventure. "Actually, there is something . . ." she began, then found herself telling him the entire story—her brother's nagging to sell Restless Spirit, her plotting to get Willa and Christian back, her matchmaking attempts. She even told him about her longing to hang up her apron and travel.

"I'm not sure your family has appreciated everything you've done for them, my dear."

Her heart skipped a little at his endearment, even as she shook her head. "I didn't do it for them," she said. "I'm not some kind of doormat."

"Certainly not."

She darted a look sideways to find him smiling wide.

"Look." He nodded toward the lake.

She glanced up to see Willa and Christian leaving the boathouse, neither looking at the other and several feet of space in between them. It was clear that they hadn't enjoyed their moonlight row.

"It's not necessarily better to be young, is it?" Weldon said.

"No." Billie sighed. "Oh, well, I guess I'm stuck here for good now," she said, thinking how selfish and sulky she sounded.

"Nonsense."

She barely heard the word, reacting to Willa and Christian's downcast expressions as they drew nearer by feeling the hurt herself. Willa walked past them with only a muttered goodnight.

Christian paused by the glider. "I tried, Billie," he said. "I even asked her to marry me. She's leaving."

She felt the air go out of her lungs and understood why people used the word *deflated* to describe a disappointment. "I'm sorry, dear," she told him. Her hand gripped his fingers and he returned the pressure briefly.

"I'll see you in the morning," he said. "Goodnight, Weldon."

"Don't forget the ceremony tomorrow," Billie reminded him. "I haven't missed putting flowers on the graves in nearly forty years."

"If it's just for family . . ." Christian began.

"Nonsense," she interrupted, unconsciously echoing Weldon. "You *are* family."

She was rewarded with a slow, grateful smile. Ah, if only there wasn't so much unhappiness behind it. For the first time since her niece had been a willful six-year-old, she felt a spark of anger toward Willa. It faded when Weldon reached out and lightly patted her hand.

Long after Christian left, she and Weldon sat in comfortable silence. He'd started the glider rocking again, and the motion soothed her. When his hand covered hers, she felt only a mild surprise before acknowledging how pleasant it felt to enjoy a man's strength, all the more so because she'd relied on her own strength for so long.

"How would you feel about adding to your family, Wilhelmina?"

Everybody was sure in a mood this morning, Rod decided as he added more milk to his coffee, wondering if he'd ever get used to the bitter taste enough to drink it straight. Christian had barely grunted to him when he'd opened the divider and passed through on the way to the bathroom. Willa was walking around like a robot low on batteries as she replenished the buffet. And he'd never seen Billie so distracted before. Just now she'd told him to get dessert from the refrigerator downstairs, and he'd had to remind her that it was still only breakfast.

He heard Freddie barking outside and wished he could take her out for a long walk through the woods. But he had to stay and help start making box lunches, so everyone could go into town for the Memorial Day observance. Today was his last day before graduation, and he knew a lot of the kids were planning to drive up to Duluth. For once, he didn't want to be with them. He'd rather spend the day here, goofing off with Freddie, helping Billie, maybe even fishing again. He wouldn't mind spending the rest of the summer like that, he decided. Maybe if he talked to his parents, tried to reason with them . . .

He moved to the window above the sink, looking over the tops of the herb plants to the driveway. Billie was outside, fussing with the plants they were to take to the cemetery later. He sensed that this day meant something special to her, something different than it did to most people. His parents had always spent the holiday at the beach or cruising down the St. Croix River on a friend's yacht. Thanks to Billie, this was the first year he'd ever thought about what the day really meant.

He wondered how it would feel to be standing next to Rick's grave with all those people around. He was so used to going there alone. He hoped he wouldn't do anything stupid, like cry or something. A band of nervousness tightened across his throat.

When it was time to go, the four of them squeezed into Willa's car. Reaching the cemetery she pulled up behind a line of vehicles, all stretched along the narrow drive cutting through the green cemetery lawn. Rod felt a moment of sheer panic. It looked like a funeral, with the solemn procession of people in their Sunday clothes. He swallowed and loosened the tie he'd had to borrow from Christian, feeling more like a kid than he ever had before. When he got out of the car, he circled around to the trunk to help Billie remove the potted geraniums.

"Thank you. It's over that way," she said, and he slowed his pace. He'd already started in the right direction, forgetting that as far as the others knew, he'd never been here before.

He turned back to see Christian, like him, balancing a flowerpot in either hand. Willa was several steps behind him, her face pale as she looked over the rows of granite markers. Rod followed her gaze and saw that up and down each row, several of the headstones were decorated with small flags, the stripes and stars fluttering in the light breeze.

He looked at his aunt in time to see her falter. He was about to say something to Billie, to tell her to slow down, when Willa looked directly at him. She was scared, he realized, like the deer he'd startled in the woods one day last week. With that understanding, his own nervousness disappeared.

"The VFW puts up the flags every year," Billie chatted on ahead of him. "On every veteran's grave. *Oh*." She slowed to a creeping pace. "Why, there are already flowers on your father's grave. Whoever could have done that?"

Christian and Willa caught up just in time to hear Billie's question. Everyone stared at the wilted grocery-store bouquet of carnations and baby's breath stuck inside one of Billie's canning jars. Rod put an end to their curiosity. "I did," he admitted.

Billie recovered first. "That was a lovely gesture, Rod."

Christian patted him between the shoulder blades before he walked ahead with Billie's flowers, letting her direct him as he set them near the headstones of her brothers. Three other markers beside Rick's fluttered with flags, a vivid reminder of how much the Mitterhauser family had given to its country.

Rod could feel himself choking up, and he hung back. Willa stopped next to him. "We need to talk about your father," she said quietly.

"I'd like that," he said, his words pushing through the lump that rose to his throat as his nervousness returned.

The minister's voice droned on. The service was ecumenical, with all the local churches participating in some way, and with a different cleric officiating each year. Willa stood to one side of the large Mitterhauser family monument and remembered the last time she'd attended, with her grandparents and Billie. Rick was overseas then, and the small rectangle of ground on the other side of the monument had been unmarked.

"Bonds, not blood, make a family," Pastor Gunderson was saying. Most of his words so far had escaped her. All she could think of was talking to Rod. What would she tell him? she wondered, drawing in a deep breath of air to give her strength.

She fixed her attention on the small dais where the minister stood. He was a young man, barely thirty, but his quiet baritone voice and prematurely receding brown hair lent him dignity and authority as he said, "Ruth knew this when she followed her mother-in-law, Naomi, promising 'where you go, I will go' . . ."

Willa's gaze met Christian's, and she quickly looked away again.

". . . and indeed, we are bonded to each other, this human family of ours." Pastor Gunderson spread his arms to include everyone, and Willa glanced around her at the dozens of people who were standing on the green lawn, listening to the pastor's remarks.

"Death cannot break these bonds."

A roaring began in Willa's ears, and the words faded

in and out. She stared at the small flag that marked Rick's grave, silently arguing with the minister's words. Rick *had* broken the bond. He'd done it by rejecting all of them.

Her breath caught in her chest, and the word *no* forced itself into her mind. It wasn't Rick's doing at all—*it was hers.*

She was the one trying to sever the bond that still linked her to her brother. That was why she tried to put the memories from her, why she rejected Christian. But after all the grief, the pain, the anger, what was left besides this square of stone set into the earth?

The service ended with the Lord's Prayer, and Willa's "amen" was hoarse with unshed tears. She could feel Billie looking at her sharply.

"You go ahead," she heard herself saying. "I'll be along in a minute."

Billie hesitated, then reached out to take Christian and Rod by the arms. "I'd like to see where my mother's folk are buried," she said, leading them away. "My third cousin—twice removed, actually—usually puts flowers there, but . . ."

Her voice faded as they walked down the row of markers, and Willa was left alone. She remembered the day they had found out about Rick, a hot, muggy day when they'd complained incessantly about the weather—until the news came, and the weather and everything else that was trivial or temporary was forgotten.

Her legs felt weak, and she sat down on the grass, feeling its coolness through her light cotton dress. She looked around, a bit embarrassed, but no one was paying attention to her. She thought of Rod coming here by himself and suddenly realized he must have done it when he was supposed to be in track.

She felt tears coursing down her cheeks, and she shut her eyes. Immediately, the image of her brother—his auburn hair and laughing gray eyes—filled her mind.

"You stupid lout," she said, but the words were without force. "I miss you. We all do. I wish you were here to see Rod. I wish—" She ran out of words.

What was left? she wondered again, staring out at the rows and rows of headstones and flowers and flags, looking for an answer. People moved in and out of the rows: little white-haired ladies saying goodbye once more to their husbands, parents explaining to children what their grandparents had been like. Her gaze landed on a bright red head. Rod's.

We're left, she thought. *All of us at Restless Spirit.*

"Ready?"

She turned to see Christian standing above her. She nodded and reached up for his hand, letting him pull her to her feet. In the distance, she saw Rod and Billie making their way to the car.

She could feel Christian watching her as she brushed the grass from her dress and wiped at her eyes. "I'm ready," she said at last.

Christian steered Willa's small car across the causeway. She'd handed the keys to him on their way back to the car, and he'd understood that she was too emotional to drive. She sat in the back with Billie, while Rod stared out the windshield on his side.

Christian honked lightly at a boat full of resort guests who waved from their spot near the causeway. *No fish there*, Christian thought absently, glancing in the rearview mirror at Willa.

All traces of her tears had gone, but she still had a

haunted look. She'd worn her hair pinned up, accenting her cheekbones and large eyes, but the morning breeze had pulled it from its knot while they were standing outside. Now, tendrils curled at the side of her neck above the collar of her pale gray dress, adding to her air of fragility. He knew that Rick's ghost was haunting her.

When they came around the curve the old house stood waiting for them, a solid reminder of all the people and events that had taken place on this island through the years. He felt a sense of comfort knowing that he was a part of it. To Billie, at least, he was family. And he was going to do his damnedest to be family to Rod, even if it meant grabbing Patrick Dane by his starched collar and shaking some compassion into the man's head.

They piled out of the car, and Christian froze when he heard Willa say, "Rod, would you come upstairs a minute? I want to show you something."

The letters.

He tried to look her in the eye, but she escaped him, leading the way into the house with Rod close at her heels. Christian numbly followed Billie into the kitchen, feeling like a death row criminal who'd just been granted an appeal.

As Willa and Rod tramped up the steps, he and Billie exchanged glances. Her eyes reflected his hope.

"Maybe now . . ." Her words trailed off.

"Maybe," Christian echoed, his gaze following Willa up the back stairs.

"I'm sorry I didn't give these to you sooner, Rod. They're from your father." They were standing in Willa's bedroom on the second floor.

He stared at the box in his hand, then looked up at her. "He sent these to you?"

"Yes. Maybe when you read them, you'll understand him a little better. You need to know—"

She broke off and went to the window, staring sightlessly across the lawn to the boathouse, where someone was sliding a small canoe down the landing. "He didn't die in Vietnam," she finally said. "He died on a military base in West Germany. He killed himself, Rod."

The silence stretched and grew until it was nearly unbearable. At last she heard him whisper behind her, "I knew it was something like that."

She turned to stare at him, surprised. "You knew? How?"

"It was the dates."

She looked at her nephew, really *looked* at him for the first time, seeing him for himself and not as a diluted reflection of Rick. The parts didn't seem to add up—the long legs and arms, the bony face and surprisingly blue eyes, the sheaf of too-long, red-orange hair. But he stood straight and looked back at her with a direct blue gaze, and she knew he was special.

She sat down on the bed, ready to listen, and he sat next to her.

"The only thing I knew about my dad was that he was in Nam, so I always listened whenever anyone talked about it, or when we studied it in school. It was probably the only time I paid attention to history class," he said with a crooked grin.

"The last American troops left Vietnam almost two years before Dad died."

"We were wrong not to tell you," she admitted. "Especially me, since I had these letters. I think he wanted me to understand. I'm not sure I did, until today."

Rod looked down at the box of letters on his lap and started to leaf through the envelopes. He pulled a handful of them out of the box. "Some of these are from Christian."

"I'd better take those." She could feel herself blushing at the thought of Rod reading them. He handed them over, but not before examining one of the postmarks, then looking at her reddened cheeks.

"You and Christian had something going back then, too?"

"Yes," she said, smiling.

He stared at her in utter confusion. "What's wrong with you two, anyway? It's been almost twenty years, and you guys still haven't managed to get it together."

"Maybe it's time to do something about that."

She left Rod to read the letters and went downstairs. Christian was sitting by himself at the table, a mug of coffee in his hands, when she entered the kitchen. He looked up, his gaze questioning.

"He's still upstairs, reading the letters," she said.

"Is he okay?"

She smiled and nodded. "You were right. He's a pretty tough kid. He had most of it figured out already." Her smile faded. "You were right about a lot of things."

"Oops," an unfamiliar voice said from the doorway. Willa and Christian looked over to see a middle-aged woman in a yellow short set, three kids lined up behind her like a family of ducklings.

"We wanted to pick up our lunches to take out on the lake. Your aunt said they were here in the refrigerator?"

"I'll get them." Willa dug through the food packed in bags and boxes on the refrigerator shelf. "Number Seven, right?" She handed over a large brown paper bag.

They trooped out of the kitchen, and Christian said, "Where were we?"

Before she had a chance to answer, more footsteps approached the kitchen from the hall.

"Let's get out of here." He stood up and took her by the arm. She followed obediently as he pulled her toward the pantry and shut the door behind them.

"There. It might not be far enough away, but I couldn't wait much longer."

The searching look in his eyes embarrassed her. He held her lightly, his hands on her shoulders, and she wished he would pull her close and kiss her instead. Right now, she needed all the reassurance she could get.

"I've decided to stay at Restless Spirit," she told him unsteadily, thinking this must have been how Rick felt when he first dove off the banks of the point into deep water. She felt Christian's hands tighten on her shoulders as he pulled her slowly toward him.

"I know you told me you would only ask once," she said, her voice husky, "but—"

Her words were lost as his arms closed around her, and his lips covered hers. The kiss drove away all her embarrassment and the last remaining shreds of uncertainty. This was home.

Not the island, not Restless Spirit, not this house.

Home was Christian's arms.

She kissed him back, feeling the bonds between them mending and strengthening. Happiness swelled inside her, and she gave herself over to it, letting it bubble up through her chest until it burst open into words.

"I love you." She didn't even know she was crying until he started to kiss away her tears, his lips warm against her eyelids and cheek.

"And I love you." He broke away to look into her eyes. His sparkled with a combination of amusement and desire. "One more time, Willa. That's it, I swear it. Will you marry me?"

"Yes!" she shouted, and they both broke into laughter.

EPILOGUE

The Fourth of July

Billie moved among the guests, pouring coffee and making mental notes on what each table needed. This one was out of potato salad; that one could use more biscuits.

They were eating out on the lawn again to celebrate. She smiled, her head filled with plans—lawn games, fireworks, maybe another visit from Hulbert. He hadn't been around in awhile. People take things for granted when they become too familiar, she had decided. Like this place, she thought, pausing between tables with the pot of coffee in her hand to look around her.

The day had dawned fresh and clear, after an overnight thunderstorm that had everyone worried except her. The lake sparkled like a bowlful of gems, and the lawn smelled green and new. She smiled. Now *this* was a celebration—the family was together again at last.

A hand closed over hers and took away the coffee-pot. "Billie, what are you doing working on a day like today?" her younger brother John scolded, his face brown from Arizona sunshine. He pulled her by the hand and led her back to their table. "Let the caterers handle it. Today is special."

Oh, yes, she thought, and turned to look around one more time before following him past tables of happy faces—family, friends, and guests, all joined together. The family's table was easy to distinguish from the others, decorated in white lace and fresh-cut flowers, with blue ribbon streamers stirring in the breeze.

"Trying to get your last licks in, Billie?" a teasing voice called, a middle-aged man who'd been coming to Restless Spirit since he was a child.

"Just making my last rounds," she replied, to scattered laughter.

She took her seat next to Weldon, winking at him. As she finished her meal, she let the conversation surround her while still managing to keep one eye on her guests. She tasted a pickle critically and set it aside on her plate. Hers really were much better, she thought, vowing to find time to have a talk with the caterers.

"Who's ready for cake?" Marilyn, her sister-in-law, asked. She was as tanned and healthy looking as John, and Billie wondered idly if she'd look that way herself once she reached her destination. She stole a glance at Weldon while everyone else's attention was focused on the many-tiered cake, frosted in white and decorated with red roses like the ones blooming near the veranda.

"It's the most beautiful wedding cake I've ever seen." It was Kerry Songstad who'd spoken, seated at Rod's side in her blue-flowered satin dress. She stared at the cake with a look of awe.

Billie's gaze went to Christian as he pushed back his

chair and stood, darkly handsome in his gray suit, and reached out his hand to Willa. They had been married on the front veranda that morning, sharing the ceremony with family, friends, and a resort full of guests, some of whom had looked on with confusion at all the excitement interrupting their Independence Day holiday.

Billie felt tears fill her eyes as Christian led Willa toward the cake, which stood off to the side on a small table of its own. Willa's loose hair stirred around the shoulders of her simple white gown made of layers of fine batiste. Billie smiled. Her niece looked like a naughty fairy princess as she tried to stuff a piece of cake into Christian's mouth. He evaded her efforts, sending everyone into peals of laughter.

She had stood next to Willa as they spoke their vows. Probably the world's oldest bridesmaid, she decided wryly, and all the more ridiculous because Rod had acted as best man. They'd made an odd pair, but tears had formed in her eyes anyway when she saw her great nephew standing next to Christian. In his new gray suit, white shirt and tie, he looked so much like his father that for a moment it had hurt to watch and think that Rick wouldn't be there to see his sister marry his best friend.

But the moment had passed, and Billie had realized then that Rick was there, in all of them. He, more than anyone else, blessed this union.

She felt something press into her hand and looked down to see that Weldon had given her his handkerchief. She dabbed at her eyes and smiled gratefully at him. "A lovely couple, aren't they?" he said, but his gray eyes never left hers. She looked away, suddenly shy at the thought of the suitcases standing and waiting by the door.

She watched as Willa and Christian served pieces of

cake to everyone seated at the family table. When Willa came to her and Weldon, Billie said, "Sit down a moment." Weldon found an empty chair and moved it closer so Willa could join them.

"I want to give you your wedding present." Billie reached into the beaded bag that matched her blue dress and handed Willa a long white envelope. She watched, slightly nervous, as Willa opened it and unfolded the piece of paper inside.

"It's the deed to Restless Spirit."

"I know that you didn't want it, at least not when you first came back. But no one ever really owns it anyway. It belongs to all of us, past and future. And I'll let you in on a secret," she said, leaning closer. "This is Hulbert's treasure. Everyone thought that he'd buried gold somewhere on the island, when all along the island was the treasure. No one saw it because it was hidden in plain sight."

"Thank you, Billie. Christian and I will take good care of it."

They looked up when Willa's father started to speak. Christian came to stand beside them, resting a hand on both Willa's and Billie's shoulder.

"I'd like to toast my daughter and her husband," John began. "I don't have a Bible handy, but maybe Paster Gunderson will correct me if I misquote," he said. "For everything there is a season and a time for every matter under heaven. A time to be born, and a time to die; a time to weep, and a time to laugh; a time to mourn and a time to dance; a time to cast away stones, and a time to gather stones together." He paused and looked around at the many smiling faces.

"This family is gathered together here today to laugh and to dance, to celebrate the marriage of Willa to Christian, who has been part of our family since they were

children together. They will have both joy and sorrow, because that is life. But may they weather their storms the same way they celebrate their joys—together."

A moment of silence followed the toast, and then everyone clinked their glasses together and cried, "Here, here!"

"Are you ready to sneak away?" Weldon whispered in Billie's ear. She felt a flutter of anticipation in her bosom.

"So soon? I thought we would stay for the fireworks this evening." She looked across the lawn at the tables of guests, realizing this might be the last time she played hostess.

"We have to drive all the way to Minneapolis to catch our flight to Santiago," he reminded her. His face fell. "Unless you've changed your mind. I know the Andes mountains are hardly the Ritz, and I—"

She touched her fingers to his lips to silence him. "I can't wait to climb mountains looking for that bird," she said.

"The Giant Hummingbird."

"That one." She pushed back her chair. "I'll just go change and get my things." She slipped away unnoticed from the bustle as guests helped to clear away tables. She felt a little sad about changing out of her pretty blue dress, but her steps quickened when she remembered the sturdy clothes she'd ordered from the Banana Republic and L. L. Bean catalogs, all packed and waiting in her suitcase.

A half hour later she rejoined Weldon on the veranda, dressed in her traveling clothes, and felt a lump rise to her throat as she looked out over the lawn. A group of noisy children played tag, while a pair of fishermen struggled to set up an old badminton net. Nearby, her brother was teaching Rod to play horseshoes.

"A fine wedding day this is," came Christian's teasing voice at her elbow. "The bride and groom stay at home while the maid of honor runs off to South America with one of the wedding guests."

Billie felt herself blushing as both Willa and Christian wrapped her in a farewell hug. She and Weldon started for the car but only made it halfway before a group of guests waylaid them by throwing handfuls of rice. Billie thought about correcting their mistake, but changed her mind when she looked over at Weldon. He was laughing with delight as rice bounced off his shoulders and stuck to his gray hair.

Who knows? she thought, as she turned to wave goodbye. Life's adventures were still ahead of her.

PHOTO BY LARRY LINDAHL

KATHLEEN BRYANT wrote everything from instruction books and technical manuals to "junk mail" copy before transferring her writing skills to fiction. She has published four previous romance novels and was named "Best New Romantic Suspense Author" by *Romantic Times* in 1991. Born in Minnesota, she currently lives in Arizona.

COULD THE PAIN OF THE PAST COST HER THE FUTURE?

To Willa Mitterhauser, the fishing lodge run by her aunt on Minnesota's Pine Lake is the place of her happiest childhood memories. It was there that she and her late brother Rick spent each summer and Willa first learned about love in the arms of Rick's best friend, Christian Foster.

Now, years later, Willa and Christian are reunited at the lodge. Though their passion is quickly rekindled, Willa wonders if it's just a passing fancy or if their time to be together has finally come.

Harper
Monogram

The Mark of Distinctive Women's Fiction

Romance

ISBN 978-0-06-108107-1

5 0 7 9 9

EAN

9 780061 081071

Ⓢ

USA $7.99 Canada $9.50